SWORD OF DARKNESS

A RELIC HUNTERS NOVEL

KERI ARTHUR

With thanks to:

The Lulus
Indigo Chick Designs
Hot Tree Editing
Dominic Wakeford Editorial
Robyn E.
The lovely ladies from Indie Gals
JMN Art—Covers by Julie for the amazing cover

CHAPTER
ONE

I t was my worst nightmare come to life.

A ladder, leading down into the deep darkness of an underground tunnel.

In truth, it wasn't so much the ladder or even the tunnel that scared me, though as a member of one of the taller branches of pixies, the cramped and often dangerous conditions in Deva's ancient tunnels did put them on my list of least favorite places to be.

No, the problem lay with the critters that so often used the tunnels as a highway to get around.

Rats, to be precise.

"Are you coming down or what?" The gruff voice rose from the dark depths below. "We ain't gotta whole lot of time to play with here."

"There're no rats, Beth," a second voice said.

That one belonged to my brother, Lugh, a six-foot-six giant of a man who had very little fear of anything. But then, he hadn't woken to discover the beady-eyed bastards running over him as a kid.

I glanced at the woman waiting on the other side of the

1

heavy metal plate we'd moved to access the ladder. She had a thick-set body, heavily wrinkled pale features, brown eyes that looked less than pleased right now, and a long plait of silver hair that ran down her back to her butt. She was also married to the impatient man below, though from the little Lugh had said about dwarven tunneling teams—whether they were freelancers or working for the National Fae Museum like these two—being married was an exception rather than the rule.

"Is that true, Brega?" I couldn't keep the trepidation from my voice. "I know these are military tunnels rather than sewers, but I can't imagine they'd be totally rat free."

She sniffed. It was a sound that managed to be both impatient and amused. "There are rats everywhere in this city, but as far as tunnels go, these are fairly clean." She looked me up and down. "Why the hell is a long streak of pixie such as yourself scared of them little things?"

Most of us are scared of something, I wanted to mutter, but resisted the urge. I suspected Brega wasn't the type to feel sympathy for childhood terrors, especially when dwarves lived, breathed, and loved the underground places of this world, be they here in Deva or elsewhere across the UK.

I edged closer to the ladder. It was surrounded by a circular metal cage that prevented you falling backward but didn't make me feel any safer, simply because it didn't prevent you falling down.

Brega glanced pointedly at her watch. "We've roughly ten minutes before security does the next pass, so you need to make up your mind—are you going down, or are you staying up here?"

I blew out a breath. "Going down."

No matter how much I hated rats, I couldn't let Lugh go to Nialle's house alone. He'd not only been Lugh's best friend since boarding school but had worked alongside him at the National Fae Museum. He'd met his death while researching Agrona's Claws, and we believed the very same people responsible for his murder had recently made an attempt on Lugh's life. They'd also firebombed the family tavern I ran and had kidnapped both me and my ex, Mathi, using him to force me to find the Crown of Shadows for them.

To top it all off, our mom disappeared six months ago. We only recently discovered her body—she'd been shot and then buried by a tunnel collapse.

At this point, though, her death didn't seem linked to Nialle's, but rather to the theft of the Éadrom Hoard, a treasure of godly relics that had been guarded by the light elves for eons. Ever since we taller pixies had lost the job, in fact.

Of course, given Nialle *had* been researching the Claws, a connection was technically possible. At this point, none of us were really certain of anything. Nothing other than the fact we'd find the bastards who'd killed Mom and make them pay.

No matter what it took.

Unfortunately, Nialle's house remained guarded by the Eldritch—a small but specialized offshoot of the Interspecies Investigation Team who generally dealt with deaths involving odd or magically unnatural causes—and that meant Lugh would need someone to act as lookout while he searched for clues as to what Nialle's murderers had been after. The dwarves wouldn't provide that service—not unless we were willing to pay an exorbitant extra fee, of course.

I turned and carefully climbed onto the ladder. Water from the brief but fierce storm we'd had during the ten minutes we'd spent waiting for the guard to pass dripped steadily down the metal, making it slick and slippery. I tried not to think of how far it was to fall and carefully went down.

I was at the halfway point when Brega dragged the cover back into place. The brief sliver of streetlight that had been guiding my way died, and darkness wrapped around me. I ignored the gathering tension and kept climbing down, the metal vibrating under my fingers as Brega followed. After a second or so, light shone up at us, high-lighting the rough-hewn stone walls while lessening the likelihood of slipping.

I jumped down the last few feet and was steadied by my brother. I gave him a nod of thanks and pulled the small flashlight from my pocket. Lugh had wanted to bring the helmets and headlamps he kept in the car, but Locryn—Brega's gnarled and surprisingly bald husband, given dwarves' reputation for hairiness—had assured us the tunnels were relatively safe.

It was the "relatively" that worried me.

Once Brega had joined us, Locryn gave us a gruff "This way" and headed down the passage, his light bobbing unevenly across the brick and metal walls. Our footsteps echoed in the musty and rather odorous air, and some-where up ahead, water dripped. These tunnels—which had once provided safe passage to and from the various under-ground military installations during the Second World War —crisscrossed large sections of Old Deva. I was willing to bet most wouldn't be in the same pristine condition as this one.

As we moved deeper into the complex, the bricks gave way to stone and water trickled underfoot. Though we passed several offshoot tunnels that showed obvious signs of collapse, ours continued to look structurally sound.

I really, *really* hoped it remained that way.

We trudged on, the air getting colder and fouler while the moss that covered the stone underfoot made each step that much more treacherous. It forced me to keep an eye on where I was placing my feet rather than what might lie ahead, and I suspected that was a good thing. Especially if what lay ahead was a collapse that would make this journey a whole lot harder than it currently was.

As we entered a three-way junction, the slightest wisp of oddly moving air caught my attention. I paused and quickly swept the light around. If I hadn't lost all sense of direction, the tunnel to our right headed toward Nialle's. While it looked passable, the same could not be said for the one directly ahead. It had partially collapsed, the bricks around the door's structure filling the doorway even though the rusted support beam remained in place. The final tunnel led into some sort of communications room, if the barely visible bits of old machines were anything to go by.

The unusual play of air had come from that direction, but it had stopped the minute I shone the light that way. Nothing appeared to be moving. Nothing seemed out of place. And yet...

Lugh stopped. "Beth? Something wrong?"

I hesitated. "I think something moved."

Brega sniffed. "It was a rat. Disappeared into that room as we came out of the tunnel."

I glanced at her sharply. "From what direction? Behind us?"

"Hard to say." She frowned at me. "Why are you so worried about goddamn rats?"

"Because I've been attacked by the bastards before." I glanced at Lugh. "And the movement in the air felt wrong."

5

Understanding ran across his expression. The ability to hear the whispers of the wind and to use her as a weapon was one I'd only recently gained. While second sight ran through our family, the storm power had apparently come from my father's side. Not that I really knew anything more about him than his name—Ambisagrus—and the fact that he and Mom had had a brief dalliance which had left her pregnant with me.

But according to Beira, he was a curmudgeon and a minor god of storms and wind. And she would know, given she was a hag—who were, just like their male counterparts, gods trapped in human flesh as a form of punishment. The only difference between the two was the fact that curmudgeons could alter their appearance to a more pleasing form while hags could not.

"We need to keep moving," Locryn said, and did so without waiting for the rest of us.

Lugh hesitated. "Keep an eye on the situation and let me know the second anything changes."

I nodded, took a final glance at the comms room, and then followed him into the tunnel. But every sense was now hyperaware, and though I couldn't see or hear anything untoward, I could feel it in the caress of the wind.

Which was annoying and scary all the same time, especially when I had no real idea how to control the wind's parameters.

But whatever had caused that slight tremor in the air was definitely following us. Either it was a very hungry rat, or it was something else entirely. The movement didn't feel large enough to be caused by human or fae—although in all honesty, I was so green when it came to understanding this particular "gift," I could be reading all the signals completely wrong—but that still didn't discount the possibility of it being some kind of shifter in his alternate form.

And rat shifters did exist in Deva. I knew for a fact there were several working for the IIT; one of them had even saved me from an attack when I'd walked into a trap to save Mathi's life. He might be my ex and a lying, cheating elf of the highest order, but I'd been well aware when I'd stepped into a relationship with him that light elves didn't view them the same way the rest of us did, and I just couldn't hate him for, well, doing what came naturally.

We eventually reached the end of the military tunnels and stepped through a break in the wall. The neighboring tunnel was low, narrow, and far older, forcing Lugh to bend at an uncomfortable-looking angle. I was ten inches shorter, but even so, had to duck fairly low to get past some of the sections. Thankfully, the ceiling height did improve as we moved further along, but it never gained the more comfortable proportions of the military tunnels. Eventually, Locryn stopped and pointed to a neat three-foot circular shaft cut into the rough-hewn stone ceiling, right at the point where it met the wall.

"There she is, just as requested," he said with obvious pride.

I shone the light up. The shaft was about ten feet deep and topped by a large flagstone; that had to be the basement's floor, given the floors in Nialle's main living areas were all lovely old oak.

Evenly spaced notches lined either side of the shaft and were no doubt intended to be foot- and handholds, though the distance between each did make them a little more suitable for dwarves rather than we oversized pixies.

I glanced at Locryn. "This must have taken weeks to create."

He smiled. "Dwarves can work quick miracles when required."

"And when enough money is thrown your way," Lugh said, his voice amused.

"That too," Locryn agreed sagely. "You still got the map back to the museum we sent you?"

"You're not waiting for us?" I asked, surprised.

"Not being paid to wait," Brega said. "And the museum's an easy enough stroll from here."

I had a feeling their version of an easy stroll was far different from ours. But Lugh simply nodded and shook both their hands.

"Appreciate the help at such short notice."

"Anytime, Lugh." Locryn's quick grin revealed multiple wrinkles and a shiny gold front tooth. "Especially at the rates you're paying."

"Enough of that." Brega lightly nudged her partner's shoulder. "Don't be worrying about the ladder, Lugh— we'll come back and get rid of it when you're done."

Given there was no actual ladder to be seen, I presumed she was referring to the small mound of rubble positioned against the wall underneath the shaft. It was just high enough to allow someone my height to step up onto the first set of footholds. They must have already removed some of the digging waste, because there wasn't enough here given the depth of the shaft. It also wasn't high enough for either of them to clamber easily into the shaft.

As the two of them disappeared into the darkness of the tunnel, I wondered if our follower was still around. The air had no tales to tell right now, but instinct suggested he or she hadn't gone away.

Of course, instinct did tend to be something of a pessimist.

I glanced at my brother. "How long ago did you ask them to do this?"

"Around the same time the fae council called a halt on the museum's investigations into Agrona Claws."

There were three items that made up the goddess's claws—a crown, a sword, and a ring. According to legend, they could control shadows, darkness, and ruin—which we were presuming meant the destruction of crops, leading to famine and even pestilence. When used together, they apparently had the power to change the very essence of the world by either extending the night or banishing it altogether.

And extending light was what we suspected the Looisearch—the people behind it all—intended. By ensuring night no longer existed, they believed the Annwfyn—who were a distant branch of elves existing in a place alongside yet apart from our world, and who considered human, fae, and shifter flesh something of a delicacy—could never again hunt in this world.

The trouble with their whole plan was the fact that, while the Annwfyn appeared to make every attempt to avoid sunshine and any form of artificial light, no one had any real data on whether they could exist within it. It wasn't like anyone could risk asking, given their culinary tastes.

We'd already lost the crown to the Looisearch. We couldn't afford—the *world* couldn't afford—to also lose the sword or the ring.

I motioned to the shaft. "Why didn't you get them to make it wider? It's going to be a tight fit in there with your shoulders."

"I've been in tighter spaces, trust me."

"That did not answer the question."

He laughed. "Because they charge by the meter and the amount of rubble removed. Besides, anything wider might cause structural problems, as we're close to the building's foundations."

"Given the number of tunnels crisscrossing the area, it'd be fairly safe to presume that if the foundations were going to collapse, they would have done so by now."

It was more likely they'd been worried about causing minor structural movement that would get noticed and maybe get them in trouble.

He grinned and didn't deny the accusation. "Shall I go first?"

"Given how heavy that flagstone looks, definitely. Me and the rat will be just fine down here."

His gaze darted back to mine, his expression concerned. "It's still following us?"

I looked back down the tunnel. "I'm not sensing it at the moment. I'm not even sure if it's the rat Brega spotted. But I have my knives."

Said knives were wickedly curved blades made of pure silver, a metal that was deadly to shifters, due to the fact it formed a poisonous compound when it came into contact with certain proteins unique to them. Even elves were wary of silver; it wasn't as deadly to them as shifters, but their legendary healers couldn't easily fix wounds caused by it.

These particular knives had been gifted to my family back in the days when we'd been their guardians and could only be used by the females of our line, though no one had ever understood why that particular restriction had been placed on them. Either the old gods had been playing one of their weird games—gifting certain humans or non-humans powerful relics and then watching the fallout was something they'd found greatly amusing, apparently—or they'd suspected we'd have more need of their powers than our male counterparts.

Of course, it wasn't only the silver that made the knives deadly. They'd been blessed by multiple goddesses and could counter all sorts of magic. If family rumors were to be believed, they were also an effective counter to the wiles of the old gods, though as far as I knew, none of my ancestors had ever tested that one out.

Lugh glanced briefly at the knives strapped securely to my thighs and then nodded. "Shout the minute you see or feel anything untoward, and I'll drop back down."

"I'll be fine."

"I know, but you are my sister and the only one I have. It's my role as a big brother to look after you. Besides, you're wound up tighter than an antique clock right now."

Echoes of Mom and Gran using the same phrase rose, and grief briefly surged. I shoved it away and forced a smile. "Will you stop wasting time worrying about me and just get up there?"

Lugh laughed, then leapt up, grabbed the first of the handholds, and then began to climb.

I stepped back as a small amount dirt showered down but kept the light shining up so that he could see the holds. "Is there any form of security in the apartment we need to be aware of?"

"Not in the basement, but it's always possible the Eldritch have added something."

He didn't sound at all worried by the prospect; it was probably why he was the relic hunter, and I ran the tavern.

Once he was near the top of the shaft, he shifted position, securing his feet and bracing his back against the wall before he reached for the flagstone. With a grunt of effort that echoed softly down the shaft, he lifted it up and slid it carefully to one side. Then he hauled himself over the edge and disappeared.

I leaned a shoulder against the tunnel's wall and crossed my arms, and just for a second, thought about Mom. About how her laughter could fill a room with joy. The gentle way she'd ruffle my short hair every morning at breakfast, no matter how old I'd gotten. The tension so evident in her green eyes even as she'd calmly assured me she'd be back before dawn. Except she wasn't, because someone had shot her in the back and buried her body under stone... Grief rose, a deep, dark void that could all too easily swallow me whole if I allowed it.

I sucked in air and pushed the images and the pain away. I'd have to deal with the grief sooner or later, but right now, I had to keep focused on hunting down her murderers. They'd taken her from us far too soon, and they would pay for that.

Lugh reappeared a few seconds later, his light all but blinding me as it shone down the shaft. "All clear. Up you come."

I pocketed my flashlight, stepped carefully onto the stone mound, and reached for the first of the handholds. "It was very considerate of them to leave this."

"It was my consideration, not theirs. Wasn't sure how much shoulder strength you had."

I snorted and pulled myself up, shoving my left foot into a hold before reaching for the next. "I haul beer barrels around on a daily basis. My shoulders are just fine."

He grinned and offered me a hand as I neared the top, helping me up and over the edge. I dusted off my fingers, then pulled out my flashlight and turned it on. The basement was surprisingly wide if the expanse of the ceiling was anything to go by, and its brick walls were bare. The air was warm and softly circulating, which suggested Nialle had put in a mechanical ventilation system—which warmed cold air while removing moisture and providing air flow. It also meant the power hadn't been turned off, though that really wasn't surprising, given his girlfriend—Dana—had lived here with him. Whether she'd remain here or simply sell the place once she was given the all-clear from the Eldritch was anyone's guess.

It was difficult to gauge how far under the house the basement ran, thanks to the metal shelving that stood directly in front of us. It was filled with all manner of antiquities, from what looked to be prehistoric cutting tools to Roman terracotta and even a few old Tudor cannonballs—or at least, that's what I presumed they were, given their size and shape.

"This way." Lugh turned and strode toward the narrow gap between the shelving and the wall.

"Do you have any idea what you're looking for? Or are we just randomly searching?"

"I daresay the Eldritch and Nialle's murderers have already done the whole random search thing."

"Yes, but it's safe to presume Nialle didn't give the latter the information they wanted, given they came after you next. And even if the Eldritch interviewed Dana, she wouldn't have been able to give them a detailed list of any artifacts that might be missing."

"She did help him catalogue a lot of the stuff here, remember."

"Yeah, but knowing Nialle, there'd be a separate stash she knew nothing about. He's sneaky, like you."

He glanced over his shoulder, his expression mildly shocked but frost-green eyes glinting wickedly. "I don't keep hidden stashes."

I snorted. "Not at the old substation, true, but that's not the only building you own, is it?"

He grinned and didn't deny it. We passed two more shelving units and came out into a wide square area that sat between the shelves behind us and the ones ahead. Three long metal tables defined the boundaries of the open area; inside this were four filing cabinets and two whiteboards. Whatever had been written on them had been partly scrubbed off; only illegible bits and pieces remained.

I walked across to the oak staircase that led up to ground floor and leaned against the end newel. Despite its evident age, the inner song of the oak remained strong, and it spoke of an ancient grove and a tree cut down before its prime by humans unable to hear her music. Very few such groves remained today, and they were fiercely protected by the pixies and wood elves who lived in or near them.

Not that humanity was generally aware we pixies were part of that protection brigade. We'd been living amongst humans longer than even the elves, but most had no idea there were five branches of us, two of whom were as tall as the elves. Which was undoubtedly why many still bought into the whole "pixies are tiny beings who fly around sprinkling golden pixie dust everywhere" folk tale rubbish. There *was* one branch who did use pixie dust during their spelling, of course, and another who used it for flight, but it was little more than showbiz razzamatazz and totally unnecessary for either. The only real magic the rest of us had was one of manipulation; we could hear the song of nature and use its inherent power, and we females could also control the actions of humans, shifters, and some fae via direct contact. The ability to force compliance on others had apparently been part of an ancient goddess gifting the pixie nation with the six virtues of womanhood—beauty, a gentle voice, sweet words, wisdom, needlework, and chastity. The Aodhán line had managed to avoid gaining the bulk of those, especially the whole chastity thing. I mean, seriously, what had the goddess been thinking?

I crossed my arms and watched Lugh open the top drawer of the oldest-looking filing cabinet. "So Nialle does have hidden storage here?"

"He has an entire hidden room."

I raised an eyebrow and shone the flashlight around again. There was nothing to suggest a hidden room here, but I guessed that was the whole point. "Where? It looks as if the basement actually runs the full length of the house."

"It does."

"Meaning he's robbed space from under his neighbors' house?"

"No. He's just gone down another level."

With the drawer fully extended, he reached in, felt around for something at the very back of it, and then grunted in satisfaction. A heartbeat later, what I'd presumed was the solid, filled-in section under the rise of the stairs slid silently aside, revealing steps leading down into deeper darkness.

"Nialle really *was* sneaky," I commented. "What would happen if someone tried moving the filing cabinet?"

"Nothing. The switch is fingerprint activated and wireless, so even if the cabinet was moved or the switch found, it wouldn't matter. You stay up here and keep an eye on things."

"Things" meaning our possible follower, I knew. I nodded and squatted on my heels, keeping my back against the newel as I pulled out my phone, checked for reception, and then began scanning the various social media sites for anything of interest.

It was a good half hour later when I caught the first whisper of unusual movement in the air. I scanned the shadows clustered around the shelving units but couldn't see anything. Yet that whisper of movement was getting stronger. The rat—or whatever else it was—had entered the room and was slowly making his or her way around the far end of the shelving units. I sent Lugh a warning text and asked him to start making some cover noise to distract our intruder, then shoved my phone away and placed my flashlight on the floor, shining its light up to the ceiling. The glow would be just bright enough for me to see where I was going when I was behind the shelving.

As a metallic clatter rose from the hidden room, I padded softly along the wall. The air's whispering kept me informed of the intruder's movements, but right now, I was more concerned about stopping him from escaping so we could question him.

Once I reached the shaft, I squatted and carefully lifted one edge of the flagstone until I could get a good grip on it with both hands. Then, with a silent grunt of effort, I thrust up and moved it back across the shaft. After placing one side down carefully on the first little ledge, I gently lowered the rest of it.

Just as the wind whispered her warning.

The shifter was coming at me.

Fast.

TWO

I glanced up sharply but couldn't tell if the figure was male or female because it was little more than a blur of movement.

I dropped the flagstone, drew my knives, and pushed backward, hitting the wall hard enough to force a grunt. As a fist skimmed past my nose, I slashed with one knife, ripping through leather and flesh with equal ease. Blood splattered lightly across my face and arm, but the figure made no sound. It—*she*—simply twisted around and came at me again. I backed away, dodging her blows, the knife blades gleaming a deep and deadly blue as I cut and stabbed in response. But I wasn't a trained fighter and, as one of her blows got through and scraped my cheek open, I knew I had to end it. Fast. Before more than just my cheek was bleeding.

I shoved one knife into its sheath and quickly gathered the air around my fingers. As another blow whispered past my chin, I flung the gathered ball of air. It hit her midsection and lifted her high, sending her crashing into the top end of the shelving unit and then down to the floor. As bits of pottery and metal rained down on top of her, Lugh appeared, grabbing her by the back of the neck and throwing her hard against the wall. She hit it with a grunt, dropped back to the floor, and didn't move.

Lugh checked her pulse and then stepped over her and strode toward me. "You okay?"

I thumbed the blood away from my cheek and nodded. "Yeah."

He gently caught my chin, moving it to one side so he could examine the wound. "That almost looks like a knife wound."

"She wasn't armed. She was just fast."

"Probably caused by a fingernail then, which is never a good thing when we're dealing with rats." He stepped to one side and waved me forward. "There's a medikit in cabinet two. Go use it while I gather and restrain our captive."

I nodded and walked down the aisle, noting the area under the stairs once again looked solid. Lugh had obviously hit the close button as he'd galloped to the rescue.

I headed over to the filing cabinets and discovered someone had thoughtfully numbered them. While I found the medikit and disinfected the wound, Lugh placed the shifter onto an office chair, then rolled her around the metal table, depositing her close to the wall.

She was thin, with a pinched face, sharp nose, and short, somewhat spiky gray hair. I might have only met one rat shifter, but she definitely fit the mold. The upper left sleeve of her pale leather jacket had been sliced open, and while blood soaked its edges, the flow wasn't strong enough to suggest I'd hit anything vital. Of course, that was neither here nor there, because if she didn't get treatment soon, the cut would fester and blood poisoning would quickly become a rather deadly problem.

"We going to treat her wound?" I asked.

Lugh wrinkled his nose. "She'll need a steady infusion of sodium nitrate to rid the toxin from her body, and that's not something medikits carry. It has to be done at the fae hospital."

Sodium nitrate—a preservative found in many processed foods, and which could be deadly in large amounts to humans and most fae—was rather weirdly the only thing found to stop the progression of silver poisoning in shifters. It apparently worked by flushing the deadly compounds from their organs and tissue.

"Then we'll need to release her sooner rather than later." We really had no other option, given none of us were supposed to be here.

He nodded as he walked over to the nearest shelf and picked something up. It took me a second to realize it was handcuffs.

Amusement twitched my lips. "Why on earth would Nialle have handcuffs here? Or shouldn't I ask?"

Lugh laughed and tugged the woman's hands behind the chair. "I'd love to say 'don't ask,' but in truth, I have no idea if he and Dana were into dominance games. Knowing Nialle, I wouldn't have thought so."

"So why are they here? They don't look that old."

"They're swing cuffs from around 1912, and he found a storeroom filled with them years ago, when he was on the dig of an old prison from that period. The museum wasn't interested in taking them all, so he occasionally sells them online." He locked them onto the shifter's wrists, then placed the key in his pocket and moved back around the table. "There's a scrub and sink area down the far end—do you want to grab a bucket of water so we can wake our captive?"

At the mention of water, said captive suddenly gained consciousness. "Don't you fucking dare."

I glanced at Lugh. "She was foxing? How did you know?"

"Felt the jump in her pulse just as I locked the final cuff." He crossed his arms and added, in a voice that was flat and cold, "Give me one good reason why we shouldn't just leave you here to rot."

The shifter snorted. "Because it would be against the law, and everyone knows you two are law-abiding citizens."

"Given I'm an antiquarian who steals for a living, it would be fair to say 'everyone' who told you that is wrong." Amusement filled his voice but didn't reach his eyes. "You attacked—and injured—my sister. To repeat, give me one good reason why we shouldn't just leave you here."

She didn't answer, instead wasting time twisting and tugging at the cuffs, trying to break free.

"You won't succeed," Lugh said. "They may be old-school, but they were designed to counter the strength of shifters."

She swore and glared up at us. "What's it going to take for you to release me?"

"Well, for a start you can tell us why you attacked," I said. "As a rat, you could have hidden anywhere and simply waited for us to leave. Why attack?"

Surprise flickered through her eyes. She hadn't expected us to know what brand of shifter she was. "Thought it was a trap."

Lugh frowned. "Thought *what* was a trap? Us leading you into this basement?"

She nodded. "It was all a little too easy, wasn't it?"

I shared a glance with Lugh. He looked as confused as I was, which made me feel a little better. "Why would you think that?"

"Neither of you reacted, even though you obviously suspected you were being followed. Then the minute I'm inside here, you attempt to lock me in."

"Replacing the flagstone could hardly be describe as locking you in, especially when pixies have no control over stone and couldn't have fused it as we can wood," Lugh said. "Besides, as a rat shifter, you could have lifted it with a pinky finger."

Her gaze ran from Lugh to me and back again. "You're pixies? Well, fuck."

"What is it with our attackers not doing their homework?" I shook my head. "Who employed you?"

She sniffed. "Don't know."

"Was it Kaitlyn?"

Kaitlyn was a part elf who operated an antiques shop in Old Deva, but it was in truth little more than a front for her more profitable brokering services. If you wanted something bought, traded, stolen, or even threatened, Kaitlyn was apparently your woman.

She'd been responsible for allocating the contract that had led to the attack on the tavern and the knifing attempt on me—though I did believe the idiot shifter when he said he'd only meant to scare me. He'd been under pixie influence—a handy little ability we females had that enabled us to control humans, shifters, and most fae except elves with voice and touch—at the time, so he'd had no choice but to tell the truth.

"No," the woman said, with perhaps a little too much vehemence.

I leaned across the table and gripped her shoulder. Her

teeth snapped toward my hand, the sound loud in the hush of the basement. She didn't get me, thanks to the fact I'd been careful to keep out of biting range. But this close, I couldn't help noticing that not only was she looking much paler, sweat now beaded her forehead. The infection had started, and that meant our questioning window was closing. I might be annoyed at her, but I didn't want her dead.

That sort of thing never went down well for Aodhán and Tàileach lines of pixies.

The fact I'd wounded her in self-defense might not invoke the whole "never shed blood except in service of the old gods or in self-protection" curse that had been placed on us eons ago, but I had no desire to test its boundaries or realities.

"You will answer all our questions honestly and do exactly as we ask." My voice took on a deeper timbre, filled with magic as powerful as it was old. "Now, tell me, was that denial the truth?"

Her face twisted for several seconds then she spat out, "No."

I released her and stepped back again. "What was the contract you accepted, and what information did Kaitlyn give you about us?"

"Nowhere near fucking enough, obviously." Sweat trickled down the side of her face, and she shook her head with quick impatience. Droplets of sweat hit the metal table, sizzling lightly on the surface before becoming inert. "And if you know anything at all about Kaitlyn's business model, you'll know we never get the name of the contractor."

"What was the job, then?" Lugh asked.

"To follow Bethany Aodhán, record where she goes and what she finds, and report back on a daily basis."

"To Kaitlyn?"

The shifter nodded.

"How many of you are in the team?" Lugh asked. "It's not a job you could do on your own."

Once again, she fought replying. And once again, it was of no use. She hissed; it was a sound filled with frustration. "Three. We do eight-hour shifts."

Meaning someone was pretty desperate to keep track of my movements, and that was odd, considering Lugh was the relic hunter, not me.

Of course, I *was* the one who'd found the crown.

I just wished I wasn't also the one who'd lost it again.

"What are their names? And yours?"

"Leina Rodden, Reid Rodden, and Eryk Rotte."

"Right," Lugh said, "you're going straight back to Kaitlyn from here and tell her you can no longer fulfil your contract—"

She made a low growly sound. "You can't make me do that."

"He can't," I said, "but I can, and you will do just that. And you will never again accept a contract that involves either me or my brother."

She somehow managed to look both annoyed and unimpressed by the restriction. A smile tugged at my lips. "And if you're thinking I can't stop your counterparts from accepting such a contract, you'd be right. But Sgott Bruhn happens to be our adopted father, and as the head of the night division of the IIT, he could make life extremely hard for them."

As statements went, it was mostly the truth. He might not have officially adopted either of us, but he'd been Mom's partner for over sixty years and had been in my life since I was two.

Whether he'd break the law for either of us was another matter entirely, but I personally doubted it. Which didn't mean he wouldn't help us—he would and had—but he'd do it within the framework of the law.

Or, at the very least, a flexible version of it.

Leina's eyes widened, alarm evident. She'd obviously had dealings with either Sgott or the IIT.

"Kaitlyn really didn't tell you anything about your targets, did she?" Lugh said. "Maybe do a bit more groundwork before you take the next contract."

She muttered something I couldn't quite catch, and then said, "What happens now?"

"We let you go," Lugh said.

"And when you do report back to Kaitlyn," I added, "you will tell her nothing about the tunnel, the shaft, or indeed this basement and whatever you might have seen here."

She swore. Long, loud, and rather colorfully.

"Wow." The corners of Lugh's frost green eyes crinkled. "Who knew there were so many different ways to say 'fuck you'?"

He walked around the table, grabbed the back of the chair, and rolled our captive across the room and down the small corridor to our shaft.

I followed, eying the shifter with increasing concern. Her breathing was ragged, and small patches of gray were beginning to bloom across her skin. It was a sign of just how rapidly the infection was moving.

As Lugh bent to release the cuffs, I stepped to one side of the chair—out of kicking range—then touched her shoulder again. "Change of plans—go directly to the hospital and get the silver poisoning treated. You can make a call to Kaitlyn and your team on the way there."

She grunted but didn't say anything. The minute she

was released, she shoved the flagstone aside and disappeared down the shaft as swiftly as... well, a rat down the drainpipe. I sent the wind down to check on her, even though she really had no choice but to obey my last directive. She'd shifted shape and was moving away at a run.

I glanced at my brother. "Looks like I'll have to go talk to Kaitlyn again."

"Yeah, because she took so much notice of your warning last time." He shoved the flagstone back into place, then grabbed the chair and wheeled it back to the working area. "Might be better if we let Sgott handle it."

"That would mean telling him we were here. Best not to, given he has to remain on a working relationship with the Eldritch."

He glanced at me. "Sgott can read you like a book."

"So you lie to him."

"It'll just be easier all around if we admit what we've done upfront. He'll find out in the end anyway." He pulled an envelope out of his pocket. "Found this in the hidden room; it's addressed to me."

"What does it say?"

"Didn't have time to check."

He sat on the table and slid a nail under the seal. I perched next to him and tried to curb my impatience as he carefully opened the envelope and removed a piece of yellowed parchment that had been wrapped around several smaller pieces of paper. He placed them on the table beside him and studied the letter.

I'd seen enough of Nialle's writing to know it was his.

Lugh took a deep breath and then began to read it out loud. "If you're in possession of this letter, then I'm dead, and you, my friend, need to be very careful. I became aware of being followed a week ago and reported it to the IIT. I

25

thought they'd dealt with it, because I didn't spot my watchers again, but if you have this, then I was wrong. We both know how much I'd hate that."

Lugh's laugh was a strangled mix of amusement and sorrow. He scrubbed a hand across his face, smearing the tears that glistened on his pale red lashes. "Yeah, we do, my friend. We do."

I wrapped an arm around his shoulders and hugged him. He rested his head against the top of mine for a few seconds, then read on. "I haven't had the chance to speak to you much these last couple of days, thanks to the fact we've both been nose deep in our own investigations. But before I head to France, I wanted to let you know what I've found, and I don't want to risk a text or leave the information somewhere a thief or intruder could easily find."

"He always was a little paranoid about his research findings," I murmured.

"And with good reason, given he did have some research stolen a few years ago. Then there's the whole singing bowl fiasco."

The singing bowl was part of the Éadrom Hoard and had reappeared in the museum's crypts a few weeks ago. How and why remained a mystery. Certainly, none of the museum's protections—magical or physical—had given any sort of clue or warning. The fae council believed it was an inside job, and they'd had Nialle and Lugh high on their list of suspects, even though both had been thoroughly questioned about it at the time by the museum's security division *and* the fae council's.

Nialle's death would not have taken the spotlight of suspicion away.

I hugged Lugh a little tighter. He gave me a wan smile and continued to read the note.

"All those months with my nose stuck in old books finally paid off—I found a reference to the Sword of Darkness in the *Book of Tywyllwch*."

"Which is?"

"A late-thirteenth century Welsh manuscript containing Old and Middle Welsh poetry attributed to a late-sixth century poet. The original is kept in the National Library of Wales, but we have a later parchment copy."

"Huh." I motioned him to continue.

"There was a poem about a black sword that cast all before it in darkness, wielded by Rostin De Clari, a chevalier who was said to be Agrona's earthly embodiment."

"Agrona was goddess—why would she embody a man?"

"Stop interrupting and we might just find out."

I snorted. "I have no patience. You should know this by now."

"Says the woman who wasted ten years of her life with an elf who was never going to marry her."

"Yes, but the sex was good, and it wasn't like there was a more suitable prospect around."

Mainly because single male pixies were something of a rare breed here in Deva, and while I had nothing against humans, I couldn't see the point of engaging in anything more than a sexual liaison with them, given their short life spans. Why set myself up for heartbreak that way?

Lugh rolled his eyes and went on. "After talking to Jacques—who is, before you cut in again, dearest sister, a French archeologist Nialle has worked with on and off over the years—I was able to contact a historian familiar with Rostin De Clari. He's been working on the family tree and believes there could be a direct descendant alive today."

"Which doesn't mean they'll know anything," I commented.

"No, but it's a start," Lugh said, and then continued reading. "I did try to convince the historian to send me the information, but it's the man's life work and he's... well, he's as paranoid as me."

I could almost hear Nialle's half laugh as Lugh read that. I hugged my brother again and then said, "Which begs the question—if Nialle was killed for that information, does that mean the historian is dead as well?"

"Jacques should be able to tell us that. I'll contact him once we're out of here." He glanced down at the letter again. There were only a couple of lines left. "If I don't come back, seek the oracle. She left a message for me a few hours ago and said she had some information on the goddess's Claws that I needed. I know you're wary of self-proclaimed prophets, Lugh, and with good reason, but there was something in this woman's voice that made me believe her. I did return her call, but she didn't pick up and, well, we'll see."

Lugh took a deep breath and released it slowly, then picked up the smaller bits of paper. One was a newspaper article with the picture of a woman with black hair, thin features, and a rose tattoo running down the left side of her face. Her name was Peregrine Stace, and she'd apparently been arrested for attempting to steal the *Book of Tywyllwch* from the Welsh National Library. Nialle had circled the woman's name in red, with a question mark above it but no explanation as to why. The other piece of paper was a hastily written note with a name—Castell—a phone number, and then the words "Oracle to old gods" and "return call" underlined.

"Oracle" was a term once used by elven mystics, though humans had purloined it long ago and since besmirched it.

28

I tapped the note. "I didn't think there were any true oracles left."

"There's none that I know of, especially not when it comes to a direct line to the gods." He grimaced. "She's probably just a half-blood clairvoyant cashing in on the term."

"Or she's actually a hag herself."

He wrinkled his nose. "That's unlikely, given how unhelpful the hags generally are. And it's not like the curmudgeons come out to play very often."

Only to procreate, and rarely at that, it seemed.

"Beira has been helpful. At least so far." But then, she did want me to take up Mom's mantle—to, in her words, 'seek what has been lost, and to confront the darkness in whatever guise it takes.'

"And helping her might well have gotten Mom killed. You need to be wary of them."

"They're old gods. It's not like I can do a whole lot if they decided to play nasty."

"Given who your father is, that's not necessarily true anymore."

I couldn't help a wry smile. "A half-blood with no real idea how to control her 'god-given' powers isn't going to be much of a threat to them."

"Then perhaps you can simply annoy the hell out of the hags until they throw their hands up in frustration and walk away. You're good at that sort of thing."

"Ha!" I said and nudged him hard.

He laughed, then rose and tucked the papers into his pocket. "We'd better get out of here."

"You don't want to keep checking the secret room in case you missed something? We may not get back here."

"There won't be anything else to find. He would have mentioned it if there were."

I slipped off the desk. "What's the plan then?"

"For tonight? We rest. And you do have a tavern to run tomorrow."

"One that is only partially open, thanks to the heritage council dragging their heels getting the ground-floor window fixed." Besides, Ingrid—who'd been the tavern's manager for more years than I could remember—was more than capable of running it. It wasn't like we were in the middle of summer and the main tourist season. "Do not think you're going to investigate any of this information without me, brother mine."

"I wouldn't dream of it."

I snorted. "Say that with a little more conviction, and I might be tempted to believe you."

He grinned, hauled up the flagstone, and waved me to precede him. I climbed over the edge, felt for the toeholds, and then carefully went down. When I'd reached the end of the shaft, I dropped down onto the pile of stones, then slid down to the tunnel floor and shone the light up for Lugh.

He replaced the flagstone and came down the shaft with surprising speed, considering how little maneuvering room he had.

"Why are we going back to the museum?" I asked.

"Because it's closer than my place, and it's easier to catch a cab from there." He pulled up Locryn's map on his phone and made it larger. "This way."

I fell in line behind him. The tunnel's ceiling remained low enough that he had to hunch his shoulders and lean forward at that uncomfortable-looking angle again.

"And tomorrow?"

"I think we'd be best served by doing as Nialle suggested and contacting this Castell."

"Without knowing anything about her? That could be dangerous."

"Every move we make from now on is likely to be dangerous."

That was a statement I certainly couldn't dispute, given we still had no idea who was really behind any of this. Just because we suspected the parents of the women murdered by the Annwfyn were the ones seeking the Claws didn't mean we were right. We hadn't yet found any confirming information, though that might change over the next couple hours, given Sgott and Cynwrig Lùtair were currently in the process of interviewing them.

If they could find them, that was.

As the stone underfoot became more slippery, I concentrated on where I was putting my feet in an effort to avoid ending up on my butt. The water trickling past my boots looked as foul as the air smelled, and while I did have a stash of spare clothes at Lugh's, I didn't have any shoes—something I'd better remedy if I was going to be spending more time there.

It took twenty minutes to get back to the museum, though the map didn't lead us directly into the main building but rather to an old stone staircase. Lugh pulled a bunch of keys from his pocket, used an old-fashioned and rather rusty-looking one to open the heavily stained wooden door at the top, and ushered me through. We came out into the Doric-style portico situated on the opposite side of the parking area to the museum.

"This way," he said, and took off quickly.

I hurried after him. We moved around the right of the gorgeous old building and through an ornate metal gate that led onto Grosvenor Road. From there, it was a quick cab ride to the old power substation he'd converted years ago. When compared to the lovely old terraces that lined the rest of the street, it was a particularly uninspiring and rather ugly single-story, brown brick building, but it had one thing they did not—plenty of storage space. In a city as old as Deva, that was as rare as hen's teeth.

He punched the access code into the security system's screen sitting to one side of a grimy black wooden door. When it clicked open, he stepped to one side and ushered me through. The building's foyer was large and airy, with only two doors leading off it; the one on the left went into the accommodation portion, while the one on the right into his office and the storage area. I went left, into the large and airy combined living and kitchen area. Unlike my place, these areas were spotlessly clean and tidy. He might be messy at work, but he was pin neat when it came to his home and even his private life—to the point where he hadn't had a serious relationship for a good ten years now. The few women he had dated never made back it back here to his sanctuary.

I was seriously hoping Darby—an elven healer I'd met at school and who'd been pining after Lugh for as long as I could remember—was about to change all that. Especially now she was aware he really *was* attracted to her.

If it was a big brother's lot in life to protect his little sister, then it was the little's sister job to ensure her brother did not end up a lonely old man.

Not that he or I could in any way be termed old. We pixies tended to live almost as long as elves.

I walked over to the kettle and flicked it on—Lugh refused to have a coffee machine on the grounds it was a waste of money when he never spent that much time here

—and then headed to his fridge. It contained a small bottle of milk, a few apples, half a loaf of bread, and some cheese growing a colorful array of mold. "When was the last time you did a proper shop?"

"Shopping hasn't been on my list of priorities over the last few days." He tugged out his phone. "Order pizza while I contact Sgott."

I did so, then made a quick call to Ingrid, telling her I wouldn't be in tomorrow and asking if she'd be able to step in. Thankfully, she was more than happy to do so.

After I made a pot of tea, I placed it on a tray with two mugs and a small jug of milk on the cusp of useability, then carried it over to the wide stone coffee table that dominated the space between the two sofas.

From what I could hear of the conversation, it seemed Sgott wasn't taking the news of our latest escapade too well.

No surprise there.

"Told you we should have lied." I placed the strainer over the first mug, then picked up the pot and poured the tea.

He shoved the phone away and dropped onto the sofa opposite. "If he'd found out later—and he would have, given his nose for lies—it would have been worse."

I picked up the milk and poured some into my mug. It didn't curdle, so that was a bonus. "I take it he's going to speak to Kaitlyn first thing?"

He nodded. "He said he's already given her one warning, so this time, he'll haul her into the station, just to remind her no one is above the law."

"That won't help, given what he's said about the strength of her lawyers." I took a sip of tea. "How are they going interviewing the relatives of the five women attacked by the Annwfyn?"

"No luck. They've talked to Cynwrig's other cousins, but Jalvi's parents and siblings have gone missing, and apparently no one knows how to contact them."

Cynwrig was a dark elf and co-heir to the Myrkálfar throne, and Jalvi another cousin. Her sister, Telyn, had been one of the victims in the Annwfyn attack that had started this whole Claws mess.

Of course, while Cynwrig might be heir to the throne, he wasn't a crown prince but rather "just" a lord. That was because, technically, there was no such thing as elven kings these days, as they'd been forced to swear allegiance to the "true" and very human royal line after they—and most of the fae—had lost the great war eons ago.

We pixies had sensibly kept out of that mess.

I drank more tea and raised my eyebrows. "And they believed that?"

A smile tugged at Lugh's lips. "Sgott certainly didn't. He requested their phone numbers and is in the process of getting a warrant so they can be traced."

"If they really don't want to be found, then surely they would have gotten rid of their phones."

"You'd think so, but we aren't dealing with hardened crims here."

"No," I said wryly, "just dark elves who have been in the smuggling business practically since creation itself."

He laughed. "They've had no luck contacting the light elf relatives, either. They've apparently retreated to the inner circle of the main encampment, and neither man can enter without permission."

Light elves—or Ljósálfar, as they were more prop-erly known—lived in a huge swath of land that lay to the east of Deva. It contained vast forests and multiple lakes and had two distinct districts. The outer circle contained the everyday administration areas, as well as the living quarters for the two lower levels of light elf society. The inner circle was the province of high bloods and contained vast houses made of living trees. Or so Mathi had once said. It wasn't like I'd ever been there.

I took another sip of tea. "Did you mention our so-called oracle?"

He nodded. "The name didn't register, but he said he'll run a search when he gets back to the office and let us know what he finds."

"And the other woman? Peregrine what's-her-face?"

He smiled. "Stace. Again, he can't provide any information until he gets back to the office."

"Well, that's just frustrating." My phone pinged, and I glanced down at it. "Pizza is two minutes away."

"Excellent." He rose and disappeared into the foyer to collect it.

I accepted mine with a grin of thanks, quickly opened it up, and drew in a deep breath. There was no finer smell than a pepperoni pizza with extra cheese. Lugh, to my ever-lasting horror, was a man of simple tastes and preferred a margherita.

There was little talk while we demolished our meal. Once I'd gathered up the empty boxes and placed them in the trash, I made another pot of tea and then said, "Is it too late to try the oracle now?"

"Probably, but I can at least leave a message if she doesn't answer." He took the scrap of paper out of his pocket, then dialed the number, putting it on loudspeaker so I could hear the call.

It rang out without giving him the option of leaving a message.

"Well, I guess it was never going to be that easy," I said.

"No." He put his phone away. "I'll try again in the morning. In the meantime, what movie do you want to watch?"

I raised an eyebrow. "You're going to sit here and watch a movie with me? Really?"

He grinned. "No, dumbass. You're going to sit here and watch a movie while I go catalogue a few things."

I snorted, unsurprised. "I might grab a shower first—can I borrow a T-shirt so I can rinse out my undies and bra?"

He raised his eyebrows. "Why not just raid your clothes stash?"

"Because then I'd have to replace them."

He rolled his eyes. "Women."

I bounced up and kissed his cheek, and then headed into the bathroom.

After the shower, I picked up the TV remote and started scrolling through Netflix until I found something I hadn't seen before. By the time midnight rolled past, my eyelids were starting to droop. I checked on Lugh, told him I was off to bed, and got a vague wave in return.

Situation normal, I thought with a smile, and headed into the spare bedroom. I was asleep almost before my head hit the pillow.

The sharp ringing woke me who knows how many hours later. I fumbled around on the bedside table without opening my eyes, then hit answer and said, "Whoever this is, you'd better have a good reason for ringing at this ungodly hour."

The laughter that rolled down the line was decidedly

sexy, and my hormones woke with a vengeance. Which did them no good when Cynwrig was at the other end of the phone rather than in bed with me.

"I would hardly call seven in the morning ungodly."

His voice was smooth, velvety smoke, and I resisted the urge to sigh in pleasure. Like most dark elves, he was blessed with not only good looks but an inner magnetism that made him nigh on irresistible. Light elves were divinely beautiful beings, but dark elves were sex on legs. They could make the iciest of maidens weak with wanting without the slightest bit of effort.

No one would ever accuse me of being an ice maiden, so it came as no surprise to any of my friends that I'd jumped into bed with him at the very first opportunity.

Of course, he was absolutely keeping me "close" to garner information about our hunt for the Claws, but that was okay. Despite the attraction that burned between us, I was in many respects doing the same thing. Having a dark elf with access to the fae council, the night council, *and* the black market—which his people basically controlled—on our side had already proven handy. I had no doubt it would continue that way as our hunt for the Claws and Mom's killers deepened.

"Especially," he continued softly, in that same sexy "I can make you come just by talking to you" tone, "for a woman who runs a business that opens at eleven most days."

I pushed upright and tried to get a grip. "I had a late night, and Ingrid is in charge of the tavern today."

"Any particular reason for either?"

It was casually said, but I couldn't help but notice the slight sharpening in his tone. We might be casual lovers, but that didn't mean he liked competition.

Not that we'd had any sort of discussion about our liaison or what—if anything—either of us were expecting out of it other than sex. We just hadn't had the time. I guessed if it went on for more than a few weeks, we'd have to. Casual was absolutely fine, but the last thing I needed was getting into another relationship where I was the only one not playing the field.

"Sgott didn't tell you about Lugh's and my adventure last night?"

"He did not."

"Why not?"

"Because our search was basically fruitless, and I went home early."

Part of me couldn't help but wonder if he went home alone, but I didn't ask the question because I had no right to. "I take it that means no one was willing to talk?"

"My people certainly weren't. I'm hoping that'll change this morning now that Sgott isn't with me. What did you and Lugh get up to?"

I gave him a quick update on what had happened and then said, "I don't suppose you know an oracle going by the name Castell, do you?"

"There was a woman who went by that name living in the Coedwig Hynafol light elf encampment in Wales, but I was under the impression she'd died some fifty or so years ago."

"Is it a common name amongst the elves up there?"

"No." He paused. "I'll make a few calls before I head off this morning. Can I take you out for dinner tomorrow evening?"

"That would be lovely. And thanks."

"My pleasure."

Hopefully it would soon be mine... I smacked the

thought away, dropped the phone back onto the bedside table, then headed into the bathroom to check if my underwear had dried out on the heated towel rack overnight. It had, so I got dressed and wandered into the kitchen to make a pot of tea.

Lugh came stumbling out just as the kettle boiled. "What the hell are you doing up at this hour?"

"Cynwrig rang. He's under the impression I'm always up early."

"Well, you are."

"Only when I'm working."

"Which is basically all the time. You're as bad as Mom when it comes to taking holidays away from the tavern."

"Darby and I holidayed in Mallorca only a couple of years ago."

"That was six years ago, dearest sister, and Darby is as bad as you are."

He perched on a stool on the other side of the breakfast bar and scrubbed a hand across his bristly face. There were large bags under his eyes, suggesting he hadn't gotten all that much sleep.

"What time did you get to bed?" I slid the cup of tea across to him, then pulled out the bread and inspected it for mold before popping it in the toaster.

"About an hour and a half ago."

"Why so late?"

He wrinkled his nose. "Got caught up in cataloguing. I don't get all that much time to do my personal stuff, what with work and all."

I grinned, and his eyes narrowed. "Don't say it."

Which was basically a dare and one I couldn't resist. "You need a live-in assistant, brother, just like Nialle had. Can I suggest—"

"No."

"But I'm sure she'll be more than—"

"Definitely not. I enjoy my bachelorhood."

"No, you don't. I've heard you complaining many a time about the lack of permanent female companionship in your life."

"Only in my weaker moments."

"Darby has all the time in the world to wait for one of those weaker moments."

He rolled his eyes. "Enough. What did Cynwrig want?"

I chuckled softly but didn't push it. "He asked me out to dinner. I told him what Nialle's note said about the oracle, and he said he'd make a few calls and try to track her down."

The toast popped, so I placed it on a plate and gave it to him, along with a knife and a jar of marmalade—the only decent spread he had in his pantry. The man lived like a monk—at least he did here. I'd seen the fridge in his office, and it was packed.

"Meaning she does exist?" he said.

I popped in two bits of bread for myself, then leaned back against the counter and crossed my arms. "He was under the impression she'd died fifty years ago."

"Interesting." He smeared marmalade over the toast and then took a bite. "Before I started cataloguing, I did a quick Google search for our would-be *Tywyllwch* thief."

"Peregrine Stace? Did you find anything?"

"According to news reports, she was released on bail pending trial and subsequently disappeared. A body was found two months later in a Conway boarding house room, and they believe it was hers."

My eyebrows rose. "Believe?"

He nodded. "Decomposition was so bad they're still searching for dental records to confirm identity."

"Did she use her own name to check in?"

"Yes, but there were no security cams to confirm it was her, and she paid cash rather than using a credit card."

"All rather convenient, don't you think?" The toast popped, so I put it on a plate and then spooned on marmalade. Lugh might like it smeared, but I preferred to actually taste the stuff. "It also doesn't say much about the hostel's cleaning roster—or the people she was bunking with—that decomposition got so bad they've resorted to checking dental records."

"They have a few individual single-person cabins at the rear. She was staying in one and asked not to be disturbed."

"Still doesn't explain why no one investigated the smell." I took a bite of toast. "When did all this happen?"

Amusement touched his eyes. "Guess."

I contemplated him briefly. "Not long after Jalvi accessed the Myrkálfar records for the Tenebrous hoard?"

While the light elves had been responsible for looking after the now missing Éadrom hoard, the dark elves guarded the Tenebrous one. Agrona's Claws had apparently been a part of it, but the dark elves had no record of how or when they'd disappeared. It wasn't a recent event, however.

I had no idea which of them guarded the third hoard. Maybe it was a joint effort.

"Got it in one," Lugh said.

I frowned. "She can't be an elf with that surname, though, so how would she be connected to the search for the Claws?"

"She might not be. She might simply have been

41

employed to steal the book. The news reports did imply she had a long and shady history."

A long and shady history meant she was better at getting caught than getting away. Surely if the people behind all this were going to hire a thief, they'd have hired a good one. There were plenty of dark elves out there who subcontracted their services.

"So why haven't they made another attempt to steal it?"

He shrugged. "For all we know, they decided it was easier to bribe one of the librarians to either scan or jot down the poem. Thing is, they might not have been able to do much with the information afterward. Not everyone can read Old Welsh."

"Why? It's not that different to the modern stuff, surely?"

"Old Welsh differs in both the way they use some words and the alphabet. Middle Welsh is closer to today's usage."

"The things you learn." I took another bite of toast. "They've had plenty of time to find someone who could read it, though."

"Yes, but they'd have to be extremely careful. The dark elves would have put an alert out on anything relating back to the Claws the minute they realized what was going on."

"Cynwrig never mentioned that."

Lugh snorted. "He's a dark elf—he's never going to tell someone he barely knows something like that."

I grinned. "I would hardly say he 'barely' knows me, brother mine."

He rolled his eyes. "I meant in the character sense, not physical."

I laughed. "Hopefully Sgott can grab the investigation report and we can see where it's at."

"It's probably precisely nowhere. These people seem to be rather good at leaving little in the way of leads."

"They'll make a mistake sooner or later. We just have to have patience."

"Says the woman who has none."

I grinned but didn't reply as my phone rang; the tone told me it was Ingrid. I hit the answer button and said, "There's a problem?"

"You could say that." Her voice was dry. "There's a rather raggedy-looking woman here who's refusing to move and is loudly proclaiming to all and sundry that she needs to speak to you as a matter of urgency."

My eyebrows rose even as my pulse rate skipped and raced on. "Did she say why?"

"No, but she did give me a name and said you'd recognize it."

"And that name is?"

But even as I asked that question, I knew.

"Castell," Ingrid said. "And she's claiming she's got an urgent message from your father."

CHAPTER
THREE

"**M**y *father?*"

"What's going—"

I held up a finger to silence Lugh as Ingrid said, "Yeah, that was my reaction too, given the wastrel hasn't been sighted around these parts since he left your mom some sixty-odd years ago."

"You knew him?" I couldn't help my surprise. In all these years, she'd never said anything, but maybe that was at Mom's request.

"Sighted him once. Had an odd energy around him."

"Does this woman?"

"No."

Which didn't preclude the possibility of her being another hag. While Beira was surrounded by a stormy and rather electric energy field, she was the goddess of winter and storms, so that was to be expected.

Still, it didn't hurt to check. It was always better to know exactly what we might be dealing with.

"Is she a hag?"

Ingrid snorted. "Well, she's old and a little scruffy, but calling her a hag is going a little far."

A comment that suggested Ingrid had no idea hags still existed. Interesting, given she was pixie—even if one from a much smaller branch—and should have at least some awareness of the old gods.

"Tell her we'll be there in fifteen minutes and give her a cup of coffee or tea."

Ingrid snorted again. "She demanded whisky."

My eyebrows rose. "Did you give it to her?"

"I got the distinct impression she wouldn't take a 'no' very kindly, and it's still too early in the day to be dealing with confrontational guests."

I couldn't help smiling. Ingrid might be small, but woe betide any customer who thought she could be easily intimidated. Still, if Castell was a hag, then caution was a wise move. Beira hadn't in any way threatened me, but I'd certainly gotten the impression trouble was only a finger-snap away.

"Keep an eye on her, and we'll be there soon."

The minute I hung up, Lugh said, confusion evident in his expression, "Her? I thought you were talking about your father?"

"Castell apparently has a message from him. She's at the tavern waiting for us."

"This whole situation is just getting weirder," he muttered and then pushed to his feet. "I'll call an Uber while you finish getting dressed."

I grabbed the last bit of toast from my plate, then ran into the bedroom to shove on my coat, boots, and knives. Once we were in the Uber and scooting through the morning traffic, I gave Cynwrig a call. His line was busy, so I left a message, letting him know that we were on our way to meet Castell, who was currently sitting in the tavern.

Ye Old Pixie Boots—the name Mom had given the tavern when she'd taken it over after Gran's retirement a hundred or so years ago—was a heritage-listed building in the historic heart of Deva's famous Rows area. It consisted of an undercroft at street level, one floor at "row" level, and our living quarters above that. Aside from a few layout changes upstairs and the necessary modernizations, it was basically the same building that had stood on this spot since it had undergone minor remodeling in the late 1400s.

I pushed open the old wooden door and clattered down the steps to the main room. Given its age, it was an unsurprisingly intimate space, with five tables in this front area and four smaller ones and the bar on the far side of the stairs. Bright pixie boots of various sizes hung from the exposed floor joists and beams, some of them real, some of them not, but all of them a nod to tourist expectations.

Castell wasn't hard to miss, given she was the only other person in the tavern. Ingrid was industriously scrubbing things down behind the bar at the other end, making herself useful as she kept an eye on our guest, as requested.

At first glance, Castell looked to be little more than a small bundle of rags. Her long silver hair was rather wild-looking and knotted with leaves and twigs. Her features were pale and heavily wrinkled by time, and her hands claw-like and spotted with age.

She sat at a table pushed up against one of the five sturdy oak posts supporting the upper floors. Its song reverberated through the floorboards under my feet, and it was a joyous, welcoming sound. It wasn't aimed at me, though, but rather the woman who leaned against it.

A woman who was as old as that post was, and who'd

known it in its prime, when it was in truth a tree rather than a mere building support.

This woman wasn't a hag.

She was a light elf. A very, very *old* light elf.

As I neared the table, her gaze snapped up to mine, and my steps briefly faltered. Her eyes were white. Completely white. There was no pupil or iris, just an unnatural milkiness that shone with luminous power.

A power that was almost godly.

I shivered but forced myself on. A smile tugged at her thin lips, and the corners of her unusual eyes crinkled. "I can taste your shock from here, young woman, and I admire your ability to keep it contained. Most folk don't have such presence of mind or manners the first time they meet me. Who's that with you?"

"My brother, Lugh."

"Ah yes, the dead antiquarian's partner. I'm told you rang last night, young man, but sadly, I was in no position to answer the call." She cackled, and it was a decidedly wicked sound. "Had the arms of earth wrapped around me and was too lost in passion to be worried about such mundane things as phone calls. At my age, dearies, desire doesn't come calling all too often, and you have to grab it while you can."

I blinked, more than a little taken back. Such candor wasn't what I'd expected from a light elf. While they were extremely promiscuous beings, even when married, they tended to be emotionally remote. It was very rare for them to share intimate sexual details with people they knew, let alone complete strangers.

"And now I've gone and shocked you both once more." She cackled again and patted the table. "Come now, sit down, because I've a message that must be delivered and not all that much time left in which to do it."

I pulled out the chair opposite her. Lugh sat next to me. "Why?" he said. "Because, if you'll excuse my candor, you may be old but don't look on death's door to me."

She laughed again. "And you'd be right, my lovely. But you two took your time getting here, and my driver is picking me up at eight thirty." She raised her left hand. "Can't exactly drive myself anywhere with claws like these."

"Then why don't you get them fixed? They can, you know," I said.

Hell, these days the fae healers were experts at not only halting but pushing back the ravages of many inflammatory diseases, including arthritis. It might not last over the entire lifetime of an elf, but for a woman in her twilight years, I'd have thought it a no-brainer.

"Because the most beautiful trees in a forest are not the ones that grow tall and straight, young woman, but rather those that are gnarled and twisted by time and life." There was a hint of censure in her voice, and it was oddly reflected in the oak post's song. "Besides, it would hardly help my ability to drive, given I'm blind, and there's no healing that."

I leaned back in my chair and studied her for a second. There was a sharpness in her gaze, an alertness, that suggested all was not as it seemed. "I'm thinking being blind doesn't mean you can't actually see."

She cackled again. She really was the strangest light elf I'd ever met.

"And you would be right, because the inner eye is always more powerful than the outer. It's just that most folk have no idea how to focus it."

"And this inner eye allows you to 'receive messages' from the old gods?" Lugh asked.

Her gaze unerringly flicked his way. "I'm tasting skepticism in your manner, young man, and I find that odd, given who your mother was."

"You knew Mom?" I asked before Lugh could reply. It wasn't that he didn't believe in oracles or prophets, just that he'd come across too many false ones in his time as a relic hunter.

And one had almost cost him his life.

"Not personally, no," Castell was saying, "but such dark news travels fast on the wind, and it carried to all those who could hear it."

"No disrespect meant," Lugh said, "but you're a light elf —a forester. The manipulation of living, growing things is your purview, not wind and storms."

"What I was born and what I became are two very different things." Her gaze came to mine, and there was a light—a warning—that twisted my insides. "As some here will discover soon enough."

"Meaning?" I asked, glad only a fraction of the inner trembling was evident in my voice.

"Meaning, young woman, that ignoring the path that stands before you will ultimately lead to a darker and far more dangerous journey."

As I stared into her unearthly eyes, something strange happened. My awareness of the tavern—and Lugh—faded, and my focus became singular. All I could see was a field of white. Then the white gave way to shadows and fire, a cowled figure standing over a sacrificial stone darkly stained with eons of bloodshed, and a knife that gleamed with an unearthly light raised high. Words filled the air. Words that trembled with power. I had no understanding of them or the spell being invoked, but I could feel the darkness in it and taste its intent. It was taking life to give life.

Then one word reverberated, and the shadows stirred in response.

Ninkil.

The spell was bringing into being the god of rats and destruction.

The knife flashed down. I glimpsed red hair and green eyes but no clear features. Then there was darkness and chaos, and I was sucking in air, suddenly desperate to breathe and survive...

The white blinked and receded, and awareness returned. My breathing was ragged, and Lugh's hand was on my arm, his grip so tight it felt like he was holding me upright. But my attention remained on the benignly smiling woman on the other side of the table.

"What the hell was that?"

She raised a pale eyebrow. "I am never privy to the visions given in the translucence. What you saw... might be nothing more than a possibility. One of many paths that might yet lie before you."

"If I don't do what you and the old gods want me to, you mean," I said, voice flat. Angry.

At her, at fate and the old gods, and even at Mom for not teaching me about the Eye, second sight, or anything else that might have been useful to help save the lives of those around me.

Castell cackled again. "I am merely a vessel for the whims and messages of the old gods. What I want is neither here nor there."

Lugh was still gripping my arm, so I smiled and squeezed his hands to let him know I was okay and that I'd explain later. His eyes narrowed—a warning that I had better—and then he released me. I returned my gaze to Castell. "And is the vision I saw what you were sent here to tell—or show—me?"

"No." She finished her whisky in one long gulp, then raised the glass and wobbled it slightly in demand. Her hands might be twisted, but she seemed to have no trouble holding that glass.

It was also notable that, despite her earlier comment, she seemed in no hurry to leave.

Ingrid—who was a short but fierce-looking pixie with curly green hair and deep brown eyes—came hurrying over from the bar and cast a questioning look my way. I nodded, and she plucked the glass from the other woman's hands and hurried off to do the refill.

"Then what message are you here to deliver?" I said.

"And what information did you have for Nialle?" Lugh added.

Her gaze flicked across to his. "I was told to warn him the Looisearch watch his movements and plan to snatch what he finds in France."

"Who told you to warn him?" I asked, once again before Lugh could say anything.

"That would be Beira." She wrinkled her nose. "She's rather cantankerous, that one."

I frowned. "Why would she go through you? The hags have sent us messages before."

"Yes, but Beira had only just heard the whispers brewing on the wind and, given the urgency of the situation and the fact she had no desire to reveal her presence to anyone else because her enemies rise, she had no choice but to avail herself of my services."

"And who the hell are the Looisearch?" Lugh asked, with a look my way. "I take it you already know?"

I wrinkled my nose. "I'm sure I mentioned them."

"I'm sure you didn't."

"Ah, well. Sorry." I waved a hand. "Cynwrig believes it's the code name for the group who are looking for the Claws and consists of the immediate families of the women killed by the Annwfyn."

Ingrid returned with Castell's drink. She accepted it with a nod of thanks and then said, "Indeed. And you need to re-steal the crown before they find the sword."

"They surely can't be any closer to finding the sword than we are," Lugh said. "There's not all that much information to be found—"

"Nialle found all that was needed. Your delay in following his footsteps has given them a head start." She raised a gnarled finger, as if to cut off any protests. "And don't be giving me excuses about it being hard to trace the steps of those who have already disappeared, because that may apply to society's eyes, perhaps, but not Eithne's."

Eithne was one of the original hags and their greatest prophet. According to Beira, Eithne's Eyes—which were her real eyes turned to stone to preserve them—held the ability to not only help find the missing treasures of the old gods but also hunt down darkness. Mom had certainly used her Eye for the former, and very successfully over the years. That Eye was now mine, but it was already evident my connection to the thing was very different to Mom's.

No one was really sure why that was or what it meant going forward. Which, to my way of thinking, suggested I need to remain extremely wary of using the thing, especially after Beira's warning that what tracks darkness also attracts it.

Lugh pushed to his feet. "Then I had better go contact Jacques straight away."

As he hurried down the other end of the tavern to make the call, Castell said, amusement evident, "I do like a man of action. Shame he's far too young and inexperienced for the likes of me."

I raised an eyebrow. "When has that ever stopped a light elf?"

"Oh," she said, expression sharpening, "I'm sensing a slice of bitterness in that comment."

I waved a hand. She might be blind, but I had a feeling she'd nevertheless see the action. "Long story, and one I have no desire to get into right now."

She studied me for a couple of unnerving seconds before saying, "Desire remains, despite the anger. It is hard to shake the sensuality that is the touch of a light elf."

"Well, luckily for me I have the touch of a dark elf to counter it."

Her gaze narrowed. "Ah, yes, Cynwrig Lùtair. Watch your heart with that one."

A smile tugged at my lips. "My heart isn't under threat from the likes of Cynwrig Lùtair."

"I like the confidence with which you say that, young lady, and I do wish you luck. The dark elves are rather pertinacious once they set their minds on a course of action."

My smile grew. "He's heir to the throne. I'm in no danger of anything more than sexual satisfaction. What do you know about the Eye? Was it you who found it and sent Beira its location?"

She nodded. "Via your father, of course. He'd been searching for it since your mother's disappearance, from what I could gather."

"Did he say where he found it?"

"No, he did not."

Of course not. "Then what was the message he sent you here to deliver?"

"Ah, yes, I almost forgot." She cleared her throat, closed her eyes, and reached. Not physically, but rather magically. And though my knives didn't react, it was an action that blew through me oddly, and it somehow felt as if my second sight was being activated without my consent. The air began to stir, and the sharp electricity of a distant storm spun around me, sending sparks dancing across my skin. Then, in a voice that deeper and more ethereal—of this world and yet not—Castell said, "What was your mother's is now yours. What comes cannot be avoided. You are the weapon but have not yet been primed. Seek she who stands with her head in the clouds at the junction of earth and sky as a matter of urgency."

A shudder ran through Castell's body, then she sucked in a deep breath and somehow looked... less. As if the otherworldly presence that had briefly swept through her had drained all her strength and power, leaving her shriveled and shrunken.

Even her eyes looked faded. Gray.

"You heard?" she croaked.

I nodded. "Understanding is another matter."

Her laugh was little more than a faint echo of its former self. "The old ones do like their puzzles."

And so did old elves, I'd wager. I repeated the last line in the message and then said, "I don't suppose you know of a place resembling that description, do you?"

She shook her head, then raised her glass and downed the whisky. "And now, I must be going."

I rose with her and half reached out as she wobbled unsteadily on her feet. "Do you need help to your car?"

She shook her head. "The lovely Tyree is about to walk in the door."

Said door opened on cue, and a big man stepped inside. Aside from being tall, he was thickset, with wild brown hair and a beard that was long enough to be plaited.

A bear shifter, I suspected.

He moved down the steps with surprising grace and tsked in concern. "Looks to me like you've been overdoing it again, Ms. Castell."

"Aye," she said, and held out her hand. "Home, dearest Tyree."

"At once, Ms. Castell."

He swept her up into his arms, and she snuggled into his massive chest. I suspected sleep wouldn't be too far away.

The big man looked at me. "If you'd be holding the door open for us, it'd be appreciated."

I nodded and quickly moved back to the tavern's entrance. "Will she be okay?"

"Aye. She always gets like this after the old gods have spoken through her. These days, it takes a week or so for her to recover, as she's not as spritely as she once was."

I opened the door and stepped to one side. "I take it you've worked with her for a while?"

He nodded. "Nigh on fifty years now, but it's a position that's been handed down through my family for generations."

"Really?"

I couldn't help the surprise in my voice, and he smiled. "Humans have always been the greatest threat to oracles, but their trigger finger has to be mighty fast to beat the speed and fury of a bear shifter."

I'd witnessed how fast and powerful Sgott was when in

full fight mode, and it certainly wasn't something you'd want to be at the other end of.

Once I'd locked the door again, I picked up the whisky glass and walked back to the bar. Ingrid had already headed back upstairs, so I tucked the glass into the underbench washer, then waved to catch Lugh's attention. He was still on the phone and talking softly enough that I could barely hear him but glanced around and raised an eyebrow. I pointed upstairs, and he nodded.

I ran up the first stairwell, then walked past the Row level bar to reach the smaller set of stairs tucked into a nook behind it. I generally kept this door locked, not only because the upper area was my living quarters, but also because there'd been a spate of thefts after Mom's disappearance. We now believed the thieves had actually been planting listening devices and that the thefts had been a cover. Which didn't make much sense to me, but Sgott had suggested that by stealing smaller items, they were distracting us from the bigger picture. He'd arranged for all the bugs to be removed, but I wasn't about to take the chance of them being replaced.

Even with the roof height lifted, the upstairs accommodation was confined. There was a combined kitchen-living area and two bedrooms—one had been Mom's and was now mine, and the other one Lugh and I had shared as kids and was now used as a spare. The bathroom was the second-biggest room in the flat, but it had to be, given four oversized pixies had at one point all been using it. Gran had moved out of the tavern when she'd handed the reins over to Mom, but before then, she'd slept in the loft, which was only accessible through a hatch and a loft ladder—something that had never worried her, as she'd been remarkably spritely right up until the day she'd passed.

I walked over to the kitchenette and filled the kettle, then unhooked the fourth of seven mugs hanging from the bottom of the overhead cupboard. Inside, stone clinked, and relief stirred. No one had found or stolen the Eye.

I rolled it onto the counter. It was as black as midnight and about the size of an oval-shaped marble. Which, given it had once been an actual eye, was about right. Though its power was currently inert, deep purple light jagged through its heart. It might not be emitting any energy, but my presence had nevertheless placed it on standby. I'd only have to touch it and it would activate.

I shivered and tugged open the nearby junk drawer. Inside, amongst all the other bits and pieces Mom had deemed too useful to throw out, was an old silk glove. It was one of Gran's, and I had no idea where the pair was, but I could totally understand why Mom had never ditched it. Even after all these years, her scent and her presence still seemed to resonate.

Using it as a shield, I carefully picked up the stone, then walked across to the coffee table and placed it down. The thrum of power was faint but gathering strength, and the jagged streaks of purple stronger. I wasn't ready to confront whatever darkness lay waiting just yet. I needed to fortify myself with tea first, and maybe even chocolate.

I made a pot of tea, then grabbed a block of Cadbury Toffee Whole Nut out of the fridge. Once everything was on the tray, I carried it over to the coffee table.

Lugh clattered up the stairs just as I was pouring the tea.

"Any luck?" I asked, without looking up.

"Yes, and in more ways than one." He dropped onto the sofa opposite and then accepted his mug of tea with a nod. "Why is the Eye out?"

"Because I thought I'd use it and see what happens."

"That would explain the chocolate, then."

I nodded. "It's never too early."

"Mom used to say the same thing." The sadness that crossed his expression echoed through me, gut-wrenching in its intensity. He took a drink and then added, "Jacques is still alive, and said Nialle was the only person who'd called asking about a historian familiar with Rostin De Clari and the legend of the sword."

Which wasn't really surprising if they'd been following him around. They could have simply talked to the historian themselves after Nialle's visit. "Does he know if the historian is still alive?"

"His name is Jules Auclair, and he's not only alive but currently in Liverpool attending an event at the World Museum this evening." Lugh glanced at his watch. "He's staying at The Duke on Duke and will meet us in the cafe next door at ten. Coffee and patisseries are on us."

I raised my eyebrows. "You've already called him?"

"Yes indeed."

"Meaning he's still refusing to give information over the phone. Does he understand just how dangerous us meeting with him could be?"

Lugh shrugged. "I did mention it. He wasn't convinced."

More fool him, then. "Did he say if anyone else had contacted him?"

"No."

Which I guess meant our competitors for the Claws either already had the information from Nialle, or they were once again sitting back and waiting for us to do the bulk of the legwork. It had, after all, worked when it came to the crown.

"So he's just going to give us the same information he gave Nialle?"

Lugh nodded. "But he said he did a little more research after speaking to Nialle and has added a few extra notes to our folder."

I took a drink and then said, "You know, maybe I'm just being overly suspicious, but this all feels a little too convenient to me."

"If it was a setup, he wouldn't be suggesting we meet in a busy cafe. That's hardly an inconspicuous environment."

"Which could be the whole point."

"It'll be fine, Beth." He hesitated. "But take your knives, just in case."

"I was intending to." I scooped up the glove, then carefully picked up the stone. "I'll tuck this away again. We haven't the time to tackle it now."

"Which Castell would no doubt say was a mistake."

"No doubt, but a few hours shouldn't make all that much difference."

And I crossed mental fingers that I hadn't just tempted the gods and fate.

As I dropped the stone back into its mug and hung it up, Lugh said, "Seriously? Could you actually hide it in a *less* secure place?"

"Someone knew about my bedroom vault, Lugh. There's no guarantee they don't know about the others."

The "vaults" were cavities that existed in the wooden bones of the old building. A long-ago, probably human, owner had repaired the old oak frame by using metal straps bolted onto the beams rather than hiring a pixie to heal the wood. Though we pixies considered it an extremely crude and inconsiderate action—something akin to ramming nails through flesh to hold broken bones together—it had at least held the rotting pieces together long enough for my great-grandmother to buy the place and start proper repairs. In the process of restoring the oak beams to their original condition, she'd created "natural" cavities behind the remade straps, thereby providing perfect hidey-holes for small items. There were four in all—one in each of the bedrooms, one here in the living room, and one upstairs in the loft.

Lugh grunted. "Mathi knew about the vaults, didn't he? Did you ever ask him who'd he'd mentioned them to?"

"No, but it'd be pointless, given Gilda was using Borrachero to milk him for information about the fae council and gods know what else."

Borrachero was a truth drug that put the recipient in a chatty sort of twilight zone and left them with no memory of the event. We had no idea how long she'd been using it on Mathi, and we couldn't ask because she'd been murdered a few days ago.

Dead ends were quite literally the overarching theme of our investigations at the moment.

With the Eye safe and the glove back in the drawer, we quickly finished our tea and headed out again, returning to Lugh's to grab his car before heading toward the M53 and Liverpool.

Roadworks slowed us down, so by the time we reached Liverpool and found parking close to Duke Street, it was right on ten.

Lugh sent Jules a message saying we'd just arrived and would be there in five, then said, "This way." We hurried down the stairs and out onto the street. The icy wind hit hard enough to blow me back a step or two before I caught my balance, and it was filled with the scent of the sea and rain. I quickly did up the coat's buttons, not just to keep the chill out but to also hide my knives from casual sight. While certain magical artifacts were legal to carry, human cops tended to get twitchy at the sight of knives. Especially when they were as deadly looking as mine.

The Duke on Duke was situated on the ground floor of a gorgeous old Georgian building. The frontage was half brick, half glass, the windows framed by wood that had been freshly painted black. The door was also wood, but like the window frames, its song was muted by multiple layers of paint.

"This looks more like a bar than a café," I said.

"It's linked to the hotel next door, so it probably acts as both." He pushed the door open and waved me through.

The inside bones of the building were exposed brick, the floor black and white tiles, and the styling modern. Pink leather stools lined the bar on one side while sapphire leather bench seating ran the length of the other. The regularly spaced tables were freestanding—no doubt so they could be moved around to cater for different-sized groups —while the chairs were also sapphire in color but did at least look comfortable. That wasn't always a given in places like this.

A waitress approached and asked if we'd like a table. Lugh explained that we were meeting a friend and gave her his name. She directed us to the back of the room and said she'd be down in a few minutes to take our order.

The front half of the room was much brighter than the rear and, as the shadows clustered around us, an odd sense of trepidation stirred. Gods only knew why.

Jules had claimed the last table at the end of the long room but didn't move or even look our way as we approached. There was a half-consumed coffee close to his right hand and a phone next to his left. AirPods were in his ears, and his eyes were closed. He looked for all the world like someone caught up in the program he was listening to.

I had a growing suspicion that was not the case.

Lugh stopped in front of the table and cleared his throat. "Jules Auclair? I'm Lugh Aodhán—I contacted you a few hours ago about..."

His voice trailed off. Then he swore softly, reached across the table, and gently pressed two fingers against the other man's neck.

He swore again, this time with more vehemence. I didn't have to ask why.

Jules Auclair wasn't listening to music or anything else on his phone.

He was dead.

CHAPTER
FOUR

"The bastards got here before us." Though Lugh's voice was low, it was filled with anger and frustration.

"It could be a natural death," I said. "Maybe he had heart problems or something."

Lugh shot me an irritated glance. "Heart attacks generally don't kill you instantly. Even in the case of a sudden cardiac arrest, there is at least a few minutes between onset, unconsciousness, and death."

And whatever *did* kill him had been superfast. The café staff would have noticed something was wrong, otherwise.

My gaze jumped to the shadows behind him. Sometimes in these sudden death situations a soul would linger, but there was no indication that was the case here. Not that I was overly sensitive to those sorts of things—no more sensitive than anyone attuned to the energy of living things such as trees was, at any rate.

I shivered and rubbed my arms. The café was warm enough, but a chill now crept through my soul. I had a bad feeling this death wouldn't be the first we'd discover.

I did my best to ignore the premonition and said, "How the hell did they know he was going to be here? We only made the arrangements a few hours ago."

"Someone had to be following him. Maybe they overheard our conversation." Lugh scrubbed a hand through his short, unruly hair. "Or maybe Sgott's people missed a bug in the tavern."

"That's highly unlikely." Especially when they'd only been removed twenty-four hours ago, and there'd been no opportunity for anyone to replace them. "It's possible Jacques lied to you. Maybe we weren't the only ones who called about Jules."

"He has no reason to lie."

"If these people are capable of murder, they're capable of dropping a threat or two to force compliance from someone."

"Jacques isn't the type who'd take any sort of threat lightly, but I guess it's possible. It still begs the question, if they wanted Jules dead, why do so now, just before he was due to meet us? They could have done it at any time since Nialle's murder and been less obvious about it."

"Maybe this was their only opportunity." I half shrugged. "Do you want to call it in while I go talk to the waitress? Maybe she saw something that could help."

"We need to search him for the information he was carrying first."

My gaze swept the table. "There's no folder, so surely that means whoever did this has taken it?"

"Yes, but it's possible the folder wasn't all he had. Historians like to keep a notebook handy just in case they need to jot down information. Keep an eye on the waitress and let me know if she approaches."

As he slipped into the bench seat next to Jules, I stepped

into the gap between the tables to block anyone's view and watched him while keeping half an eye on the waitress's movements.

He quickly but efficiently went through Jules's overcoat then moved onto his blazer and eventually pulled a small notebook free from an inside pocket.

He slipped it into his jacket, then nodded and rose. I moved back to the other side of the table just as the waitress headed our way.

"Everything okay?" she asked in a breezy and unconcerned way.

"I'm afraid not." I lightly touched her arm. As my power surged, I added, "Please don't panic, but it appears our friend has passed. My brother is calling in help, but I need to know, did anyone approach this table before we did?"

She licked her lips, her expression horrified as she stared at Jules. "A woman did. She ordered them both a coffee but left without finishing hers."

Thankfully, she didn't seem aware that I was compelling her to answer. Or maybe she was just the naturally chatty type and saw no reason not to. "How long were they talking?"

There was a slight hesitation. "Maybe ten—fifteen—minutes. She left not long after the coffee arrived, which was slightly odd."

"How long ago was this?"

She wrinkled her nose. "I think he arrived just after nine thirty, and she walked in a few minutes later and asked for him. He did say he was expecting someone."

The timing suggested either this woman had been following him or he'd planned to meet with someone other than us. My gut was voting for the former rather than the latter. "Are you able to give me her description?"

"Well, she was a dark elf, about so tall." She raised a hand, indicating a height a few inches over my five eight. "And she was wearing really gorgeous earrings."

I raised my eyebrows. "You noticed her earrings?"

She flashed me a grin, but it faded quickly as her gaze returned to Jules. "I love amber, and hers were shaped to look like a bee."

"Was there anything else that stood out to you?"

"About her? No."

"And him? Do you know if he gave her anything? Like a file?"

"She did leave with a folder." She frowned. "Why are you asking all these questions? You cops?"

"No, just curious." Given the last thing I needed was her realizing she was being compelled, I quickly added, "You'd better go inform your boss what has happened, but don't tell anyone else and don't mention my questions to either him or the cops."

I pushed the enforcement of that last bit, and she nodded. "You're staying here? You won't touch anything?"

"The police will want to talk to us, given we found him, so yes, we'll stay. And no, we won't touch anything."

She hurried away. I glanced at Lugh. "The cops and ambulance on their way?"

He nodded. "Though it's too damn late for the medics to be of any help."

I crossed my arms and studied Jules for a second. "If the woman is behind his death, what could she have administered to make it look so natural?"

"I don't know." He glanced around. "There're no security cameras, so I guess we'll have to rely on a postmortem giving us at least some answers."

I nodded. While we wouldn't get those results, Sgott would look at them if we asked.

The cops arrived at that point, and the manager escorted them down, giving the two of us side eyes as he explained the situation. One of the cops took our statements and details while the other began to photograph the scene. As the medics bustled in and we stepped out of their way, the officer said, "You're free to go. If we have any further questions, we'll contact you."

"Thanks, Officer," Lugh said, then motioned for me to lead the way.

Once back outside, I drew in a deeper breath and then said, "What now?"

"We go to the café across the road and take a look at the notebook while keeping an eye on developments here."

"I'm thinking the only developments will be the medics removing his body and the cops leaving after doing a few more interviews. On the surface, there's nothing suspicious about his death."

"Maybe, but I need a good strong coffee to keep me awake enough to drive home. Besides, we really can't plan our next move until we read Jules's notes."

"Good point." I motioned for him to lead on and, after waiting for a couple of cars to pass, we ran across the road and headed for the other café. But as Lugh pushed the door open, a frisson of awareness hit. I stopped and looked around but couldn't immediately see a reason. Aside from the nosy parkers still clustered around The Duke, there were few other people out on the street. I suspected the fact it was so damn cold was one reason for this; the other would be the ominous and rather dark cluster of clouds gathering overhead. While I could feel the thunderous power of the storm deep inside, all any sensible person had to do was take one look up and know it was either get inside or get drenched.

As if to emphasize this point, the sky rumbled, a deeply ominous sound that rolled through the air and echoed through my being. A few seconds later, lightning flashed. It was in that momentary streak of brightness that I saw him.

He was tall and dark skinned, wearing a black trench that emphasized the width of his shoulders and muscular arms. He moved with a grace and power that drew the eye, and I wasn't the only one to notice. There might not be many of us out on the street, but more than one woman cast a second glance his way.

"Beth?" came Lugh's question, "What's wrong?"

"I just spotted Cynwrig. Go grab us a table, and I'll be there in a minute."

He cast a glance up the street, then nodded and made his way inside. I hurried after Cynwrig, not wanting to call out until I got closer. But he must have sensed my presence, because he stopped abruptly and turned around, his gaze unerringly finding mine.

The slow, delighted smile that stretched his lips sent my hormones into a feverish dance. I watched him approach, enjoying the sensuality evident in every step.

"Well, well," he murmured, sliding a hand around my waist and pulling me closer to his big, powerful body. "What an unexpected delight to find you here in Liverpool."

I didn't reply. I just tangled my fingers in his thick, dark hair and pulled his lips down to mine. Our kiss was all heat, passion, and promise, and it made me wish we were some-where—anywhere—else, so we could explore the desire that burned around us.

By the time I released him and stepped back a fraction, neither of us was breathing very steadily.

"That, dear Bethany, was a cruel thing to do to a man when we're in the middle of a street."

I laughed and rose on my toes to drop another, much quicker kiss on his lips. The desire I could taste on them only made me want him more. "What are you doing here?"

"I was right in my suspicions that Sgott's presence was the reason we weren't getting answers. Jalvi is here, in Liverpool. You?"

She was here at the same time as our historian? That was interesting timing—especially given the waitress's description. "We were supposed to meet someone in The Duke, but he was murdered before we got there."

He studied the café across the road for a second. "I take it this person was connected to the search for the Claws?"

I nodded, swung around, and offered him the crook of my arm. "Can I buy you a cup of coffee? Or do you need to resume your hunt for Jalvi?"

He smiled. "Jalvi wasn't at her hotel when I checked. I have my people watching the foyer while I head down to the docks to talk to our team down there. But that matter isn't urgent, and I'd much rather spend time with you."

A smile tugged at my lips. "Good answer."

"Truthful answer." He hooked his arm through mine, his big body radiating heat and desire as we walked back to the café. "I take it Lugh is also here?"

"Grabbing a table as we speak."

He pushed open the door, then ushered me through. The café was more homely and inviting than its competition across the road, the chairs a retro sixties style and the matching tables covered by cheery red-and-white checkerboard tablecloths.

Lugh had found a table next to the front windows and

flashed Cynwrig a welcoming smile. "I've ordered drinks and croissants all round."

"Excellent," I said as Cynwrig pulled out a chair for me, then sat beside me. His knees brushed mine, and his smokey silver eyes gleamed wickedly. He knew exactly what that oh-so-light connection was doing to my pulse rate. "What did the notebook say?"

Lugh gave me the look. The one that said I needed to be patient. The same one he knew I'd ignore. "Unfortunately, Jules wasn't only using shorthand, but his writing is minute and verging on unreadable. It's going to take a little time to transcribe the whole thing."

"A historian with unreadable writing? Unimaginable," I said dryly.

"If people can't read it, people can't steal it," Cynwrig said, amusement evident. "It's a motto my people have lived by forever."

And one that had obviously stood them in good stead, given how successful they'd been in black market trading for absolute eons.

The waitress arrived with our pastries and said cheerily, "The coffee will be here shortly."

"Thanks," Lugh said. Once she'd left, he added, "From the little I've read, Rostin De Clari was female, not male—"

"Ha!" I cut in. "Told you the goddess wouldn't work through a male."

"In this particular case, it would seem you're right." It was said in the tone a teacher would use on an irritating student. "Though there are plenty of examples through time where gender didn't seem to matter."

"And who, pray tell, is Rostin De Clari?" Cynwrig asked.

As Lugh explained, I reached for the chocolate croissant, took a bite, and almost groaned in pleasure. There weren't many places outside France that did a perfect chocolate croissant—in my opinion, anyway—but this place got pretty damn close.

I licked some chocolate from my lips—very aware of the sharp increase of intensity of Cynwrig's gaze as I did it—and then said, "Did they know she was female? It was unheard of back in those days for a woman to be a chevalier, wasn't it?"

"Yes, but she presented as male throughout her life and had female lovers, so none were the wiser. They only discovered the truth on her death here in England."

It was likely her servants knew—it would have been extremely hard back in those days to successfully conceal your periods. But if she had female lovers, then maybe they were used as decoys when that time came around. Plus, period syncing was a known—if not studied—phenomenon.

"If she fought and lived in France, why did she die on English soil?" Cynwrig said. "That's an extremely unusual choice, given England and France were very often at war during the Middle Ages and Early Modern periods."

"It seems to have had something to do with the sword, and De Clari's wish for it to be concealed, never again to be raised by the hand of humanity."

"It's the Sword of Darkness, so why not simply wrap it in shadow? And why come to England to do that? It's not as if the old gods were continent restricted."

"Depending on what year De Clari came to England," Cynwrig said, "it's possible that we were already guarding the crown and the ring. The sword was the last of the Claws to be placed in the Tenebrous Hoard."

"Would she have known that though?"

Cynwrig shrugged. "It would depend on her connection

with the sword and the goddess herself. Does the notes say anything in regard to the Claws?"

Lugh reached for the crème pâtissière-filled croissant, leaving Cynwrig the cinnamon apple. He didn't seem to mind. "Unfortunately, that's as far as I've gotten with the notes, so I have no idea what other information there might be."

Cynwrig glanced at me, silvery eyes dark with barely banked desire. "Were you able to question the café's staff before the police arrived?"

"Yes." I hesitated, but there was no point in avoiding the matter any longer. "Tell me, does Jalvi wear amber earrings that resemble bees?"

He stilled for a fraction of a second and then sighed. It was an annoyed and regretful sound. "Yes, she does, and it would certainly explain why she was absent when the hotel staff insisted she hadn't left yet."

I frowned. "How could they be sure? There's usually more than one way in and out of a hotel, and it's not like they'd keep an eye on everyone coming in and out."

The smile that tugged briefly at his luscious lips held little in the way of amusement. "In this case, it's a boutique hotel with only a dozen rooms, so they're familiar with all guests. Both the internal stairs and the elevators deposit guests into the lobby; there are three exit options from there, but all are visible to check-in and anyone seated nearby."

"So how did she leave without being seen?"

"There's an external fire escape that's kept locked unless there's an emergency. It is easy enough to disengage the alarms and unlock a door if you have the knowledge."

And Jalvi obviously did. "Is it possible her family

warned her you were on the way and she simply absconded before you arrived?"

"Yes, though they were warned against it."

If his tone was anything to go by, there'd be hell to pay if they had.

"However," he added, "the fact that the woman seen with your historian before his death wore the same earrings as Jalvi does makes it unlikely. They were handmade and one of a kind. She wouldn't have been foolish enough to wear them if she in any way suspected she was being tracked. And she certainly wouldn't have done so if she thought her presence could be linked to the historian's death."

His tone was flat and it yet somehow contained a deep wash of anger and sorrow. Or maybe it wasn't so much his voice but rather the deep connection that flared between us, allowing me to sense his emotions.

"I'm so sorry, Cynwrig." I slipped a hand over his thigh, and his muscles jumped under my touch. Just for a moment, his natural magnetism surged, making it hard to breathe.

A difficulty that only increased when his hand slid over mine. The sheer force of this man's presence was definitely dangerous to my health.

"You have nothing to apologize for," he said softly. "Jalvi seeks vengeance, and that's an extremely dark and slippery slope—one from which very few return."

There was something in his voice—an edge that spoke of experience—that made me wonder if it was a slope he or someone close to him had gone down. But the grimness in his expression suggested he wasn't about to explain it.

Not yet, and definitely not in this place.

The waitress returned with two coffees and my tea. I

gripped the handle and wiggled the little pot back and forth for a few seconds to strengthen the brew, then poured it into the cute teacup. "Given the likelihood that whoever killed Jules—be it Jalvi or someone else—might still be out there watching us, what's our next move?"

Lugh tucked the notebook back into his pocket. "We find a temporary shelter while I sort out the notes. Should only take a few hours, and we can decide what to do next based on the results."

"I can be of some assistance there." Cynwrig picked up his coffee—a very strong black—and took a drink. "My family owns an old warehouse close to the West Coast Shipping Hub. It has twenty-four-hour surveillance and top-notch security, with the upper living accommodation only accessible to my siblings and myself. Jalvi—or anyone else who might be watching—will not get near the place."

"As long as it wouldn't inconvenience either you or your family, it sounds ideal," Lugh said.

"Given it's in my family's best interests to solve this puzzle and bring these people to justice as quickly as possible, it definitely wouldn't be an inconvenience."

His gaze met mine as he said that, and it had me melting and breathless in an instant. The man definitely had plans for more than providing a safe place for Lugh to work.

It was all I could do not to jump to my feet and demand we leave straight away.

By the time we finished our drinks and croissants, the storm had unleashed, the rain so heavy the gutters were struggling to cope.

Cynwrig called for a car, and a few minutes later, a black BMW pulled up at the café. A tall dark elf climbed out, raised a large umbrella, and ran around the back of the vehicle to the café's doors.

Once the bill was paid, we headed out, the chauffeur escorting us to the car one by one so we didn't get soaked. Traffic was light, and it didn't take us long to get across to the warehouse. It was an old red brick building—one of many that dominated this area of the docks—that was three stories high and had large, vaguely boat-shaped, multipaned windows. A red metal roller door opened as we approached, giving entry into a surprisingly large and bright parking area. A wall of double-height windows to the left separated this area from what looked to be offices and meeting rooms, while two elevators and a set of metal stairs lay at the far end within a cage that resembled glassed-in bear claws. A series of sturdy-looking bollards stood in front of that. Cynwrig's family was seriously intent on ensuring no one could successfully make a ram-raid entry.

The driver pulled to a smooth stop in the parking bay closest to the cage. Cynwrig thanked him, then added, "We shouldn't be needing your services for the rest of the day, but you'd best take the car home, just in case."

"Will do, sir," the older man said in that genteel sort of tone chauffeurs the world over seemed to use.

He climbed out to open the door for Lugh while Cynwrig did the honors for me, offering me a hand to help me out, then keeping hold of it as he led me toward the bear claws.

"I take it the glass used here is bulletproof?" Lugh asked as the BMW reversed out and left.

"All the glass in this building is." Cynwrig pressed his free hand against a reader set into the wall to the left of the cage. "When you're major players in the black market trade, you never can be too careful."

Light swept his hand and, a heartbeat later, one of the clawed panels slid seamlessly aside. He repeated the process with the elevator panel, and it arrived with a soft chime. I'd expected it to be all gleaming steel and glass, but it was in fact quite functional, more like a cargo elevator than one designed for humans.

A few minutes later, we were on the top floor and stepping out into a massive area that reminded me of those expensive New York loft apartments you often saw in glossy design magazines. Floor-to-ceiling black metal windows dominated the raw brick wall opposite, providing a vast view over the docks and the shipping lanes beyond. There were exposed metal pipes and beams everywhere, and this central section was cathedral-like, rising high to the exposed trusses. Black metal stairs lay to the left and right, leading up to an upper floor that no doubt held bedrooms. A huge kitchen was tucked under the area on the right, while there appeared to be a number of more intimate spaces to the left.

Cynwrig took off his coat and then helped me with mine, placing both in a cleverly concealed cupboard to one side of the elevator. Once Lugh's coat had joined ours, Cynwrig said, "I remotely turned the heating on, but it may take a while for the space to warm up."

"I've worked in much worse conditions, trust me," Lugh said.

"If you'd like to work in an office, there's several down the hall to our left. Help yourself to any stationery that you need."

Lugh raised an eyebrow. "Here's perfectly fine, unless you want me out of the way for other purposes."

Cynwrig laughed, the sound so deep and warm that desire skittered across my skin. "I'm actually intending to whisk your sister upstairs, if neither you nor she has any objections."

"*She* certainly doesn't," I said, voice dry. "And my brother has no say."

"But he'd certainly be grateful if you did. Otherwise, she's going to be pacing the floor telling me to hurry the fuck up."

I laughed, though it was nothing but the truth.

"Then I shall ensure she's occupied for several hours at least." He tugged me forward. "Oh, and feel free to help yourself to anything you need in the kitchen or bar, Lugh."

He nodded and walked across to the U-shaped sofa that dominated this central section, his somewhat absent expression suggesting he was already working on the translation task even if he hadn't yet got the book out. Cynwrig hustled me across the vast space to the stairs on the right.

"How many bedrooms does this place have?" I asked.

"Six—three on each side. All ensuite." He cast a wicked look over his shoulder as we headed up the stairs. "And all fully soundproofed."

"I take it past lovers were... vocal?"

"Some," he said easily. "But the soundproofing is also in place for everyone's comfort. My parents no more want to hear their children having sex than we want to hear them."

"How many siblings do you actually have?"

He cast me a wry glance. "You haven't googled already?"

"Didn't occur to me." We clattered up the stairs together. "I take it past lovers have?"

"Mainly those who weren't elf. It's usually one of the reasons they rarely lasted more than a week."

The first floor remained a vast and airy space, thanks to the double width of the hall and the fact that the walls to our left weren't full-length plaster to the vaulted ceiling, but rather a third glass, which allowed the light from the building's main windows to filter through the rooms into the hall.

"In this day and age, with so many weirdos about, googling the background of a date is pretty common practice," I said. "Why do you consider it grounds for splitting?"

"Because if they want to know anything about me, all they have to do is ask. If I'm fucking you, I'm into you, so questions are acceptable."

I raised an eyebrow as he opened the door to the room at the very end of the hall. "So, if you're not fucking them, questions are unacceptable?"

He laughed, a warm, vibrant sound that sent another wave of heat flooding through my body. "That depends entirely on the person and the situation, but basically, yes. Especially when it comes to my family."

"Huh." I stepped inside and looked around. Like everything else in this place, the room was vast. There was a bathroom to the left, a seating area in the middle, and to the right, against the raw brick external wall, a bed big enough for six people to party in.

I couldn't help but wonder if in the past six people *had*. He'd certainly had that sort of reputation during his youth, even if he'd apparently "calmed down" now that he was basically running his father's empire alongside his sister.

My gaze returned to his. The desire so evident there made my knees buckle. "I notice you didn't actually answer my question."

He laughed and tugged me close to his warm, hard

body. "Aside from my twin, I have three younger sisters and a younger brother."

I rose onto my toes and brushed a kiss across his lips. "But only six bedrooms here?" I murmured. "That's rather inconvenient for one sibling, isn't it?"

"Rhiryd is the rebel in our family. He's declared he has no intention of joining the family 'business' and has run off to some artist's enclave in France, where he has multiple lovers of both sexes and, as of last week, one child on the way."

A smile tugged at my lips. "So, while he's not participating in the family business, he's doing his best to enrich the family's wicked and wanton reputation?"

"If that," he murmured, his lips so close I could taste them, "is your roundabout way of asking if I have any children, then the answer is no. And I will not—not until I meet the woman with whom I'll spend the rest of my life."

Which wouldn't be me, sadly. But I had him for now, and that was better than nothing. I kissed him urgently, with all the pent-up fire and hunger that had been building since the moment I'd spotted him on the street.

"I do so love a woman who unashamedly takes what she wants," he murmured when he could.

"That's good to hear, because right now she wants you badly, but you're fully clothed, and all that material is just getting in her way."

"That," he said, with a rumbly and rather amused growl, "is easily fixed."

He pressed his fingers against my shoulder and lightly pushed me back a couple of steps. Then, with agonizing but glorious slowness, he stripped off, until he was standing there naked. He was perfection itself, from the well-muscled planes of his chest to his washboard abs and the happy trail of dark hair that drew the eye to his long, thick, and oh-so-ready for action cock. Even his damn legs were perfect—long and lean, holding the muscular strength of a runner rather than a weightlifter.

I sighed in pleasure, and he raised an eyebrow, his expression lazily amused. "The offering meets with your approval?"

"Always."

I hastily began to undress, only to be stopped by a firm hand. "Allow me."

He proceeded to strip me, and oh, it was such an erotic sensation. It wasn't just the way his fingers brushed my skin, but the way he teased and tasted each newly revealed piece of flesh. By the time he slipped my panties from my hips, I was quivering with need and as wet as hell. Then his fingers slid over my clit, and all I could do was groan and arch into him, wanting, needing, more than just that too-brief caress.

I reached between us and stroked his erection. "I need this," I growled. "In me. Now."

He made a low sound deep in his throat, slid his hands down to my butt to lift me, then pressed my back against the door. A heartbeat later, he was in me, filling me, liquefying me. I groaned in sheer pleasure and wrapped my legs around his waist, but despite the desperate, aching throb, didn't immediately move. There was something very perfect in the press of our bodies and the heat of him deep inside. I'd had other lovers—hell, I'd been with Mathi for nigh on ten years, and he was as close to perfection as a light elf could ever get—but sex was very different with Cynwrig. It felt *real*. Promised *more*.

Then his lips claimed mine, and thought disintegrated. He began to move, gently at first, then with more urgency.

Delicious sensations washed through every corner of my mind as desire merged with need and swiftly became a wave of utter pleasure that would not—could not—be denied. I gasped, tightening my legs around his waist, drawing him even closer, wanting it faster, needing absolutely everything he had to give. Then my orgasm hit, and I couldn't think, couldn't breathe, as wave after glorious wave of pleasure rolled through me.

He came a heartbeat later, a low groan torn from his throat as his body stilled against mine and his heat flooded deep inside.

For several seconds, neither of us moved, then he sighed and captured my lips, kissing me gently. "Just to confirm things here, you are fully protected against pregnancy, aren't you?"

I laughed and released my grip on his waist. He immediately lowered me to the floor.

"Yes, I am," I said. "Like you, I want to find the right man before I even contemplate children. And given the dearth of suitable pixie men in this goddamn shire, that could be centuries away."

He grinned, caught my hand, and led me toward to the party-sized bed. "I can't say I'm sorry to hear that. It gives us plenty of time to fully explore each other's sexual desires."

"It does indeed," I said sagely. "Shall we start with a voyeuristic one? I've always had this thing about windows..."

~

It was close to two in the afternoon by the time we headed back downstairs, and the storm had well and truly swept past, leaving the streets clean and gleaming.

Cynwrig headed into the kitchen while I dropped down beside my brother and said, in a teasing tone, "So, you managed to transcribe it yet?"

He rolled his eyes at me. "We're not talking about a few pages needing to be transcribed here, you know. It's the whole notebook, and it holds far more than just information of De Clari. It actually feels like a lifetime's work."

"Why would he be keeping a lifetime's work in a ratty old notebook?" I said, then looked at my brother. "Oh, hang on, asking the wrong person that."

Lugh snorted. "I do *not* keep my work solely in notebooks."

"But you do use them."

"Because a pen rarely runs out of juice at the wrong moment, and notebooks are easier to carry around than cords and power packs. And you know this."

I grinned. I did, because I'd teased him about it often enough in the past—especially when said notebooks had gotten damaged after ill-advised journeying into damp caves and other god-forsaken places.

"So, what other sort of information does it contain?"

"So far it's mostly been a lot of history about the De Clari line, both before and after Rostin."

I noted the "mostly" and knew that was a deliberate wording choice, but nevertheless asked, "She had children? How, given the life she was leading?"

"It happened after she set up here in England. I'm still working through that section of the notes, but that's not what is interesting."

"Is he always this roundabout when it comes to

revealing information?" Cynwrig asked. He placed a tray containing two coffees, a pot of tea, and a packet of chocolate digestives on the coffee table. "Sorry about the biscuit choice—they're my father's favorites and all we have stocked in the pantry at the moment."

I reached for one of the biscuits. "Digestives are fine. And yes, it's a rare moment when Lugh doesn't take the long road to say something."

"You two have no sense of the dramatic," Lugh growled, though the twinkle in his eye countered the edge in his tone. "But fine, spoil the buildup if you must. If Jules's notes are to be believed, and the people behind the theft of the crown and the search for the remaining Claws *are* the families of the six elven women killed by the Annwfyn, then finding all three items will do them absolutely no good."

Cynwrig handed out the drinks and then sat on the coffee table. "Why not?"

"Because it appears only a spellcaster of great power can unlock the combined might of the Claws."

"Meaning De Clari was a spellcaster?" I asked.

Lugh nodded. "Jules doesn't believe it was a coincidence that not only was she the first in her line to have such power but also the first to raise the sword." He glanced at Cynwrig. "It means that, unless elves suddenly gain spellcasting abilities, there *has* to be someone else behind this sudden push to find the Claws."

"Someone who's taking advantage of their grief," Cynwrig said grimly.

"It would certainly explain why we keep running into spellcasters." I hesitated, wondering if Lugh would mention that Rogan—his boss at the museum—was a spellcaster of some repute and possibly a good place to start asking questions. Not that I thought he'd be involved in this plot. Aside from the fact the man had never lost anyone to the Annwfyn as far as we were aware, he wanted the Claws for the museum. It was his life and his one true love. But Lugh remained silent, so I added, "Do you think Maran Gordon could be the brains behind it all?"

Maran was a spellcaster who not only specialized in the theft of antiquities but ran a profitable sideline in concealment and body morphing spells. She was also the bitch who'd fire-bombed the tavern. I'd given chase on the night but had basically ended up walking right past her when she'd cast the morphing spell aside and resumed her normal form.

"It's possible, but unlikely," Cynwrig said. "Maran doesn't get involved in *anything* unless there's a major monetary payday behind it."

"But she'd know who hired her," Lugh said. "All we have to do is find her."

"*That* is the problem of our lifetime," Cynwrig said. "My family has been trying for decades, and the IIT have an active arrest warrant out. She has neatly evaded all of us."

"Not really surprising, if she magically alters her form at will," I said.

"Yes, but no caster can maintain a false identity for more than a few hours; it simply taxes their bodies too much. It's more a case of the spellcaster community being small but insular in Deva. They protect their own."

"They're hardly the only ones doing that," Lugh commented.

Cynwrig shot him a hard glance. "I don't like the implication behind that comment."

"And yet it's a truth you don't deny."

Cynwrig raised an eyebrow, and it somehow conveyed cold amusement, even if his expression remained friendly.

"Tell me, would you have so readily cooperated with the IIT if it had been revealed your mother was behind the theft of the hoard?"

"*That* is a stupid question, given we both know Mom spent her life trying to find stolen artifacts," Lugh snapped. "But seeing we're firing them at each other, did you inform Sgott that you've found Jalvi? Or are you intending to track her down and talk to her first?"

"Speaking of Jalvi," I said hurriedly, wanting to cut the deepening argument off, "do you think she'll be able to tell us who's actually running the Claws search? Because she's acting more like a soldier than a leader."

Cynwrig's gaze cut to mine and, just for a moment, there was nothing except cool distance in those silvery depths. It was yet another reminder that I needed to tread a little more cautiously with this man. No matter how well I knew him physically, he very much remained a stranger.

Then he blinked, and warmth returned. It didn't in any way ease the slight tremor of … not unease. Wariness, perhaps.

"You're right in thinking Jalvi wouldn't be anything more than a foot soldier in this particular war," he said. "But whether she'll know the identity of the man or woman ultimately giving the orders is unknown."

"She should at least know who is coordinating the elven side of things, though," I said.

"I would hope so." His phone rang, the noise sharp in the vast space. He drew it from his pocket, then rose and walked away. "Edvard? There's news?" There was a few seconds of silence, then, "Keep an eye on all exits. I'll be there in ten minutes."

He hung up, made another call to request the car, and then swung around. "Jalvi's just turned up."

Lugh rose. "We'll get out of your way then."

Cynwrig frowned. "There is no need to leave. The warehouse is far more secure—"

"You'll be wanting to use it to interview your cousin, and we both know you'd prefer to do so without an outside audience." Lugh's reply was blunt. "We'll head home. You can contact us when and if you have anything you want to share."

Cynwrig hesitated, glanced briefly at me, and then nodded. Disappointment coursed through me. I mean, he could have put up a *token* protest, just to make me feel better.

But then, why would he? No matter how intense the connection between us, we were in the end just bed buddies. Amazing bed buddies, granted, but that was all.

I finished my tea, grabbed my purse, and followed the two men to the elevator. Cynwrig helped me into my coat, his warm fingers brushing my neck but for once not sending the usual tremor of delight through me. Disappointment, it seemed, was a great dampener of lust.

He guided us out of the building, and though he made no move to kiss me goodbye, his gaze lingered on my spine as I walked away.

When we rounded a corner, I glanced up at my brother and said, "So what was all that shit about?"

His gaze met mine evenly. "What shit?"

I snorted. "Don't play innocent to me, brother mine."

He rubbed his nose, his expression unrepentant. "He's using you to keep an eye on our search—"

"I'm well aware of that."

"Yes, but he's not being totally honest with us. He's not telling us everything he knows."

"He's a dark elf—"

"That's no fucking excuse in this case, Beth, and you know it. If we're laying all our cards on the table, then he should too."

"But are we laying all our cards down? I'm thinking we're not, given how eager you were to leave the warehouse just now."

The sudden twinkle in his frost-green eyes suggested I'd guessed right. "Well, as a matter of fact, we never did get around to discussing the most interesting fact I uncovered."

I raised my eyebrows. "Shall I do a dramatic drumroll before you make the announcement?"

He laughed and nudged me lightly, just about knocking me into the nearby wall. "Idiot."

"Just spit it out, brother."

"Well, it would appear that not only has Rostin De Clari's bloodline survived into *this* century, but there's also a direct descendant living not three shops away from the tavern."

FIVE

I stopped and stared at him. "Seriously?"

He nodded. "You know that little lithomancy and spell shop in the undercroft near Debenhams's main entrance? She owns that."

Lithomancy was a form of divination by which the future was told using specialized stones or the reflected light from those stones. "If she's still in the magic business, she could be our missing link."

"And might even know where the sword is."

He began moving again, and I hurried after him. "Surely it can't be that easy."

"No, but wouldn't it be nice if it was?"

It would, but nothing in this quest so far had been, and it was hard to believe that would change any time soon.

We retrieved his car and returned to Deva. Once he'd found parking near the tavern—never an easy task in the narrow streets surrounding its historic old heart—we walked down Eastgate Street until we reached the little shop. It was situated in one of only five basement-level crofts still in use, and the stone steps that led down to the doors had been hollowed out by centuries of foot traffic. The heavy—and probably original—medieval-looking doors were locked. I stepped back to scan the area and noticed the bronze plaque on the wall to the left. It read "Alinda's Lithomancy and Minor Spells. No appointment necessary." Under that was a list of opening times.

"It's closed for the day, but reopens tomorrow," I said. "I guess we come back."

"I guess we do." Lugh motioned me to precede him back up the steps. "In the meantime, we should head back to my place. I need to scan this notebook in case word gets out we've got it and someone attempts to grab it."

"Cynwrig's the only one who knows about it, and he isn't going to tell anyone," I said. "Why would he, when you're the best person to transcribe the thing?"

"I know, but caution is nevertheless warranted given everything that's happened."

A statement I couldn't argue with. "I'll also need use the Eye at some point."

"Why don't you grab it now and take it with us? You can do the reading while I scan."

My gut clenched at the thought. Castell might have urged me to use it, Beira might claim I needed to understand its power, but there remained a reluctance deep within. I wasn't entirely sure why, though I did suspect it had a whole lot to do with stepping into Mom's shoes and the fact that I just didn't feel worthy, let alone ready.

"I'm not staying over at your place, Lugh. The tavern is my home, and it's perfectly safe."

He snorted. "The tavern's been firebombed, and you've been attacked in your own bedroom, so *that* is a ridiculous statement."

"Well, yes, but Sgott now has his people watching the

place. The shifters will react to anyone acting suspiciously in the area, and I can seal the door to the upper stairs. I'll be perfectly fine."

He sniffed, an unconvinced sound if I'd ever heard one. I grinned but was saved from having to argue any further by my phone ringing.

The tone told me it was Mathi, so I hit the answer button and said, "I take it you're fully recovered from the kidnapping and out of the hospital?"

"Yes, and I'm planning a little day trip to see a certain spellcaster in Elsmoot—"

"Aram?" I said. Lugh's gaze shot toward me, but he remained silent. "Wouldn't he have skedaddled by now? Kaitlyn would have sent him a warning that we wanted to talk to him."

"She hasn't. I've just finished speaking to her."

I raised my eyebrows. "And why would you be doing that rather than your father?"

"Because my life has been placed in jeopardy twice now and there will not be a third."

"That doesn't explain why your father isn't undertaking the search."

"I'm sure he is, but I refuse to sit around and wait." His tone was flat and cold. This was the light elf speaking, not the man who'd been my lover for nearly ten years. "If helping you out with the search for the Claws gains us the names of those behind the attacks all that much sooner, then join the hunt I will."

I wasn't sure that was a good thing, given the likely tension between him and Cynwrig. Still, that wasn't my problem, and they were both adults. They could work it out.

"And what about your day job? Don't you have the family business to run?"

The Dhār-Val family ran one of the largest forestry growth businesses in the UK. Basically, they tripled the growth rate of plantation forests in order to protect the remaining old growth forests from harvesting. Though Mathi was the son of a second son, his uncle had retired some eight years ago without male issue. From what the little I'd gleaned about the situation, Ruadhán was ineligible for the position because his ability to manipulate the energy of living flora was considered below acceptable levels, and the board would not have accepted his tenure even if he *had* been interested.

I personally doubted Ruadhán would have accepted the position anyway. He had his own little kingdom to run in the form of the daytime IIT division and seemed to enjoy the power it gave him over *all* races.

"The board can cope well enough without me for a few days," Mathi said. "This is more important."

I was betting neither the board nor his uncle would see it that way. "And you want me along because...?"

"Your knives counter magic. I think it a prudent step, considering we're about to confront a spellcaster capable of who knows what. Besides, I have a council meeting I need to attend tonight, so the added protection will not go astray."

A smile twitched my lips. Mathi was nothing if not practical. "What time are you going?"

"That depends on where you are."

"We're just leaving the tavern and about to head over to Lugh's."

"I'll meet you there."

He hung up. I shoved the phone away and said, "Well, that was unexpected."

"What was that about Aram?"

"Mathi's intending to complete our interrupted quest to talk to the man. He wants me—or more specifically, my knives—along."

"And I bet he didn't even try to soften that admission."

"Nope."

Lugh shook his head. "I take it you're going?"

I nodded. "It's worth a trip. If he's there, he will give us answers."

"If he had any sense, he'd have disappeared by now. They might have kept the kidnapping of you and Mathi out of the mainstream news, but I doubt it'd be a secret in underground circles."

"Maybe, but Mathi said Kaitlyn didn't send Aram a warning about us wanting to talk to him."

"Well, of *course* she'd say that."

I quirked an eyebrow at him. "It's to her benefit to tell the truth, given she's admitted she regularly passes information onto Ruadhán for certain... allowances."

Surprise flitted across his expression. "Really? I can't imagine Sgott being party to something like that. Especially given what he said about the woman being as slippery as an eel."

"Maybe that's *why*. Maybe Ruadhán uses his position to downgrade certain charges."

Lugh frowned. "I know you don't like the man, but I can't imagine he'd pervert the course of justice."

"He's a light elf; they never think in terms of black and white. If he thought perversion would get the desired results, he'd do it. Legalities wouldn't come into it."

Lugh's expression suggested he didn't agree, but he

didn't argue any further. He clicked open his car and, once we were underway, said, "Just do me a favor and keep an eye on who's behind you this time? I don't need the stress of another phone call saying there's been an accident, there's blood all over the car, and you're missing."

"Keeping an eye on who's following us didn't help us last time."

He gave me *that* look. "You know what I mean."

"I do, and I'll be fine."

He harrumphed but didn't say anything else. It was close to five by the time we arrived at Lugh's, and Mathi was waiting, as promised, his arms crossed as he leaned back against the driver side of the car. He didn't move as we pulled up behind him, nor did he smile. Serious Mathi was in full control. It'd be interesting to see how long it lasted, given how desperate he was to get me back in his bed.

I was betting it would take maybe five minutes with me in the car. Ten at the most.

"Send me a text when you get to Elsmoot," Lugh said as he switched off the engine. "At least I'll know you got that far safely."

"I will." I leaned across and dropped a kiss on his cheek. "You make sure you lock and bar the front door. We both know how lost you can get in research."

A smile twitched his lips, but he didn't deny the accusation. I grabbed my coat and bag, then climbed out the car and walked down to Mathi.

Like most light elves, he was lean and sinewy, his body powerful without holding the obvious muscular strength of the dark elves. His hair and skin were golden, his face so beautifully perfect it would make angels weep, and his eyes the color of summer skies.

I wasn't an angel, and I didn't weep, but my body

nevertheless reacted to the sight of him. I'd been with the man for nigh on ten years and was *very* familiar with just what all that perfection was capable of. I might not want us to be anything more than friends, but habit and proximity were sometimes difficult to ignore.

His gaze scanned me, then rose to meet mine; some of the frost had definitely retreated. "You're looking well this afternoon."

I stopped a few feet from him and shoved my hands into my coat pockets so he couldn't grab one and tug me closer. "Thanks. I take it there's no lingering problems from the knock on the head?"

He pushed away from the door, then turned and opened it. "No more than usual, at any rate."

I laughed and climbed into the car. He closed the door, then ran around to the driver side and got in. "I'm told you saved my life. Again."

"Hardly again. The men who kidnapped you that first time weren't intending to kill you."

He pulled out of the parking spot, then raised his eyebrows at me. "It sure felt the opposite at the time."

"They roughed you up to make a point. The people who ran us off the road were holding you hostage against my good behavior."

"And did they get what they wanted?"

I quickly updated him on everything that had happened in the twenty-four hours since I'd last seen him. "We currently have no idea who has the crown, because the people who ran us off the road were killed, and not by me." I glanced at him. "Your father didn't mention any of this?"

"I haven't talked to my father."

I frowned. "That's a little unusual, isn't it, even for your dad? Your injuries were pretty serious, and you are his only son and all."

He smiled, though it was a ghostly echo of its usual self. "He did, of course, enquire about my status. He was assured I would be perfectly fine, so why would he visit?"

"Because..." I stopped. Light elves really didn't do emotions. Or, at least, the highborn ones didn't. They could be warm and funny once you knew them, but love wasn't a concept they believed in, not in the same way the rest of us did. Marriage was nothing more than a contract benefitting both parties, and children a means of continuing the line. "Never mind."

His smile was a fraction warmer. "He's a very busy man."

No doubt, but it still seemed a little odd to me.

After Mathi navigated the traffic and we were once again on the motorway heading toward Elsmoot, he added, "The fact the historian was killed before you arrived suggests someone is still watching your every move."

"They have a history of employing the services of bird shifters, but there's nothing we can do about that."

"Actually," he said, "there is."

I raised my eyebrows. "How?"

"Via a spell." He cast me an amused look. The frost was definitely fading. Flirtatious Mathi wouldn't be that far away now. "Birds can't follow what they can't see."

"I take it you've purchased one such spell?"

"Indeed. As I said, I have no intention of being run off the road or kidnapped again, so this car is fully shielded to any who might be tailing us, be they in the air or in another vehicle."

My knives hadn't reacted, but that wasn't surprising, given they only tended to come to life if the spell was aimed at me. The spell on the car was external rather than internal, and directed outward rather than in.

"Shielded how, though? A light screen won't work, because the speed we're going would shred it."

"It's a mix of an invisibility and mirroring spell. Those above will see empty road and those behind will see the car ahead. I activated it when we left Lugh's, and it will last long enough to get us to our destination."

"That must have cost a packet."

A smile tugged at his lips. "My family isn't exactly poor, Bethany."

"No." Just for an instant, our gazes met, and it felt like old times. Which was damn dangerous when it came to this man. Give him an inch, and he'd take advantage of it.

I tore my gaze away, and he chuckled. "You cannot fight it forever."

"Oh, I can and will."

"We had something special."

"So special you were fucking multiple other women."

"That doesn't lessen what we had."

"It does for me."

"Ah Bethany, were you but an elf."

"If I were an elf," I said, voice dry, "you still wouldn't take me seriously or consider me contract worthy, because I'd probably be servant class."

"A truth I cannot deny, as much as I might wish to."

I snorted and moved the conversation to safer subjects.

It took us twenty-five minutes to get to Elsmoot, even with the slow down for roadworks in several spots. Mathi already had Aram's address in the GPS, so once we were close, he hit the button and followed the instructions. They led us to a long row of rather ratty-looking glass-and-brick three-story buildings. Aram's place was sandwiched between a pawn broker's and a Subway. The latter was open, but most of the other premises had closed for the night.

"This doesn't look the sort of place a high-profile spell-caster would be using," I commented, somewhat dubiously.

"Which is the perfect cover, if you think about it." Mathi parked and unbuckled his seat belt. "I'm betting most of his main business isn't done in the shop, but rather the floors above it. That middle floor certainly looks more like an office than accommodation."

He might have been driving, but he'd taken in a whole lot more detail of the premises than I had. I sent Lugh a text to let him know we'd arrived safely, then tugged on my coat and climbed out of the car. Thunder rumbled overhead, and the heady scent of rain filled the air. We had three minutes to get undercover before the storm unleashed.

I thrust my hands into my pockets, a little unsettled by the certainty of that thought, and quickly followed Mathi across the road. Aram's premises was narrow, with one metal-framed window sitting either side of the entrance. "Spells For All Occasions" was blazed in gold letters on the top part of the door and, underneath that, "Appointments Not Necessary."

Mathi tested the handle, but it was locked, so he peered in through the window. I did the same but on the other side of the door. Getting too close to the man wasn't advisable, given the thawing was nigh on complete.

With the deep darkness that now haunted the interior, there wasn't all that much to be seen. I could make out a service counter on the left, and two shelves—one free-standing, one against the right wall. If he followed the setup used by other practitioners, they'd both be filled with an assortment of ready-made potions and minor spell scrolls, while at the back of the room would be a screened-off area where the private consultations and spells would happen.

"It's too dark to see if there's any stairs, but it might be worth checking the rear of the building, just to see if there's a rear door or external access to the upper floors."

Mathi nodded. "This way."

He set off at a good clip without waiting for me. I hastily caught up, and we strode past the remaining shops in the row and then down the side street. As he'd guessed, there was a loading lane at the back of the building and concrete stairs that gave first-floor access to all the shops lining the main street.

Mathi walked along until he found the rear door into Aram's. It, too, was locked.

"Well, that puts an end to adventures today," I said.

"No, it does not." He motioned me back several steps. "Use your lovely body to block anyone passing by seeing what I'm about to do."

"It's dark and it's about to piss down. I doubt anyone will." I nevertheless crossed my arms and turned around to watch the street—a dangerous move where he was concerned. "I take it you're about to break in?"

"Breaking isn't the right term. I'm merely unlocking the door with a pick rather than the key."

"Law enforcement would still call that breaking and entering."

"My father would argue it depends entirely on the situation."

A couple walked past the lane. I tensed, but they moved on without pausing. The street remained too damn busy for my liking, however. "I take it that means your father occasionally allows his people or their sources to side-step the law as a means of getting information?"

"Warrants can take forever to process, and that can sometimes be detrimental to certain cases."

"And to making charges stick in court, no doubt."

"That would depend on the case making it to court. Some don't."

"Meaning he's keeping the Complaints Commission extra busy?"

"No more so than usual."

I wondered what "usual" was. And whether that meant few dared to even raise a complaint against Ruadhán.

A gentle curtain of rain began to fall, but if the weight of clouds was anything to go by, the curtain would soon become a torrent. "You having much luck there? Because you have thirty seconds before the sky opens up and we get drowned."

There was a soft click as the lock opened, but before I could turn, he slipped his hand around my waist and pulled me back against his strong, sinewy body.

"You always were impatient when it came to entry," he whispered, and brushed a kiss against my neck.

A wave of delight shivered through me, but I somehow manage to catch the sigh of pleasure before it could leave my lips and instead thrust back with an elbow.

He laughed and jumped back out of the way. "I'd offer an apology for taking advantage of your inattention, but we'd both know it would be neither sincere nor true."

A smile tugged at my lips. "You're incorrigible."

"When it comes to luscious women, that is most certainly true." He pulled two pairs of silicone gloves from his coat pocket and hand me a pair. "You want to check if there's any spells clinging to the door or the handle before we go in?"

I pulled a glove onto my left hand and tucked the other into my pocket. I had no idea if holding the knife with silicone gloves on would make any difference to the way it reacted to magic, but I wasn't about to take the chance.

The minute I drew it from the sheath, light flared down its length. There wasn't just one spell here, there were multiple. I touched the point to the middle of the metal door, and there was a short, sharp explosion. A sulfurous, slightly metallic smell briefly stained the air. I touched the knife's tip to the door handle and got the same result.

As the rain began to pelt down, I warily grasped the handle. When nothing happened, I turned it and then pushed the door open. It revealed a short corridor with a second door to the left and third ten feet directly in front. Both were closed.

I couldn't see any more spells, and the knife wasn't reacting, but I kept it out regardless. Better safe than sorry when walking into a spellcaster's lair.

I stepped inside, then paused again. The flooring was vinyl, and though it had been laid over the top of real floorboards, their song had long ago been silenced. They couldn't tell me if anyone stood in the rooms beyond either door.

"I can't hear movement or conversation," Mathi murmured.

"No." But that didn't mean there wasn't anyone here. For all we knew, there could be a goddamn army in either the room ahead or on the second floor.

I forced my feet on. When we reached the first door, Mathi cast a gaze my way, eyebrow raised in question. I lightly touched the knife to the middle of the door and, when nothing happened, nodded. He turned the handle and carefully pushed the door open, revealing a small laundry. It contained little more than a wash basin, a very old, very rusted top-loading washing machine, and, on the window side, a string line on which two pairs of men's socks and half a dozen men's underpants were strung.

"Tighty-whities," I murmured. "I'm thinking we're dealing with an older gent."

"Especially since said whities are more yellow than white. The man needs to employ some bleach."

"Says the man who does none of his own washing," I said, voice wry.

"Doesn't mean I don't know the basics, dear Bethany."

He motioned me on. There was no obvious spell on the next door, and the knife remained inert. And yet... something was off.

The closer I got to the door, the more that sensation of wrongness grew. Power tickled across the outer reaches of my senses, a caress that was familiar and yet not.

I reached for the doorknob, but a heartbeat before I gripped it, I saw it.

Pixie dust.

I swore, and Mathi immediately said, "What's wrong?"

I glanced at him, my expression grim. "The knob is covered in pixie dust."

"Ah."

"Yeah."

There were two kinds of pixie dust—the gold stuff that was generally nothing more than the detritus from the magic smaller pixie lines used to fly, and which could, in certain circumstances, be reshaped into a spell that was a lot more dangerous.

Though not deadly. Never deadly. No pixie line was

immune to the blood curse for causing unwarranted harm to others.

The other kind was blue and was found in ancient forests under a special type of mushroom that only sprouted during a blue moon. It was generally used to replenish the dust trees from which both the Malloyei and Gadahn pixies—the two lines that used magic to fly—drew their power, but it could also be used as a spell augmenter and rejuvenator.

"Any idea what its function is?" Mathi squatted to study the knob but made no move to touch it. While elves were immune to the "obedience touch" of we Aodhán women, they could be affected by pixie dust. "I'm not seeing the usual glitter that accompanies reshaping."

"That's because it's blue and means it's been deliberately placed here."

I squatted beside him. The hall wasn't exactly wide, and my leg pressed against his. Heat flared between us, and I once again found myself restraining the instinctive urge to do more than just *press*. I mean, seriously, my hormones needed to be bitch-slapped. It wasn't as if they were starving for attention or touch these days. Not with Cynwrig around.

A knowing smile tugged at Mathi's lips, but he didn't otherwise react. "If there was a pixie spell on that door, wouldn't your knives react?"

"I honestly don't know." I somewhat tentatively raised the knife and touched its point to the knob. Nothing happened. "Maybe they were never designed to respond to pixie spells. They are a rarity these days and generally mild in nature."

"If there's a pixie spell on this door, I'm thinking it's not mild."

And I was thinking he was right. I rose. "The door hasn't got a lock, and the knob doesn't look particularly strong. I think the best way around the situation is for you to kick the door in."

"That will alert anyone who may be inside."

"A chance we'll have to take if we want to get some answers." I wrinkled my nose. "But I don't think we'll find the pixie responsible for this in there. It's lost some of its shine, so it's at least a couple of hours old."

Whether Aram or anyone else was inside was another matter, but something within me doubted it. While smaller pixies did magically downsize their bodies in order to allow flight, the restrictions of weight and mass ratio meant they remained visible to the eye.

If someone *had* been inside, they would have seen her. Or him. So, either the pixie was a client—unlikely—or she'd been sent here after something. Gadahn pixies, who were the smallest of the two flighted lines, did have a special love of stealing.

Mathi rose and booted the center of the plywood door. It crashed back hard enough to send plaster dust flying. The pixie dust remained on the knob, which was basically confirmation there was some form of ill-intent behind it.

The room beyond was small and, despite the two large windows facing the main street, full of shadows. Thunder rumbled ominously, and the rain was torrential, hitting the glass so hard it was hard to hear anything else. A table sat in the middle of the room with four chairs around it—three at this end, one at the other. To the left was a small office area, and to the right, stairs leading up to the next floor.

The area looked and felt empty, but I nevertheless entered warily, scanning the floor for any indication of traps or further pixie dust. Nothing.

I walked across to the office, but it contained little more than a desk, a chair, and a filing cabinet. The drawers had all been opened and obviously searched, given the number of files dumped on the floor and paperwork strewn about. Of course, it was possible that our spellcaster was the world's messiest record keeper, but I doubted it, given how neat the top of his desk was. I squeezed past Mathi and walked around to the back of the desk. There were three drawers, and they were all open. Blue dust decorated two of the locks; our pixie had definitely been looking for something.

"We can check this mess out later," Mathi said. "We need to get upstairs and see what our pixie has done up there."

I nodded and followed him out the door. Once we neared the stairs, I again took the lead, keeping my back against the wall and my gaze on the floor above as we slowly climbed. My knife remained inert, but there was a sprinkling of pixie dust on the newel cap. At least this time it was gold rather than blue; our pixie had taken flight here, though whether she'd gone up or down, I couldn't say.

I pulled the spare glove from my pocket and carefully scraped some dust into it. Flight dust wasn't entirely universal—there were always some minor tells that could lead you to the pixie it had come from. Whether there were enough tells in this scraping was another matter entirely— and something only a dust specialist could tell me.

There were two halls leading off the landing. The one directly ahead was empty and held four closed doors. I carefully peered around the corner. One further door and window down the far end.

I slipped around, knife held at the ready even though I had no sense of immediate danger. There was no pixie dust on the first doorknob; Mathi pushed it open, revealing a generous-sized bathroom.

Which left the doors down the other hall.

The inner tension cranked up a notch, but I didn't say anything. The first two doors were unmarked by dust, and the rooms—which were bedrooms—empty.

The third doorknob had the faintest sprinkling of golden dust. Our pixie had gone in here. I touched the knife tip to the knob, just to be sure there was no spell, then tugged my coat sleeve over my hand and opened the door.

It was another bedroom, but this one was messier than the others, and the film on the half-finished black coffee sitting on the right bedside table suggested someone had been in here fairly recently.

One room to go.

Mathi led the way down but stopped short of the door. I soon realized why. The whole thing was covered in dust. The blue kind.

And the energy rumbling across the outer reaches of my senses suggested this wasn't a spell either of us should be messing with.

"We can't risk kicking this door in." Mathi's voice was grim. "Not with the amount of dust on it."

I nodded. "I'll call in a specialist to deal with this. Do you want to head back to the office? Hopefully we can uncover some clues as to what she was searching for."

He nodded. "I'm not liking the feel of that spell, though, so be careful and don't get too close."

"I'm sometimes irrational but I'm not stupid."

He smiled, touched my arm, and then walked back to the stairs. I bent and placed the knife on the floor, keeping it pointed at the door just in case whatever spell had been layered over that door activated. It might not help, of course, but I felt decidedly safer.

I dragged my phone out and googled dust specialists. They could be found in all major cities and towns, but Elsmoot was a port, and pixies tended to avoid the sea—even the Malloyei, whose element was water rather than the usual variant of flora control.

Google told me there were a couple in the area—one in Deva, who I actually knew, and one in Warrington. While Deva was the closer of the two towns, the amount of traffic on the road coming up here meant the Warrington specialist would probably get here faster.

But before I could ring her, light jagged down the knife's blade. It was just a brief flash, but my tension and pulse rate nevertheless leapt.

My gaze swept the door, but I couldn't immediately see any change. I warily stepped closer, and that's when I saw it. The gentle specks of blue had begun to move and form tiny clusters. Each of these was then drawn into the next, becoming larger and more visible each time. The vibration of their energy grew at the same rate, becoming sharper, hotter, stronger. As the door paint began to blister in multiple spots, a memory hit. Gran, regaling us with the time a friend of hers—a Gadahn pixie—accidentally exploded a small smattering of blue dust while she and her family had been out collecting it. Though it had been just the dust from under one mushroom, she'd ended up with singed clothes and hair. Of course, Gran had never said how she'd set the dust off, but the description of the event was close to what was happening here.

I swooped for the knife and ran down the hall to the stairs, taking them two at a time. When I hit the first floor, I shouted, "Mathi, we have to get out—now!"

He looked up but didn't question the order. He simply followed me across the room and down the short hallway.

We were at the external door when there was a soft *whoomp*. A heartbeat later, a huge wave of hot air lifted us up, flinging us past the concrete walkway and over the old metal railings down to the wet cobblestones below.

CHAPTER
SIX

I hit the stones hard enough to knock the breath from my lungs, then skidded along for several meters, only stopping when I crashed sideways into a dumpster. Pain flooded my body and for several minutes, I struggled to breathe, let alone think.

"Bethany?" came Mathi's croaky question. "You okay?"

"Yeah. You?"

"Winded, lumps of skin missing, but otherwise alive."

I forced my eyes open. Saw him, pushing upright. His pants were torn and there was a bloody scrape on his chin, but nothing appeared to be broken and he could move, even if he winced as he hobbled toward me.

My gaze went past him and widened in shock. The roof and the top floor of the building had disappeared. Only a few rafters remained, their blackened bones reaching for the sky as if desperate to escape the fire that burned below them. The shops either side appeared untouched by the explosion—blue dust gave spells a high degree of accuracy —but it was unlikely they'd remain that way if the fire brigade didn't get here quickly enough to get the flames under control.

"So much for them not getting a third shot at me," he grumbled.

My laugh caught somewhere in my throat and sat there like a lump that briefly made breathing difficult. I pushed into a sitting position but didn't get any further as muscles I didn't even know existed vehemently protested.

After several, somewhat useless, deep breaths that didn't do a whole lot to ease the waves of pain, I said, "This explosion wasn't aimed at either of us. It was set to get rid of evidence."

"Meaning we might have found Aram's body had we been able to get past that blue dust coated door?"

"I'm guessing there'll be the remains of a body but only the coroner will be able to tell us if it's Aram or not."

"Then I'll ask my father to keep me appraised of their findings."

"And maybe ask him to find out more about Aram."

He nodded and somewhat gingerly squatted in front of me. "The cobblestones might appear smooth, but it seems they hold plenty of hidden grit and other sharpish bits."

"And we appear to have hit a whole slew of them."

"Apparently so." He reached out and gently thumbed moisture away from my cheek. It had a bloody hue. "That scrape is pretty nasty."

"So's your chin."

"Yes, but your face will attract far more attention." He reached behind me to grab the coat's hood and tug it over my head. "That should conceal it from a casual glance, as long as you keep your head down."

He rose, offered me a hand, and then pulled me up

easily. Pain rose yet again, but it was at least a little less brutal this time.

Once we were on the move, Mathi hooked my right arm through his and pulled me closer. For once I didn't object, simply because my legs remained damnably shaky. Reaction more than pain, I suspected.

Rather surprisingly, no one in the buildings that lined this portion of the lane had come out to check what had happened, and I couldn't see anyone peering through rear windows. Either the buildings were empty, or explosions were an everyday part of life around these parts.

A fire engine had arrived by the time we got back to the main street, its blue emergency lights washing brightly through the wet darkness. Several firemen were busy unwinding hoses while others pushed spectators back. More sirens could be heard in the distance; I guessed they'd probably be police and ambulances.

There was glass and debris scattered all over the pavement and street, and the cars parked in front of the shop had sustained heavy damage. Lady luck had definitely been looking out for us when the lack of parking spaces had forced us farther away from the building.

We took a wide berth around the area and made our way back to Mathi's car. He helped me into the passenger seat and then hobbled around to the driver side.

He didn't start the car, however, instead pulling a handkerchief from his pocket and offering it to me. "There's no first aid kit in the car, so this is the best I can offer to stop the blood."

"From getting on the leather?" I teased.

A smile tugged at his lips but didn't quite reach his eyes. "Between the two of us, the poor leather is going to need complete detailing."

I glanced at his leg. Though his pants had ripped as he'd slid along the cobblestones, they'd held up enough to protect him from more serious damage. The blood was coming from a cut on his upper thigh that looked more like a puncture wound than a scrape. He'd obviously landed on something sharp and pointy. "I think the handkerchief is better used to put pressure on that."

He raised his eyebrows, mischief dancing across his expression. "Are you offering to go down and provide administrations?"

"My days of going down on you are long over, my friend."

His sigh was long and sorrowful. "Such a shame."

I rolled my eyes. "And you've only yourself to blame."

"Sadly, that is very true."

He folded the hanky and pressed it against the puncture wound, then used his belt to hold it in place.

As he started the car and reversed out, I flipped the vanity mirror down to check out my cheek. He was right about it being nasty; I'd basically scraped the entire right side of my face open and couldn't even remember it happening. I tugged my sweater sleeve over my hand and cleaned it out the best I could.

"I think you might need to call Darby and see if she can meet us at the tavern," Mathi said.

"Wouldn't it be better just to go straight to the fae hospital?"

"It probably would, but I'm not in the mood to be waiting in the emergency room right now."

I snorted. "As if, as a highborn, you ever had to wait for anything in your entire life."

"That doesn't dismiss the initial comment." He glanced

at me. "Did you know that Darby warned me off trying to seduce you back into my bed?"

Amusement ran through me. "Did she now?"

"Yes. She claimed you now had a nice man in your bed and that I need to give up and just get on with finding someone else."

"Sound advice, if you ask me."

"You know me far better than that." His voice was wry. "But unless you've gained a third suitor, it's a long stretch to call Cynwrig Lùtair a nice man."

"You would of course say that."

"You don't know him."

"Odd. He said the same thing about you."

He sniffed. It was a disdainful sound. "Myrkálfar cannot be trusted."

"And Ljósálfar can? I believe I've evidence to the contrary. But it doesn't matter, because I'm just sweeping out the cobwebs until something better comes along." I paused. "Something other than *you*."

He gave me another of those sniffs, and I couldn't help grinning. "Do you have another hanky? You appear to have developed a sniffle."

He didn't look amused. I laughed, tugged my phone from my pocket, and rang Darby.

"Hey," she said in a bright voice that thankfully said I hadn't woken her. I knew she had the next week off work because her sister-in-law was expected to give birth at any minute, but she'd been working late shifts until last night, and that usually meant she slept solidly through most of her first day off. "What's up?"

"Just wondering if you're available for a little wound patching."

"What the hell have you gotten yourself into this time?"

"Nothing much."

"Nothing more than a magical explosion that destroyed two stories of a building," Mathi said dryly.

"Is that who I think it is?" Darby grumbled. "Please don't tell me you're letting him back in."

"This is purely a business venture."

"A fact I can sadly confirm," he added.

"Well, good, but why the hell were you both in the vicinity of an explosion? I mean, I can understand someone wanting to blow Mathi's annoying self up, but not you."

"It wasn't aimed at either of us. We were at Aram's—a spellcaster involved in one of the attacks at the tavern—and it was just a matter of bad timing."

"That seems to have become a habit lately." I could almost see her shaking her head. "Are you heading for the tavern?"

"No, Lugh's."

"And he's there right now?"

Her tone had gained a little extra excitement, and my grin bloomed again. "He is."

"Excellent," she said with obvious relish. "I'll pop over there immediately."

I almost felt sorry for Lugh. Almost. "How's Talein? That boy of his decided to greet the world yet?"

Of all of Darby's older siblings—and she had plenty, as the forester class, who were the elf equivalent of traders and included medics and arborists, didn't have the fertility problems that assailed highborn lines—I probably knew Talein and his wife Shona the best. There were only a couple years difference in age between us, and Darby and I often went out for dinner and movies with them. Mathi, it had to be said, had often come with us despite his natural highborn inclination to look down on the lower-born lines. Though he'd also been known to comment that he often felt like a fifth wheel.

Up until now, all of Darby's siblings had produced baby girls. Finally having a boy to carry the family name forward another generation meant the pressure was off Darby to marry an elf and produce an heir. She really *could* marry Lugh if she wanted to.

"He greeted the world quickly and raucously at seven this morning," Darby said. "I've been with them all day at the compound; he's such a lovely wee thing once fed."

"Please give them both my love and congratulations and tell them I'll pop in once they're back at their city apartment in a few weeks."

As much as I would've liked to see them earlier, light elves—especially first-timers—gave birth within the home compound and generally stayed there for the first month or so after a baby's birth. It gave new parents time to acclimatize to looking after the child while ensuring there was plenty of help and support available.

"Have they named him yet?" I added.

"Ruairí Veon Talein Riagáin. Named after his maternal grandfather, and it definitely suits him, as he's inherited his red hair." She sighed. "He really is the cutest damn thing I've ever seen, despite the strength of his lungs."

"Is Lugh aware how clucky you're getting?" Mathi said.

Darby laughed again. "We haven't even gotten to first base yet. Let's not scare the man unduly."

"And declaring your intention to marry him certainly wouldn't have done that," I said wryly.

"Well, he does need to know my intentions are honorable. Unlike that lout in the car with you."

"If you're not careful, I'll speed up and give you less alone time with Lugh," Mathi said, his tone lazily amused.

"No, you won't, because that'll cut your time with Beth."

He smiled and didn't deny it.

"We should be there in half an hour or so," I said, "depending on the traffic."

"No problem. See you there."

She hung up, and I put the phone away. After swiping at the trickle of blood near my chin, I glanced at Mathi and said, "Did you happen to find anything worthwhile in the office before the thing was destroyed?"

"It appears our pixie was searching for a specific file." He reached into his coat pocket, pulled out the jagged edge of a manilla folder, and handed it to me.

I frowned and accepted it. "Why just the edge?"

"Because that's all there was. It must have gotten stuck on the back of the cabinet and ripped when the drawer was pulled open. I couldn't find the folder on the floor, so it was obviously taken."

"Huh." I turned the scrap around. A name had been written along the edge, though it was incomplete. "Elivista? Does that ring any bells?"

"It's a traditional first name used by multiple Ljósálfar highborn families, but more than that, no."

"Do you know if either of the two Ljósálfar families who lost loved ones in that last Annwfyn attack has a member who runs by that name?"

"No, but I can ask." He paused, concentrating on the traffic as a car up ahead did an illegal turn, causing havoc for those immediately behind him. Or her, as the case might be. "If there *is*, then it's more than possible she's our equivalent of Jalvi."

"It would certainly explain why someone was hired to steal her file and erase any other evidence, possibly including Aram."

He nodded. "I'll talk to my father tomorrow. He'll know."

"While you're chatting, ask him how many highborns deal with Aram."

"If Aram is a mid-class spellcaster, he's more likely to have dealings with the healer class than us." He glanced at me. "How hard will it be to track down the pixie who did this? Will the dust you collected help?"

"Yes, and if you want to detour to George Street before we get to Lugh's, I can drop the sample off at Nati's. She lives near the bus terminal there."

"Wouldn't it be better to wait until we're both patched and dry?"

I wrinkled my nose. "It can take a few days to pin down and track back the specific dust details, so it really would be best if the search is started ASAP."

"Before anything else gets blown up, you mean."

"Well, yes." Especially given someone had already tried to firebomb the tavern. I didn't want a pixie adding any more damage.

Mathi swung onto Liverpool Road and then said, "I don't recall a Nati ever being mentioned during our relationship."

A smile tugged at my lips. "Is your memory going, old man? Because we went to dinner with her and her boyfriend on several occasions. I believe you commented that sex would be an interesting challenge given the height difference between the two."

"Anyone would think I was sex-orientated."

"Wonder where they'd get that impression?"

My voice was dry, and he laughed. "Is she a cute, well-developed woman just under three foot tall, with green hair and eyes and a six-foot partner who's bald?"

"That's them."

He glanced at me, blue eyes glimmering with amusement. "You have to admit, it was an interesting dynamic. They still together?"

"I haven't seen her for a couple of years, but last I heard they were."

He grunted and returned his attention to the road. Peak hour was always hell in Deva, and by the time we reached George Street, there was absolutely no parking near Nati's. Mathi scooted into Oulton Place and stopped just long enough for me to clamber out.

"I'll park illegally around the next corner and wait for you there," he said, and zoomed off the minute I slammed the door shut.

I hastily did up my coat then shoved my hands into my pockets in a vague attempt to keep them warm. Though it wasn't raining anymore, the night was absolutely bitter. I hobbled more than ran down the street, then darted through the at-a-crawl traffic. Nati's place was a small one-up, one-down red-brick house, but its unimpressive looks were deceiving. Like most of the places along this side of the street, they'd been able to extend at the rear without compromising the size of the backyard, thanks to the fact it ran down all the way down to an old canal.

I rang the doorbell, heard it chime deep inside, and shifted impatiently from one foot to the other until I heard footsteps approaching. They were too heavy to be Nati's.

A light came on, then the door opened, revealing a

hulking figure of a man with a thick red beard and bald head. He stared down at me for a heartbeat before recognition stirred.

"Bethany? This is a surp—" The rest cut off as his gaze centered on my cheek. "What the hell happened?"

"Tripped and fell—is Nati home?"

"No, she's out on a job." He glanced at his watch. "Should be home in ten or fifteen, if you'd like to come in and wait."

"I can't." I fished the glove out of my pocket. "Can you give this to her and ask if she can ID the dust inside for me?"

"Sure thing. I take it your phone number hasn't changed?"

"No. Can you please tell her it's urgent?"

"I will. You sure you won't come in? She'll be disappointed to have missed you."

"I'll catch her later. Need to get over to the hospital for this." I lightly tapped my cheek, and he nodded.

"I'll get her to call you, then."

"Thanks."

I darted back through the traffic and made my way back to Mathi. Once inside the car, I switched up the heat and held my hands out to the vents. My fingers were like blocks of ice.

"Success?" Mathi said as he reversed out of the lane.

"She was out on a job, but Jessup was home. I gave him the glove and said we needed it evaluated urgently."

Mathi gave me a long look, something I felt more than saw. "I don't suppose she could be the pixie we're hunting?"

"Nati? No way."

"You're sure?"

"Nati's a tracer—"

"And knowing dust and their spells inside out is a necessary part of their job. It wouldn't be the first time a legitimate tracer has had a sideline business."

"I know, but Nati wouldn't do something like that."

He hesitated, then nodded. "I'll trust your judgment."

"Thanks."

My fingers had thawed out by the time we reached Lugh's, but the shivers assailing the rest of me hadn't eased. I doubted it was the cold, because it was damnably warm inside the car right now. I suspected it had something to do with second sight and the certainty that more trouble loomed on the horizon.

Of course, that could also be my naturally pessimistic streak coming to the fore.

Darby had parked in the second of Lugh's parking spaces, which forced Mathi to find a spot several houses further along. As thunder rumbled overhead—signaling not only a renewal of storm activity but also seeming to place an emphasis on the growing sensation of trouble—we hastily made our way back to the old power station.

A wave of warmth and laughter washed over me as we entered. I led the way into the living area and saw Darby perched on a stool one side of the counter while Lugh sat on the other. Between them was a half-finished bottle of Penfolds Grange Hermitage. If the color of the label was anything to go by, it was a fairly old one too.

"Good grief," Mathi said, in a shocked sort of voice. "Is that a '51 red?"

"A new arrival should always be celebrated with a very fine wine," Darby said cheerfully. She was typical light elf in looks—tall and slender, with long pale gold hair plaited into a thick rope that ran down her spine. Her eyes were the color of summer skies, and her features sharp but ethereally beautiful. "Would you like some?"

"That is the stupidest question ever, but why on earth would you waste such a rare wine on an unappreciative lout like Lugh?"

Though his voice suggested annoyance, his eyes twinkled. Lugh laughed and raised his glass. "Because she knows the fastest way to this man's heart is via his stomach."

Darby rolled her eyes. "As if."

I walked over and gave her a quick hug. "Congrats on becoming an aunt again."

"Thanks." She wrinkled her nose. "You both look and smell like shit and need to go shower. I cannot fix this"— she waved her hand up and down my length—"until you're clean."

Mathi's gaze immediately met mine, intentions obvious. I held up a finger. "No."

He sighed and glanced at Lugh. "Do you mind the imposition of us using both showers?"

"Better that than having to put up with the smell for any longer than necessary," Lugh said. "Seriously, did you both get caught in a stink bomb?"

"No; blue dust explosion."

"Almost as bad." Darby made a shooing motion. "Go, now."

I headed into the spare room and had a quick hot shower. Various bits of me protested the water's touch, but it was definitely worth it because I felt so much better after.

Thankfully, my coat had protected the top part of me

from both the storm and the blast, so I was able to get back into my sweater, shirt, and bra. My jeans were pretty much a write-off, however, which forced me to raid the drawer of spare clothes.

Mathi was sitting beside Darby sipping on the red when I came out. She'd already patched him up, because there was no sign of the wicked cut on his chin and no indication of a bandage underneath the sweatpants he was wearing. Lugh's, obviously, as Mathi did not—and never had—keep a cache of spares here. He also generally would never be caught dead in anything resembling sweatpants.

"Right," Darby said, sliding off the stool, then patting the seat. "Prop yourself here while I do my stuff."

I obeyed, then swung the stool around to face her. She pulled gloves from her purse, snapped them on, then pressed her fingertips against my temples. "Remain still while I do a full scan."

"It's mainly my face."

"Yeah, that's why you're walking like an old woman. Just shut up and let me do this."

I shut up. Her gaze narrowed, and her magic rose, a warm and bright caress of energy. It washed from the top of my head down the length of my body, then returned at a slower pace. After a moment, she nodded and stepped back. "Plenty of bruises and scrapes, but you're right, your cheek is the worst of it. The rest is mainly bruising."

She quickly healed them all, then picked up her red and moved around the counter to stand beside Lugh. He didn't move, which was one step up the ladder of acceptance in my opinion.

Darby's too, if the twinkle in her eyes was anything to go by.

I took a sip of the red—and by gods, though it would generally be considered past its peak of drinkability, it was still a lovely drop—then said, "I take it Mathi's updated you on events?"

Lugh nodded. "I called Rogan when Darby arrived, gave him the bare bones, and asked if he could help us out tracking Aram down. He's outraged at the possibility that such a lout—his words—could be responsible for the Claws not appearing in his museum."

Which was almost funny, given that during his time as a relic hunter, Rogan had gained a reputation for his shady methods and loutish behavior when it came to acquiring artifacts. "Does that mean if Aram is still alive but in hiding, Rogan will be able track him down?"

"He has good guild links, so he has more chance than the rest of us," Lugh said. "He also mentioned that the first of the two new antiquarians has accepted the job offer and should be arriving in the next day or so."

I raised my eyebrows. "I know Nialle has to be replaced, but hasn't that happened a little too quickly? Antiquarians with the relevant experience aren't thick on the ground these days."

Lugh shrugged. "He's been trying to fill the additional positions for a few months now and had recently increased the rate of pay being offered to attract better candidates. It obviously worked."

"Maybe so, but it still feels wrong."

"With Nialle gone and the Claws continuing to take most of my time, we really need the extra help. The Claws isn't the only search the museum is running, and right now, they've all stalled."

And that was never a good situation when you were dealing with fragile antiquities and a black market hungry to consume them. "Did you mention the notes to Rogan?"

"Notes?" Mathi said, glancing from me to Lugh and back again. "What notes?"

Lugh glanced at me. I shrugged. "You might as well tell him. He's declared intentions of tracking down the bastards who keep damaging him, and given they're the same bastards we're trying to find, we might as well join forces."

Lugh quickly updated both Mathi and Darby, though he omitted the fact he'd scanned the notes to keep a secure copy. And that was probably prudent. While I absolutely trusted both, Borrachero had already been used on Mathi in order to get information, and while both he and the council had taken steps to ensure it couldn't happen again, there was no guarantee.

"And no," Lugh added, "I didn't mention them to Rogan. It's pointless until we know for sure whether they're actually useful or not."

"So, what's our next step?" Darby said.

Lugh glanced at her in surprise. "Our?"

She gave him a deadpan look. "If I'm going to be the medic on call, I want to be included on the hunt. And I will *not* take no for an answer."

"Well, I guess that means you're in." He didn't look concerned by that prospect. Maybe her declaration had finally helped him realize she was *utterly* serious about wanting a sexual relationship with him. Of course, whether he'd take the logical next step was another matter entirely.

"I'll transcribe the rest of the notebook tonight," Lugh said, "and tomorrow, Beth and I will talk to Alinda and see if she knows anything. We'll decide our next step from there."

Mathi nodded. "I'll talk to my father and see if he's

gained any further information from the men who
kidnapped me or those who forced us off the road."

I frowned. "The men who kidnapped you were after the
rubies belonging to the Shield of Hephaestus, not the
Claws."

"And the shield is?" Darby asked.

"It belongs to the Greek god of smiths, fire, and volcanoes and gives control over the latter two elements," Lugh
said. "It's missing because the Ljósálfar guarding the hoard
it was a part of dropped the ball."

"*That* remains a debatable point," Mathi commented.
"And you should not be talking openly about it. The council
would not be pleased."

"Given the council basically accused me of being part of
that theft, they can go fuck themselves as far as I'm
concerned."

"I do love the polite manner you two use when
speaking about the council."

"When they show me some respect," Lugh grumbled,
"I'll show them some."

"And I would think the situation we find ourselves in
deserves more understanding and tolerance from *all* parties
involved." Mathi glanced at his watch, then downed the
rest of his wine. "I have a meeting to get to and need to
detour home to dress more appropriately. Beth, would you
like a lift home?"

I shook my head. "It's not raining here yet, and I really
need to stretch my legs."

He nodded. "Then I'll call tomorrow, and we can
arrange a meeting to compare notes."

As he rose and quickly left, Darby's gaze caught mine
and glared at me rather pointedly. I smiled, finished my

drink, and slid off the stool. "I should probably get going too. I've tavern accounts to do."

Lugh followed me across to the door. "I know what you're doing."

I grinned and patted his arm. "I shouldn't be the only one in this little family group getting rid of the cobwebs, brother mine."

He rolled his eyes. "I cannot—"

"You can. You just have to give in to the inevitable."

"Some things are worth taking time over. I believe this might be one of them."

Which was probably as much of an admission of intent as we were likely to get at the moment. I rose onto my toes and kissed his cheek. "Just don't take too much time. Women only have a finite measure of patience when it comes to these matters, and you've already wasted a whole lot of hers."

He opened the door and ushered me out. "You're a troublemaker."

"Nope. Just want to see you happy."

"A man can be happy without getting married, you know."

"Who said anything about marriage? I was talking about sex, brother. Just sex."

He muttered something under his breath, and though I didn't entirely catch it, I suspected he was calling me names again. I laughed, shoved my hands into my pockets, and walked away. The night remained cold enough for my breath to frost the air, but it nevertheless felt good to be out in it with a storm rumbling overhead.

Thankfully, the rain remained several kilometers away, which meant I'd get home before it unleashed again.

But as I neared Eastgate Street, I became aware of smoke riding the strengthening breeze. Fire. There was a fire somewhere close by. I couldn't see any flames, but I nevertheless broke into a run, my heart beating a tattoo as fierce and loud as my footsteps. I swung into Eastgate Street and came to a sliding stop when I saw multiple fire engines and police cars.

This time, it wasn't the tavern that had been hit.

It was Alinda's.

CHAPTER
SEVEN

Heat washed across the night, and smoke stung the air, catching in my throat and making me cough. Entwined within that smoke was an acridness that smelled a little too familiar; this fire, like the one at Aram's, had been started by a blue-dust spell.

But why? What had Alinda known—or maybe even held—that required this sort of action? And was she safe? Her shop had been closed today, and none of the basement-levels had accommodation, so unless she'd come back here this evening, she should be.

Of course, the way things had been going lately, nothing was guaranteed.

The police had set up a wide no-go zone that prevented me—and any possible customers—from getting into the tavern from the street. I'd have to retrace my steps and use the rear entrance, but customers weren't likely to do that. I dug out my phone and rang Ingrid.

"Hey, boss," she said, "everything is fine, but there's been a wee bit of excitement here this evening."

"Yeah, I'm standing out front watching it. The tavern didn't get any damage from the explosion or fire?"

"No. The power has been cut, but the generator kicked in and we're fine."

My gaze jumped to the streetlights. They were on, which had to mean the grid had switched to battery backup in this portion of Deva. It was a necessity given the possibility of an Annwfyn attack, and a luxury previous generations never had. "Are there any customers?"

"The only people here are Jack and Phil, so it might be worth closing early."

Jack and Phil were a couple of old pixies who were basically a part of the Boot family. I remembered seeing them in the booth at the back of the first-floor room as a kid, and Mom had once told me she had the same memories.

"It's looking likely they'll have the street sealed off for the rest of the evening, so yeah, close up. And give Jack and Phil a bottle of Dog Point to ease the pain of being sent home early."

She laughed. "Do that, and they'll be wanting to be sent home early every night."

They wouldn't, because for them, it wasn't about the alcohol but rather the company. There were probably only a hundred or so pixies living here in Deva, and no enclaves at all, so there was little family or community support for those in their autumn years. The tavern, which had been pixie-owned for generations, had become something of a meeting point for many of our elders. We did what we could for them, but I was well aware it wasn't enough. And petitioning the council to do more had so far produced little result.

Movement caught my attention, and I looked around. A

man wearing a dark trench coat had moved out of the walkway opposite and was striding toward the crowd that had gathered to watch proceedings. No, I realized after a moment, he *wasn't* heading for the crowd but rather a dark-haired, pale-faced woman standing away from the rest of the crowd. Normally that wouldn't have bothered me, but there was something unnerving about the intensity with which he watched her. Something that had the hairs along the back of my neck rising.

The earlier premonition of trouble jumped back into sharp focus. With most of my attention still on the stranger, I said, "Ring me if there's any problems, Ingrid."

"There won't be. Do you want me to open up again tomorrow?"

"Yes, thanks." By all rights, I should be able to do it, but better to be safe than sorry, given the growing sense of alarm running across the trouble radar.

I shoved the phone away and moved after the stranger, keeping to my side of the road and a little farther back so as not to draw his attention. He stopped a few meters away from the woman, and though he continued to watch her with an intensity I found increasingly creepy, he no made no immediate move on her.

Was he waiting for something? Or some*one*?

I scanned the surrounding buildings and then the crowd but couldn't see anything that pinged my instincts. The woman's attention remained on the basement and the firemen battling to contain the blaze. Her face was pinched and pale, and her body language distressed.

Alinda. It had to be.

Which meant I had to get to her before that man did something.

But as I walked toward them, my knives began to pulse. They were sheathed and covered by the length of my coat, so the glow that usually came with an activation this strong was concealed from casual sight. But I could feel their heat through my jeans, and that meant the spellcaster was close.

I stopped again and looked around more carefully. I couldn't spot anyone casting, but if there was ill intent behind the spell, they'd hardly be standing openly out in the street. Humans might not be able to sense spell work, but they weren't the only ones gathered in the crowd.

I scanned the upper levels of the nearby buildings and, after a moment, spotted a woman standing in the shadows to one side of an open window. The only reason I saw her at all was thanks to the wash of light from the emergency vehicles making her bushy red hair glow.

Maran Gordan had hair like that.

I was striding toward the building's entrance before I'd even really thought about it. If it *was* Maran, then I'd be damned if I let her escape me again.

But dare I chase her and risk losing Alinda?

We'd already lost the crown to Maran and her allies. We couldn't afford to lose the sword as well, and Alinda might hold the clues we desperately needed.

I swore vehemently and stopped again, this time in the shadows of the building's elevated walkway, out of Maran's line of sight. I had no idea what the intent of her spell was, but— The thought froze as I looked back toward the gathered crowd.

Alinda and her watcher had disappeared. I scanned the street but couldn't see them anywhere. Which could only mean that the spell Maran had cast was a concealment shield, though not one I'd come across before. There were generally two types—light and shadow, meant to be used in either day or night—and they were designed to hide a person from normal sight. But shadow shields were generally the less hardy of the two and could be unraveled by the faintest caress of light. Given the wash coming from all the emergency vehicles in the street, it should have been rendered nigh on useless.

Which meant this particular spell had been combined with something else—something that gave it a more robust nature, allowing its use in this sort of environment.

The knives were still reacting to that magic, even if more faintly, so the concealed shifter was still in the area. They would have reacted more strongly had the shifter and the woman walked past me, so they must have slipped under the tape and walked through the emergency vehicles to the other side of the exclusion zone.

I darted back to the tavern's side of the road and raced up the steps leading to the first-floor level of The Rows. Once I'd run past the cluster of vehicles and the taped-off area on the street below, I paused and looked over the ornate metal railing, scanning for the vague shimmer that sometimes indicated the presence of a shadow shield. Nothing. But the knives' pulsing remained constant, which suggested I was going in the right direction.

I hurried to the end of the Row and down the exit steps before pausing to look in either direction before taking a guess and heading right. The knives' pulsing sharpened abruptly.

Overhead, thunder rumbled ominously, and my skin prickled with its power and the awareness of the storm. I hurried on, gaze sweeping the street, looking for a shimmer in the air or some other indication I was drawing nearer to the man and the woman. Still nothing.

Another rumble, louder and closer, and this time the

force of it rolled through me, otherworldly and fierce. For one heady moment, my senses sharpened, and I saw not only the bubble of distortion that was the shadow shield, but the vague outline of a figure within it; a figure that was running at pace and carrying another.

He was *fast*. Shifter fast.

I swore again and ran after them. As I did, the storm unleashed and the rain hit, a deluge of water that not only made it difficult to see but the old cobblestones dangerously slippery. But at least it would cover the noise I was making.

Lightning split the dark skies. In that brief but fierce illumination, I again spotted the bubble and its occupants. They were turning left into the lane up ahead.

Behind me, someone shouted my name, but I paid them no attention. I didn't have the time to pause or even risk a look behind me. If I slipped, I'd lose my quarry for sure.

The lane was narrow and lined with old and rather unglamorous-looking brick buildings. A small parking area dominated the far end, and there were three cars parked down there. As I sprinted after my quarry, headlights came on, bathing the lane in light and ripping the shadows from the stranger.

He was whip-thin and bald, and carrying the woman like she was nothing more than a sack of potatoes. The way her head was flopping about had me worrying about neck injuries—but unless I stopped the shifter before he reached that vehicle, neck injuries might be the least of her worries.

The stranger must have finally realized I was behind him, because he looked briefly over his shoulder. He didn't seem all that concerned to see me, and a second later, I realized why. Something—some*one*—barreled into my side and sent me flying. I hit the road hard and skidded along the wet stones for several meters, my breath leaving in a painful whoosh. The air stirred around me, whispering of incoming movement—which it could have fucking done *before* I'd been tackled.

I scrambled upright and turned to face the man who'd sent me flying. He was large, fast, and furious, but he never reached me a second time, because suddenly there was someone between us. Someone my hormones recognized even if I couldn't see his face. A second later, my attacker was on the ground, the rain washing the blood pouring from his mashed nosed down his cheeks and onto the stony ground as he howled in agony.

Cynwrig spun around, his gaze sweeping my length and coming up relieved. "You okay?"

I nodded. "Take care of my attacker. I have to catch the other one."

I didn't wait for an answer and bolted after the stranger with as much speed as I could muster. But they were only meters away from that car, and I wasn't going to get there in time. Wind played around my fingertips, as if inviting me to use it. It was certainly tempting. But the likelihood of injuring the woman in the process of tripping her abductor up was relatively high, especially given he was unlikely to fall in a manner that would protect her.

Sadly, the amount of wind I could gather wasn't likely to affect the vehicle. But Beira had declared I could use the power of storms, not just the wind, and she of all people should know what was and wasn't possible. Lightning *would* stop the car, even if it just fused all the electricals.

I had nothing to lose by trying. Nothing except my life, perhaps. But I was the daughter of a storm god; surely that should count for something.

I slid to a stop and thrust my left hand toward the sky,

physically reaching for the forces that roiled above me. Nothing happened. I swore, closed my eyes, and this time mentally imagined what I wanted, what I intended.

Power punched down from the sky, hitting my fingertips before surging down into my flesh. It burned through every cell and fiber of my being, expanding me, changing me, making me a being that was ethereal and translucent, of flesh and yet not.

Lightning flashed, fierce and bright. Not across the sky, but rather inside me. Through my torso, down my right arm and into my fingertips, where it ripped past flesh and streaked across the wet night. It left with such force that I fell to my hands and knees, my breathing ragged, my muscles weak, and my body feeling as if it were on fire. But somehow, I found the strength to lift my head. My lightning streaked past the stranger and hit the roof of the car. There was a small explosion, and tiny sparks flew as the force of the hit caused fragments of metal to melt and burn. Then bright light ran across the defrosting wires embedded in the rear window, and it shattered, sending glass fragments spearing across the night. A heartbeat later, two tires exploded. As smoke began to flood out from the grill, a woman scrambled from the front of the car and bolted away.

The stranger followed her.

I pushed upright, but my legs wouldn't support my weight, and I fell back down again. I screamed in frustration, but my throat was raw and little sound came out. And my vision was going in and out of focus.

Cynwrig appeared in my fading field of sight. "Stay still. I've called in—"

"You need to stop that shifter," I croaked. "You need to retrieve the woman he's carrying. She's vital to our search."

"Bethany—"

"Fucking go," I growled, though it came out little more than a painful rasp. "*Now*."

He went.

I collapsed.

~

It was the sharp vibration of displeasure humming through the building's structure that finally stirred me. As I crawled toward full consciousness, I realized that though the storm still raged above me, I was no longer in the midst of it but rather in my own bed. Wood song told me there were two people in the living area and a third in the other bedroom, but the thunder was so damn loud I couldn't hear any conversation.

I suspected that was deliberate.

Because there was a fourth person here, and she was not only in the room with me but the source of both the noise overhead and the displeasure that sang through the building.

"You can stop foxing, young woman" came the harshly guttural comment. "I know you're awake."

A smile twitched my lips, and I opened my eyes. Beira was perched in a chair drawn up close enough to the end of the bed for her to rest her feet on it. She was on the short side—though far too slender to be a dwarf—with sharp brown features, a thick nest of wiry steel-gray hair, and rather large wart on the end of her nose. But it was her aura —which sang with the ferocity of the storm that raged outside—that caught attention and made most people fear her.

I wasn't most people, and I'm not sure what that said about me.

"And there's nothing quite like waking to your dulcet tones."

She snorted. "I'm not here to cosset you, young woman. You damn near killed yourself—what the hell were you thinking, calling down the lightning like that?"

"You're the one that told me I could use the wind and the storms."

"Yes, but I didn't mean for you to jump into the deep end without first learning to swim. If you'd died—and you came close—we'd all be in serious trouble."

"'All' meaning hags? Or everyone in general?"

I gingerly pushed upright. My body no longer burned, but there was an odd tightness to my skin—the sort of tightness that came from newly healed flesh. I glanced at my fingers. The tips were baby pink; obviously, the lightning burning out of my fingertips had been a physical reality rather than a mere sensation.

"Everyone," she said crossly. "Hags aren't immune to world events, you know, and the wrong people getting their mitts on the Claws would disadvantage us just as much as you lot."

"How? You're all goddesses—"

"Trapped in flesh suits that need to be fed and watered just the same as everyone else. Hard to do if these bastards disrupt the natural order."

"Yes, but it's not like you can have a heart attack or die of old age."

"That does not negate my comment." It was snarkily said, but her dark eyes twinkled.

"So why are you here? As you've said, you're not the cosseting type."

"No, but I was the only one able to save your life." She shook her head. "Did you not listen to the warning Castell brought to you?"

I raised my eyebrows. "You know about that?"

She waved a hand. "She mentioned it. Matter of professional courtesy."

And maybe a desire to avoid annoying the old goddess who had a vested interest in me. Thunder cracked overhead, and the building shivered under its force. It was almost as if the sky had heard and agreed with that silent thought.

"Her warning didn't make a whole lot of sense. I mean, who the hell is 'she that stands with her head in the clouds at the junction of earth and sky'? How am I even supposed to find something like that?"

She tsked. "Are you not aware there is something called Google these days?"

"And such an undefined search is likely to bring up nothing more than books and all manner of random facts on the horizon."

Another tsk. "I can see Castell will have to advise your father to speak plainer in future messages."

My eyebrows rose again. "Do you think there will be future messages?"

She shrugged. "Who knows? He's obviously beavering away in the background to help you, but what his intentions are overall, I cannot say. And it's not like he or his fellow curmudgeons have revealed themselves to us. Not for centuries."

"Then what am I missing? I take it you do understand what my father meant?"

She sighed. It was a very put-upon sound. "I suspect he meant Beinn Nibheis—or Ben Nevis, as it is more commonly called these days. It's a mountain in Scotland and the highest in the UK. Over the centuries it has been called many things, including the mountain of immortality, the mountain with its head in the clouds, and even mountain of heaven."

"And someone lives at the top of it?"

"No."

"Then why am I being told to seek she who does?"

Beira hesitated. "I can't explain, because I can't even be sure anything will happen, despite your father's demand you go there. The junctions of heaven and earth don't often open to those who are human."

"Which I'm not."

She waved a hand and said crossly, "Figure of speech, as you're well aware."

A smile tugged at my lips. "Does that mean this junction is some kind of portal? Is it the place old gods go to move on?"

"No. It's more a... confluence."

"Well, that makes total sense."

"It will when you get there." She handed me a glass of rather murky-looking water. "Drink that. It'll help with the lingering aches."

I tentatively accepted it. "What's in it?"

"Herbs and crap. Stop being juvenile about it, and just drink it."

I quickly did so. It tasted as murky and horrible as it looked. I half gagged but managed to keep the wretched stuff down. I handed her the glass and then said, "Why were you the only one who could save my life? Darby's a healer—"

"And no healer can heal without touching, and touching you would have been deadly."

I blinked. "Why?"

"Because the forces you called down continued to roil through you."

"I remember the sensation of burning—was that in fact a reality?"

"Other than the entry and exit points of the lightning, your skin wasn't *actually* burning. But you were so hot that touching you would have almost instantly melted *her* skin."

"If I couldn't be touched, how did I get here?"

"Via the wind. I heard your call to the storm and had her sweep me to your location. We brought you here once it was safe to do so."

She used storms as a means of transport? That was interesting—and handy if it was a skill I could master. Though mastering *anything* right now was still some ways off, given my somewhat tenuous control over the wind.

"Shouldn't the fact that I'm the daughter of a storm god have provided me at least some protection?"

"It did, because you're alive to tell the tale when most others wouldn't have even survived that initial blast. But eventually your insides would have boiled away because you've not the knowledge to dissipate the force you'd gathered. You're here now because I was close enough to reach you and do that for you."

"Well, thanks."

"As I said, it would be rather inconvenient if you died just yet." She lowered her legs and pushed upright. "Now that you're awake and as sensible as you're ever likely to get, I'd best be going. Just remember, don't call on the lightning again until you've gone to Beinn Nibheis."

"Is it safe to call the wind?"

"Yes, as you definitely need the practice. But do not, under any circumstances, reach for anything else. I don't need to be skedaddling across the countryside siphoning heat to save your life. I do have other matters to attend to, you know."

I was tempted to ask what matters, but her expression made me think better of it. There were obviously some things a mere pixie—even one with the blood of a god running through her veins—should not enquire about.

"I'll inform your brother you're awake. And don't forget, the Eye is a weapon you must use in this fight, even if you're scared of it."

She marched out without waiting for a response. I stared after her. How the fuck had she known I was afraid to use the Eye? Was it simply a guess thanks to my lack of usage, or was there a deeper connection to between my Eye and theirs than what they'd said?

Knowing Beira, the latter was probably true.

The floorboards hummed with movement, the depth of the song telling me it was Lugh. He ducked into the room and stopped beside the bed, his hands shoved deep in his pockets. It made me suspect he was battling the urge to reach for me just in case I was still heat fragile.

"Good to see you finally awake," he said. "I really thought I'd lost you for a while there."

And that fear was right there in his eyes, along with relief and love. I reached out a hand, and he silently caught it. For several seconds, neither of us moved or said anything. We didn't need to.

Then he squeezed my fingers and released them with a smile. "You up to eating? Darby says you should."

I nodded. "How long was I out? And what happened to Alinda? And Cynwrig?"

"Just over twenty-four hours has passed, and Cynwrig left a couple of hours ago to attend the council meeting."

"Another one? Something drastic must have happened."

Lugh shrugged. "He didn't say, but then, we aren't exactly high-ranking pixies."

"Maybe, but we *are* a part of the two relic hunts the council is currently involved in. I'm thinking that should change."

"Oh, I agree, and I daresay he might have told you had you been awake, but... you know what elves are like."

I certainly did. "And Alinda? That is who it was, isn't it?"

He nodded. "She's asleep in the spare room. She's been bound by some sort of sleeping spell, and we don't want to risk getting in an unknown spellcaster to dislodge it. Not until we know who's involved in all this."

"What about Rogan? He should have been able to do it, surely?"

"Yes, and if you'd remained unconscious for much longer, we would have called him."

"So aside from still being spelled, she's okay?"

He nodded. "Darby's been monitoring her vitals, and while there has been slight deterioration in the half hour, it's not yet dangerous."

"I'm surprised they haven't hit the place to retrieve her. If the spell is strong enough to last this long, it's strong enough for them to track it."

"Sgott has placed guards and sniffers out front and back. No one is getting in here without them knowing about it."

"That's going to be great for trade," I muttered.

"Given the general shittiness of the weather, trade has been nonexistent anyway. I told Ingrid to close down early tonight. It's pointless paying staff to stand around twiddling their thumbs. I've just made a fresh pot of tea, if you'd like a cup."

"Make it a barrel and we've got a deal."

He laughed, then bent and carefully hugged me. "Don't be scaring me like that again. Ever."

I returned his hug fiercely. "I'll try not to."

"Good." He dropped a kiss on the top of my head. "Pizza arrived five minutes ago, so there should be some left."

"If there isn't, there will be hell to pay."

He laughed again and left. I got up and slowly got dressed. My body might have healed, but my muscles still felt dodgy. No doubt it was more a result of being knocked sideways than calling down the lightning. My knives were sitting on the bedside table along with my phone, which—despite the slightly singed look to the cover—appeared to have come through okay. I sent a message to Cynwrig to let him know I was awake and okay if he wanted to drop by after the meeting, then put the phone into my pocket, grabbed the knives, and walked out.

Darby immediately leapt up from the sofa and ran over to give me a hug. I hugged her back and said, "I'm fine, really."

She harrumphed. "I'll be the judge of that, but first, you'd best have a cuppa. I know how grumpy you get if you don't have a regular intake, and it has been twenty-four hours."

I laughed. "Luckily for you, I've been unconscious all that time."

"And we all know that doesn't make a difference."

She grabbed my free hand and tugged me toward the sofas. There was indeed plenty of pizza left. I grabbed a plate, loaded up three slices, then plopped down and started eating. "What's happened in the time I was unconscious?"

"Nothing much," Darby said, though the twinkle in her eyes suggested some inroads had been made on the whole relationship quandary. "Cynwrig got pretty badly burned when he shifted your position to help your breathing."

I frowned. "I was having trouble breathing?"

Darby nodded. "Your body heat was causing your trachea to swell. Luckily, Beira got there before the ambulance, because they wouldn't have been able to help you."

"What about the shifter who kidnapped Alinda? And the one who assaulted me?"

"The latter is being held and questioned. The former threw Alinda at Cynwrig and then escaped." Lugh placed a tray containing our largest teapot and three cups on the table. "I've managed to transcribe the rest of the notebook. It's basically a family tree with as much detail as he could find on each of De Clari descendants."

"But nothing on the sword?"

"No, but that is hardly surprising if De Clari *did* come here under the goddess's guidance to hide it."

"Surely someone in the family must know. If not Alinda, then someone else."

"There is no one else. She's the last of the family in this generation."

"Of course," I muttered. "I mean, why would anything be that simple."

"Nothing ever is when it comes to relic hunting," Lugh said. "It takes time and patience to uncover long-hidden clues."

"Which is why you're the hunter and I run the tavern."

Something that would have to change, at least until we sorted out the Claws mess. Neither of us said that out loud, but it was pretty evident we were both thinking it.

I grabbed a slice of pizza and bit into it. "Has Sgott managed to talk to Kaitlyn yet?"

Lugh shook his head. "Not as far as I know. But there is some news on the men who kidnapped Mathi."

There was something in his tone that had my eyebrows rising. "I'm thinking it's not good news."

He poured the tea and slid one cup across to me. "They were found dead in their cells."

I blinked. "They were being held by the IIT—how the hell is that even possible?"

"From what Mathi said, that's a question currently under investigation. They suspect magic—"

"Impossible," I cut in. "All important government buildings—and I would imagine cells—are protected against spellcraft."

"Yes, but what has been woven can also be unwoven if you know what you're doing," Lugh said. "There's no gaps in the CCTV footage, so it wasn't an inside job."

"Did that footage show the moment they were attacked?"

"No camera can pick up magic."

"But they would pick up the reactions of the men to being attacked."

"Except it happened at night, when they were both asleep."

"Inconvenient."

"I suspect they'd agree, were they still alive."

His voice was droll. I demolished the rest of the pizza slice and picked up another. "When were you talking to Mathi?"

"He rang up this morning and was going to pop around. I told him not to because I wasn't up to dealing with the pissing contest he and Cynwrig would undoubtedly have gotten into."

A smile tugged at my lips. "Two alpha men going at each other for dominance doesn't sound all that bad to me."

"You weren't conscious at the time so had no say in the decision."

"I'm thinking the decision would be the same even if I had been conscious."

"Possibly. I've no time for that sort of bullshit right now."

"Or ever," Darby said. "That's not your style."

"No, it's not," I agreed. "His style is to take forever to tell the woman he's interested in he's interested, and then take more time to actually make a move."

He rolled his eyes. "Seriously? Could you for once try for subtlety?"

I wrinkled my nose. "Not my style."

"And he *has* moved forward a fraction," Darby said, eyes twinkling. "We have a date."

So had I, I suddenly remembered. Except Cynwrig was now in a council meeting, and I'd only just awoken, and in all truth wasn't really up to doing anything too energetic. "An official date? As in, going out to dinner?"

"And dancing."

"Are you sure you're feeling okay, brother mine?" I leaned over the table and felt my brother's forehead. "No fever—"

He laughed and slapped my hand away. "Like you weren't angling for this very result when you left us alone the other night."

I grinned. "Yes, but you're often so slow on the uptake I didn't actually think you'd use the time wisely."

"He didn't," Darby said. "I asked him."

"Well, at least he said yes rather than internally debating it for the next week or so."

"Will you two please stop talking about me like I'm not here? It's a rather annoying habit."

I laughed but made no promises. Once I'd finished my pizza and cup of tea, I picked up my knives and rose. "Let's go wreck that sleeping spell and see what Alinda has to say."

The two of them followed me across to the spare bedroom. The knives started pulsing the minute I entered, though it wasn't a particularly strong reaction and suggested the spell could be wearing off on its own accord. Still, given who'd cast it, we really couldn't risk letting it play out naturally.

Darby moved to stand on the other side of the bed while Lugh remained just outside the doorway. The room wasn't large, and his big frame would have dominated the space.

I drew one of the knives, then glanced across to Darby. "Be ready, because I have no idea what will happen when I kill the spell."

She nodded and flexed her fingers. I carefully touched the flat of blade against the exposed portion of the woman's chest. Light ran down the fuller, and energy crackled briefly around the blade's edges, but for several seconds, nothing else happened.

I sheathed the knife as Darby leaned across and pressed her fingers either side of Alinda's temples.

"There's nothing's physically wrong," she said. "Heart, pulse, brain activity all normal. There are a few final spell cobwebs in the process of being dispersed—"

She never completed the sentence, because Alinda drew

in a sharp breath and her eyes popped open. Her gaze was blank for a second or two, then she blinked, and awareness returned.

She glanced quickly around but stopped when she came to me. "Bethany Aodhán. It's about fucking time you showed up."

CHAPTER
EIGHT

To say that was not the first thing I expected from her would be the understatement of the year. Century, even.

"I'm sorry—"

"So you should be," she said, somewhat crossly. Which seemed to be a reoccurring theme when it came to my interactions with fortune tellers or old goddesses. "The stones said you'd be showing up weeks ago. Why didn't you?"

I raised an eyebrow. "If it was so damn urgent, why didn't you just walk across the road and speak to me?"

"What the hell are you talking about?" She pushed into a sitting position. Darby must have stripped off her wet clothes before placing her into the bed, because she was now wearing one of my old T-shirts. "And where the hell am I?"

"You're in my living quarters above the tavern across the road and just down from your shop."

"Would have been handy if the stones had clarified *that*

little detail. So why am I here?" She waved at Darby and Lugh. "And who are these people?"

I introduced them, then explained what had happened.

"And the shop? How bad is it?"

Her manner was matter-of-fact rather than angry, and that surprised me.

"The front of your shop has been gutted," Lugh said, "but from what we've heard, the rear portion was untouched by the fire and only has minimal water damage."

"Which is something of a miracle, given the amount of water they were pouring in," I added.

"No miracle but rather good spelling. I had an inkling there would be a flood and piled on countermeasures." She wrinkled her nose. "Didn't foresee anything about a damn fire, though."

"It wasn't an accident," I said. "It was the result of a blue dust explosion."

Her gaze sharpened on mine. "And how do you know that?"

"Smelled it in the smoke." I pulled the chair a little closer and sat down. "Why would anyone want to destroy your place and kidnap you, Alinda?"

"Perhaps for the same reason I was expecting to see you —they were after information on the goddess's sword."

"You *have* Agrona's Sword?" Lugh said, somewhat incredulously.

"Well, of course not," Alinda said. "That thing was hidden eons ago, and with damn good reason. They don't call it the Sword of Darkness for nothing, you know."

"We're aware it can give the user control over—"

"Night is the least of its abilities. It's a beacon for all the evil that lives within darkness."

"Does that mean it calls to the Annwfyn?" Lugh asked.

"They can sense its activation, yes, so be wary when you touch it." Her voice was grim. "But it also calls to those who worship the darker gods. Why do you think it was hidden so completely?"

"Was it ever a part of the Tenebrous hoard? We're aware the Myrkálfar had both the Crown of Shadows and the Ring of Ruin."

"They did at one point unite the Claws, but an ancestor managed to relieve them of all three items and successfully re-hid each. There are few in this world that can wield the sword, let alone the Claws united."

"Rostin De Clari managed to use the sword quite successfully, from everything we've read."

"She was a mage of great power, and yet even she paid the ultimate price."

Lugh frowned. "How? Didn't she live to a grand old age?"

"To the extent anyone ever did back in those days, yes. But her soul had been stained by the long years of using the sword, and it was claimed on her death by the stygian."

In human legend, the stygian was the river presided over by the boatman Charon, who'd ferry across the souls of the dead on their way to the underworld of Hades. In truth, there was no river, and the stygian were the souls of those charged to bring fresh fodder to whatever dark god they served.

"It is a fate that applies to all her bloodline," Alinda continued, "and the reason I will never have children. This evil destiny ends with me."

And she certainly didn't want sympathy for a decision she'd willingly and knowingly made. Her expression made that very obvious.

"If you're not holding the sword, do you know where it is?" Lugh asked.

"No, but I can gift you with the puzzle of its location—beyond the steps of the gods, in Tywyll's temple, at the altar of darkness."

"And here I was thinking it was only in Hollywood movies that important relics can only be found by solving a location puzzle."

Lugh's voice was dry, and her gaze shot to his. "If one does not want every power-hungry fae or mage imaginable to seek and claim dangerously powerful items, it's only sensible to make finding them as difficult as possible. Which is why there's an added caveat on the puzzle—only a pixie gifted with prescience can unlock the final door."

"Meaning an Aodhán, because there's no other pixie line gifted with that talent."

She smiled, but there was something oddly unsettling about her gaze all of a sudden. It was almost as if the soul that now shone out of it was that of someone not of this world but the other. Someone who'd been dead for a very long time. I shivered and resisted the urge to move the chair a little farther away from the bed and the presence who now shared Alinda's body.

"What the elves seek to ignite must be extinguished," she said. "What was once your duty must be again."

That voice definitely wasn't Alinda's, and it not only spoke of great age and wisdom, but also never-ending regret and agony.

Could it be Rostin De Clari herself? Was Alinda some kind of channeler with a direct connection back to the only mage who'd ever wielded the sword successfully?

I swallowed heavily and said, "Pixies never guarded the

sword or the other Claws. We were never responsible for the relics of the dark gods, only the light."

"If that were true," she said, "you would still be in the service of the gods. But this mess was started by one of your kind, and you must finish it."

I blinked. "A pixie stole the sword?"

"Not just any pixie, but an *Aodhán*. An ancestor of yours."

"Well, fuck," Lugh muttered. "There goes the family myth that we were the innocent party in that whole sordid affair."

It also meant Beira had either lied about not knowing the truth of what had happened or that she had, in fact, truly believed we were the innocent party.

But why would she call the theft of the Claws only a minor transgression? Especially given her comments only an hour ago that their use could affect the hags just as much as humanity itself.

The only way I'd know was to ask the source herself, and there was no guarantee she'd actually give an answer. She might be intent on helping us, but I was betting there was a whole boatload of stuff she wasn't telling us.

I returned my attention to Alinda and the entity speaking through her. "What are we supposed to do with the Claws once we find them? Give them back to the elves to guard? Because that's already proven unviable for weapons this dangerous."

"They must not remain in this reality."

"Meaning we destroy them?" I asked.

"You cannot destroy what the gods have made."

"Then what the hell are we supposed to do with them?"

"You move them beyond mortal reach."

I snorted. "Yeah, that's going to be easy to do."

"You are a godling. You can walk where mortals cannot. This is a destiny that has been waiting for your arrival into this world, and it is one you cannot avoid."

"I may be the daughter of a storm god," I growled, "but it's not like he's provided any sort of parental guidance on what I can and can't do."

"You don't need his guidance. You have the goddess's gifts. But beware—even the gifts of light can sometimes exact a bloody price."

"Meaning what?" Why couldn't these people just speak *plainly*.

She made no reply, and the omniscient presence in Alinda retreated. She blinked several times, reminding me somewhat of a dreamer surfacing to full consciousness.

"Well, that was definitely unexpected," she said, her voice wavery and weak. "Channeling is usually at my request, not hers."

"Does that mean it *was* Rostin De Clari speaking through you?" I asked.

"Rostin or one of the other ancestors. It varies, but the knowledge is shared so it matters not."

"How is something like that possible? I mean, their souls were taken by *dark* gods," Darby asked.

"Taken, not consumed. They might be forced to forever serve their dark masters, but they are not owned by them. The connection of the past and the present is so strong in our line that they can break through the veils that conceal the otherworld when necessary."

And while De Clari had obviously deemed this moment necessary, I just wished she'd been a little clearer as to why. It was all well and good to tell me the Claws must be removed from mortal reach but aside from the dark gates— and there was no way in hell we could ever risk stashing the

Claws anywhere near the Annwfyn—there were few other possibilities.

Unless, of course, she meant to returning them to the goddess herself. Was that why I'd been advised to seek she who stands with her head in the clouds? Had both Castell and Beira misunderstood my father's message? Was it less about me learning to use the power of the storms and more about the confluence itself and the ability to confront the goddess?

If it were the latter, dare I go there until we *did* have the Claws? I had no fucking idea. Which seemed to be a standard state for me of late.

Alinda looked around for a second and then said, "Where are my clothes? It's not safe for me to be here any longer than necessary."

"We can protect—"

"No," she said, cutting Lugh off. "You cannot. You have a task to complete. I'm well able to protect myself now that I am aware the shadows move my way. They will not find me a second time, I assure you. My clothes?"

"They're in the dryer—just let me fetch them," Darby said, and headed out.

"Thank you," Alinda said, then returned her gaze to me. "There is one more thing I need to impart, and it comes from me—or from my reading of the stones—rather than my ancestors."

"And that is?"

"Seek the monolith that has no eyes in the forest with no voice; she will help you unite the goddess gifts."

The image of a standing stone wreathed in old man's beard, the tufted balls of white ringing the stone's top making it seem as if it was wearing a crown, rose. It was one of the things I'd seen in the Eye when I'd first done a reading with it, and I doubted it was a coincidence. Not when the threads of fate seemed to be woven through everything at the moment.

"I daresay that statement makes little sense," Alinda continued, amusement evident, "but as the saying goes, if the path was easy, everyone would be on it."

I snorted. "A saying that was no doubt coined by the old gods who often got their jollies making paths as difficult as fucking possible for their followers."

She laughed. "That is undoubtedly true, but hey, adversity does strengthen the spirit."

"Don't believe that one either," I said.

She laughed again. "I do like you, Bethany Aodhán, but I have taken enough of your time. I must leave."

Once Darby returned with her clothes, I pushed the chair back and left, closing the door behind me to give her some privacy. None of us said anything. The walls in the old tavern might not be paper thin but they didn't exactly stop sound from carrying, either. It was better not to discuss our next step until Alinda had left, just on the off chance she was caught.

Lugh made another pot of tea while Darby and I plopped down onto a sofa and grabbed another slice of pizza.

Alinda came out a few minutes later, her steps a little unsteady and her face drawn.

I frowned. "Are you okay?"

She waved a hand. "The price of channeling is always higher when it is initiated from the other end."

Darby rose. "I can boost your energy reserves—"

"No," Alinda said quickly. "It is the price we pay and one that should not be avoided. Is there a rear entrance to your tavern? I don't think I should risk going out the front."

"You couldn't anyway, as the area remains blocked off," Lugh said. "They're still investigating the cause of the blast."

Alinda glanced at me. "I thought you said it was blue dust?"

"It was, but it's not a scent most humans are sensitive to, and any trace of it would have been erased by the ferocity of the fire."

And whatever remnants *had* remained would have been washed away by all the water they'd poured in.

She grunted. "If you can show me the exit, I'll get out of your hair."

Lugh nodded and placed the tea pot on the table. "Have you a car nearby? Or need a cab?"

"No, but I called a friend, and he'll be waiting for me in St. Werburgh Street."

"Then I'll accompany you, just to ensure you reach him safely."

Alinda looked him up and down, then half smiled. "As impressive as you are, you are not immune to magic, and if they attack, that's what they'll use. I'd rather not be responsible for them snatching you alongside myself, if that's what awaits out there."

"I didn't save your ass from one kidnapping only to have them make a second successful attempt," I said.

"You have more than enough on your plate, young woman," she said, more forcefully this time. "Just show me to the door. I promise, I'll be all right now that I'm aware of the situation."

Lugh's gaze met mine. I half shrugged in response, and he moved past me, leading Alinda across to the stairs and then down. I sat, poured the tea, and said, "So, does the fact you now have an official date mean there was no good use of the alone time I gave you two?"

"With all the shit that's happening at the moment, that's the question you ask?"

"The happiness of my brother and best friend is more important to me than said shit, even if it does involve the fate of the world as we know it. So, was there kissing?"

She grinned. "Hell, yes. And can I just say, your brother is a master of the art."

"Excellent news."

"It's fair to say I'm very definitely looking forward to the next logical step."

"He may take a while getting down to the whole sex thing. He seems intent on taking it slow."

"After waiting for the man to do *anything* for how many goddamn years now, I'm totally okay with slow, trust me."

I laughed, held out my teacup, and clicked it lightly against hers. "Here's to slow progress and eventual satisfaction."

"Amen to that," she said solemnly, a twinkle in her eyes.

"Amen to what?" Lugh said as he clattered up the stairs, the old wood humming under his weight.

"Nothing you need to worry about," I said.

"A statement that only makes me worry more." He grabbed his teacup and sat down beside Darby. "Any clues as to what Alinda's last statement meant?"

"Maybe." I wrinkled my nose. "Did you ever look at the search results you were running for the standing stone I saw in the Eye?"

"No, forgot all about it, to be honest." He pulled his phone from his pocket and, after a few minutes, grunted in satisfaction. "It came up with a dozen stones that fit the description."

"Only a dozen?" I said, in a wry sort of tone.

He gave me a "don't be daft" look. "You are aware just how many standing stones there are on this fair isle of ours, aren't you?"

I smiled. "Does the search come with images? It might save us some driving time if I can pin down possibilities beforehand."

"Hang on." He fiddled with his phone for several more seconds, then held it out to me.

I flicked through the images on the screen, spotting at least five that could have fit the bill. But it was the second last one that had my instincts twitching. I flicked the screen around to show him. "We need to visit this one first. Where is it?"

He plucked the phone from my grip and, after another few seconds, said, "Nercwys Forest."

"Is it far from here?" I asked.

He raised an eyebrow. "Does it matter if it was?"

"Well, yes, because if it was a fair drive, we could leave now and get there in the morning."

"It's in Wales, and probably only a forty-minute drive. It can wait until the morning."

I nodded. "What time do you want to leave, then?"

He shrugged. "Six? We can beat the traffic and the bulk of the mountain bikers who apparently use the area."

I nodded. "You staying here, then?"

He shook his head. "I'm too long for that damn bed. Besides, someone needs to walk Darby home."

Her cheeks dimpled. "Someone doesn't have to feel obliged, but it would nevertheless be appreciated."

Lugh nodded and swiftly drank the rest of his tea. "What are you going to do?"

I shrugged. "Watch some TV for a while." Maybe do what I'd been avoiding up until this point and use the Eye.

"In other words, wait for Cynwrig to call," Lugh said, amused.

I smiled and didn't deny it. He rose and held a hand out to Darby, then tugged her upright. "I'll see you in the morning."

The two of them left hand in hand. I'd never seen a bigger smile on Darby's face.

Once I'd locked the external doors, I fused the stairwell frame and door together to provide extra protection, then walked over to the kitchenette and plucked the cup holding the Eye free. I didn't touch it—not then, and not when I'd sat back down. I simply rested the cup in between my crossed legs and watched the play of purple lightning through the black stone's dark heart.

The Eye was waiting to be unleashed.

I should have grabbed the chocolate from the fridge to shore up my courage, though I wasn't sure if even that would have helped.

I finished my tea, poured another, then munched on the last piece of pizza. Basically, doing everything I could to avoid the inevitable.

But the growing wash of power coming from the Eye suggested avoidance would not be tolerated.

I put my cup down, drew in a steadying breath, then dropped the stone into my palm.

The minute it touched my skin, it came to full life, flooding my senses with power as it swept me away to distant places... *The pounding of waves and the whir of leathery wings. A cave created long ago by unknown hands. Bats that hung from the jagged rafters of the ceiling, forming long runs of gold across the darker stone. A path that could have been made by giants, the long steps winding up to a door whose wood was so old and broken that its song had fled long ago. Beyond lay a cave that jutted out toward the wild seas, the dark stone ceiling providing shelter for the moss-ridden remains of the church that hunkered underneath it. Most of its walls had been broken by the elements and time, but it somehow remained beautiful. Only the chancel end of the church stood whole, and its simple stone altar was a stark contrast to the ornate and beautiful stained-glass window that rose behind it. The vision snapped forward, directing my eye to a pane that lay in the middle of the glass-work. It was a plain black sword. Blood trickled down the length of its fuller and dripped slowly from the tip onto the stone chest that rested underneath it, hitting with enough force that it cracked the top open...*

The vision was swept away, replaced by sound.

Jalvi's late, a woman said.

It reminded me a little of the voice I'd heard in the visions that had risen the last time I'd used the Eye, but this woman's tone was deeper and lacked the inherent warmth.

Jalvi's been captured. This second voice was that of a man and held the snap of power.

Cynwrig?

Yes.

He's becoming a problem.

You should not have attacked his sister.

The comment was greeted by a grunt. *It was thought necessary to gain the information we needed.*

And now means we'll be forced to deal with him.

Yes, though I'm loath to kill him. That'll only bring the full attention of the dark elves onto us.

Agreed, although his disappearance will draw just as much attention.

True. There was a pause. *Will Jalvi talk, do you think?*

Undoubtedly, but what can she truly tell them that they don't already know?

She is aware who keeps the crown.

Kendrin has already been dispatched to move it.

Ah. Good. And our newly woken seeker?

The bugs have been removed. We are currently reduced to following her.

That is another situation we may be forced to rectify.

The vision shifted with sickening abruptness, and this time, the voices were familiar. It was the man and woman who'd been discussing my mother's murder in the last vision.

Did you manage to question Gilda's counterparts? the man asked, his voice cold.

Yes, permission was given.

Permission was given? Did that mean the woman was a member of the IIT branch? Or a lawyer?

Uncover anything?

They do not know how Gilda came across the ruby.

Then why were they seeking the others?

They were told to.

Whom by?

They did not know.

And you believed them?

I gave them Dahbree. They could not lie.

If Gilda's partners had been given Dahbree—the drug Lugh had been given the night this shit all started for us and a poison that forced truthfulness even as it took your life—then it was no wonder their deaths were still under investigation. It was so rare that it generally wasn't tested for, though surely it would show up in the autopsies.

So the risk you took in interviewing them was for naught?

I wouldn't say that, the woman said drolly. *It would*

appear that our dearly departed Gilda had formed a close bond with Kaitlyn.

Indeed? the man said. *Then perhaps we should have another discussion with our broker, and soon.*

The visions faded, and I somehow found the strength to release the still pulsing Eye. As it dropped back into the mug with a clink, I gulped in air. My heart pounded so fiercely, it felt as if it were about to tear out of my chest, and hot pokers of pain were shooting through my brain, making my eyes water and lose focus. Mom was definitely made of sterner stuff than me.

It took a good ten minutes before my breathing and pulse rate settled into something approaching normality. I gulped down my tea and then tugged out my phone and rang Sgott. Thankfully, he answered.

"Bethany," he said. "How are you feeling, darling girl?"

"I've just used the Eye, so not fantastic."

"Ah," he said. "I thought you ringing me this late could only mean trouble. What did you see?"

"You're aware that Mathi's kidnappers were killed in their cells recently?"

"Of course, but what has this—"

"They were questioned before their deaths by a woman. I have no idea what she looked like, because the vision was sound not images, but she gave them Dahbree before she questioned them."

Sgott sucked in a breath. "I'll check the tapes and notify the coroner immediately, although it may already be too late. Dahbree dissolves in the body pretty quickly after death."

"The woman also said she was given permission to be there."

"Not by me she wasn't."

"Ruadhán, then."

"I'll check. Anything else?"

"Have you talked to Kaitlyn yet?"

"No. With everything else that has gone on, she hasn't been a priority. Why?"

"Well, you might want to do it sooner rather than later, because the woman who killed Gilda's partners is now intending to go after Kaitlyn."

"I'll send a unit around immediately," he said. "That it?"

"Whoever stashed the first lot of bugs in the tavern could be planning to place more of them."

"I'll get the team to run regular checks, and we'll also place some discreet motion sensors on the stairs to your living quarters and link the alarm to your phone and mine. It won't stop them, but at least we'll know when someone enters your quarters uninvited."

"Great, thanks." I paused. "Does the name Kendrin mean anything to you?"

"Offhand, no. Why?"

"He's got something to do with the missing crown. It's rather vague, I know, but..."

"But your instincts are twitching, and just like your mother, you can't ignore it."

The sadness in his voice made my heart ache. He and Mom might never have married but they'd been in a committed relationship for over sixty years, and he'd probably taken her disappearance harder than even Lugh or me, simply because with all the resources he had at his disposal, he'd been unable to find her.

"I'm afraid so."

"I'll see what a search comes up with." He paused. "You're feeling okay now? You had me very worried there for a while, lass."

"I'm fine, Sgott. Really."

"Well, good," he said, somewhat gruffly. "But please don't be doing anything like that again. I've already lost your mom. I don't want to be losing you as well."

Tears stung my eyes, and I blinked them away quickly. He was my father in all ways except by bloodline, and I wish he was standing here with me rather than at the other end of the phone, because I really wanted to hug him.

"I'll do my best to ensure that doesn't happen," I said softly.

"I appreciate that, lass," he said in that same gruffly emotional tone and then hung up.

Almost immediately, the phone rang again, the tone telling me it was Cynwrig.

I hit the answer button and said, "You survived the council meeting then?"

"Yes," he said, with a seriously sexy drawl. "And so did Mathi."

I raised my eyebrows. "You and Mathi had words? Over what?"

It couldn't have been about me. Not at a council meeting, anyway. They were both too professional—and too elven—to air personal grievances in a public space.

"He wanted the council to issue a warrant for Aram's arrest."

I frowned. "Can the council order something like that? Surely that's the province of the IIT?"

"For crime-related matters, it is. But the council can issue warrants in specific cases that deal with the overall safety of the town or its people."

"Which I guess does apply in this situation, given the Claws can destroy the balance of light and day."

"Yes, but the point is, there's no clear evidence Aram is

involved in either the theft of the Claws or the Hoard in any way other than helping secure the moonstone from your tavern. Besides, if the council does issue a warrant, it might only succeed in driving him further underground."

"If he's not already dead, that is."

"We have no evidence of that."

"They'd still be sifting through the rubble of his shop and wouldn't be able to confirm that yet, surely."

"That doesn't nullify the point of a warrant being worthless. It would be far better to set a seeking spell onto him."

"Seeking spells don't usually work against spellcasters."

"It depends on the spellcaster and the strength of the spell. Aram is a strong caster, but he's not among Deva's elite."

"But Deva's elite may well be protecting him," I said. "There's a theme of family protecting family running through this whole situation."

For several seconds he made no reply, though I had a deep sense of him being surprised by the comment. It might well have been nothing more than imagination, but I suspected he hadn't expected me to call him out on his response to Jalvi's appearance when we'd been at the warehouse.

"I know Lugh was angry," he said slowly, "and I under-stand his reasons—"

"Do you truly?" I cut in bluntly. "Because from where he's sitting, you're using our sexual relationship to gather information—"

"I made no secret of the fact the council appointed me as your liaison as an information gathering exercise."

"Yes, but I thought we'd had an understanding that it was to be a two-way street."

"We do—"

"Except when it comes to family," I cut in again.

He sighed. "No matter my personal feelings on the matter, I'm obligated to protect her until an internal interrogation is undertaken. I could not allow either of you to be a part of that."

"Is that why you didn't inform Sgott of her whereabouts?"

"He was informed that we had her."

"Was he informed about everything she told you?"

"Most of it, yes. The only information held back related to family."

"That's a very convenient excuse."

"I'm an heir to the Myrkálfar throne. That comes with certain obligations, and it means I sometimes have to walk the tightrope between what I might want and what I am expected to do."

"Given Jalvi is working with the very same people who attacked your sister, I'd have thought protecting her from external interrogation would have been the last thing on your mind."

"It is not so much a matter of protecting her from the IIT but rather those she's working with, as they have a habit of murdering their underlings. That would be inconvenient, given it's possible she holds answers to questions we haven't yet got enough information to ask."

"If one of those questions is the crown's location, you can ignore whatever she told you. It's already being moved."

"How do you know this?"

It was sharply said, suggesting either he or possibly the council had ordered a raid.

"Heard a conversation via the Eye."

He cursed, meaning my guess had been correct. "Did you hear anything else?"

"Two things—a man called Kendrin was dispatched to move the crown from its current location, and you've now become enough of a problem to those hunting the Claws that they're considering kidnapping you."

"The latter doesn't surprise me, especially given Jalvi's involvement in this plot. There will be plenty of her kin sympathetic to the Looisearch's cause, even if they do not fully understand the consequences."

"It does mean you'll have to avoid deserted alleyways and the like for a while, though."

He half laughed. "I was in the middle of a main street—in the middle of a fight—when I was dosed with Dahbree, and even then, they didn't manage to snare me."

"Yeah, but you did end up facedown in a canal full of hungry ellul," I said, voice dry. "I might not be around the next time to haul you out."

"Then perhaps I should endeavor to keep you *very* close indeed." His voice was so low and seductive that an image built of our naked bodies entwined around each other, sweaty flesh glowing as pleasure rose... I gulped and barely even heard him add, "One never knows when one might need... saving."

I was the one who'd need saving if I wasn't very careful. The man could get addictive in all the delightfully wrong ways...

I pushed the—admittedly delightful—images from my mind and said, "Does the name Kendrin ring any bells?"

"No, but I will make inquiries." He paused again "And yes, I will let you know the results."

Unless it involved another relative, no doubt. "Who won the battle over Aram?"

"Neither of us. The council has instead requested Marjorlaine Blackguard—the spellcaster guild's leader—appear before them."

"And will she?"

"Yes. The guild cannot risk losing their licenses to practice within old Deva."

That made sense. Old Deva was a tourist hot spot for nine months of the year, and a good portion of the city's spellcasters made the bulk of their living within that time.

I hesitated and then said, "Darby told me you burned your hands fairly extensively after I called down the lightning."

"Yes, but they were healed without problem at the fae hospital. What of yourself?"

"I'm tired, naturally enough, but other than that, came through it without any further side effects."

"Beira was quite annoyed that you'd had the audacity to reach for that which you could not control," he said, amusement evident. "Of course, she also called me a fucking idiot because I'm old enough to know better than to reach for someone who'd been storm lit."

Curiosity stirred and I couldn't help asking, "So how old are you? You've never actually said."

"In elven terms, I'm two hundred and seventy-three years old."

Elves as a race were very long-lived, and it wasn't unknown for their elders—or statesmen, as they were called—to reach their millennium year before death finally took them. It also put him right on the cusp of breeding age for elves, which was generally between the three and five hundred years old.

Of course, there was a quasi-fertile thirty-year period before they hit the three-hundred-year mark, which, given I was nearing my own fertile period, was why I'd always ensured I was fully protected. Aside from the fact I'd seen firsthand how elves treated half-bloods, I had no desire to bring a child into this world just yet.

We pixies weren't as long-lived as elves, but at sixty-two, I was also close to a fifth of the way through my lifetime—although given the seed of a storm god had given me life, there was no saying how much that would affect my lifespan. Especially given we Aodhán tended to be longer-lived anyway.

"Any plans for tomorrow?" Cynwrig asked.

"Lugh and I have to check out a standing stone in the morning, but other than that, no. Why?"

"Shall we try to go out for dinner again?"

"That depends," I said, dropping my voice a notch, "on what dessert is."

"Dessert can be anything you wish," he said in that low and oh-so sexy tone again.

"Anything?" I drawled. "That could get dangerous."

"I'm very well equipped for dangerous."

I laughed and was tempted—very tempted—to invite him over tonight. But as much as I burned for his touch, I also needed to rest. Just because I felt fine didn't mean my body had fully recovered from the aftereffects of lightning containment.

"I'll ring you tomorrow to confirm a pickup time, then."

"Perfect," I said. "Sleep well."

"As if I could," he drawled, "given the overwhelming impact the mere act of speaking to you has on my libido."

I laughed again. "I'm sure you've plenty of lovers in the wings more than willing to give your libido a hand."

"A harem is of little use when there is only one your body aches for."

His comment not only had all sorts of wanton images stirring but also enflamed the fires of wanting. And not by accident, I suspected. The man was a dark elf, after all, and they were well known for their sexual appetites.

"Oh, I bet that line has worked a treat for you over the years," I said, deliberately keeping my voice light.

"Given it's not something I've ever said before, I wouldn't know. Sleep well, dear Bethany."

With those oh-so-sexily said words ringing in my ears, he hung up.

Ensuring that I didn't, in fact, sleep well.

The minute I jumped into the car, Lugh handed me a coffee and a paper bag containing an egg and cheese McMuffin and a couple of hash browns. "Thought I'd save some time."

"Always appreciated." I plucked one of the hash browns from the bag and munched on it happily. "Did you have any success searching for the other two things Alinda mentioned in her vision after you dropped Darby home last night?"

"If that's your roundabout way of asking if I was invited in to stay the night, then no, I was not."

I'd have to commend Darby on her restraint the next time I saw her. "It actually wasn't, you know."

He cast me a wry glance. "Most people would believe the solemnity with which that was said, but I've spent my life listening to that very tone and know far better."

I smiled and plucked the other hash brown free. I'd had enough time to make myself a bacon butty before Lugh had picked me up, but I was still as hungry as hell. A lingering aftereffect of calling down the lightning, I suspected.

"Your private life is your own business, brother. You don't need to be telling me anything if you don't want to."

He snorted. "Since when has *that* been a working rule? Besides, you two are as thick as thieves, and there appears to be *nothing* you keep from each other. I couldn't get away with lying in this situation even if I wanted to."

"*That* is very true."

He snorted again. "A sensible man would run far, far away—"

"You have been for years. Time to give in to the inevitable and just see if it works. It may not."

"And if it doesn't, where does that leave you and Darby?"

"As long as you don't break her heart—"

"What if she breaks mine?"

"I doubt that's going to happen."

"No relationship in history is ever one hundred percent guaranteed to succeed, Bethany."

"I know, but I'm thinking you're in a far more secure position heart-wise than I am with Cynwrig."

He glanced at me. "I'd have thought that, after Mathi, you'd know better than to fall for another elf."

"I do, and I won't. But shit happens, you know?"

He laughed. "Let's get this conversation back on a sensible track—I googled Nercwys Forest this morning. It's a thriving woodland through which hikers and cyclists roam."

"I take it that means our standing stone is off the main tracks?"

"Yes." He glanced at me. "What are you going to do if it *is* the right stone?"

171

"Alinda said we had to speak to it."

"While there are as many theories about the purpose of standing stones as there are stars in the sky, none of them have ever mentioned the provision of wisdom or guidance."

"But most theories center around the belief that they were religious or ceremonial meeting points, which does imply that priests or mages were involved. It's more than possible that some of them were either communing with specific entities through them or simply using them as some kind of access point to the energy of the earth itself."

"Manipulating the energy of the earth has never required the use of third-party devices such as stones."

"As far as recorded history is aware, but since most standing stones were placed in the Neolithic period, how would we actually know? It's not like they wrote anything down."

"Does this mean you *do* have a plan? Or are we just winging it once we get there?"

"That depends entirely on whether this stone is who I think it might be."

"Which is Eithne, I take it."

I nodded. "If I'm right and this standing stone is hers, then as the latest user of her Eye, I should be able to talk to her."

Or, at the very least, be able to connect with whatever wisdom or power still remained in her monument.

"It's possible that you might need the Eye to do that—I don't suppose you thought to bring it?"

I patted the front pocket of my jeans. "I did indeed."

He shook his head. "You can't keep placing the thing in mugs and pockets. Given its increasing importance, it might be best if we have it made into a piece of jewelry. It's a disguise few would question and a means of keeping it close."

"Jewelry can also be stolen or lost. Besides, the damn thing activates every time it touches my skin, and that would send me around the bend all too quickly." I finished the rest of my McMuffin, then tossed his now empty cup into the bag along with mine and dropped it into the rubbish bag behind the driver seat. "There's a reason Mom never carried it around with her, you know."

Not that I'd actually known about the Eye, let alone seen it, as Mom had kept it well hidden from me. Hell, it had been Beira who'd told me what it was.

He contemplated that for a moment, then said, "What if we wrap it in some sort of wire frame to keep it off your skin but still accessible to touch when it was needed?"

I hesitated. While I really didn't like the thought of wearing the thing, instinct was whispering that it might be a good idea.

"As long as it's not fugly."

"I don't do fugly, Beth."

"You did once."

He rolled his eyes. "That was an expensive and rather exquisite Egyptian piece."

"That was as fugly as hell."

"You were sixteen. It's a well-known fact sixteen-year-olds have barely developed common sense, let alone good taste." He glanced at me. "I take it you haven't tried to read the Eye again yet?"

"Actually, I did."

I quickly described the cave and the old church I'd seen, and he grimaced. "There is nothing in that description that helps pinpoint the place."

"There surely can't be many temples named after a goddess called Tywyll."

"That's presuming we *are* dealing with a goddess. She could be a mere saint for all we know."

"But there surely can't be that many medieval—or older—church remnants sitting on the edge of a cliff—"

"Trust me, there *are*."

"Yes, but this one is in what looks to be an old cave that sits above a bigger cavern."

"We still need something more definitive to pin a location."

"What about the bats?"

He glanced at me, eyebrows raised. "What about them?"

"Well, I've never seen golden bats—have you?"

"I've never actually paid any attention to them, but I'll contact Barry—he's a wildlife biologist I met through Nialle and specializes in bat conservation. He should at least give us some idea where we'd find such a bat."

"Knowing our luck, they'll probably be everywhere."

"You've become a pessimist of late, sister dearest."

"I was always a pessimist. It's just become a more noticeable trait of late."

He laughed and returned his attention to the road as the traffic increased. Once we'd finally reached Nercwys Forest, we pulled into the small parking area and stopped. There were only half a dozen other cars here, so hopefully that meant there wouldn't be too many people either walking or cycling along the trails. I really didn't want an audience when I attempted to commune with the standing stone.

I grabbed my backpack and coat, then climbed out of the car. The morning air was fresh, and I took a deep breath, drawing in the sharp but sweetly refreshing scents of the nearby conifers.

Lugh walked around the back of the car and said, "This way."

He took off toward a set of old iron gates that led onto a wide walking track. The surrounding wood was filled with birdsong, but there was little other noise. The wind was light, barely stirring the conifer needles, and there was little animal movement through the undergrowth. It was a peaceful and beautiful area, and there was a part of me that wanted nothing more than to sit under the canopy of one of the soldier-straight conifers and draw all that peace into my soul.

Because there wasn't going to be a whole lot of it in my near future.

I shivered and rubbed my arms as Lugh pulled a map and a compass from his coat pocket, did some calculations and stuff, and then said, "We'll need to head off the track in a few minutes."

"There are things called GPSs these days, you know. Far easier than compass tracking."

"But sometimes not as reliable." He cast a wry glance my way. "Have you not complained numerous times over the years about Google Maps leading you astray?"

"Well, yes, but it really doesn't happen all that often."

"And it doesn't happen at all if you're proficient at compass hiking. This way."

He moved off the track and cut through the lines of conifers at a good clip. I followed several meters behind, concentrating more on the soft songs of the regimented beauty surrounding us than where we were actually going. But after a while, the plantation trees gave way to more natural wilderness, and Lugh's pace slowed, then finally stopped. I stopped beside him. A misty sort of fog had descended while we'd been in the conifers, and it made the area ahead look decidedly otherworldly. The ground was thick with fallen branches, and brambles scrambled over everything. The trees were thin and in a very poor state, the song of the few still struggling to survive full of distress. Deeper in, there was nothing but death.

"A forest with no voice," Lugh said softly.

"What would cause this sort of destruction to a woodland?" I said. "It's not as if the Nercwys Forest is uncared for."

"There's been a bit of movement of late to allow portions of woodland to return to their natural state."

"This isn't natural," I said.

"Trees do die, Beth."

"But not usually this many in the one area. There's something wrong here."

"Maybe." He moved across to a thin, twisted tree that still maintained a scraggly crown and placed a hand on its trunk. It might still have a song, but I couldn't hear it from where I was standing, and that was unusual.

"You're right," he said, after a moment. "They're being poisoned."

"By what?"

He hesitated, briefly closing his eyes as he deepened his connection to the tree. "The cause is seeping down the hill. This tree remains alive because it sits on the outer reach of the flow."

"Is it natural, do you think? Could it be mining or farming runoff affecting the area?"

"The controls on both are very strict these days, so I doubt it."

I swept my gaze across the foggy deadness, and

another chill ran through me. If it wasn't human actions killing these trees, then the cause might well be magical. The die-off couldn't possibly be caused by Eithne's stone, because it had been around for eons. What had happened to the forest in this area was more recent, but whether that meant it had happened in the last few years or had taken decades, I couldn't say. It generally *did* take a longer time for older, more established trees to die, but most of these were little more than saplings. Until we found the cause of the poisoning, we couldn't be certain about anything.

Not even if this area could be restored.

Lugh led the way forward again, but the going was slow thanks to the fact that we had to scramble over the remnants of fallen trees or skirt around thick thickets of brambles—which were always happy to thrive where nothing else could. The further in we got, the deeper the sense of wrongness became.

As yet another thorn snagged my coat, I grumbled, "If this is simply a re-wilding of woodlands, why the hell would they allow the brambles to explode?"

"They usually don't. Something is definitely happening here—something aside from the trees dying." He glanced over his shoulder. "Can you feel anything?"

Magically, he meant. "No, but my knives are in the backpack, so maybe I won't."

"It might be best if you get them out and strap them on. I'm really not liking the feel of this place."

I immediately did so. And felt weirdly safer for their weight, even if they remained inert.

"Anything?" Lugh asked.

I shook my head. He grunted and moved on. As the ground rose, the trunks of the nearby trees became more bleached, suggesting whatever caused this had been happening for quite some time.

A sharp ringing echoed across the odd stillness and made me jump. Lugh stopped, dragged out his phone, and hit the answer button. "Rogan? Is there a problem?"

I stopped close but couldn't hear the other side of the conversation, which was a little annoying.

After a minute or so, Lugh said, "Why can't he just catch a cab?"

More silence. I shifted from one foot to the other and scanned the trees again. Something had shifted. Or perhaps it was more accurate to say that something had now woken. There was now an odd sort of awareness in the dead blanket of fog surrounding us, and though my knives continued to remain inert, my second sight was giving me all sorts of bad vibes.

"What time does his plane come in, then?" Lugh growled. "Not soon, I'm hoping."

More silence, then, "Fine. Text me the details."

As he hung up, I said, "What's happened?"

"Rogan wants me to pick Eljin up from the airport. He's arriving at two, apparently."

"Who the hell is Eljin?"

"One of the new antiquarians." He headed off again, but not before casting me a look that I knew from long experience meant trouble headed my way. "Actually, maybe *you* should pick him up."

"Why would either of us be doing that? Rogan has a boatload of underlings he could ask if he didn't want his new relic hunter catching a cab."

"He said to consider it a team-building exercise and a chance to get know each other in a non-work environment."

I snorted. "How long has he known you?"

"So long he's forgotten I detest such pleasantries. You, on the other hand, are excellent at them."

"I'm not doing your dirty work, Lugh."

"Oh, in this case, I really think you should."

I glared at his back. He must have felt the heat of it, because his shoulder blades twitched. "Why?"

"Because Eljin is not only a very single pixie, but also only a couple of years older than you."

"And you know all this how?"

"Rogan always gives me the files for an opinion on prospective employees."

"And you're matchmaking me with this man even though you've never actually met him?"

"He's a pixie, Beth. He can't be all that bad."

I snorted. "Yeah, because aside from your good self, we have so many fine representatives of pixie males in Deva at this particular moment."

He laughed and dragged out his phone. A second later, mine dinged. I pulled it out of my pocket and opened his message. It was a picture of a man with shaggy mahogany hair and golden eyes. He very definitely wasn't just *one* step up the ladder when it came to pixie talent in Deva but a veritable *dozen* of them. I wasn't about to admit that to Lugh, though.

"A Tàileach pixie? Gods, Lugh, you know how they feel about us."

"He's French. Different line, different attitude. And remember, you're not the only single pixie woman in Deva looking for decent talent. Best to get a jump on the competition while you can if you ask me."

"And no one did."

But he did have a point. I glanced down at the picture

again. Presuming Eljin was into women rather than men, and that there was the necessary spark that happened when potential lovers first met, why not test the possibilities out anyone else could?

"Fine," I muttered. "I'll pick the man up. But you'll have to lend me your car."

He laughed and glanced over his shoulder. "I knew you'd never be able to resist a pretty face."

He'd barely finished that comment when the knives came to life, the heat of them so fierce it burned through my jeans and scalded my skin.

But before I could warn him, there was a blast of light and a loud *whoomph*. A heartbeat later, we were hit by a wind so fierce it swept us up and sent us flying.

CHAPTER
NINE

I hit the ground with a pain-filled grunt and slid down the hill for several yards before spotting the looming thicket of brambles. I grabbed desperately at nearby tree roots, breaking several before I found one sturdy enough to hold my weight and stop the slide.

I drew in a shuddering breath and winced as pain slithered down my left side. It wasn't bad enough to suggest I'd broken anything, but I'd undoubtedly have a colorful array of bruises tomorrow, given the ground was as rough as old boots. Fragmented spell threads rained all around me, evidence to the strength of the spell Lugh had somehow triggered...

Lugh.

I sat up and looked around, my heart somewhere in my mouth. After a moment, I spotted his crumpled figure half wrapped around a moss-covered rock.

And he wasn't moving.

I scrambled over, dropped onto my knees behind him, and tentatively reached out to feel for a pulse.

He had one, which was a relief. It didn't do a whole lot

to ease the overall fear pulsing through me, though, as having a pulse didn't mean he wasn't seriously injured.

"Lugh?" I said in a slightly quivery voice. "You need to speak to me. *Now*."

His eyelids flickered but didn't open. The fear ramped up a notch. Aside from the fact he'd undoubtedly hit the rock with some force, he'd been far closer to the spell than me and would have caught the explosion's full force. While I couldn't see any obvious injuries, I couldn't discount internal ones.

I grabbed my phone to check for reception. The signal wasn't great, but it did at least exist. I could call an ambulance, but I'd probably have to go meet them, and I didn't want to leave him here unconscious and alone. If he *did* have internal injuries, it was possible he could suffer some sort of medical event while I was gone. But more worrying was the fact that I had no idea if tripping the spell would bring whoever had set it here to investigate. Them finding him defenseless and alone probably wouldn't be in his best interests.

"Lugh? You need to wake up. I need to know you're okay. Please."

He stirred, and this time, his fluttering eyelids opened. The frost-green depths were filled with pain, but his pupils weren't dilated, and there was no sign of confusion.

"Fuck," he muttered, "did you catch the number of that bus?"

I half laughed, half sobbed. "Are you hurt?"

"Don't know." He shifted and almost immediately hissed. Pain swept across his face, and beads of sweat broke out across his forehead. "It would appear I've damaged my arm."

"Damaged how? Bruised? Broken? There's a big difference you know, brother."

"Speaking from previous experience, I would say broken."

"Then don't move any more. I'll call in the medics—"

"I'm not about to leave this area without discovering what the fuck that spell was protecting."

"You can't—"

"I can and will. It wouldn't be the first time I've broken something on a hunt, and I daresay it won't be the last. You got anything in that pack resembling a medical kit or bandage?"

His expression said he was set on this course of action, and past experience said there was little point in arguing about it.

Which had never stopped me before and damn well wouldn't now.

"If you won't agree to calling an ambulance, then at least let me call Darby."

He hesitated. "She's with her brother and his new bub—"

"And if you don't think she'd abandon them all to patch you up, you're a bigger idiot than I thought."

"That's *not* what I meant."

A fact I knew well enough. "She appointed herself troop healer, and she was utterly serious about it. Trust me, she'll get *very* annoyed if we don't call her."

He rolled his eyes. "Fine, but not until we know what that spell was hiding."

"Deal." I pulled the backpack around and unzipped it. "To answer your earlier question, I don't have a medical kit, but I do have a couple of scarves."

"Why on earth do you have scarves?"

"Because it's winter and my neck gets cold. Obviously."

His half laugh ended in a grimace, and more sweat rolled down the side of his face. "We'll use one to tie on a brace and the other as a sling. Do want to find a couple of straight pieces of wood while I lever myself into a sitting position?"

I nodded and rose. There wasn't much in the way of straight wood in the general area, but I picked up a couple of suitable-looking branches that still held an echo of life, even if it was fouled with whatever poisoned this area. I chased that foulness away, then carefully manipulated the wood fibers into a straighter, stronger form. Strangely, despite the fact both branches had been shed from their parent long ago, their song increased in intensity after my touch. Whatever ailed this area *could* be fixed with a little pixie help.

Lugh was bathed in sweat by the time I returned, and his expression pinched with pain. I knelt beside him and carefully braced his arm without bothering to remove his coat. He assured me there weren't any bones sticking out, that it was at worst a simple break, and I took him at his word. Even if it weren't true, there wasn't much more I could do than what I already had.

Once I'd made the second scarf into a sling and secured it around the back of his neck, I rose and offered him a hand. He gripped it with his good hand and allowed me to pull him carefully to his feet. Fresh droplets of sweat trickled down his cheeks, but he didn't say anything, despite the pain I could see in his eyes.

"Onward and upward, sister dearest," he said. "And this time, you and your knives had better lead."

I drew them both, then turned and carefully moved back up the hill. When I neared the area where the explosion had happened, I paused and scanned the area. Tiny threads of fractured magic still played about on the breeze, but I had no sense of further threat, and the knives weren't reacting.

I walked on, carefully picking my way through the wild undergrowth. The further up the hill we went, the deeper the developing fog became and the thicker the brambles grew. They alone seemed to thrive in the foulness of this place, and I suspected that was deliberate. Thick patches of brambles certainly provided a barrier few people would venture into, and it meant the spellcasters wouldn't need to leave as many traps.

There *was* a path through the brambles, but the higher we climbed, the narrower it got. Thankfully, the knives were razor sharp, and I could hack away the worst of the thorny tentacles before they snagged us too badly.

Then life began to pulse down the knives' fullers, the color a deep, threatening purple.

Dark magic lay ahead.

I stopped and once again scanned the area. It was hard to see anything thanks to the blanket of fog, but I had a weird feeling we were close to the hill's top even if we couldn't see it.

I glanced back at Lugh. "There's magic ahead. You'd better stay here."

He hesitated and then nodded—something I could see only thanks to the knives' eerie glow. "Try not to get yourself blown up."

"You just don't want the odious task of picking up your new coworker at the airport," I said lightly.

He half laughed. "I'd rather pick him up than pieces of you, so be careful."

"I have a dinner date and the promise of hot sex waiting

for me tonight. I'm not going to let any kind of spell get in the way of that, trust me."

And I crossed all things that I hadn't just tempted fate. Like all the old goddesses, she really did enjoy fouling expectations and plans.

I continued on cautiously, feeling more than a little exposed without my brother's looming presence behind me. The steady pulse of light down the blades echoed through their hilts, giving me an odd sort of feel for the spell's location. The closer we got, the more the blade's purplish glow spread, pushing the fog back and allowing me to see a little of what lay ahead.

It wasn't brambles. It was a barrier. A magical barrier. One that pulsed with foulness. I stopped and said, "I might have found the source for the poisoning of this wood."

"Magic? Or something else?"

"Magic." I glanced behind me. The knives hadn't just cleared a path ahead, but also behind. "It's another barrier."

"A twin to the one I hit?"

"No, because the knives didn't react to that one until you'd already hit it."

"Is it safe to come up?"

I quickly re-checked there were no other traps except the one that lay ahead and then said, "I think so."

He trudged up the hill and stopped behind me. "Will the knives be able to destroy it?"

"Maybe, but I'm not liking the feel of the spell, and I really don't want to get that close to it."

"Then throw them. I know you've a shitty arm but even you can manage to hit a wall that damn big."

"Gee, thanks for the confidence boost, brother."

He laughed, a soft but bright sound that felt like

sunshine in the surrounding gloom. "Given what happened last time, I suggest we hug the ground and cover our heads."

I waited until he'd done so, and then raised my arms and launched both knives toward the darkly pulsing barrier ahead. Then I threw myself down beside Lugh and twisted around to see what happened.

The blades flew straight and true, the pulsing purple fire spinning from their points seeming to guide them toward their target. They slid easily into the magic before coming to an abrupt halt at their hilts.

For several seconds, nothing happened.

Then cracks began to appear in the wall, radiating out from the point where the knives were buried. At the same time, a deep and decidedly off-sounding humming bit through the air, starting low but increasing in intensity until it was absolutely painful.

Then, with little other warning, the wall exploded, sending a wave of broken magic and debris flowing down the hill.

"Cover!" I yelled, and buried my face into the ground, my hands covering my head as much as possible.

The wave hit, so thick with foulness that for several seconds it was difficult to breathe. But it didn't deposit its load of debris and magic on top of us, instead rolling on down the path.

A path I could now see clearly.

The explosion had swept away the fog.

I blinked, then twisted around to look up the hill.

A line of skeletal oaks ringed a hill that was topped by a solitary standing stone. A stone that held the dead remnants of what once had been old man's beard.

Eithne's monument.

"Well, fuck," Lugh said. "We found it."

"We did indeed, and in the first place we looked for a goddamn change." I pushed to my feet, then helped him clamber to his. "Now we just have to hope that the spell placed around her clearing hasn't actually sucked the life from her stone as thoroughly as it has the rest of the area."

I moved up the hill and picked up my knives. They'd dropped to the ground when the spell had exploded and weren't damaged in any way, which I guessed was not unexpected, given magic didn't affect them. It did make me wonder what else they were capable of, though. After all, they'd been gifted to the women of my line back in the days when the Aodhán had been the warrior guardians of their hoards, and I wouldn't be surprised if, over the centuries, we'd simply forgotten the greater extent of their capabilities thanks to the fact we'd concentrated on the one aspect we'd found most useful.

I sheathed them, then cautiously approached the stone. The dead grass crunched under my feet, but as I got closer, the faintest hint of green began to appear, softening the sound and giving me hope that all was not lost in this place. The old man's beard that had looked dead from a distance held a few tiny shoots of green, suggesting that at least some part of the climber still clung to life.

I hoped that also meant the monument—and the consciousness or power that resided within it—remained viable.

I stopped a meter or so away from it and looked up. It was a massive thing, wider in girth than Lugh and at least half his height again. It was made of the same black stone as the Eye but lacked the thrum of power I'd immediately sensed in the smaller stone.

Lugh did a slow circle around the base of the stone.

"You know, from certain angles, it has the attributes of a woman."

I raised my eyebrows and walked around to join him on the other side of the stone. From this point, it did hold a womanly shape, though her facial features were worn and without definition, and the woody stems of the mostly dead old man's beard basically hid the mounds of her breasts and the voluptuousness of her body.

Eithne might have been the first hag, but if this stone was anything to go by, she hadn't been tarred by the same unkind fate that subsequent goddesses had.

Unless, of course, this stone was commemorative of the goddess she'd been before misdeeds had cast them all into flesh form.

"Are you getting anything from it?" Lugh asked.

I shook my head. "But I didn't really feel the power in the Eye until I touched it."

"And you're afraid to touch the monument?"

"Yes." I raised my gaze to where her eyes would have been. There was no indentation, nothing to suggest the Eye in my pocket had been carved from this stone, even if they appeared to be the same.

"You saw this image in the Eye for a reason, Beth. It might be important, it might not, but I'm thinking the only way you're going to find out is to touch the thing."

I drew in a breath then blew it out. "I know. It just that—"

"Touching the Eye results in being physically drained, and you don't want to risk that when I'm injured," he finished for me.

A somewhat bitter smile twisted my lips. "Well, yes. One of us does have to be fit enough to drive home."

"No, because Darby will be meeting us in the parking

area, remember, and I'm more than capable of helping you down the hill if need be."

A statement that didn't in any way ease the inner trembling. I sucked in another breath and then said, "I guess if Mom was here, she'd be telling me to pull up my big girl britches and just get on with it."

He laughed, a soft sad sound. "Yeah, she definitely would."

I thrust my hand into my pocket and drew out the little silk jewelry bag I'd shoved the Eye into. After tugging the drawstring loose, I rolled the black stone into my right palm, wrapped my fingers around it, then stepped forward and placed my left hand on Eithne's stone.

A deep pulse ran through the standing stone. It was a low, somewhat tenuous sensation, not unlike that of a heart struggling for life.

There was a long pause, then another beat, stronger this time.

Energy crawled through the Eye in response, oddly expectant in feel. No images flowed into my mind from its dark surface, and I wasn't sure if that was a good thing or not.

The deeper pulse continued to gain strength and ramped up my tension and fear. The energy flickering through the Eye deepened, and purple light began to leak between my clenched fingers. I had no immediate sense that the Eye was, in any way, drawing down on my strength, yet my body trembled, and I had the oddest feeling of standing on the edge of a precipice. That I was only one step away from not only the unknown, but something that would change my life in undefined ways.

It was all I could do not to run. Only the knowledge that

the key to finding Mom's killers might well lie in whatever was about to happen kept me still and connected.

As the deep heartbeat grew stronger, warmth began to flood the exterior of the standing stone. Way above my head, the old man's beard stirred, the dry rustling quickly softening as green flooded the dead branches and buds and leaves appeared along the vines.

"The stone is coming back to life," Lugh said, in a hushed, almost awestruck tone. "Are you all right, Beth? It's not harming you in any way?"

I shook my head but didn't otherwise reply. Couldn't, in fact, reply. The energy that pulsed through the Eye and echoed through me was now eclipsed by that of the standing stone, and it was a force that dragged me, ever so slowly, toward that unseen, unknown cliff.

Then it dragged me over.

I fell, not physically but metaphorically—spiritually?—through utter blackness and had the oddest feeling that I was also falling through time and space.

When I stopped, I was in a place that held no sound beyond that solitary heartbeat and no light other than the very distant flash of purple lightning that was the Eye. Instinct told me she was my connection to reality and my only means of getting back.

The air was still and close, and I was weightless and ethereal in a place that was connected to the sky and the earth even though it existed in neither.

Then, like distant thunder, a voice said, *Who enters my megalith?*

The question held such a deep note of authority that terror skittled through me. *My name is Bethany Aodhán—*

You are the inheritor of my Eye?

Yes.

Why do you not use it as you should?

I was never taught—

Learning comes from experiencing, young woman. Experience can only be achieved via connection and use.

There were echoes of Beira in that statement, and amusement slithered through me. But before I could reply, the voice added, *What is it you wish?*

What makes you think I want something?

Few can find this monument. Fewer still can access her heart. Only those who seek answers to the unanswerable ever try.

A statement that didn't make a whole lot of sense, but then, I was talking to an old goddess who'd passed from this world long ago. I was probably lucky she'd even deemed me worthy of speaking to. *A vision sent me here. I'm unsure why.*

You cannot direct or interpret the Eye's visions?

No.

There was a long, seemingly surprised pause. *The Triune should make that impossible.*

Confusion stirred through me and seemed to echo across the black stillness. *What's a Triune?*

There was a ponderous sigh. *The Aodhán line has fallen far, it would seem.*

Meaning it's another gift from the gods?

The Triune is three—foresight, protection, and knowledge. They were designed to give the Aodhán all the tools they might need to fight those who seek the rebirth of the dark gods in the tangible world. You have the Eye and the knives—I can feel the presence of both.

I do, but I had no idea they were part of this Triune. What, then, is the third part?

It is the codex—a book that holds the vast knowledge of all creation.

No book would ever be large enough to contain all of that.

No book ever written by man or woman, true.

And can you tell me where this book is?

What once was gifted to your line remains in it. Look to the west.

West of what? As clues went, that was damnably vague. But I had a feeling she would give me nothing more, and I was right.

Finding it is of the essence, she continued. *Darkness rises in the East. Ninkil is the first but far from the least of your problems now that the relics are again unleashed onto the world.*

You know about that?

I am gone, but I am not entirely forgotten. I hear.

Don't suppose you know who stole them or where they might be hidden?

Those questions are for you to answer. It is your destiny— your purpose. Keep faith with the Eye, complete the Triune's circle, and pay the price to make them your own. You will be far better equipped to deal with what comes.

What price?

She didn't answer. She simply said, *I wish you luck. You will need it.*

Her presence retreated, and I was dragged back through the black, the distant flash of purple growing clearer and brighter.

Then I was in my body and on the ground, sucking in air as every muscle trembled and it felt like a freight train was moving through my head. Lugh was sitting beside me, his good arm resting against my spine, holding me up.

I rubbed my temples in a vague attempt to ease the pain. "That was *not* what I'd expected."

"Talking to the old gods never runs the way you expect."

"You say that like you've done it."

"I did once, in Greece. It's not an experience I want to repeat, but then, he was the god of war and, well, warlike."

He offered me a small, uncapped flask. I took a swig and immediately started coughing. It was whisky, not water, and it burned all the way down even as it chased the worst of the tiredness away.

"I called Darby when you were thrown back from the stone," he continued. "She'll be waiting for us both at the parking area."

A smile tugged at my lips. "She could be waiting a while. I'm not sure either of us are in a fit state to walk back down."

"With the spells gone, it should be far easier to go down than it was to come up. Besides, she's still at least half an hour away, if not more, given she wouldn't have been able to leave the elven compound straight away. What happened with the standing stone?"

"I talked to Eithne." I frowned. "At least I presumed it was her. She never actually said her name."

"Did she say anything useful?"

"Do old goddesses ever?"

He laughed. "More riddles, then?"

"Kind of."

I quickly updated him, and he said, "Meaning the goddess's gifts Alinda mentioned wasn't referring to the Eye itself, but rather the Triune it's apparently a part of."

I nodded. "Did Mom ever say anything about it?"

He shook his head. "It's a term that's generally used in conjunction with the holy trinity in Christianity. As far as I'm aware, it's never been used in our family."

"And you've never seen Mom use this codex she mentioned?"

"No." His frown deepened. "I do remember walking in on an argument between Mom and Aunt Riayn not long after Gran died. If memory serves me right, it was over a small, leather-bound book."

"She left us not long after that," I commented. "Maybe that argument was the reason."

He nodded. "It's also possible she took it with her when she left."

I wrinkled my nose. "Why would she have, though? Mom was the first-born female—the gifts of the old gods were hers to inherit."

"Aunt Riayn never did have a high opinion of that particular inheritance law." His voice was dry. "It's why she tried to buy Gran's share of the tavern multiple times before she'd died."

I raised my eyebrows. "But she hated the tavern."

"She hated the thought of Mom inheriting everything all the more."

"But she didn't—Aunt Riayn did get the bulk of Gran's other investments, including her property in Galway."

"Yes, but our history in Deva lies within the very walls of the tavern."

Because it had been in the family for three very long-lived generations. It had witnessed births, deaths, and everything in between. The building's structure sang with generations of love, laughter, and grief. It was far more valuable emotionally than all those other investments combined.

I took another sip of whisky, then handed him back the flask. After taking a drink himself, he replaced the cap and tucked it away. "Did Eithne tell you where to find this codex?"

"She said in the west."

"Helpful." He paused. "Although I guess Aunt Riayn is technically in the west."

"It's probably a very long bow we're drawing, but if the book is with her, it would be so much easier."

"If she *does* have it, she'll demand high compensation for it."

"Then maybe we need to talk to Vincentia instead."

I hadn't seen my cousin for over twelve months now, and rather rarely before that, but we did at least get along.

"She might well confirm whether or not they have the book, but if you think she's any less mercenary than her mother, then she's pulled the wool over your eyes."

A wry smile tugged at my lips. "I'm well aware of her mercenary tendencies, but she *is* in the family business even if she only accepts private commissions, so it does go with the territory."

The family business, of course, being relic hunting rather than tavern running. It was usually the males of our line who turned to that side of things, but over the centuries there'd been a few women who'd bucked that trend.

"And let's be honest here," I added, amusement bubbling through me. "You've never really forgiven her for beating you to Vesta's patera."

He sniffed. "She sold it to a private investor. *That's* what I couldn't forgive."

I laughed and pushed slowly to my feet. "We'd better get out of here. You need to get that arm healed, and I've a new antiquarian to pick up from the airport."

His gaze skimmed me and came up concerned. "I'll ring Rogan and ask him to get someone else onto it. You need to rest—you've also a hot date to prepare for, remember?"

"Darby will do a full medical check. If she says I need to

rest, you can call Rogan." I offered him a hand and helped him upright. "You're the one who said I couldn't risk missing meeting possibly the most eligible pixie bachelor to appear in Deva for decades."

He smiled. "I'm sure I can arrange a fortuitous meeting further down the track."

"Yes, but as you also noted, better to get a jump on the competition while I can."

"Who knew my own wise words would come back to bite me in the butt?" he grumbled.

I laughed. "And you'd better get that butt moving, because if Darby has to hang around in the parking area for too long, she *will* come looking for us. And you know how much she hates hiking."

"For an elf, she's not very woodsy."

"She's a city girl and a healer to boot, but you've plenty of time to convert her."

He snorted and didn't bite. We made our way slowly through the brambles and eventually picked up pace as we neared the main track.

Darby was leaning against the side of Lugh's car when we finally arrived back at the parking area but pushed off and walked toward us as we moved through the old metal gates.

"You two both look like crap—what on earth have you been up to?"

"Breaking magic, breaking bones, and talking to a goddess in a standing stone," I said. "You know, the usual stuff."

She snorted and planted herself in front of me, forcing me to stop. "I'll tackle you first. You look the easiest."

"Um, can't it at least wait until we get to the car?"

"Well, no, because you need to get yourself home

straight away and make yourself presentable for the future husband. And presentable means a nice dress, not jeans and old boots, by the way."

I gave Lugh a long look. "You told her?"

"Well, of course. You're not the only matchmaker in this family. I also sent a message to Rogan and asked him to inform Eljin that you'd be picking him up because I broke my arm."

"And with that all sorted, how about you two stay silent and let me work my magic?"

I smiled but stood still as Darby pressed her fingers against my temples and her magic unfurled through me. After a couple of minutes, she made a satisfied-sounding grunt and stepped back. "You had some bruising along your ribs, which I fixed, and your energy reserves are a little low, but a good cup of tea and a decent meal would soon fix that."

"Decent meaning not take-away," Lugh said, giving me the eye. "So bypass McDonald's and grab something at the tavern before you go back out."

"Hey, I'm versatile. I can do both."

He rolled his eyes and tossed me the car keys. "Go. Darby will drive me home once she patches me up."

I glanced at Darby. There was a definite glint of mischief in her blue eyes, and I rather suspected she was going to use Lugh's injury to remain in his company for the rest of the day.

"Luck," I murmured, just soft enough for her to hear, and left them to it.

The drive home was uneventful, and I definitely felt a whole lot better after a long hot shower. I heated up some baked beans, then poured them over a couple of slices of grilled cheese on toast. I wasn't sure it would fit Darby's definition of a decent meal, but I couldn't be bothered cooking something more complex.

After booking a short-term parking space online, I headed over to Liverpool Airport to pick up Lugh's new partner in crime. The plane arrived on time, and I stood at the back of the lounge area, my arms crossed as I scanned the people pouring off the plane.

Eljin was nigh on the last to come out, and I had to say, his photo didn't do him justice.

Like most Tàileach pixies, he was golden-skinned and lean in build. His face was sharpish but handsome, his eyes the most delicious shade of old gold I'd ever seen, and his mouth definitely made for kissing. He moved with the confidence of a man very sure about his place in the world, and yet there was nothing in his energy output or expression that suggested this confidence was in any way overbearing or egotistical.

His gaze came to mine, did a quick circuit down my length, then rose again. The smile teasing his lips was polite, but his eyes gleamed with appreciation.

Which made me even gladder I'd taken Darby's advice and worn a dress—albeit a heavyweight winter one. First impressions counted.

"Bethany Aodhán?" he said, in a voice that was accented just enough to be sexy. "I'm Eljin Lavigne. It is a great pleasure to meet you."

"Same." I shook the offered hand. His fingers warm against mine and held just the right amount of pressure. "Do you have much in the way of baggage?"

"A suitcase, nothing more. The rest will follow once I've sorted permanent accommodation."

"Ah, good. This way, then."

He fell in step beside me, close enough that I could feel

the heat of his body while still respecting the boundaries of personal space. "Do you also work at the museum?"

I smiled and shook my head. "No, though I *am* helping Lugh track down some relics at the moment."

"Unofficially and unpaid, I take it?"

The amusement in his tone had my gaze rising. His golden eyes—which held deeper flecks of buttery brown—glinted with understanding. "Yes. Why?"

His soft laugh ran across my skin like a caress, and while it didn't have the same fierce impact of Cynwrig's, it was nevertheless a pleasant sensation. "I have a sister gifted with foresight and used to drag her into my searches all the time. Unpaid, of course."

I raised my eyebrows. "It's rare for Tàileach pixies to hold second sight."

"There's Aodhán in our bloodline."

Meaning Lugh was right. The French lines didn't hold the same animosity.

"She no longer helps you now, I take it?"

He shook his head. "She married ten years ago and has three young children. I'll not place her in any sort of danger, even if her foresight rarely leads to a dangerous situation."

I couldn't help wishing *mine* didn't. "She your only sibling?"

He nodded and lightly touched my back, guiding me around a luggage cart that erupted out of a corridor. He removed his fingers almost immediately, but my spine seemed to retain the heat of them for a little longer than was usual.

There were definite possibilities here... and yet something within wasn't entirely convinced. Of course, it was probably the same something that was still very much in lust with all things Cynwrig and wasn't currently interested in other possibilities.

"My mother wanted more children but was never blessed," he was saying. "My father was much older than her. It happens."

It did, especially in both the Aodhán and Tàileach lines. It was the price we'd apparently paid for our height and our longer-than-pixie-norm lifespan, and the reason why there were eleven years between me and Lugh.

"Is your brother off on a hunt now? Is that the reason you've been tasked with picking me up?" He paused, a mischievous glint entering his eyes. "Though I am in no way complaining. The photo Monsieur Rogan sent me of you was pretty, but in person, you are exquisite."

Amusement rather than desire bubbled through me. "And that is a fabulous pick-up line, Monsieur Lavigne—does it often work?"

He laughed. "Sadly, no. Women are so suspicious of a compliment these days."

"Probably because past experience has given them reason."

He hesitated. "It was sincerely meant, but I apologize if it made you uncomfortable. That was not my intent."

"You didn't, but thank you anyway. Where are you staying?"

"At the Chapel Boutique Apartments, in Albion Street."

I didn't know the apartments, but Albion Street was roughly halfway between the tavern and the museum and definitely within walking distance to both. Which could be handy if things did kick off between us.

We continued to make pleasant small talk as we picked up his bag and then walked across the road to the multi-story car park. The trip back to Deva didn't take all that long, and it was with a vague sense of regret that I pulled into the small parking area opposite the Chapel Apartments.

"It has been a pleasure to meet you, Bethany Aodhán," he said, with a friendly, polite smile. "Would it be too forward of me to ask for your phone number?"

"Not at all." I gave it to him, then added, "Feel free to call if you need help with anything while you're settling in."

A devilish glint entered his eyes. "Such an open invitation could invite abuse. I am a stranger in this place, after all, and I do find it difficult to make friends."

"Oh yeah, I can totally see that."

His laugh was warm and easy. "I perhaps exaggerate just a little, but I would truly like to see you again. Can I take you to dinner in appreciation for picking me up?"

"I'm a little busy with the hunt at the moment but I'm sure we could work something out. Even my brother has to sleep sometime."

"Sleep is very underrated," he murmured, a wicked glint in his eyes. "I'll talk to you soon, Bethany."

He climbed out, collected his suitcase from the rear of the car, and gave me a salute as he went past and walked across the road to the apartments. I enjoyed the view from behind—he really did wear jeans particularly well—then sighed, started up the car, and headed home. After finding a parking spot relatively close to the tavern, I sent Lugh a message to inform him where it was and that I'd leave the keys on the coffee table in my living area. Then I headed to my computer to get in a couple of hours of paperwork before getting ready for my date.

≈

Cynwrig opened the car door, then offered me a hand. I accepted it gratefully, swung my legs out of the chauffeured car, then rose. The dress was figure-hugging and ankle-length, though the split to my left thigh did make movement easier. A soft breeze ran around my stockinged legs but contained no scent of rain. Not that I was cold; even if my heavy woolen coat had been unable to keep the cold out, the heated appreciation emanating from the suited man standing to one side of me would have been more than enough to keep the chill at bay.

Of the winter-induced kind, anyway.

He switched his grip from my hand to my spine, his touch sending my pulse into a chaotic dance. There was a part of me that half wished we could skip dinner and jump straight into the dessert potion of the evening, but the saner part of me was having none of that. Our destination was none other than Viridis, the latest dining sensation in Deva and one of only twenty-three restaurants in the UK to be given a Michelin green star for high levels of gastronomy and sustainability. I'd been wanting to come here for ages but, despite the astronomical prices, the wait list was at least eight months long.

"Who did you threaten to get a table here at such short notice?" I asked.

He laughed, opened the door, and ushered me in. "I'm good friends with the maître d' and have inside information when it comes to cancellations. Luckily for us, a table did tonight. Otherwise, it would have been dinner at the nearby pub."

I seriously doubted *that*, given the classy burgundy dinner jacket, crisp white shirt, and black pants he was wearing.

The room we entered wasn't particularly large, but

filled with Victorian splendor. The tables were well spaced, the lighting muted, and there was no evidence of a bar, though there was obviously one here given that at the nearest table, a waiter was uncorking a bottle of Moët.

A dapper-looking older man approached, took care of our coats, and then said, "This way, Lord Lùtair."

"Thank you, Henrick." Cynwrig pressed a hand against my spine again, guiding me after the older man.

Given said older man wasn't wearing a badge, this was either Cynwrig's friend or he did in fact come here often enough to be on a first-name basis with all the staff.

We were led through the stylish and beautiful room to a staircase near the back. I ran my fingers across the worn and obviously original volute at the base of the stairs and let them drift along the curved oak handrail as we moved up. Its song danced through me, and I couldn't help smiling. This building had been a long and happy resting place for the wood in this staircase, and there were very few left in Deva of this age that could make such a boast. Most had inevitably suffered damage over time, even the stairs in the tavern—though at least they'd had the advantage of pixie owners who could and did repair anything done to them.

We continued past the first floor and up to the second. This was a more intimate space set under the roofline, with a large and rather ornate Victorian fireplace dominating one wall and five discreetly placed tables—two at either end of the room and one in the middle. Henrick led us to one under a window on the street side and, once he'd seated us, handed us a drink menu. "Shall I come back?"

Cynwrig glanced at me and raised an eyebrow. I placed my purse under the table, then skimmed the menu and said, "I'll have the Macallan 18, please."

"Make that two." Cynwrig waited until Henrick had left

and then said, continuing the conversation we'd been having in the car, "Marjorlaine Blackguard has agreed to appear before the council tomorrow morning."

"Whether she actually cooperates is another matter entirely."

"Oh, she will. The spellcasters' guild cannot afford to get on the wrong side of them."

"Those members who play by the rules, for sure, but I'm thinking there's quite a few who don't."

"Blackguard is not one of them."

Henrick reappeared with our drinks, placed them on the table, and then handed us food menu. As he once again slipped away, a voice said, "Cynwrig Lùtair? As I live and breathe, it's been absolutely *ages*."

My gaze shot right. The woman approaching was tall, dark-skinned, with long, curly black hair, and a figure to die for. She was also a dark elf, although from a different line to Cynwrig, given her eyes were a silvery green.

"Orlah," he said, voice filled with warm surprise. "What are you doing here? I thought you were seeking greener marital pastures over on the continent?"

He rose and kissed the offered cheek. Hers dimpled in pleasure.

"Sadly, said grass was not greener, and I have returned." She glanced at me, her expression friendly enough. "Do you mind if I steal him for a second or two? I want to introduce him to my friends."

"Would it matter if I said I most certainly *do* mind?" I said mildly.

She blinked, obviously taken aback, then wrinkled her nose. "I'm sorry, I didn't mean to be presumptuous or to intrude. Cynwrig, I'll ring you."

If she was hoping to make me feel bad, she succeeded.

But hey, this was my time with him, not hers. She could introduce him to as many friends as she wanted another day.

She kissed his cheek again and then sashayed across the room toward a table where two other women waited. Cynwrig's gaze briefly followed her before returning to mine. There was little to be seen in his expression, but his eyes flickered with desire.

I wasn't sure if it was for me or his friend, and I certainly wasn't sure how I felt about the possibility of it being the latter.

Which was a lie but one I was fully supporting right at this moment.

I leaned back in my chair and swirled my whisky. The ice clicked lightly against the glass, a bright sound in the warm shadows that surrounded us. "Can I ask who that was?"

"Just an old friend."

"Old bed friend?"

"Yes." He studied me speculatively for a moment. "Why?"

"Just curious."

"Curious? Or jealous?"

Oh, there was definitely jealousy, but it wasn't like I'd ever be stupid enough to admit that to this man. "We're both free agents, are we not?"

"Yes—"

"And we're both free to pursue pleasure elsewhere, are we not?"

"Yes—"

"Then I have no reason to be jealous."

"No, but it would nevertheless warm my cockles if you were."

Amusement twitched my lips. "I think your cockles get more than enough attention without my input."

His laugh was warm and deep and sent delight skimming across my skin. "But my cockles *adore* your attention."

"Hmmm" was all I said to that.

He laughed again then reached across the table and twined his fingers through mine. "If ever I decide to get into a serious relationship, you will be the first to know. I promise you that."

Mathi had made a similar promise and broken it at first chance. I knew dark elves took a vow more seriously than light, but there was a part of me that was wary of trusting too much.

Probably the same part that had trusted Mathi too much.

"And I promise *you* the same courtesy."

He raised his eyebrows. Though amusement played around his lips, there was something a whole lot more... dangerous... in his eyes. "That sounds like there's competition in the wings."

"There is."

"Not Mathi, I would hope."

I laughed. "Mathi can pursue me all he wants but he will never again grace my bed. But there *is* a new pixie in town, and he's rather... lovely."

Cyn's amusement grew, as did that dangerous glint. This man did *not* like the thought of credible competition, and my hormones skipped along in giddy delight.

"If you called *me* lovely," he said, "I'd be offended."

"Lovely is more likely to be long-term. Sexy and dangerously hot is not."

His gaze narrowed fractionally. I picked up my glass to hide my amusement and wondered if his other lovers had partners on the side. I suspected not. Something in his manner and the way he was studying me suggested he wasn't used to sharing.

Not that it mattered. I was never going to be his "one," and while I was more than happy to be "one of a few," I couldn't let the intense sexual attraction that burned between us distract me from finding *my* "one." That might or might not be Eljin, but the only way I was going to find out was by testing the relationship waters with him.

"Do you have a date with this pixie?" Cynwrig asked.

"Yes."

Which was only a partial lie, because we had agreed to dinner. We just hadn't set the date yet.

"I wish you a good time, then." He paused, then added with a wicked smile, "But not too much of a good time, of course."

I laughed and changed the topic. "Have you any luck tracking down who Kendrin might be?"

"Yes and no."

I raised an eyebrow. "Meaning?"

"There is a Kendrin Mason I believe might be the man we are looking for, but he has, unfortunately, disappeared."

"Not surprising, given he's been tasked with hiding the crown." I took a sip of whisky. It was lovely, both soft and velvety on the palate with just enough notes of orange citrus, vanilla, and cinnamon to tease the taste buds. I was definitely going to find a bottle or two for my own collection. "Mason isn't an elven name, though."

"Because he's only half. His mother was human who was killed in a Annwfyn attack some five years ago."

"You know, given that is becoming a major theme when it comes to the Looisearch, it might well be worth tracking down the families of all those who have been attacked or taken in attacks over the last decade. We might just find the names of everyone involved."

He smiled. "The council is already onto that. What do you wish for dinner? Henrick will return to take our order in a few minutes."

I studied the menu for a few seconds and then put it down. There were too many perfect-sounding choices. "You've obviously been here more than a few times, so how about you decide for us both?"

"There is no dish that could ever be called bad in this restaurant, but I would be honored to choose."

I smiled. "Meaning, I take it, that previous guests picked their own?"

The sudden heat in his eyes had my toes curling. "It would be safe to say that the appetites of previous guests were not as... hearty as I might like."

I smiled. "Perhaps they simply preferred not to exercise on a full belly."

He laughed and, when Henrick glided over, proceeded to order what amounted to a banquet. It was just as well I hadn't eaten all that much over the day. And that I'd never suffered reflux or anything else more violent from "exercising" after a good meal.

Conversation moved on after that, and we talked about everything and anything, from weighty subjects like the current political situation to lighter ones like our weird dealings with the public during the course of our work. I might have found Eljin easy to talk to in the brief time I'd been with him but sitting here with Cynwrig really was on another level altogether.

It was just such a shame he was elf rather than pixie.

The meal ended with coffee close to midnight, and my offer to pay my share of the hefty bill was brushed aside. As we followed Henrick back down the stairs to collect our coats, he said, "Do you wish me to call the car? Or would you prefer to walk?"

I knew without even looking that, despite the chill in the breeze and the clouds shrouding the stars, there was little risk of rain. Not tonight, anyway. "Walk. But the bigger question is, to your place or mine?"

He smiled and slid his hand from the middle of my spine to my rear, briefly cupping it. "I've been doing nothing more than admiring your lusciousness all evening and I really, *really* need to touch. Which means my place. It's far closer."

I laughed. "Smooth. Real smooth."

He raised an eyebrow, his expression curious. "Why is it that you always greet a compliment with sarcasm and disbelief?"

Henrick held out my coat. I handed my purse to Cynwrig and shoved my arms into the sleeves. "I don't know."

He gave me a long look. "Oh, I think you do."

I didn't bother denying it, but I also wasn't about to bring down the mood by talking about past hurt and self-protection. "It was all a *long* time ago and not worth a mention."

"A lie I can all but taste."

I smiled and tucked my arm through his as Henrick opened the door and ushered us out. "Shall we talk about breakfast? Because I'm thinking there definitely needs to be croissants this time."

"As ever, m'lady, your wish is my command."

The conversation moved on, and we strolled through the semi-deserted streets unhurriedly, simply enjoying each other's company on this cold, wintery night.

Until I felt the tension in him, that is.

I silently studied the well-lit street ahead but couldn't immediately see a reason. But the comments I'd heard in the Eye rose, and apprehension stirred.

"Is something wrong?" I asked softly.

"You could say that." His gaze met mine, his expression annoyed more than anything else. "We're being followed."

CHAPTER
TEN

I didn't question his certainty. He was a dark elf, after all, and the old cobblestones were a superhighway of information to someone who could command stone as easily as I did wood.

"How many?"

"Four."

I frowned. "Four isn't many considering what happened last time someone attacked you. Or rather, foolishly attacked your sister while you were in the vicinity."

"It's possible there's more up ahead—closer to my apartment—and that those behind us are merely reporting our location." He glanced down at me. "I don't suppose you brought your knives along, did you?"

"Why do you think this purse is so heavy?"

I'd also brought the Eye, though it was sitting in its little silk purse under my left breast, as that was the best way I could think of to keeping it close without spoiling the look of the outfit. I'd expected it to be annoying, but it surprisingly wasn't.

His smile briefly crinkled the corners of his eyes. "I do

like a woman who comes fully prepared for all eventualities."

"One has to, given what's happened to me in the recent past. What if they use Dahbree again?"

"If this is the kidnapping attempt you saw in the Eye, they're more likely to use something that will take us down faster—another reason to handle this situation before we walk into any trap that might be waiting."

"Meaning you have a plan?"

"I *always* have a plan." The mischief dancing in his eyes suggested he wasn't just referring to the current situation. "Can you fight in those shoes?"

I gave him a long look. "Have you not seen the size of my heels?"

He glanced down. "Yes, and while they are pretty, they're not very practical for purpose."

"Maybe not for the purpose you're proposing, but they were perfect for an evening of seduction. Which," I added with a sigh, "I can sadly see slipping away."

"It won't take long to deal with the four behind us."

"What if there's more ahead?"

"There's a lovely little boutique hotel in that lane we just passed. We can spend the rest of the evening there while any would-be attackers up ahead waste time looking for us."

Which didn't take care of the overall kidnapping problem, but we could only deal with one situation at a time.

"Stop a moment so I can take off the heels."

He did so, holding my elbow lightly to help me balance as I removed both shoes and then attached them to my purse. The strap was a thickish chain, so it wouldn't break easily, even if I was forced to use the bag as a belting weapon. Men generally had little respect for the dangerousness of a purse in the right hands, but then, few realized how much crap women carried in them and just how heavy they could be.

We walked on for several minutes, the cobblestones smooth and cold under my stockinged feet. There was a bit of me that wished I could hear the murmurs of the stone, though not so much because I wanted to know where our trackers currently were but rather *what* we might be dealing with. Four shifters would be a very different prospect to four humans.

"There's a walkway just ahead that will take us through a retail courtyard before coming out onto a lane that eventually meets up with Watergate," Cynwrig murmured. "We'll take that instead of remaining on the main road."

Watergate being the street where his apartment was located. "I take it the lane provides a perfect ambush area?"

"It does indeed. Shall we proceed?"

"Definitely. These people need to learn not to fuck with me when I'm on a promise."

He laughed, a warm, rich sound that ran across the silence and oddly eased the tension in me. We entered the walkway, which wasn't very long but filled with lovely old Victorian buildings, then on into a lane that was far less enticing.

We quickened our pace, him so lightly he made no sound, and me with only a slight whisper coming from my stocked feet. About halfway up the lane were several large metal dumpsters on wheels, their lids up and both empty. Behind them was a brick wall and a small alcove holding a couple of plastic wheelie bins. Cynwrig lifted them up, placed them beside the metal bins to provide additional cover, and then motioned me into the alcove. The wall was only half-height, so we both had to hunker down to ensure we wouldn't be seen the minute the four men entered the lane.

I dropped my purse onto the ground and pulled the knives free. They weren't active, but I nevertheless left them sheathed, just in case they came to life and gave us away at the last moment.

"Where are the men now?" I asked softly.

My pulse rate was sky-high, and tension pounded through me. I was well able to stop a fight, and I could certainly defend myself—Mom had made sure of that, even if my training had been untraditional by most standards. But I'd never actively attacked anyone, and it was... well, scary.

"Two are entering the lane now," Cynwrig murmured. "The other two are hanging back."

"They're being cautious."

"As they should be. Only a fool would dare track a Myrkálfar without taking all possible precautions." He paused, his gaze narrowing a little. "They're close to the lane now. We attack once all four have passed us. Okay?"

I nodded and swallowed heavily, but it did little to ease the sudden dryness in my throat. Cynwrig's hand wrapped around mine and briefly squeezed. I glanced at him. His smoky silver eyes glittered dangerously in the darkness, and an air of anticipation hovered around him.

I smiled, feigning a confidence I didn't exactly feel. He nodded and released me. The seconds stretched into minutes, and the frustration of waiting clawed at my insides. I tried to keep my breathing soft and even, but it was a hard task.

Then Cynwrig raised two fingers and motioned toward the metal bins on the other side of the wall, indicating where the first half of our targets were. I tightened my grip on the knife hilts, my breath caught somewhere in my throat. For several seconds, there was nothing, then came a sound that was little more than a piece of grit skittering across the cobblestones.

They were close. Damnably close.

Cynwrig touched my leg, making me jump slightly. He silently indicated that he'd go up and over the wall then motioned me toward the plastic bins. When I nodded, he raised three fingers and, after a second, dropped the first one.

Tension slithered through me and my grip on the knife hilts was so tight I'm surprised the two people on the other side of the wall couldn't see the glow of my knuckles.

The second finger dropped.

I slightly shifted, reading to thrust up and run around the bins.

The third finger never dropped.

My phone rang, the sound sharp in the tense silence.

Cynwrig swore and surged up and over the wall. I raced out of the nook, saw the flash of movement, and hit the last plastic bin hard, sending it tumbling into the path of the man running straight at me. He did an awkward half leap and landed heavily, stumbling for several steps before turning to come at me again.

I flicked the knives from their sheaths, dodged his fist, and then slashed sideways and back with the blade in my right hand. He swore and leapt back. The knife point skimmed the front of his coat, slicing open the leather but not skin.

Movement, behind me.

I instinctively ducked, then swung around, sweeping with one foot, knocking my second assailant off-balance and tearing open the side seam in my dress. Saw this assailant throw out a hand, as if to stop himself falling. I quickly sheathed one knife then grabbed his fingers. "Don't move, don't attack, don't say anything."

As my magic surged between us, something hit me from behind and sent me sprawling. I hit the ground on hands and knees, managing to keep grip of both knives at the cost of skinning my knuckles on the old cobblestones. The air stirred lightly around me, but it wasn't a breeze; it was movement. I swore and half swung around, lashing out with one knife. Felt the shudder of it connecting echoing back through my arm as I followed through with the movement, slicing through muscle and bone as easily as butter. As the stench of burning skin stung the air, my assailant's severed hand dropped to the pavement, and his warm blood spurted across my face.

I scrambled back, gagging, as he raised his head and howled. Then his shape began to shimmer, shift, and instead of a man standing in front of me, there was a wolf with a front foot missing.

Shifting didn't—*couldn't*—replace severed limbs, even if it did hasten the healing process for them.

I raised my knife and held it at his eye level. "This is silver. Unless you want to die of blood poisoning, I suggest you—"

I never finished, because the bastard turned and ran. A second later I realized why. Cynwrig appeared from behind the bins, his big body airborne as he launched after the fleeing wolf.

He hit the shifter hard, and the two of them rolled across the cobblestones, growls, curses, and snapping teeth filling the air. I scrambled upright and ran over, but before I could touch the shifter, he stopped moving.

Cynwrig grunted and, as the unconscious wolf's form

shimmered back to human, pushed him off and rose. There was a cut along his right cheek, but otherwise, he seemed unhurt. His gaze skimmed me, then he reached out and lightly brushed his fingers down my cheek. "You're bleeding."

"It's not my blood." I scraped my coat sleeve across my face and tried not to think about the stickiness that remained behind.

"The blood on your hands is."

"I scraped them when he knocked me over. Nothing to worry about." Even if they did hurt like a bitch now that the adrenalin rush was easing. "Sorry about my damn phone going off at the wrong moment. I should have thought to turn the damn thing down."

"Next time."

"Don't know about you, but I'm seriously hoping there *isn't* a next time." I glanced around but couldn't see the two men he'd tackled. "What did you do with the others?"

"Threw them in the first bin and fused the latch. They'll keep until the IIT arrive."

While most Myrkálfar could manipulate the earth and the metals that came from it to some degree, they usually concentrated on one particular element to ensure precision. But from the little Cynwrig had said about his family, they could easily and accurately manipulate pretty much *all* the earth's elements.

I lightly toed the shifter at our feet. "This one won't—he's a shifter, so he's going to need medical help to combat silver poisoning pretty damn quickly."

"Then I'll call the IIT, you call the medics."

I nodded and did so. Cynwrig then picked up the shifter, dumped him in the second metal bin, and fused this latch down as well—though I did have to wonder for how long it would remain attached if shifter got serious about escaping.

After I'd picked up the knife sheaths, we walked over to the person I'd frozen in place. I was rather surprised to discover it was a woman. The multiple layers of clothing on top of her thickset form did a good job of concealing the fact from a cursory glance.

I briefly gripped her hand again and said, "You will now answer all our questions openly and honestly. Understood?"

Her dark eyes glittered dangerously, but she obviously knew she had little choice in the matter.

Cynwrig crossed his arms and studied her for several very long seeming seconds. She couldn't move—my previous order still held true until I said otherwise—but I think if she could have shifted in discomfort she might have.

"Who gave you the commission to follow us?" he asked eventually. "Was it Kaitlyn?"

"No," the woman growled. Her voice was on the harsh side of husky, making me wonder if it was the result of damaged vocal cords. The ugly scars down the left side of her face and neck suggested it could be. "The broker has stopped taking contracts that involve *her*."

That last bit was said with a sneer and obviously directed at me. "So you *were* after me, not Lord Lùtair here?"

"Yes."

"Then why not wait until I was alone? You must have realized his presence upped the risks."

"Yes," she repeated. "But a contract has just gone out for tender, requesting his temporary removal from Deva and—"

"You figured you'd take advantage of the situation and,

in the process, jump both the queue *and* the competition," Cynwrig finished for her.

"We *never* land the bigger contracts," she muttered.

But they'd landed mine, which meant someone considered me less worthy than Cynwrig. Which was odd, really, given my newly emerging talents were of use to both the Claw group *and* the Hoard stealers.

"Who gave you the contract for me, then?" I asked.

"I only know her first name."

When she didn't continue, I raised my eyebrow and said, "And that name is...?"

"Minnie Mouse."

"Really?"

My voice was disbelieving, and she smiled. "Of course it isn't, but it's not like I can tell you otherwise."

There was only two ways to prevent someone speaking the truth when compelled by a pixie. One of them was via telepathic control, and I seriously doubted we were dealing with that here. "I take it the contractor was a pixie?"

"Yes."

Which meant I couldn't countermand or even dissolve the other's pixie's orders. The controlling magic just didn't work that way. "If you're under a pixie order you must have met her—can you give me a description?"

"No."

My frustration grew stronger, though again it wasn't an unexpected answer. Any pixie ordering anything illegal of another would ensure their identities were well and truly hidden. And it wasn't like we could track the "feel" of the obedience magic as we could pixie dust, because although the compelling magic in every pixie line did have share certain characteristics, it was impossible to pin it down to a particular family or person.

"You're putting a lot of trust in a woman you don't know," I commented.

"That's how these sorts of contracts work," Cynwrig commented. "The person responsible for funding the contract will not renege, as that would get them blacklisted."

"Huh." I looked at the woman again. "What were you supposed to do with me once you had me?"

"Ring to arrange pickup and payment."

"Do it now," I said. "Tell her you've got me sedated but you're two men down and it'll just be you coming to the exchange point."

As the distant sound of sirens invaded the air, the woman pulled out her phone and made the call. When the number started to ring, I reached across and hit the speaker button.

"I take it your mission has been successful given that's the only reason you should be ringing this number."

The voice was low and had a somewhat tinny sound to it, suggesting some sort of voice moderating app was being used. It was obviously a woman, but more than that, I couldn't say.

"Yes," our captive said.

"Any problems?"

"Well, she really wasn't happy about the possibility of being kidnapped. It took some doing to get her under control."

The woman laughed, and there was something vaguely familiar about it. "I did warn you she could fight."

"*That* is something of an understatement. The bitch took out two of my men."

The woman laughed again, and that sense of familiarity

strengthened. Damn it, who did I know who laughed like that?

"I take it she's now trussed up tighter than an antique clock?"

Familiarity sharpened to recognition and, for several seconds, I couldn't breathe. All I could do was stare at that damn phone and wish, with everything I had, that I was mistaken. That one of the closest living relatives Lugh and I had left *wasn't* betraying us.

I certainly hoped she hadn't betrayed Mom.

Because that term was one rarely used outside my small family unit. Or, more specifically, my gran, my aunt, and my cousin.

Gran was dead, and despite the voice modulations, it didn't sound sharp enough to be my aunt.

Which left only one possibility.

Vincentia.

It would explain not only the multiple break-ins at the tavern over the last six months, but also Mom's reaction the fateful night she'd disappeared. *This* would explain why she'd left the tavern without taking the knives, as she usually did. She'd deliberately left them behind so that they wouldn't fall into the wrong hands.

The hands of the niece she'd known was betraying us.

It was all I could not to reach out, grab the phone, and unleash every bit of anger and heartbreak at the woman on the other end of that phone.

But that would only give her the chance to hide—not that there was *anywhere* in this world that was now safe for her. I'd find her, no matter how long it fucking took, and tell her *exactly* what I thought of her.

And she'd spend eternity wishing she'd never walked betrayal's path.

"We've force fed her tranqs," my captive was saying, "she won't be any trouble for hours."

"Ah, good. Exchange at Churton, as agreed?"

"Yes."

"Understood. Thanks."

There was amusement in Vincentia's modulated tone, and the urge to vent was so damn strong again that I half reached out.

I forced my hand down and said, once our captive had hung up, "Where's the meeting point?"

"There won't be one." The satisfaction so evident in her reply practically oozed from her skin. "Not now."

"Churton was a code for capture?" Cynwrig asked.

The woman glanced at him, her expression scathing. "Do you think either of us are fucking stupid? We knew who we were dealing with and were well aware capture was a possibility."

"Giving her a warning means you won't get paid," I noted. "All you end up with is a prison sentence."

"Our agreement included compensation for possible capture. As I said, I'm not an idiot."

I swore and scrubbed a hand through my hair. "Where was the original exchange point?"

"I would have been told if I'd replied negatively to Churton."

"Well planned indeed." Cynwrig took the phone from her hand and glanced at me. "We'll get the number traced, though it's likely to be a burner and will probably be dumped."

"Probably." I glared at the woman's smug features for a second, and an idea that was very much tied to the base need of revenge stirred. "What sort of car do you drive?"

"White Ford Transit Courier."

Which was the perfect little van for this sort of work, because while it was of the smaller cars in the Ford fleet, it processed a decent load space and good fuel economy. I knew this because I once had a date who was seriously into little vans and who regaled me about their benefits while I was trapped in said van with him going to dinner.

"And did your pre-arranged code word also account for the possibility of us taking possession of your van?"

"No—"

"Good." I made a give-me motion. "Keys, location, and parking ticket if there is one. Also, are there only the four of you involved in this kidnapping stunt?"

"Yes."

"Then for future reference, neither you nor your people will bid on or accept a contract involving me, my brother, or Lord Lùtair here—understood? And if Vincentia—the woman you know as Minnie Mouse—contacts you, you are not to tell her—or anyone else, for that matter—that we now have your van. In fact, you're not to say anything to her about anything you've seen or heard here tonight."

She scowled at me and, as I repeated the give-me motion, handed over the three items I'd requested.

"I take it you have a plan," Cynwrig said.

I nodded and glanced around as the specialized ambulance finally arrived. Several IIT cars followed it into the lane, one Sgott's.

"I'll explain everything later. We need to deal with this lot first."

While Cynwrig led the fae medic over to the bin holding the wounded shifter, I retrieved my purse, shoved my sheathed knives back into it, then pulled out my phone to see who the ill-timed call had been from.

It wasn't a call. It was an alert from the newly installed

movement alarm in the stairwell leading up to my living quarters.

Only a pixie could have gotten past the wood fiber alterations I'd made to the door to lock it in place, and it didn't take a fucking genius to guess who the likely intruder had been.

But even if Vincentia *wasn't* behind tonight's break-in, even if she'd guessed I'd put the call on speaker to hear what was being said, with the voice modulation in place, she was unlikely to guess I'd recognize her. And if she hadn't changed past habits, she'd leave Deva and let the hullabaloo settle down for a few days while she regrouped and replanned.

And that gave *us* an advantage.

A big one.

I swung my purse over my shoulder and walked across to Sgott. He was a big bear of a man—fitting given he was a bear shifter—with thick, wiry brown hair, brown skin, and an untamable beard.

"At least all this explains why you didn't respond to the alarm at your tavern." He planted his big body in front of me and scanned me critically. "I take it that blood isn't yours?"

"I was attacked by a shifter, but he soon regretted it. I gather you didn't catch whoever set off the alarm?"

"No. We believe they went out a rear window as we were coming in. Bird shifter most likely, because there was no sign of a rope and no easy means of getting down to street level from that window."

Vincentia wouldn't have needed a ladder. She could simply have created her own from the building's ancient oak framing.

"Anything damaged?"

"Not that I could see, but it's obvious they were searching for something."

I suspected that something was tucked in silk under my left breast, especially given what Lugh had recently told me about Aunt Riayn.

"You'd best give me a statement for this attack, then go home to check if anything is missing."

"The latter can wait. I've got to see my aunt."

Sgott's eyebrows rose. "At this time of night? Why the sudden urgency? She basically cut you all off decades ago."

"I know, but we got some information that makes me believe she may have a book that'll help me understand the workings of the Eye."

"If that were true, your mother would have retrieved it. She did want you to continue her work after her death."

Except that she didn't. Not for most of my life, anyway. It was only toward the end, when I'd finally began exhibiting the signs of second sight, that she'd started talking to me about it.

"I still need to see her. If she hasn't got the book, then maybe she knows what happened to it."

He frowned. "Then why not just ring her?"

"Because she can ignore a phone call. She can't ignore me turning up unexpectedly on her doorstep."

"I wouldn't bet on that." He cocked his head slightly and studied me through slightly narrowed eyes. "The book isn't the only reason behind this sudden urge to go see her, is it?"

I half smiled. "Once a cop, always a cop."

"I think it's more the fact you've a face that's not designed for lying."

I laughed, though it sounded a little forced even to me.

"I think the person behind the break-ins is none other than Vincentia."

His eyebrows rose again. "What makes you think *that*?"

"Because she's behind this abduction attempt."

He swore. "I'll put out an APB immediately—"

"Do that, and she'll know we know she's involved. As it stands, she thinks she's done enough to elude us."

"That may change once we do a full interview and charge your assailants."

"No, it won't, because the woman I've frozen in place is Tia's contact point and has been magically muted."

"By you or by Vincentia?"

"Both."

"Then why are you so sure it's Vincentia?"

Bitterness twisted my lips. "Because, despite the app she was using to disguise her voice, she used one of Gran's favorite sayings. It's her, trust me."

He grunted. "We'll still need to go after whoever brokered the deal."

"It wasn't Kaitlyn. I asked."

"That still leaves a handful of others."

"Whoever it is, they won't hand out the contract details without a court order, and that'll take at least twenty-four hours, won't it?"

A knowing smile tugged at his lips. "If needed."

"Best to be safe," I said.

"Fine but that doesn't alter the fact that your trip to Galway might well pointless. Tia *will* warn her mother what's happened."

"That's presuming Aunt Riayn is aware of Tia's involvement in all this. She might not be. I have to give her the benefit of the doubt, Sgott, if only for Mom's sake."

They might well have drifted far apart after Gran's

death, but they'd once been thicker than thieves. Until I could prove otherwise, I refused to believe she would condone any action that would have led to Mom's death.

Sgott studied me for a second, his expression giving little away. "You do know why Riayn left for Galway, don't you?"

"Lugh said it happened after an argument they had— one he believed was over the book."

"That may well be true," Sgott said gravely, "but the fracture came when Riayn learned you'd inherit the goddess's gifts even though Vincentia was the stronger talent."

And at the time, she had been. Hell, she might still be given mine had only just appeared and I was very much struggling to understand it.

"Meaning it's utterly possible Vincentia isn't involved in the hunt for the Claws," I said. "Maybe she's simply trying to reclaim what she's always been told is rightfully hers."

There was a part of me—the same part that was locked tightly down, refusing to grieve until revenge had been had —that really hoped that was the case, and that the timing of the break-ins was simply coincidence.

"Whatever the truth," Sgott said, "you can't go there alone."

"I won't. Cynwrig's coming."

"Why not Lugh?"

"Not enough seating in the van we're using. Besides, he was injured this afternoon and he's home with Darby right now, suffering her tender ministrations."

He laughed. "In other words, you're matchmaking again."

"Not again. Still."

"He's not going to be pleased about being left out."

"I know, but he needs to hunt down an old church with possible connections to the sword, and he can't do that if he's constantly gallivanting around the countryside with me."

"That won't alter the fact he'll be unhappy."

I grinned. "Which is why Darby's there."

He rolled his eyes and squeezed my shoulder. "Be careful and keep me in the loop."

I nodded and followed him across to my captive. Once I'd released her from my initial "stand-still, don't speak" order, he motioned his people to take care of her, then walked over to the bins and talked briefly to Cynwrig. The latter's gaze met mine, and I felt the impact of it deep in my stomach.

It was a shame, really, that I'd just committed us to a journey of more than six hours in a small van.

After speaking to Sgott for a few more minutes, he walked toward me in that confident and very sexy manner of his, instantly ratcheting up my desire level. I mean, seriously, the man needed to come with a heat warning.

"I'm told we're off to Galway."

"And may also need to check out Killiney."

He twined his fingers through mine then tugged me toward the lane's exit. "What's there?"

"A holiday house. Vincentia showed me the details for it some ten years ago, during one of the few times we met for dinner. If she's going into hiding for a few days, that might be where she goes."

"You can remember the address of a place you were briefly shown ten years ago? I'm impressed. And scared."

I raised my eyebrows. "Why scared?"

"Because it means you'll be able to name the time and

date of any transgression I might make, no matter how much time has passed since said transgression."

"The obvious solution is not to do anything you don't want flung back in an argument."

He laughed, which to me suggested there would certainly be transgressions and he really didn't care what I did with them. "What's the connection between you and this Vincentia?"

I quickly explained. He released my fingers and wrapped an arm around my shoulders, his hug brief but caring. "The gods really aren't being kind to you and Lugh at the moment, are they?"

"No, they're fucking not." I leaned into the warmth of his body. It was a comforting sensation more than sensual, which was a little surprising given the desire that still zinged between us.

"Neither of us are dressed appropriately for a long car journey," he said, "so why don't we head over to your place so you can grab a change of clothes, then go back to mine and grab some sleep?"

"Is sleep a new euphemism for hot monkey sex?"

His laugh was low and sexy, and my pulse skipped along quite happily. "Sadly, it is not. But the journey to Galway does include a three-and-a-half-hour ferry trip, and a private room would not only be possible but advisable. If your cousin is heading home, then she could be on the same ferry."

"I hadn't actually thought that far ahead."

"Realizing you've been played for a fool by a family member does tend to short-circuit plotting capabilities, even if only momentarily."

And he'd know, though his cousin's actions were far worse than Vincentia's. Presuming, of course, Sgott was right, and she was simply after the Eye rather than being deeply involved in the search for the Claws.

"That being the plan, why don't we leave the van where it is and call your car? If we're still being watched, it'll be safer."

He immediately rang his chauffeur. Five minutes later, the car arrived, and we were quickly driven across to the tavern.

To say it looked as if a tornado had hit my living quarters was something of an understatement. Obviously, when Tia hadn't found the Eye in the storage cavities, she'd opened all the dresser drawers, wardrobes, and even the linen press, and basically just tossed everything on the floor. The kitchen hadn't escaped the messy search, but it was interesting to note that all the mugs remained on their hooks. If she'd checked them, she wouldn't have bothered putting them back given she hadn't done it anywhere else, and that suggested my hiding spot was a good one. I was nevertheless thankful I'd shoved the Eye under my bra rather than giving in to temptation and leaving it behind. And until we were able to make a jewelry cage for it, that was probably my best option going forward.

I picked through the mess, found an overnight bag, and packed a couple days' worth of clothing in case things went wrong in Ireland and we had to stay longer.

Once we were back in the car, I put the phone on speaker and rang Lugh to update him.

"As much as I'd like to confront Riayn with you," he said when I'd finished, "I agree it would be better if Darby and I concentrate on unravelling Alinda's clues and see if they help to find that old church you saw. We can't risk losing another relic to these bastards."

"They only got ahead of us last time because they had

the tavern bugged and heard what I'd said about the cave. They haven't got that advantage now."

"No, but they might not need it if Vincentia *is* working with them. Her second sight was as strong as Mom's."

"Without the Eye to focus it, though, she'd be of no use to them."

"There are other means of focusing the gift, Beth. She could be using one of them."

"If she was, she wouldn't have torn the tavern apart looking for the Eye."

"That's presuming she *was* looking for the Eye and not the knives. They're possibly even more useful to someone involved in relic hunting."

I sniffed and changed the subject. Until we caught up with Vincentia, this was all nothing more than conjecture. "Even if they do beat us to the sword, it appears they're intending to wait until they have all three Claws before they unleash. They haven't used the crown yet, and it can extend or retract the shadows of dawn and dusk."

"Perhaps they're merely awaiting the arrival of a mage powerful enough to unlock its power," Cynwrig said.

I glanced at him. "They wouldn't have started this quest for the Claws without a strong enough mage to use them."

"They might not have known about the requirement for a mage. It would certainly explain why they're hiding the crown rather than using it."

"It's also not dusk they want to erase, but rather darkness, and they can't do that without the sword," Lugh said.

"Then here's hoping they *haven't* found a spellcaster," I said. "Because the council's current focus on the guild will surely make it more difficult to hire one."

"The underground trade in the dark arts is almost as

strong as the black-market trade in goods," Cynwrig said, voice dry. "The council controls neither. Trust me, hiring a caster would not be the problem. If there *is* a problem, then it's more likely to be logistical—getting them into the county without either the fae council or the spellcaster's guild becoming aware of their presence."

"Let's hope that's the case," Lugh said, somewhat grimly. "It at least gives us more time."

Amen to that, brother. "I'll keep you posted on how we go. Make sure you do the same."

"Oh, I'm sure Darby will if I don't."

His voice was dry, and I laughed. "You know what my response to that statement is going to be, don't you?"

"Yes, and I *will* remember to leave time for a little fun. But I'm thinking my definition will probably be different to what you and Darby are hoping for."

"Not the painting," I said in mock horror. "You're not going to get the easel out, are you?"

"Well, she might as well know just how intense it can get when I'm lost to the pull of the oils."

I laughed again—though in truth, he could easily lose hours if not days on those rare occasions when the painting muse struck him—then said goodbye and hung up.

Cynwrig's apartment was situated on the top floor of a three-story, double fronted, and very gorgeous old Georgian building owned by his family. Unlike many other apartments developed in these grand old buildings, his was one large and airy space divided by furniture into three main zones—kitchen, dining, and living.

The bedroom was upstairs, in the loft, and the only way to access it was via the secret stairwell behind the bookcase to the left of the vast old fireplace.

We walked across the room, and he pulled down the

disguised door release—a rather ratty-looking dictionary. There was a soft click, then the bookcase silently swung open. He motioned me through, closed the door behind us, and followed me up into the large open area in the eaves that catered to both his work and sleeping needs.

"You have first shower," he said, motioning toward the vast bathroom directly ahead. "I'll check the ferry timetable and book some tickets."

I nodded and headed in. Once I'd stripped off and tucked the Eye safely into the carry-all's side pocket, I ran the cold water in the sink to wash the blood spots from my dress, then grabbed a flannel and wiped down my coat. Thankfully, I'd been wearing a trench rather than one of my woolen ones, and that meant it'd be dry in time to use tomorrow. Or today, as the case actually was.

After a long, hot shower that had the unfortunate side effect of ushering in weariness, I dried off and yawned my way out of the bathroom.

Cynwrig was sitting in one of the lounge chairs near the sliding glass doors that opened out onto a lovely balcony area, but rose when he saw me, his eyes skimming my nakedness and coming up heated.

He met me halfway and kissed me with all the heat and desire a woman could want, then pulled back just as it was getting interesting.

"I've booked a private room on the eight-fifteen ferry," he said, voice delightfully husky. "It should only take us an hour and a half to get across to Holyhead from here, so we'll leave at six."

Which gave us close to four hours to fill. I wrapped a hand around the back of his neck and pulled him down into another kiss. "I'm thinking that leaves plenty of time for both play and sleep. Shall I meet you in that boat you call a bed?"

The heat in his gaze just about set me alight. "Deal."

But even heat couldn't combat tiredness, and sleep found me before he did. I had a vague memory of him gathering me in his arms and tucking me close into his big warm body, and felt oddly cherished more than aroused.

The former was nothing more than a sleep-fueled illusion, of course, but it was still a lovely one.

The seas were as rough as fuck, and I quickly discovered it was a *very* different experience to sailing on calmer seas—all I'd done up to now. I didn't puke, but I kept the sea sickness bags close and was utterly thankful for the private room. If I'd been in the general area amongst other seasick travelers, my stomach might well have unleashed.

The crossing seemed to take forever, but the captain did eventually announce our arrival into port before asking those of us who were driving to make our way down to our cars.

And finished it all by cheerily saying, "I hope you all had a lovely journey and please enjoy the rest of your day."

"Is he fucking serious?" I muttered. "How could anyone in their right mind enjoy a trip like that?"

"Many did. There were only a handful who appeared on the green side when I went out for coffee." Cynwrig rose from his chair and offered me a hand. He'd spent the majority of the last three and a half hours regaling me with nonsense stories to take my mind off things, and it was probably that as much as me lying down that had prevented a full-on revolt from my stomach. "You think you can make it back to the van, or do you want me to carry you?"

"You can't carry me. It'll throw you off-balance."

"The seas are easing as we speak. I'll be fine."

"So will I." His raised eyebrow suggested skepticism, so I added, "Truly. As the seas ease, so does the sickness."

"Well, here's hoping the next time we need to catch a ferry, you'll have learned a little more about storm control and can make the crossing a lot less rough."

I shifted my feet and let him pull me up. "Personally, I'll just be catching a damn plane the next time I have to come to Dublin."

He laughed, kissed me tenderly, then handed me my purse and gathered up our overnight bags.

We joined the queue of people heading down to the car bay, and though I kept an eye out, I didn't see anyone resembling Vincentia, though there were a number of redheads sprinkled amongst the mostly brown-haired crowd. Not surprising given—despite what a lot of people thought—only around ten percent of the Irish human population had red hair.

Once the ferry had docked and the ramps lowered, we got underway. My stomach immediately felt better once we were back on solid ground, though I was reluctant to test it out with anything stronger than a cup of tea.

It was very *large* cup of tea, though.

We took the fastest route out of Dublin, and once we were nearing Galway, I punched my aunt's address into the GPS and let it guide us from there. She didn't actually live in the city, but rather on the outskirts of a little village called Menlo, in a two-story stone farmhouse surrounded on all sides by a forest. I'd never actually been there, but I'd employed the power of Google Maps and will admit to feeling a wee bit of jealousy at the location's perfection. I loved where I lived, but that didn't mean I had no desire to retreat to the forests every now and again. Or maybe even retire to them.

As the GPS indicated our destination was ahead on our left, Cynwrig pulled over onto the narrow verge and stopped. "How do you want to handle this?"

I hesitated. "To be honest, I have no idea how she'll react when she sees me. I'm guessing it'll depend on whether she knows what Vincentia is up to."

And whether Vincentia had beaten us here, however unlikely that might be.

"Then we need to be ready for all possibilities. You should wear your knives."

"My aunt isn't going to attack me—"

"You can't say that with any real degree of certainty," he said. "You don't know either of them very well, remember. Not anymore."

A truer word had never been spoken. "I'll tuck the knives behind my back rather than strap them on. That way, Aunt Riayn won't see them and take offense."

"Wearing your knives is hardly a reason to take offense."

"It suggests I don't trust them."

"Well, you don't."

"But they don't need to know that straight away." I paused. "It might also be an idea if they don't know you're with me. That way, if things go wrong in there, you can ride to the rescue."

He nodded, and we climbed out of the van. I walked around to the back and, after he dropped a quick kiss on my lips, watched him walked across to the head-high stone wall that divided the property from the road and disappear over it. I continued on to the driver side, shoved the van back into gear, and drove through the open metal gate.

The driveway was long and narrow and wound through a forest of lovely old trees. They were a random mix of pine, rowan, and ash, and the desire to stop and sit at their feet, drawing in their song and their beauty, was so strong I actually lifted my foot off the accelerator.

It was a good minute or so before the house finally revealed itself. It was a long, stone-built gable-ended farm-house centered in a small clearing, with chimneys either end, a whitewashed front, and a bold red door. There were two windows either side of the door on the ground floor and five above. Wisteria covered the front of the building, and though it was bare now, it'd be postcard perfect in spring.

There was a car sitting in one of the bays of the open-fronted shed to the right of the farmhouse, so I stopped in front of it. If anyone in that house intended to run, they certainly wouldn't be using the car to do so.

I dug my knives out of my purse, tucked them through my belt at the back of my jeans, then pulled my sweater and shirt over them. I really didn't expect my aunt or cousin to whack me with magic, but it was always better to be safe than sorry, especially until we knew exactly what we were dealing with.

Thunder rumbled a warning overhead, so I grabbed my coat and climbed out of the van. The air was cold and filled with the promise of rain, but I had plenty of time before it unleashed. I walked across to the other car and pressed my fingers against the hood. There was no heat coming from the engine, suggesting it hadn't been used for at least a couple of hours. That didn't mean Vincentia wasn't here, of course, just that she hadn't arrived in this car.

I slung my purse over my shoulder and walked over to the front door. The curtains hadn't moved, but I nevertheless had the vague sensation of being watched.

I paused at the doorstep and didn't immediately press the bell, briefly frozen by uncertainty and perhaps a touch of fear. Mom had been betrayed by someone she trusted; I didn't want that person to be my aunt. I really didn't.

I took a deep breath to get a grip of my fears, then pressed the doorbell. A chime rang deep inside, but for several seconds, there was no response.

Then, finally, almost reluctantly, footsteps approached.

I forced a smile. She was my aunt. I owed her respect, at least until I knew for sure she wasn't worthy of it.

The door opened and, once again, it felt like someone had punched me. For several seconds, I just stood there, staring at my aunt, my eyes wide and stinging.

She looked like Mom. *So* like Mom, and I just hadn't expected that.

She had the same silver-streaked red hair, drawn up into a messy bun. Same careworn but beautiful face. Same green eyes. Hell, she was even wearing the same shade of red lipstick.

Only the body shape differed. Mom had been a couple of inches shorter and more bosomy—something I'd inherited.

I swallowed heavily, forcing down the ache, and somehow croaked, "Aunt Riayn?"

Her smile was friendly enough, and nothing lurked in her gaze to raise suspicion. It stirred through me nonetheless, and I had no idea why, let alone if it was deserved.

"Bethany? It's been a very long time. Please, do come in."

She opened the door wider, then stepped to one side,

keeping well out of touching range. I wasn't the only one who wasn't completely willing to trust.

I moved to the left and quickly looked around. The hallway was surprisingly spacious, with stairs that led up to the next floor directly ahead, and doors to the left and the right. Wainscoting lined the walls and ran up the stairs, the wood painted but its song so strong and vibrant I couldn't resist reaching out to caress it.

My aunt had taken good care of this building. Even the timber framing sang, and with so much health and vibrancy it could have been harvested a few years ago rather than decades.

She closed the front door, then, with a brisk "Coat on the hook," walked into the room on the right.

I hung up my coat as ordered, then followed her into what was a typical farmhouse kitchen running the full width of the building. An old green AGA dominated the massive brick fireplace directly opposite the door, heating the room and providing a resting place for the gently steaming kettle. Kitchen cabinets ran both to the left and the right of this, while more cabinets and an old butler sink lined the rear wall. The long, well-used oak table sitting in the middle of the room was surrounded by a cheerful variety of mismatched wooden chairs.

Aunt Riayn moved around them and said, without looking at me, "Would you like a cup of tea?"

"Yes, please."

I stopped behind one of the chairs but didn't pull it out or sit down. The whole situation just felt... odd. She was acting like me dropping in unexpectedly was a regular occurrence rather than something that had *never* happened.

Maybe she was just being polite. In all truth, Mom

would have acted in exactly the same manner had the situation been reversed and Vincentia had turned up on our doorstep unannounced.

She made the tea, pulled a brightly knitted cozy over it, then brought teapot and a couple of mugs over to the table. Once a jug of milk and a little container of sugar had joined it, she motioned me to sit and then did so herself.

I hesitated, then moved around to a chair that didn't leave my back facing the door. One that was, once again, beyond touching range.

A smile twitched her lips, but she otherwise didn't comment. After pouring the tea, she offered me the milk and the sugar and then finally said, "To what do I owe the honor of this visit? It has been, what? Decades since I last saw you?"

"I think it was at Gran's funeral."

She nodded. "You're right, though I believe you have seen Vincentia a few times since then."

"Yes." I paused. "Do you know where she is now?"

My aunt raised a pale eyebrow. "If you came here looking for her, I'm afraid you'll be disappointed. I've not seen her for a couple of months now."

I heard no lie in that, and yet a big part of me just didn't believe it. Probably the part that was silently grieving and angry and looking for someone to blame for Mom's death.

I picked up the jug and poured milk into my tea in an attempt to calm down and not blurt out anything I might regret later.

"Has she contacted you at all?"

"Not really." She studied me for a second, green eyes knowing. Once again, I was struck by the similarities to Mom, and I had to look down at my tea to control the tears. "You didn't drive all the way here for a pleasant little catch-up, Bethany. Not after all this time. What do you want?"

"Several things."

This time, the smile that tugged her lips failed to crease the corners of her eyes. "Like what?"

I hesitated, but there was little point in beating about the bush. "Did you send Vincentia to the tavern at any time over the last six months to retrieve the Eye?"

She raised an eyebrow, her expression coldly amused. "So, your mother has finally told you about it? Because for far too many years she was reluctant to do so, something I found rather incongruous given her desire for you to follow in her footsteps."

She didn't add "however unlikely that would be," but it nevertheless hung in the air between us.

"You didn't answer the question, Aunt."

"Because it's an obviously stupid question. Your mother made it very clear Tia would never get the Eye despite the fact she'd inherited the family gift and you had not."

That suggested she wasn't aware my second sight was now emerging, and I had no idea if that were true or if she was simply a good liar. I just didn't know her well enough to tell.

"Then you weren't aware that she's now broken into the tavern several times?"

"She wouldn't—"

"She's a relic hunter," I cut in dryly. "Breaking and entering comes with the territory."

"Yes, but she wouldn't... not to family."

It was said in a way that suggested even she didn't believe it to be true.

"Unfortunately, evidence says otherwise."

She frowned, though she didn't actually radiate any real

concern. "Well, I can't say I'm surprised, given she'll get far more use out of the Eye than you. I am, however, taken aback by the fact that Meabh sent you here to chastise me rather than simply picking up the phone. We might be estranged, but we are still family."

I stared at her, seeing annoyance and perhaps a little anger, but absolutely no deceit. She didn't *know*. She really didn't know that Mom had disappeared six months ago.

But how could that be? She'd inherited second sight, even if her gift wasn't as strong as Mom's. At the very least, familial ties should have told her Mom was in trouble, even if it didn't clarify the reason.

I took a hasty sip of tea as I searched for the best way to tell her and, in that moment of silence, a phone rang upstairs.

My gaze jumped briefly to the ceiling before settling on my aunt's again. "I thought you said Tia wasn't here?"

"She isn't."

"Then who's upstairs?"

"A guest." She half shrugged. "This farmhouse is too large for one person, so a year ago I renovated a couple of rooms and opened up a B&B. It's been quite successful."

"Why on earth would you need to open a B&B? It's not like you need the—"

She gave me a dead eye look that was so similar to the one Mom used to gift me when I said something dumb that it stopped me in my tracks.

"It's not about the money, dear child, but the company. Meabh would totally understand, I'm sure."

No doubt she would have. I took a deep breath and released it slowly. "There's something you need to know."

"Meaning there *is* a point to this visit other than telling me Tia raided the tavern in what I presume was an unsuccessful attempt to steal the Eye?"

Her voice was dry, and something in me snapped. "If you hadn't constantly harped on the fact that *she* was true heir rather than me, she wouldn't be in the deep well of shit she's now in."

"The theft of a stone—one that has little value to anyone *other* than the women in our family—could hardly be described as deep shit. Even Sgott, as protective as he is of your mother and yourself, would be hard pressed to make serious charges stick."

Her use of present tense rather than past had the anger dying again. I took another deep breath and then said, "What I came here to tell you..."

I stopped, momentarily unable to complete the sentence, and she raised an eyebrow. "Do you pause for dramatic effect? Because I'm well past such things."

My gaze met hers. I wasn't sure what she saw in my face, but hers went pale.

"What's happened?" she whispered.

There was no gentle way to do this. "Mom has been missing for six months. A few days ago, we found her body. She was murdered."

Her head snapped back so abruptly, I might well have slapped her. With a shaking hand, she clutched her cardigan across her chest and whispered, "No. That can't be. I would have known."

"I'm afraid it's true. I saw her body." I hesitated. "I also found Egeria's Coin at the entrance of the tunnel we found her in."

"Egeria's Coin never drops by mistake."

"No."

"Why would Meabh release it? It is a symbol of wisdom and good fortune and has never failed our family."

"Perhaps Mom didn't want the goddess's coin tarnished by betrayal."

"Betrayal? You can't think... I won't believe..." She half hiccupped; half sobbed. "It's *not* possible."

"I'm not saying Vincentia murdered her, Aunt. There's no physical evidence to suggest that at *all*."

"But you do think she's involved with those who did this?"

I hesitated. "She's involved in something bad—that's the only thing I'm sure of at this point."

Her face crumpled, then she thrust to her feet and walked to the other end of the kitchen before disappearing into what looked like a pantry to the left. Tension rolled through me, and I was tempted to reach back for my knives, though if my aunt had gone in there to get a shotgun, knives would be of little use.

Thankfully, she reappeared a few seconds later holding nothing more than a couple of tissues she dabbed her eyes with.

She sat back down, took a drink of tea, and then said, "How did Meabh die?"

"She was shot in a tunnel, and her body buried under stone."

She briefly closed her eyes, but tears nevertheless squeezed past. She dabbed them again and said, "That suggests she was on a hunt. Do you know what for?"

I hesitated. While I had no doubt her emotions were real where mom was concerned, that didn't mean she wasn't aware Tia was involved in the hunt for the Claws— even if she didn't know exactly what they were and what it involved. I had to be careful about what I said, especially until we knew *which* theft Vincentia was involved in.

"No. She rushed out without saying where she was going and just... disappeared."

"Why didn't Sgott use her phone to track her?"

"Because by the time we realized she was missing, her phone was dead."

"Surely the location of her car would have given him at least some idea where to begin the search."

"She didn't use the car. Someone picked her up and drove her."

"That someone *wasn't* Tia. She's not a murderer." It was coldly but also desperately said. "If you believe otherwise, you can get out of this house right now."

I held up my hands. "As I've already said, I don't believe Tia was involved in Mom's murder. Her death is separate to the theft I believe Vincentia's involved it. But after the break-ins and the attempted kidnapping—"

"*What* attempted kidnapping?" Riayn cut in.

I told her, and her face lost what little color had remained. "I can't believe—"

"Ring Sgott. He has the would-be kidnappers in custody and can confirm what I've said."

"They could be lying—"

"I truth spelled the ringleader and forced her to contact the contractor. It was Vincentia who answered."

Riayn rubbed her eyes. "She would not kidnap you in order to get the Eye. She is not that desperate for it."

I rather suspected she was but was using her contract with the Looisearch as a cover. "Our current theory is that the people behind the kidnapping are aware that I won't use the Eye to help them, so they've contracted the next best option. I really need to talk to Vincentia before this whole situation gets any worse."

Her gaze met mine, her green eyes haunted and filled with grief. Yet determination lurked in the deeper depths, and that worried me, if only because I didn't understand it. "*Can* the situation get any worse?"

"The people who've contracted Vincentia are behind several murders, a kidnapping, and an explosion that wiped out at least one person and almost killed two others."

"Guilt by association is not a chargeable offence in the UK."

"It is if it can be proven that the associate had foreseen their accomplice would commit the crime."

"She is a contractor. That ruling would not apply."

I had no idea if that was true or not so didn't bother arguing the point. "The thing is, one of the people kidnapped and almost blown up is a light elf on the council, and he wants revenge. Bad."

"Light elves don't do emotion."

"Light elves don't consider revenge an emotion but rather a duty."

"As I said, she's contractor, and that provides immunity from the actions of her employers. At worst, she would only receive a light prison sentence."

"We are talking about a council hell-bent on catching everyone involved in both a major theft and a string of murders. And there are worse punishments than mere prison time."

She studied me for a moment, then sniffed. It was a somewhat disdainful sound. "The council haven't applied the red knife for centuries."

The red knife was a symbolic and physical cutting of

ties, and it was the ultimate punishment for a pixie. "There hasn't been a situation like this for centuries."

She didn't say anything. Not for several minutes. Then she sighed and said, "I don't know where she is, but I could call her—"

"No," I cut in. "You mustn't. It will only warn her that I know she's involved—" I broke the rest off as my knives burned to life. Magic was being cast. I jumped to my feet and said tensely, "Who else is in this house, Aunt?"

She stared at me like I'd just gone crazy. "No one other than my guest. Why?"

I unsheathed a knife. The whole blade was alight and pulsing. "*This* is why."

Her eyes widened. "The knives respond to you?"

"Obviously." I ran around the table, drew the second knife, and stood behind her. The magic was reaching its peak; the spell was about to be unleashed. "Don't move. Don't touch me or attempt to control me, or goddess help me, I'll use these fucking knives on you."

Her eyes widened. "You can't think—"

"Quiet."

I raised the knives and crossed the blades. Their pulsing light flared and formed a shimmering dome of protection, purplish blue—an indication there was dark intent if not dark magic behind the spell.

A heartbeat later, that spell exploded into the middle of the kitchen, the force so strong the dome briefly buckled. A thick, yellowish gas crawled across the air, its putrid-looking fingers creeping across the dome's surface, seeking a way in. I had no idea what it was, and absolutely no doubt that breathing it in would not be a good thing.

"Cynwrig," I yelled. "I need you smash the kitchen

windows and get airflow happening. We've a caster upstairs, and she's just unleashed some sort of gas spell."

A heartbeat later, the rear windows were broken. He reappeared around the front and smashed those windows in with a long bit of wood. Air flowed through, and the yellowish gas began to dissipate.

He stepped away from the window, then growled, "Are you both okay?"

"Yes." I glanced up as the wood song on the floor above changed, indicating movement. "The caster's on the move. Watch the back of the house—I'll head upstairs."

"And me?" my aunt said.

"Head out the front. If you see anyone other than the man who was at that window a second ago, run."

She nodded and drew in a deep breath. I did the same, then lowered the knives and bolted through the gassy remnants to the kitchen door. As my aunt went left, I swung right, my footsteps echoing on the old floorboards. I flicked the knife in my right hand to my left as I hit the stairs and ran my free fingers across the beautiful old wainscoting. Its song was as fierce and bright as before, but it was the connection to the framework of this building I needed rather than the paneling itself. I pushed past the surface music, and an interconnected network of power and music appeared in my mind's eye. I ran mental fingers along golden arteries that bound the building together, found the caster's location, and quickly entwined the fibers of the windows in that room to the main structure, sealing them shut.

A scream echoed, the sound feminine rather than masculine, then glass smashed. But the windows in this place were multipaned double sash, and though the glass broke, the muntins held.

For now.

But magic was once again rising.

As the knives began to pulse their warning, I leapt up the final few steps and raced down the hall to the end door. It was locked.

I took a step back, raised one foot, and kicked it with every ounce of strength I could muster. The old lock gave way, and the door crashed back against the plaster.

Just as the caster unleashed her spell.

I swore and raised the knives again. A glittering shield of bluish-purple rose in front of me, but the force of the caster's spell pushed me back several feet even though the knives split the spell asunder.

As broken threads of magic fell around me, movement echoed through the floorboards. The caster was charging toward the door.

I stepped back, out of her immediate sight, and pressed my fingers to the door frame. Then, with a quick apology for what I was about to do, I ripped the side of the frame away from the wall and smashed it directly into the path of the caster.

She half leapt, half stumbled over it, her arms flailing as she desperately battled to remained upright.

She failed.

As she tumbled in an ungainly manner onto the hallway's floorboards, I stepped forward and pressed the point of the knife against her neck, just hard enough to draw a drop of blood. She stilled instantly.

Then I knelt, placed my hand on her arm, and said, with the force of my controlling magic behind me, "You will not spell, you will not attempt to flee, and you will answer any and all questions given. Otherwise, this damn knife will do more than just prick your skin. Understood?"

"Yes."

"Good. I'm going to step away, and you will rise and face me. Clear?"

She didn't immediately answer. I pressed the knife just a little bit harder into her skin, and she quickly said, "Yes."

I moved back but held the knives at the ready. She couldn't cast with my orders riding roughshod over her free will, but I wasn't about to take chances. If she was here to target me, then she more than likely knew what I was and could have developed a spell or acquired some other means of short-circuiting my orders. There were psi-repelling tokens out there, though they were a bit hit-and-miss when it came to pixie controlling magic.

She climbed slowly to her feet, a slight hiss escaping her lips suggesting she might have been injured, then turned. She had black hair, thin features, and rose tatt running down the left side of her face.

I knew her.

Or more precisely, knew who she was because I'd seen a newspaper article about her.

Our spellcaster was none other than Peregrine Stace.

The woman from one of Nialle's newspaper clippings. A woman who had supposedly died.

CHAPTER
ELEVEN

"Well," I said, "I'm guessing you didn't die after all."

She raised her eyebrows. "What the hell are you talking about, woman?"

"You're supposedly dead. Obviously, that's untrue, because here you are."

"I think you've got the wrong—"

"You know," I cut in, "if you're going to fake your death and claim a new identity, why not go the extra step and erase—or at least change—the very identifiable tattoo on your face?"

She didn't answer.

My gaze narrowed. Granted, I hadn't started off asking specific questions, but that bit about her tatt had been one, and she shouldn't have been able to ignore it. That could only mean she was at least partially protected from pixie directives.

"Are you in possession of a magic counter or token?"

More silence. She was definitely on possession of a token of *some* kind.

"Raise your arms to shoulder level and stand utterly still."

Again, no obedience. I repeated the order, this time with more magical force, and she finally raised her arms. I stepped close, carefully patted her down, and found the token lightly sewn into her right sock. I sliced it free with the knife and then studied it. It was an air-dried clay coin about the same size as a penny and had multiple tiny symbols etched onto its surface.

"Bethany? You still upstairs?" came Cynwrig's voice.

"Yes."

I stepped back, dropped the token onto the floor, and crushed it under my heel until there was nothing left but dust.

And could feel the anger pouring from her.

As the stair treads shivered under Cynwrig's weight, I became aware of another type of emotion—one of distress, radiating from the doorway to my right... fuck, I'd forgotten to repair the damaged I'd caused. I shoved my knives away and hurried over the frame. After pushing the shattered edges back into place, I placed one hand on each breach point, then carefully wove the fibers of wood back together, healing the breach and enabling the golden river of power to run unimpeded once again.

I wiped a trickle of sweat from my forehead, then moved back to my captive. Cynwrig appeared, his dark hair wet and coat soaked. Surprise stirred, and I looked toward the window at the far end of the hall; rain sheeted the glass. I'd been so intent on our caster, I hadn't even noticed the storm breaking.

He moved around my prisoner, then stopped beside me, his left arm pressing ever so slightly against my right. "Who have we here?"

"Peregrine Stace, who was released on bail for attempting to steal a very old, very valuable book from the Welsh National Library. She was supposedly found dead in a Conway boarding house a few months later, but the decomposition was so bad they were unable to confirm identity."

"I take it dental records were conveniently absent?"

"They're still searching for them."

"Huh." He glanced at Stace. "Why are you here?"

Her face contorted, but she had no choice except to reply now that I'd destroyed the token. "I was sent here to monitor Riayn Aodhán's movements and contacts."

"Why?" I asked.

"I wasn't told. I was simply meant to report any and all contacts she had."

"Meaning you were listening in to her phone calls?"

"Of course."

Just as well I hadn't called before arriving then, because I might have been greeted with a very nasty surprise. "Do you keep a log of calls?"

"No. Once I make a report, everything is erased."

Of course it was. "Who were you reporting to?"

"Seryn Morrisa."

Tension rippled through Cynwrig's big body, though his voice remained even as he asked, "Have you a means of contacting her?"

"Yes."

"Phone? Texts? Or some other means?"

"Usually texts, unless there's something major to report."

"Her number?"

She reeled it off. I glanced at Cynwrig. "Familiar?"

"No."

I studied him for a second, wondering if that were actually true, then returned my gaze to our captive. "Why did you attempt to steal the *Book of Tywyllwch*?"

"I didn't."

"Well, obviously, because you were caught before you could take it."

She didn't say anything because it wasn't a question. But the amusement that flared briefly in her eyes had suspicion rising. "Were you actually supposed to take it? Or was it a ruse?"

"Neither."

"Then what were you supposed to do?"

"Photograph the appropriate pages."

"How, when books of that age and value are kept behind glass and magically protected?"

"All magic can be countered if you have the knowledge. I do."

"The fact you were caught suggests you do not," Cynwrig said, voice dry.

Anger flashed briefly through her expression. "That was *not* due to lack of skill, but rather a lack of information from our source."

"Meaning?" I asked.

"I was unaware the museum had recently added a sensor under the book's stand. When I moved the pages, it altered the weight balance and set off the alarm."

"Meaning you were unable to finish photographing the pages?"

A pleased smile touched her lips. "No."

"What pages did you photograph?"

"Some poem about the black sword of Rostin De Clari."

It was no surprise, then, that the Looisearch were several steps ahead of us when it came to the Claws search.

Peregrine had photographed the book six months ago. That would have given them plenty of time to find someone to transcribe the text and grab all the clues.

Though it did beg the question, why did they wait until *after* Nialle had contacted Jules Auclair to approach—or rather kill—the man and steal the notes folder Jules had prepared for Nialle? I doubted there'd be too many historians researching the history of the Rostin De Clari line, as she wasn't exactly a well-known figure, especially here in England.

"Who were the images sent to?" Cynwrig asked.

"Seryn Morrisa."

Once again tension rippled through him. He definitely knew the woman. A relative, perhaps? Or, more precisely, a close relative of Jalvi's? They'd apparently made themselves scarce, so that wouldn't be surprising.

"How often do you report to her?" I asked.

"Nightly."

I glanced at Cynwrig. "I'm thinking we need her to keep doing that."

"I'm thinking you're right."

I stepped close to our captive again and touched her shoulder. My gaze met hers, and if looks had the capacity to burn, I'd be a cindered mess on the floor right now.

I smiled coldly. "You will head back into your bedroom and continue reporting to Seryn Morrisa. You will not leave this house, and you will remain within the boundary of your bedroom and the guest bathroom facilities up here. You will go nowhere else and will say nothing to Seryn or anyone else about our presence here or anything that you've seen or heard while we were here today. You will not do or say anything to make Seryn suspect we were here today. You will not answer any of my aunt's questions should she ask them, and you will not perform any sort of magic, no matter how minor, until I release you. Understood?"

That last bit was only said out of courtesy. It didn't matter if she understood or not, because it played no part in her being forced to obey.

She swallowed heavily and said, "Yes," in a faint, quivering tone.

She'd no doubt realized that if I didn't release her, she'd never be able to perform magic again.

"Give me your phone."

She did so. I added my number under an alias, sent myself a text so I'd have her number, then showed it to her. "Anything you send to Seryn you will copy to me separately. Is that clear?"

Another faint "Yes."

"Good." I returned the phone. "Go back into your room right now. You are free to move around and do as you wish within the boundaries of my already stated restrictions."

She turned and left. Once the bedroom door had closed, I glanced at Cynwrig and said, "Who is Seryn Morrisa?"

"Jalvi's mother, and my aunt on my father's side. I would have said our families were close, but obviously, I was mistaken."

Because they'd attacked his sister and poisoned him. I touched his arm. I might well have been touching steel. "I'm so sorry, Cyn."

The amusement twitching his lips didn't erase the dark fury in his eyes. That fury wasn't aimed at me, but I nevertheless felt its chill. "Well, finally."

I blinked, caught off guard by the comment. "Finally *what*?"

"You just used my nickname, and that, to me, signifies a definite thawing in our relationship."

I snorted. "Our relationship cannot, in any way, be described as frosty."

He pressed a hand against my spine and guided me toward the stairs. "On a physical level, no. In fact, even describing it as deliciously explosive does not do justice to what we share. But emotionally? There's a definite barrier."

"Well, yes, because you're a dark elf prince and I'm a not-too-important pixie, and never the twain shall meet at the altar."

"That doesn't mean we can't have a long and meaningful relationship. You did enjoy ten years with Mathi, did you not?"

"Yes, but that's different."

He glanced at me, his expression bemused. "How?"

I waved a hand. "He's safe."

He laughed, a sound so rich and warm it did weird things to my heart rate. "I guess 'safe' *is* the last word that could be used to describe me."

"Yes, indeed."

The front door opened, and my aunt peeked around. "Can I come back in?"

"Yes, I have her under control."

"Then you know who she is and why she's here?"

"Yes."

When I didn't continue, she gave me the same sort of look Mom used to bestow when I was being economical with answers, and tears rose again. Damn it, I needed to get these emotions under control. I couldn't afford to unleash my grief, because I suspected if I did, I might not be able to stop it.

"And?" Riayn snapped, as she marched into the kitchen.

"Do not play me for a fool, Bethany. Not when my family is involved in... well, whatever this is."

I followed her in and quickly updated her on what we'd discovered while avoiding any mention of the Claws.

"Does this mean I can now speak to my daughter—"

"No, because while she may have nothing to do with spying on *you*, she's involved in something bad. Otherwise, why arrange a kidnapping?"

"Maybe after trashing your place, she decided it was best means of getting the Eye."

"Unlikely, given she was trashing the place at the very same time as the kidnapping was happening. Besides, do you really want to risk her ending up being shot in the head and buried under a pile of rocks like Mom?"

It was a brutal thing to say, but I was beginning to suspect it was the only way to get through to her.

She clutched her cardigan again, her face pale but determined. "Tia is *not* working with the people who shot your mother. I am sure of that, if nothing else."

"There's more than one game afoot here," Cynwrig said. "And both are leaving a trail of dead people behind them."

"No pixie dare risk the blood curse, and my daughter is no fool—"

"Then by all means, please, do contact her. But if she ends up dead, don't be claiming you weren't warned or come crying to your niece."

Though his voice held little inflection, the air around him fairly crackled with anger. I suspected it had less to do with this situation, and more his own.

Riayn flexed her hands; fighting the urge to attempt a compulsion on us, I suspected. "Fine. We do it your way."

There was an unspoken "for now" at the end of that,

but I wasn't about to push it. That we'd gotten any agreement out of her was an achievement.

Cynwrig nodded and glanced at me. "I'll wait for you in the car."

I watched him leave. The man was definitely *not* happy.

"What happens now?" my aunt said.

"You keep doing what you've been doing."

"And if Tia calls?"

"You talk to her. Just don't mention anything we've told you. Don't mention we've been here."

"Wouldn't it be better if I simply told her she needs to talk to you as a matter of urgency?"

I rolled my eyes. This woman just wasn't listening. "You've a woman in your house who has been keeping track of everyone you speak to. No doubt they've a similar watch placed on Vincentia. If they realize we know she's involved, they'll kill her before we can get to her."

She took another of those shuddering breaths then nodded. I suspected she still hadn't taken our warnings to heart, but there was little I could do it. Compelling her was out of the question, given the minute I stepped close enough, she'd probably attempt the same on *me*.

"What of my guest?"

"She'll remain here and keep making her reports."

"Is that safe? What if Tia rings and she reports the conversation back to this Morrisa person?"

"Anything reported to her will be relayed to me. If I think you're in any danger, I'll let you know."

"Am I not endangered by her very presence?"

"She can't perform magic, and she's restricted to her bedroom and the guest bathroom. That does mean you'll have to take her meals up."

A cool smile touched her lips. "I'm guessing you also ordered her not to answer any of my questions."

"The less you know, Aunt, the safer you'll be."

I slung my purse over my shoulder, then motioned her to lead the way out. She opened the door and then said, her expression a mix of frustration and grief, "Tell me, when your mother was murdered, did they take the Eye? Is that why Tia couldn't find it?"

I collected my coat and then looked at her. There was something in the way she worded those questions that made me think she was not as unknowing as she'd have me believe. "Yes."

Which was nothing other than the total truth, but I was mighty grateful she hadn't asked if it had been found since then. As has been noted by multiple people, I wasn't the world's greatest liar.

"Then why do you have the knives? Meabh rarely went on a hunt without them."

"She left them behind. I don't know why because I never got the chance to talk to her before she left."

Never got the chance to say good-bye or tell her that I loved her.

And now I never would.

I blinked and looked down at my shoes to get the damn tears under control again. "What about close contacts? Has Vincentia any friends or boyfriends she's likely to contact or stay with?"

She gave me a couple of names, then added softly, "If Vincentia does contact me, I'll let you know. But she hasn't for months now, so don't be expecting miracles."

There was an edge of hurt in her voice, and sympathy stirred. But only briefly. If she hadn't built her entire world around Vincentia after her son's death and, in the process, filled her head with all sorts of half-truths, then maybe she wouldn't be in the trouble she was now in.

I forced a smile. "I gave up expecting miracles a long time ago."

I was out the door and about to step from under the cover of the porch when I realized I hadn't asked one of the questions that had driven us here.

I turned and said, "Lugh tells me that just before you left Deva, you and Mom were arguing over an old, leather-bound book."

She raised a pale eyebrow, her expression cooling. "What has that got to do with the current situation?"

"Did you take it when you left Deva?"

"And what if I did? The goddesses' gifts were never meant to be sole property of the firstborn female child."

"Family tradition would say otherwise."

"Traditions can change, especially now that my sister is dead and there's only seconds between your birth and Tia's," she said. "You have the knives. It is only fair my daughter retains the codex."

But Mom was older than my aunt, and that's what actually mattered. It was Mom's firstborn daughter who inherited the Triune, not my aunt's.

"Meaning she can use it?" If she could, then it was also possible she could use the Eye. Or maybe the Triune could be used by those who weren't the firstborn in our line.

She hesitated. "It's not fully unlocked—it hasn't been for a very long time now."

Even partially unlocked, it would certainly explain how Vincentia had become such a renowned relic hunter—she'd had additional godly help. And there was no saying that it would totally unlock for me, even if I did unite the three items.

It did make me wonder *why* our family had forgotten the importance of the Triune. Why had my ancestors concentrated more on the abilities of the Eye and the knives rather than the codex?

Was there something the goddess had failed to tell us?

Most likely. They did like their games and fun little tortures, after all.

"Do you have it here?"

"If you think to reclaim it, think again."

"Is it here or not?" I growled.

She studied me for a moment, the frost in her eyes increasing. "Why is it so important?"

"Because it plays into the trouble Tia is in."

"That explains nothing."

"As I've said, what you don't know can't kill you."

"My daughter would hardly kill me."

"No, but the people she's working with just might. Trust me, Aunt, they're after vengeance, and they don't care who or what they have to destroy in order to get it."

"Bethany—"

"*Riayn*, have you got the book or not?"

Her gaze narrowed, but after a moment she said, "Tia took it with her when she moved out a few years ago."

I took a deep breath and released it slowly. "Where does she live now? At one of Gran's other investments?"

"No, I sold them all except this place long ago."

"Why would you do that?"

"What business is it of yours?" she snapped. "They were mine to do as I wished, just as the tavern is now yours to keep or sell."

The edge on that statement told me Lugh was right. She *had* wanted the tavern—probably to sell, given its location meant it was worth a sheer fortune.

"Where does she live?" I repeated.

"Dublin." She gave me the address. "Tell her to ring me if you do see her."

I pressed my fingers to either side of the bridge of my nose. Had she not heard anything we'd said? "Sure," I said, with no intention of doing so. "Just... be careful who you invite into your house, Aunt, especially if they're elves."

Which was probably telling her too much, but I couldn't walk away and not give her at least *some* warning.

She stared at me for several seconds and then said, "Fine."

Everything was a long way from fine, but I simply nodded, held my coat over my head, and raced for the van. Cynwrig leaned across and opened the passenger door for me. As he started the van and headed down the driveway, I flipped down the vanity mirror. My aunt remained in the doorway, watching us leave.

Ensuring we did so, perhaps.

Which was undoubtedly a catty thought, but I nevertheless suspected it was also true. While she seemed to believe me about Mom, I couldn't see the same depth of belief when it came to Vincentia.

When the trees stole the final glimpse of her, I flipped the mirror back up and glanced at Cynwrig. "Why were you angry with her?"

He raised his eyebrows. "What makes you think I was angry?"

I waved a hand up and down his body. "You're very good at facial and voice control but your whole being practically bristled."

He laughed. "It's just as well my enemies cannot read my body language as well as you do."

"Maybe I'm just more... intimate... with your body's language than your enemies."

"And maybe the connection between us goes deeper than the mere physical."

"Wouldn't matter if it did," I said lightly. "And you neatly avoided the question."

A smile tugged at his lips, but the brief glance he cast my way was contemplative. Something within twitched uneasily, though I couldn't have said why.

"She wasn't taking either you or the situation seriously."

"She has never taken me seriously."

"That doesn't excuse her actions." He paused as we reached the gates, waiting for a tractor to trundle past before pulling out onto the road. "Her daughter is in serious trouble, and she seemed unable or unwilling to see that."

"And there's nothing either of us can do about it. I did get Vincentia's address from her, though. She lives in Dublin."

"And you believe it's her actual address?"

"We'll find out soon enough, I guess."

He grunted, then switched the conversation to something lighter. It took over three hours to get back to Dublin, thanks to the fact it was now late afternoon and we were hitting peak traffic times. I punched the address my aunt had given me into the GPS and silently crossed all things that she wasn't playing me for a fool.

Or, worse yet, that it was a carefully orchestrated trap.

As it turned out, it wasn't.

But it wasn't Vincentia's residence either, but rather a charming little bed-and-breakfast. The proprietor had never heard of Vincentia and had never seen anyone fitting the description I offered.

Either my aunt was lying to us, or Vincentia had lied to *her*.

"What do you want to do?" Cynwrig asked as we climbed back into the van.

I wearily scrubbed my eyes. I had the beginnings of a headache, no doubt due to the stress of the situation and a decided lack of both sleep and food, and I really wasn't up to more galivanting about the Irish countryside, no matter how green and gorgeous it was.

But what other choice did we have? Especially when there was no guarantee my aunt *wouldn't* ring Vincentia and warn her. Riayn wasn't a stupid woman, but she was more than a little blind when it came to her now only child.

"I guess we can try Killiney," I said. "It's the only other place I'm aware of that they own."

His gaze swept me, a caress of warmth I felt rather than saw. "What about we stop for coffee and something to eat first? You're looking worn out."

"'Worn' being a polite way of saying 'haggard'?"

He caught my hand with a laugh and raised it to his lips, kissing each of my fingers. Delight shimmered through me, though it was definitely a pale imitation of the usually fierce wave. Tiredness, it seemed, was also affecting my libido.

And *that* was a shocking state of affairs needing to be remedied as soon as possible.

"There was a lovely-looking pub a kilometer or so down the road," he continued. "Why don't grab a meal and something to drink there?"

"Sounds like a plan. And if we get to Killiney and she's not there, we can find somewhere to stay the night. I need to fortify myself before I tackle that ferry trip again."

His grip tightened lightly on my fingers, then he tugged

me closer and kissed me, long and lingering. I sighed regretfully when his lips left mine, and he chuckled softly. "I know, but now is neither the time nor the place."

"We should have stolen a larger van."

He laughed again, turned the van around, and headed back down the road.

Luckily, our arrival at the pub coincided with the beginning of the evening dinner service. We both ordered steak and veg, a side of chips to share, and strong coffees. As much as I would have liked a pot of tea, I need the extra shot of caffeine to keep me awake.

I did feel marginally better with good food in my belly, but the tiredness hadn't really eased. The rain had swept back in while we were in the pub, and it made the night—and the road conditions—pretty horrid.

Not that I saw a whole lot of it, because I snoozed most of the way there, waking only when the van stopped.

I yawned and then said, "We there?"

"We certainly are, sleeping beauty. It's the end terrace across the road."

I leaned forward to look past him. Though it was very hard to see anything clearly thanks to the ferociousness of the rainstorm, it looked to be a small, single-story, semidetached cottage. There was no car in the driveway, though there were plenty parked along the narrow street. Unfortunately, I had no idea what sort of car Vincentia was driving these days.

Cynwrig glanced at me. "Can't see any light peeking out from under the curtains."

"I can barely even see the front yard, and the streetlight is directly above it." I wrinkled my nose. "How good are you at breaking and entering?"

"I'm offended you even asked that question."

I laughed. "Sorry."

"Apology accepted." His tone was amused. "There's no evidence of a physical alarm system, but there could be magical."

He was obviously seeing the cottage a whole lot more clearly than me, but then, dark elves generally had excellent night sight.

"It might be an idea if we loop back around and park further down the road," I said. "That way, we can approach the back of the house from the park and not alert the neighbors."

He nodded, and twenty minutes later we were parking opposite the park's fully lit entrance. The wildness either side of the path was wrapped in darkness and, in this weather, seemed somewhat threatening.

I tugged on my coat, tied its hat down, and then, with a deep breath to ready myself for the abysmal conditions, grabbed my backpack and climbed out.

Abysmal wasn't doing these conditions justice.

The wind howled, and the rain sheeted sideways, and it was all I could do to remain in the one spot and not be blown backwards. I half raised a hand to reach for—and maybe calm—the wind, then clenched my fingers and tucked them into my jacket pockets instead. After Beira's warning, I wasn't quite ready to risk reaching for *any* part of the storm, just in case things went wrong again.

I slung the pack over my shoulders, then made my way to the front of the van and caught Cynwrig's offered hand. He led me across the road, his big body leaning into the wind and seeming to have little trouble moving forward.

Maybe the wind just had it in for me. Or maybe my father was using the storm to tell us we were on the wrong track.

Of course, if that *were* the case, it would be handy if he could also tell us where exactly the right track was.

We moved past the old hip-height stone wall, through the metal bollards, and then followed the well-lit stone track until we were into the first circle of trees. Cynwrig immediately went left, moving through the long, wet grass with the certainty of someone who could see very well.

The streetlight out the front of the little cottage dimly reflected on the half-height stone wall that separated the house's backyard from the park. Cynwrig climbed over, helped me, then walked around the newish-looking extension that had been built onto the park side of the house. An unconnected and very rustic-looking stone shed sat on the opposite side of the yard, creating a nice little courtyard area protected from the prying eyes of neighbors.

Cynwrig stepped onto the covered deck, then stopped. After studying the rear of the building for a few seconds, he said, "I'm not seeing any physical alarms. Are there any magical ones?"

I drew a knife and stepped closer to the building. There was no reaction, so I pressed the point against the bifold's lock. Again, nothing.

"It's clear externally. There could be sensors or magic inside, of course."

He moved up beside me and pressed his hand against the metal doorframe and lock. Energy rose, its feel dark and weighty, as if it were coming from deep within the earth itself. The air shimmered around his fingers, and a heartbeat later, he smiled and slid the door open.

"Wow, that was easy," I muttered. "I'm surprised the world hasn't gotten around to inventing plastic locks just to keep you buggers out."

"Oh, they have."

"Then why aren't they widely used?"

"Because we keep destroying the research and sending them back to the drawing board."

"That's not nice."

"Myrkálfar have never been nice." His eyes glimmered in the storm-held night. "Or did you not get that memo?"

"Obviously not." I motioned him forward. "After you, my dear thief."

He stripped off his coat and shoes, leaving them to the side of the bifold door, out of the way but still undercover. He stepped inside and then paused, obviously scanning the area for sensors and alarms, then gave me a nod. After stripping off my own coat and shoes, I stepped into the spacious combined kitchen and living area. The floor was polished concrete, and there was no sign of heating—no fireplace or radiators—suggesting the extension might have an underfloor system. There were two doors on the right—one led into a laundry and the other, which was closer to the kitchen, looked to be a pantry. The wall to our left was lined with bookcases. I walked across, but it was too dark to read the spines.

I glanced at Cynwrig. "Will it be safe to use the phone's light?"

"Out here it should be, but keep it dim. I'll go check the rest of the house and make sure it's safe."

As he disappeared through the door that led into the main section of the house, I dragged out my phone and turned on the flashlight app. After dimming the light, I lightly ran my fingers across the rows of lovely old books. I had no idea whether the codex would react to my presence or my touch, but given evoking the power of both the knives and the Eye involved the latter, it was probable that the codex would too. Unless, of course, by using it, Vincentia had somehow tuned it to *her* energies.

But if that *was* what had happened, why was it only partially active?

We wouldn't know until we found the damn thing.

I finished inspecting the last bookshelf, then quickly looked around the rest of the room. As expected, no sign of the codex.

I walked to the junction between the old cottage and the extension and pressed a hand against the doorframe. It was new, so while its song was stronger, it didn't hold the weight or memory of the older building. I skimmed the twin rivers of power, looking for any alterations that might have been made—spaces created within the building's frame or hidden under floorboards, perhaps. There didn't appear to be any, and that was rather unusual in a pixie-owned house. We generally did love our little nooks.

I glanced up as the floorboards hummed. A second later, Cynwrig appeared.

"Anything?" I asked.

"No physical alarms or sensors. I'm not magic sensitive, so if there *are* any magical alarms here, I've probably sprung them."

He didn't seem overly concerned about the prospect, so I kept my own fears in check. Dark elves might not be magic sensitive, but they could see the ebb and flow of earthly energies—particularly at night—and many spells interfered with that. Besides, they'd hardly be the dominant force in black market trade if they could be easily stopped by a spell or two.

"I'll have to search the place. The wood song isn't giving me anything."

He nodded. "I'll keep watch."

I followed him into the room on the left, which turned out to be a small sitting area dominated by the fireplace. He twitched the curtains open a fraction, then crossed his arms and stared out the small gap, his attention on the street, though I had no doubt he was very aware of my movements.

There were no bookcases, and little in the way of furniture aside from the old sofa that sat against the wall opposite the window and a well-padded chair close to the fireplace. There was a side table beside this, and on it lay a stack of old magazines. Novels sat on the floor underneath, but they were mostly paperback romances.

I made my way out of the room and headed past the front door. There were three rooms off the hall on the other side of the cottage. Two were bedrooms, and the third a rather small bathroom. Neither the first bedroom nor the bathroom yielded anything, and it was with fading hope that I approached the final room. It was the biggest of the three, with a window front and back, though the latter looked out onto the old shed's wall and really wouldn't have provided much light, even during the day. I paused in the doorway and glanced around, not seeing anything that twinged my instincts, then stepped inside.

The minute I did, the Eye burned to life.

The codex was here.

I drew in a deeper breath in a useless attempt to calm flaring excitement, then tugged the Eye out from my bra and wrapped my fingers around its silken bag. I could still feel its pulsing, but the material seemed to be keeping my second sight from responding. At least for now, anyway.

I slowly made my way around the room, using the Eye as a guide as to whether I was getting closer or going further away. It drew me toward the small, two-door wardrobe whose wood was so heavily covered by decades of paint that its music had been lost. I frowned and wondered why a pixie would hold such a lifeless piece in her room, then opened the door and swept the eye across the hanging space and the shelves. The book wasn't inside; it was above.

I stepped back and looked up. There were a number of boxes sitting in the gap between the top of the wardrobe and the ceiling, but the pulsing pulled me to the left. I rose onto my tippy-toes, pulled the small stack of boxes down, then carted them across to the bed. The first two held a collection of wooly hats and scarves, but in the third was a rather worn and very plain leather book the size of a note-book—and a small one at that.

It couldn't be the codex. It simply didn't look big enough to hold the sum of all knowledge.

The Eye was definitely disputing that thought. It burned so brightly I could see the purple flares of its light-ning through the dark blue silk of its bag.

It was tempting, very tempting, to put the lid back on the box, tuck it into my backpack, and deal with the whole thing later. But instinct immediately suggested *that* would be a very bad idea, and while I had no idea why, I wasn't going to ignore it. Not this time. Not for something as important as this.

I hesitated, then drew both my knives. I'd barely pulled them clear of their sheaths when they began to pulse, but this time their light was unlike anything I'd seen them emit.

"Bethany? Everything okay?" Cynwrig asked.

"I think I've found the book, but goddess only knows what's going to happen when I pick it up."

"You want me in there?"

I hesitated, tempted, but if things did go wrong then one of us needed to be alert and mobile. "Best to keep watching the street, just in case me touching the codex sets off a spell or an alarm."

"Have you checked it?"

"The knives are reacting to its presence, but not in the same way they would if there was a spell attached."

He grunted. "Be careful."

I half smiled. "I suspect me being careful isn't going to alter what happens when I touch this thing."

"Then don't touch it," he said. *I don't want you hurt* was what he meant.

I had no idea where that insight came from.

"This book is part of my heritage, Cynwrig. I have to do this if we're to get any answers. I'll be fine."

He didn't say anything, but his concern continued to wash through the air.

I undid the silk bag and rolled the Eye into my palm. Then, before I could think about the wisdom of what I was doing, I followed gut instinct, pressed the Eye against the knife hilts, and then touched their points to the book.

The reaction was instant and explosive.

Light erupted from all three items, a kaleidoscope of color that whirled around me with dizzying force, blinding me, burning me, even as it swept me up and then swept me away. Not physically. Not exactly. I could still feel the carpet under my feet and the tremor of wood song beyond that, but those sensations were growing weaker with every passing beat of my heart. It felt as if I was falling into a maelstrom of color in the same way that I had fallen into darkness when I'd visited Eithne's monument. Except there was no heartbeat here, just the light. Light that was drawing ever closer to my being, as if it meant to consume me.

Fear surged. I tried to move my hands, tried to yank the knife points away from the book, but to no avail. The vortex's grip just strengthened, and it swept me away without mercy, until all I could see, all I could feel, was its whirlwind.

Then, abruptly, the light died, and there was only darkness.

And that darkness held a heartbeat, just as it had before. Only this time, there were three rather than one. Two of those beats lay in my hand. The third was distant but drawing closer.

I could see nothing. I could feel nothing. No heat, no cold, no life.

And yet, there *was* power here. Gathering power. A storm that lay in wait.

For what?

Then I remembered the comments Rostin De Clari had made through Alinda; *the gifts of light can sometimes exact a bloody price.*

Was that the key? Did the Triune demand tribute in the form of blood to fully unite all three items?

Possibly. I mean, there had to be some reason the codex hadn't been fully utilized by my ancestors—so underutilized, in fact, that they'd actually forgotten it was part of a set.

But how could I unite *anything* when in fact I didn't exist in this place? It was a reality beyond the confines of time and space, just as Eithne's stone had been.

The third heartbeat was now so close I could reach out and touch it. I hesitated, then raised my hands, offering the two heartbeats sitting within them to that third. It joined the two in my hands, but I had absolutely no idea what to do next.

I obviously had to do *something*. I could feel it in the storm, in the gathering weight of expectation.

Eithne's words rose unbidden; *Keep faith with the Eye, complete the Triune's circle, and pay the price to make them your own.*

Meaning that technically, the triune was not complete even if the three heartbeats were sitting in my hands. So, what was I missing?

How did I pay the price?

Make them your own... exact a bloody price. Different ways of saying the same thing, perhaps?

I might not have a body in this place between worlds, but I did have a spirit or a being or whatever the hell this part of me was. I couldn't physically draw blood, but I could draw the hearts that sat so lightly in my hands into my spirit, into my heart. A heart that was beating so loudly, so fiercely, it felt like it was going to break.

I could only try. The frantic beating of my heart suggested I couldn't remain much longer in this place between worlds. It would kill me if I did. I was certain of that, if nothing else.

Without thinking any more about it, I dragged my hands in close and pressed the three beating hearts against my own. For an instant, nothing happened.

Then the distant storm of power suddenly wasn't, and as four became one, the darkness exploded. The heartbeats disintegrated, and I was tossed violently through the kaleidoscope of color and back into the world of the living.

And found myself sitting on the floor amongst the debris of the bedroom's back window, my heart still feeling like it was about to shatter and every breath a shuddering, wheezing effort. There was moisture running down my stomach, blood on the tip of the knives, and the Eye's pulse matched the frantic pace of my heart. As for the codex—the old leather was now mirror black.

As awareness deepened, I realized there were hands on my shoulders, and a voice, urging me to be calm even if he seemed far from it.

I drew in a shuddery breath and said, "It's okay. I'm okay. Everything's okay."

"No, it's fucking *not*," a harsh but familiar voice said. "Move, and I'll shoot you both."

Vincentia.

Fuck.

"Shoot either of us," Cynwrig said, "and you *will* regret it."

Though his voice was flat and without emotion, once again the air around him crackled, and his fury was so strong, I could taste it. He squeezed my shoulder, his gaze telling me to remain still, then carefully shifted around, straddling my legs so that he faced her while shielding me from her sight and actions.

"And how to you reckon that?" Her voice—and no doubt her expression—was filled with sarcasm. "I'm merely using reasonable force to protect myself against intruders in my own home."

I was tempted to lean sideways and look at her, but it was better if she thought me out to it. Besides, unless I put all possible energy into calming the horrid racing of my heart, I wouldn't be able to react if she *did* do more than merely threaten us.

"Shooting us dead will land you in prison," Cynwrig growled. "Which is where you'll no doubt end up anyway, given your failed kidnapping attempt *and* your involvement in several murders."

"Oh, I don't want either of you dead. But maimed? That's definitely appealing." This time, the sarcasm was mixed with amusement. "While I can't deny the failed kidnapping—though I am curious as to how you knew it was me—I'm not involved with Aunt Meabh's murder. I'm hurt you could even think that, Bethany."

Meaning I'd been right—Aunt Riayn *had* called her almost as soon as we'd gotten out of the gate. If she truly *wasn't* involved, it was the only way she could have known about Mom.

I carefully released the knives and then, with small movements I prayed she wouldn't see past the wall of protection that was Cynwrig's torso, tucked the Eye into my bra. There was no way I could let her see it; it was better for all of us if she—and the people she worked for —thought it lost. Then I pressed my hand against my chest in a useless attempt to slow my racing heart and rapid breathing. Moisture continued to seep down my stomach, and there was a wispy ache under my ribs. I couldn't help but wonder if the action of drawing the Triune into my body on the metaphysical plane had somehow transferred to the physical. It sure as hell felt like it, even if there wasn't the level of pain I'd have expected from being stabbed. But then, I'd stabbed myself while helping out in the tavern's kitchen once; the wound had been fairly deep, but I'd simply bandaged it, shoved on a glove, and kept going. It hadn't hurt until hours later, when the food prep had been completed and the shock had worn off.

"Why isn't she answering?" There was just a touch of exasperation in Vincentia's voice this time. Me being unconscious would undoubtedly make things a whole lot more difficult for *her*. "What's wrong with her?"

"Even if I knew, I certainly wouldn't be telling you."

"Step away from her."

"What are you going to do with her? And me?"

"My clients wish to speak to her."

"And your clients are?"

"That is none of your concern."

"And do these clients also wish to speak to me?"

"I don't know, and I don't care. Move."

"No."

There was a soft but deadly-sounding click. I didn't know a whole lot about guns, but I rather suspected that was the sound of a safety coming off.

"Move, or I *will* shoot you—and maybe in the process, hit her. I mean, bullets have been known to go straight through one person and lodge in the body of whoever is standing behind them. I suspect neither of us really want that."

"And I suspect neither the gun nor the ammo it uses has the capacity to do that."

"Maybe not, but are you really willing to risk her life testing that theory out?"

Even if he *was*, I certainly wasn't. I lightly touched his spine and croaked, "It's okay."

Tension rolled across his back, then he stepped over my legs and squatted next to me, his shoulder resting against mine and his hands behind his back, pressed against the rear wall's white-painted stone.

Power rose. He was calling to the stone, and my gaze shot to Vincentia's. She hadn't sensed it; she was too busy staring at me.

"You need to stop this," I wheezed. My heart rate and

breathing were definitely slowing, but I was still finding it difficult to talk. "Nothing good will come of your continuing involvement in the quest for the Claws."

She raised an eyebrow. "And walk away from a contract? A rather large and very profitable contract? Hardly."

"You'll end up dead, Tia."

She smiled. "That's not what I've seen in the codex."

"The codex doesn't tell fortunes. It doesn't see the future." I paused, sucking in air, stretching my response to give Cynwrig more time. "It is the sum of all known information—a library of all godly artifacts and their uses, if you like."

"Whoever told you that was feeding you misinformation."

"I'm sure the goddess who helped create the Triune would dispute that statement."

Her eyebrows rose, her expression one of disbelief. "You talked to the goddess?"

"Several of them."

The power Cynwrig was raising now moved around the room, following the cottage's foundations as it crept cautiously toward Tia. I needed to keep her talking and prevent her from noticing.

"How?" she said. "You don't even have second sight."

I smiled and raised one of the knives. It was still pulsing, though it was losing the shine it had gained in that luminous vortex. "Guess what? I'm a late bloomer."

Her gaze narrowed, and just a fraction of... unease?... skirted through her expression. "It matters not. The codex is my inheritance, not yours. It's not something your mother ever wanted or needed, but it helps me hunt relics and it will help the heir I will one day have."

"Mom never used it because she couldn't, Tia. She didn't perform the appropriate binding ceremony."

That was a guess on my part, but surely if Mom *had* understood the codex's importance—or even performed the ceremony—she wouldn't have allowed my aunt to steal let alone keep it.

She snorted. "The codex doesn't need a binding ceremony to work. One simply holds it and imagines the item you need information on."

Handy to know. "If the codex is so informative, why are you having so much trouble tracking down the Claws?"

She scowled at me. "Because like all things goddess given, it is unpredictable by nature."

"Or perhaps the goddess is right. Perhaps you have to bind the Triune to use its full resources."

"That's the second time you've mentioned this Triune —what the hell are you talking about?"

"The Triune is foresight, protection, and knowledge— the Eye, the knives, and the codex respectively. All three need to be tuned to each other for them to work fully."

The power running along the building's foundations reached a peak, and tension flickered through Cynwrig's body; he was getting ready to attack.

"Well, that's patently untrue, as your mother used the knives and the Eye for years, and I've been using the codex without restriction." Vincentia paused and frowned at the nearest wall. That suggested she was aware of the energy running through the stone, and yet she didn't move away from it. Was she unaware that dark elves could control stone as easily as we controlled wood?

Gods, I hoped so.

"You're lying to yourself, Vincentia," I said, a little louder than necessary to draw her attention back to me.

"Even your mother knows the codex is only partially unlocked."

She rolled her eyes. "My mother wouldn't have a clue. Where is the codex?"

"Show her," Cynwrig said.

Distract her, was what he meant.

I drew in a deeper breath and then said, "Fine."

I shifted the knife to my left hand and then tugged the codex out from under the other and raised it. "Here it is."

"What the fuck are you playing at?" she growled. "That's not—"

She got no further, because the stone behind her exploded, the force enough that half the wall disintegrated, showering the front portion of room with rocks and knocking her clean off her feet. As she disappeared behind the bed, Cynwrig thrust to his feet and raced toward her. There was a low sound that could have been a growl of frustration or pain from the other side of the bed, followed by the sharp retort of gunfire.

Cynwrig stumbled, his momentum briefly halted. Fear surged through me. I slapped a hand against the old flooring and felt Vincentia's location in the oak's fading music. Through it, I grabbed the legs of the bedside table and brought it down on across her chest and shoulders. It provided just enough of a distraction for Cynwrig to lunge forward, grab the weapon, then point the business end at her.

"Move and I *will* fucking kill you."

The deep edge of violence running through his voice sent a chill through me. I had absolutely no doubt he *would* go through with the threat.

"I'm thinking my cousin wouldn't be too pleased about *that*."

Her tone was amused and unworried. Either she wasn't reading him very well or she knew something we didn't.

"Right now, your cousin couldn't give a damn." My voice was so damn weak it really didn't sound like mine. "You're working with the people who poisoned my brother. I'll never forgive or forget that."

"I had nothing to do with—"

"Guilt by association is enough for me," I cut in. "And I suspect it'll be enough for Sgott."

She snorted. "Even Sgott has to follow the rules."

"He might, but I certainly don't," Cynwrig said. "Your employers came after my sister, and that is *never* a good idea."

If Vincentia had any sense, she be panicking right about now. But there was nothing in the way of unease or concern coming from her. Was she killing time? Had she called in help before she confronted us? Given what she'd said about her employers wanting to speak to me, it seemed more than likely.

I silently reached for the wind and started paying more attention to the sounds and movement running underneath the storm.

"Again, I had nothing—"

"Then there's the fact," Cynwrig continued flatly, "that your employers kidnapped and almost killed Ruadhán's only son."

"Who the hell is Ruadhán?"

"Sgott's daytime counterpart. He has a well-earned reputation for having a very loose interpretation of the law."

"None of those events can be traced back to me, and even the IIT can't manufacture evidence."

An admission that she'd at least known what the Looisearch was up to even if she wasn't a participant.

Cynwrig laughed, a sound so cold a chill shivered across my skin. "Oh, how little you understand the real world, little pixie."

It was said with such condescension that I couldn't help but wonder if that was an opinion that stretched to *all* pixies.

The wind stirred again. This time, there was whispers of movement; lights, approaching fast. I leaned my head back against the wall and closed my eyes, trying to sharpen the image I was being shown in order to see what exactly we faced. It remained rainswept and hazy, which was annoying.

"Don't be sliding into unconsciousness, Bethany," Cynwrig said sharply. "Not until we're sure you haven't got concussion after being blasted against the wall."

"I haven't. I'm just listening to the wind."

"A statement that doesn't reassure me in any way. Open your eyes, Beth."

I drew in a deeper breath and forced my eyes open. His silvery gaze was filled with worry, and it warmed my aching heart.

Then the wind stirred anew, and the glare of those approaching lights grew stronger, closer.

"Tia," I said. "Did you call in help before you confronted us tonight?"

Her snort was contemptuous. "Yes—do you think I'm stupid or something? I mean, seriously, cousin, did you not remember that I'd be able to sense your presence through the hum in the wood?"

I actually hadn't, and I'd put that gaffe down to tiredness.

"If your employers attack us, we'll simply use you as a shield," Cynwrig said. "More than happy for you to take the bullets meant for me."

"They're not going to kill me. They need me."

I laughed. "They need the Eye, Tia, and someone capable of using it. That's me, not you."

"And if you're dead, I'm their only option."

"Logic isn't your best attribute, is it?" Cynwrig drawled. "If you hand Bethany over, why then would they need you?"

She didn't say anything. Perhaps that thought hadn't occurred to her.

"How long have we got before your friends arrive?" he continued.

She shrugged. "Five, maybe ten minutes, if you're lucky."

"More likely a minute or two, if I'm reading the wind correctly," I said.

"Then we need to move." He glanced at me. "Do you want to weave your magic on her while I set up a little welcome surprise for our guests?"

Vincentia's gaze jumped to mine, her expression fierce and angry. "I've been cooperating, and there's no need to employ controlling magic. Besides, it's against the code to do so to kin."

"So my brother tells me." I pushed slowly to my feet and walked over. "I take as little notice of him as I will of you."

She took a step forward, intending to gods only knows what, but stopped when Cynwrig pointed the gun at her nose.

He didn't say anything. He didn't need to.

"Remember that whole spiel you gave about shooting and jail?" she said. "That applies just as much to you, bud."

285

Cynwrig's smile was as far from pleasant as you could possibly get. "Except I'm Myrkálfar. Trust me when I say that there are pits in this world so deep and dark your body will never be found. And I can access them from this house if I want to."

I had no doubt he meant every word and, finally, so did she. Her face paled and she quickly said, "There's no need to magic me. I'll do whatever you want."

"Of course you will," I said and reached for her.

She jumped back to avoid the touch, caught the edge of bedside table, and stumbled. Cynwrig lunged forward to grab her but wasn't fast enough. She smacked her head against the wall dividing this cottage from its neighbor and crumpled to the floor.

Cynwrig knelt next to her, checking the back of her head then feeling for a pulse. "No obvious sign of damage. Hopefully she's just knocked herself out."

Relief stirred through me. Despite everything, I didn't want her dead. Locked up in jail for the next ten years or so? *That* had definite appeal.

He made the gun safe, shoved it through his belt at the back of his jeans, and then reached for a couple of rocks, quickly fashioning them into hand and leg cuffs.

Just as he finished securing them, the wind shared the sounds and images of what lay outside. The lights had stopped. Shadowed figures now moved with intent through the storm-swept darkness, heading to this house.

"Cynwrig, we're about to have company."

"How many?"

"Three approaching the front of the house, and another two in the park."

My gaze jumped to the window. The curtains were drawn, which at least meant they wouldn't see us. Of course, if we were dealing with shifters rather than humans, curtains wouldn't really matter, as a wolf's nose was so sensitive it would have no trouble scenting us through these thick old walls.

"Then we need to get moving. Grab your things, then see if you can open the other window. I'll arrange that greeting for them."

"What about our coats and boots?"

"No time."

I spun around, scooped up my backpack, then placed my knives and the codex into it. The book didn't react to my touch, and the light had faded from the knives, but the Eye —which I hadn't placed back in the silk bag—continued to pulse in time to my heart. Was it the link? The bridge between me, the knives, and the codex? And was the Triune coming back online the reason the Eye hadn't activated my second sight despite the fact it was pressed against skin?

It was frustrating that I had absolutely no idea. And no time to even ponder it.

A tremor ran through the cottage's external walls as the old building reacted to whatever order Cynwrig had given it, then stilled. But an odd sense of doom now hung in the air. It was almost as if death strode toward us, and I wasn't entirely sure if it was ours, our would-be captors', or that of the cottage itself.

I threw the pack over my shoulders, then unlatched the rear window and slid the bottom sash up, using just enough of my connection to the wood to ensure it made no sound. The wind blew the curtains back with greater force, but it was doubtful the men standing in the trees beyond the cottage's fence line would see the movement, thanks to the ferocity of the storm and the close presence of the old stone shed.

287

But the men at the front were readying to come in. We had, at best, a minute or so.

I climbed through the window, then turned and helped pull Tia through. Cynwrig climbed out, slid the window back down, then quickly brushed his fingers across the glass to lock the metal latch. Whether it would give us enough time to get away was something we'd soon discover.

He took Vincentia from me and murmured, "This way."

The full force of the storm hit the minute we came out from behind the shed. The rain pummeled our bodies and soaked us to the skin in an instant.

We climbed over the half wall separating Vincentia's cottage from the next and padded down its length, keeping close to the shadows haunting the rear walls. Thankfully, there was no lightning in the area despite the fierceness of the storm. One flash might well have ended any hope of escape, because the men who'd been in the trees were now moving into the backyard.

Cynwrig slipped around the end of the next cottage, then stopped and leaned back against the wall. I raised an eyebrow and said softly, "What are we waiting for?"

"Chaos."

Anticipation filled his voice and, a second later, I understood why.

Vincentia's cottage quite literally blew apart.

CHAPTER
TWELVE

L ights immediately came on in the few visible
buildings on the other side of the street; front doors
opened, and exclamations of surprise and horror filled
the air.

Cynwrig grunted in satisfaction, then said, "This way."

He climbed over the next half wall and continued on
down the line of two-by-two semidetached houses. Though
the lights shone in several of the windows, everyone
seemed to have gone out the front rather than the back.
Luck, it seemed, had finally decided to pay a visit.

"Where are we going?" I murmured.

"There's no one in the end cottage. We can use it as a
refuge until the hubbub dies down."

"How do you know it's empty?"

"I communicated with the stone via the earth." His
smile flashed briefly, bright in the darkness. "I wasn't just
preparing the wall to attack Vincentia, you know."

"A man who can do two things at once," I murmured.
"Color me shocked."

He chuckled softly, and we continued on. Once we

reached the last house, he shifted Vincentia's weight, then pressed his right hand over the doorknob. A heartbeat later, we were inside.

It was probably colder inside the house than it was out, but then, these old places tended to lose heat very fast unless the ambient temperature was kept reasonably high during the winter months. Obviously, the heating system here hadn't been used for a while.

We moved through the laundry into a combined kitchen-dining area, and it was then I realized he was limping and remembered he'd been shot. "How bad is the wound?"

He shrugged. "The bullet went straight through the fleshy part of my thigh, so no major damage done."

"An assurance I'm not convinced by," I said in an echo of his earlier statement.

He half laughed. "I've been shot before and do know a little about bullet wounds. Trust me, this is only minor."

I stopped and leaned against the nearby doorframe, listening to the building's gentle song to orient myself. The cottage's floor plan was fairly simple—there was a living room to the right, two bedrooms and a bathroom to the left. The furniture was old but well looked after, and there were plenty of photos and holiday keepsakes scattered around to suggest this was a home rather than a holiday rental.

"Who shot you those other times? A rival for a woman or someone who objected to the way you were going about your black-market business?"

"Would you be surprised if I said both?"

"Not at all."

He laughed again and began opening drawers, eventually finding, and claiming, a roll of duct tape. After walking down to the smaller of the two bedrooms, he laid Tia on the double bed, then wound the tape around her mouth and head. It was going to hurt to get off, and that mean inner part of me was greatly cheered by that fact.

"Can you order her not to move from the bed while she's unconscious?" Cynwrig asked.

I wrinkled my nose. "Don't believe so."

"Ah, well, duct tape it is."

He wrapped the tape around her ankle cuffs and then looped it multiple times around the end of the bed. She wasn't going anywhere in a hurry. He quickly patted her down, removing car keys and a phone from her pockets.

He placed both in his own and said, "I'll go check if the water and electricity have been turned off and then start the boiler. You might want to get out of those wet things and into something warmer."

I nodded and headed into the main bedroom. It wasn't much larger than the other one, though the bed was at least a queen size. On the opposite wall was one of those two-door freestanding wardrobes with a couple of drawers at the base. I opened the doors and discovered a range of summer clothing—a woman's on the right, and a man's on the left. The two drawers were similarly divided and contained warmer sweaters, pants, and even a couple of coats, which was very handy given we'd left at the other cottage.

Behind the bedroom door, hanging from metal hooks, were two fluffy dressing gowns—the perfect clothing solution until the water was hot enough for a shower.

After grabbing a couple of towels from the small closet in the hall, I stripped and, after safely tucking the Eye in the backpack, checked my stomach for wounds. There was a cut just under my right ribs the same width as my knife blades, but the wound had almost fully scarred over and was no longer bleeding. Which made sense—the goddesses behind the Triune would hardly want the very ceremony meant to unite all pieces of the puzzle killing off the only person who could wield them.

I dried off, then reached for the pink fluffy dressing gown, only to pause as bedevilment stirred. With a quick grin, I grabbed the blue one instead.

Cynwrig walked into the room, his gaze quickly skimming me and coming up appreciative. "The power is on, the boiler's lit, and there's a dryer in the laundry. It'll probably take thirty or forty minutes before we have hot water, though."

"And longer than that for the radiators to start producing any heat."

He nodded. "But I've put the kettle on, so we can have a cuppa while we wait."

He removed keys, phones, and his wallet from his pockets, then quickly stripped off. His dark skin gleamed like black silk in the shadowy darkness, and fingers itched with the need to explore every muscular and perfect inch. Sadly, now was neither the time nor the place. We couldn't afford to be distracted when there were emergency and police vehicles screaming in from all directions.

I tucked my hands under my armpits to keep them out of mischief. "There's another dressing gown on the back of the door, but I couldn't find any socks or slippers."

"It's doubtful there'd be any in my size anyway." He half closed the door, then cast me a wry glance. "Pink?"

"It'll look better on you than me. Us pale-skinned redheads just can't do it justice."

He snorted, tugged it off the hook, and pulled it on. It was thigh-length on him, so it not only revealed the long, magnificent length of his legs but also the still-bleeding bullet wound.

"We need to find a first aid kit and treat that," I said, motioning toward it.

"There's one in the kitchen. You can make the tea while I patch myself up."

He scooped up our wet clothes and headed for the laundry while I checked on Vincentia. Her pulse was strong, and there was movement under her eyelids, suggesting she was either close to waking or maybe even foxing. I was tempted to pinch her cheek to see what happened but decided to grab a cuppa first. It had been a long, tiring day, and it wasn't over yet.

Cynwrig looked up as I walked into the kitchen. "She awake yet?"

"I think so but pretending otherwise." I shrugged. "I decided my need for tea is stronger than the need for answers right now."

He chuckled softly. "There are some needs that should never be ignored. Tea is one of them."

I raised an eyebrow, amusement bubbling through me. "Dare I ask what the others are?"

His smile was soft and smokey, and my pulse did its usual dance. "I suspect you should not. Not until we have time to cater to said needs, anyway."

"'Cater' is such an unromantic word."

He briefly pursed his lips. "Deal? Minister? Treat?"

I grinned. "See, this is the problem with having a natural magnetism that can make a maiden weak with wanting without even trying—you lose the ability to verbalize desire properly."

He laughed and tied off the bandage on his leg. "Then I

shall definitely concentrate on verbalizing my wants and desires when we have more time for such things."

"Something I very much look forward to," I said lightly. And hoped like hell that the gods would give us a break *and* some time—although I daresay we'd already had our allotment of luck tonight.

I found a couple of mugs and some tea bags and made our drinks. There was a packet of those little long-life milk pods in the pantry, which I generally avoided except in cases of emergencies.

This could definitely be classified as an emergency.

By the time we'd finished our tea, there were definite sounds of activity coming from the second bedroom. I sighed and met Cynwrig's gaze. "Shall we get this over with?"

Cynwrig plucked the scissors from the first aid kit and rose. "It'll make it easier to decide our next step."

"And what to do with her." Or even if we *should* do anything with her.

She was sitting up in bed trying to unpick the tape around her mouth when we walked in. Her gaze flashed toward mine, her green eyes furious. She said something incomprehensible thanks to the tape, but I had a feeling it was neither pleasant nor polite.

I stopped near the bed just out of her reach and crossed my arms. "If we undo that tape, you going to behave yourself?"

She nodded vigorously. I didn't for one second believe it. Obviously, neither did Cynwrig. He grabbed her hands and pressed them against her stomach, then wrapped his other hand around her neck, effectively immobilizing her.

I stepped forward and pressed my fingers against her other shoulder. She screamed, but the tape muffled the sound, and it was unlikely to be heard given the hubbub still happening outside.

"You *will* answer all of our questions honestly," I said softly. "You will not scream or otherwise try to attract attention. You will not attempt to escape, you will not attack either of us, and you certainly will *never* attempt to magically enforce your will on either of us or my brother."

I didn't bother asking if she understood, because her glare said everything that needed to be said.

Cynwrig released her, produced the scissors, and then said, "Hold still while I cut the tape away or risk being cut."

She stilled. He carefully slid the scissors between the tape and her skin, cut down, then tugged the tape away from her mouth but not the rest of her head.

"Bitch," she immediately growled, with another glare my way. "You will pay for this."

"Says the women trussed tighter than an antique clock and staring at the possibility of a very long prison sentence."

She didn't say anything, but understanding flickered through the frustration briefly evident in her expression. She knew that simple saying was what had given her away.

"Who is your Looisearch contact?" Cynwrig asked.

Her gaze jumped to his, surprise evident. She obviously wasn't expecting us to know even that much.

"Seryn Morrisa."

No surprise there, given she was also Peregrine's contact. But was she the brains behind this plot? I didn't believe so, though there was nothing more than gut instinct telling me that.

"And you're assisting them to find the Claws?"

"Yes."

"Why did you attempt to kidnap me?" I asked.

"I told them I'd be more successful if I had the Eye. I couldn't find it at the tavern, so we decided to go directly to the source." She paused. "Is the Eye truly gone?"

"Yes," I said. "And you could have simply called me instead of running the risk of outing yourself. I would have told you I didn't have the Eye. Hell, I didn't even know what it was until a week or so ago."

She sniffed. "Mom said you'd never hand it over."

"And she's right. But I'd nevertheless have told you it had disappeared with Mom."

She hesitated. "I am sorry for her loss, Beth. You have to believe me; I really didn't have anything to do with that."

I glanced away and blinked back those blasted tears again. She might be involved with the Looisearch, but it was becoming evident that it was the theft of the horde Mom had been trying to stop rather than that of the Claws. The crown— and indeed the sword, if the visions were to be believed— hadn't been stored anywhere near the tunnel we'd found her body in, and Mom had been using the Eye in combination with her second sight for so long that she wouldn't have made such a simple location mistake. I had no idea who had betrayed her, but I really didn't believe it was either Aunt Riayn or Vincentia.

"What do you—or the people you work for—know about the Sword of Darkness?" Cynwrig asked, with an understanding glance my way.

"Only that it was hidden by its original wielder and now lies in Tywyll's temple."

Surprise leapt through me, though it really shouldn't have given the strength of her second sight. Riayn hadn't really been wrong when she'd said that Tia was the better candidate when it came to the Eye. "You saw this in the codex?"

"No. In my focus stone."

"Then what did you see in the codex?"

Her gaze came to mine. "Your death."

For several seconds, I could only stare at her. I'd seen death too, though it had been unclear whether it had been mine or Lugh's.

"Did it involve a sacrificial stone darkly stained with eons of bloodshed?"

"Yes." Her gaze swept me. "You've seen it?"

"I saw the ceremony. The face was unclear."

"Ah. Well. That's the difference between strong sight and weak. You'd best back away from this hunt, Bethany, or that death *will* claim you."

For no real reason, my gaze rose to Cynwrig's, and an odd sort of strength ran through me. I wasn't entirely sure why, but I suddenly knew that for as long as this man stood by my side, that death would not find me.

The problem was, of course, that he would not always be by my side.

I crossed my arms and lightly rubbed them in an effort to ward off the chill creeping through my veins. "While I might not be able to fight that destiny, it has nothing to do with this hunt."

She raised an eyebrow. "You're sure of that?"

"Yes. Do you know where Tywyll's temple is?"

"At some place called Draig Y Môr."

"And where is that?" Cynwrig asked.

"Fucked if I know."

"Your focus stone or the codex didn't provide a location?" I asked, a little surprised. While I understood the codex being of little use, she should have been well versed in understanding and mitigating the limitations of a focus stone. They were, in most respects, a lesser version of the Eye.

Not that I knew or understood a whole lot about either. And that made me a little mad at Mom. She should have told me so much more about my heritage even if she'd truly believed I would never be a part of it.

"No," Vincentia said. "But it won't matter, because there can't be too many places named after sea dragons in the UK."

"Did you see anything else? Like where in the temple the sword might be stored?"

"No, but it shouldn't be too hard to find. Temples dedicated to minor gods or saints generally aren't too big or complicated."

"You've passed on the information to your employers?" Cynwrig asked.

Her gaze flicked to his. "Of course."

"When?"

"A few hours ago."

Meaning they might not be too far ahead of us for a change. "What about the crown? Do you know where it has been shifted to?"

Her face screwed up for a second, but she couldn't escape the compulsion to answer. "It was being taken to some vault in Deva."

"Deva?" I said, surprised. "Why?"

"Because the best place to hide something is also in the most obvious place."

I glanced at Cynwrig. He nodded. "It's also true that most thieves keep track of the items they steal—"

"I didn't steal the crown," she cut in. "I only secured it."

"Secured it from who?" I asked. "Raen?"

"Yes."

"And did you kill her after taking delivery?"

Contempt rippled through her expression. "I'm not being paid to murder, Bethany."

Meaning she *would* have—not only tempting fate but risking the pixie blood curse—if they *had* paid her enough? That was not only rather scary but made me wonder if I'd read my aunt utterly wrong. Maybe she was a fucking good actress and had played me for an utter fool. After all, for the better part of our existence, the Aodhán line had either guarded the relics of the old gods or spent our lives retrieving and securing them. It was only in the last few generations that my family, at least, had settled in as innkeepers—and even then, Lugh had carried on the family business. But Aunt Riayn had always had a mercenary streak, and it had definitely been sharpened in her daughter. Perhaps deliberately so.

"Who did you give the crown to after you took it from Raen?" I asked.

"A spellcaster."

"Aram?"

"I wasn't told his name and didn't ask."

"Can you give us a description?" Cynwrig said.

"No. He was shadow bound."

Meaning it might not even have been a man, but a woman using a voice manipulation spell.

A woman like Maran Gordan, perhaps.

"Do you know who ordered him murdered?"

The surprised that flitted through her expression looked real. "No, I do not."

Meaning we'd have to hope Nati came through with some answers sooner rather than later, and I made a mental note to contact her when I could.

"Which brings us neatly back to a thief never losing

track of their things," Cynwrig said. "What vault did they take it to?"

"I don't know."

An answer that rang of the truth and yet... wasn't. I studied her for a second and then said, "Then have you a means of tracking the crown's location?"

Her face screwed up again before she ground out, "Yes."

"Tell us how."

"I put a tracker dot on it, which is activated by my phone."

"An action that suggests you don't trust your employers," Cynwrig said.

"More like she intended to use it as a bargaining chip if she got caught," I said.

If she'd taken the crown from Raen, then she'd more than likely witnessed the other woman's death. She'd know that might well be her own fate if she didn't play her cards right.

"What about the Looisearch?" he asked. "How do you contact them and where are they located?"

"My only contact—aside from that one meeting with the spellcaster—is with Seryn Morrisa."

"You have her number?"

She rattled it off. "It won't do you any good. She'll change it the minute she realizes I've been caught."

"Then we'll have to ensure she doesn't become aware of that fact." Cynwrig glanced at me. "Can your controlling magic erase memories?"

"Don't you even fucking *try*," Vincentia growled.

I met her gaze. I wasn't sure what she saw in my expression, but her face went pale. "I can certainly prevent her from giving anything we've said or done here away, but releasing her will nevertheless be dangerous."

No magic, no matter how powerful, was without fault or problems. And when you were dealing with a human mind, well, those problems just multiplied.

"Yes, but throwing her in prison will only drive the Looisearch deeper underground. We have more chance of finding them if Vincentia remains free. It also means we can use her as our inside source."

"Even if the all-encompassing depth needed to totally control my actions and thoughts were possible," Tia growled, "it'll come with unwanted side effects."

That was no doubt true, given full telepathic control over another mind was considered dangerous for *both* parties. And there had to be a reason why magicking kin was against the code.

But we didn't really have many other options right now. Even if the control didn't hold for all that long, even if it did come with risks, a few hours breathing space might be the difference between us finding the sword and the Looisearch.

"Do it," Cynwrig said, and held her down again.

She opened her mouth and sucked in a deep breath, but I'd already curtailed her ability to scream, and no sound came out. She silently seethed instead, her gaze promising retribution and worse as I wove a tight network of orders around her, allowing her to work *and* send us information without giving the game away to either her employers, her kin, or her friends. Then I forced her to sleep. By that time, my head was booming, and I was so damn weak my knees were threatening to buckle.

I scrubbed a hand across my face and said, "The orders will come into play when she wakes up. She'll remember up to the point of the bedroom wall exploding and nothing after that."

At least, that's what I hoped. I'd never attempted this depth of control before and had no idea if I'd done it right.

"Perfect," he said. "How long will she sleep for?"

"Half an hour."

"Then I'll untie her and drop her back into her car."

"Isn't that a risk, given what's happening at the other cottage?"

"It's the events at the other cottage that makes this the perfect time. It's doubtful many will be paying attention to this end of the road." He moved around the bed, tugged me close, and wrapped his arms around me. I could have stayed there forever, drowning in his heat and strength. "You, my dear woman, need to grab a shower to chase the chill from your skin and then climb into bed."

"You'll join me?"

"As much as I'd love nothing more, it's better I keep watch. Besides, you're dead on your feet, and I really do prefer my partners fully awake and participating."

I laughed softly. "If they fall asleep during sex, you're not doing it right."

"Something I have never been accused of," he said, with a laugh that rumbled through his chest. He kissed the top of my head and then stepped back. "Go. Before desire gets the better of common sense."

I smiled and went. A hot shower definitely leached the ice from my skin if not my soul, and the covers on the bed thick, heavy, and toasty warm. Sleep found me within minutes.

~

A soft ringing woke me who knew how many hours later. I blinked owlishly as sleep gave way to consciousness, then realized the ringing had been replaced by talking.

And it was coming from the kitchen.

I flipped the heavy bedcovers off. The clothes I'd been wearing yesterday had been neatly folded and stacked on the nearby bedside table, but I grabbed fresh clothes from my pack and shivered my way into them. The cottage was definitely warmer than it had been when we'd broken in last night, but there was condensation on the windows, and the wind howled around the building even if the storm no longer raged.

Which did not bode well for the ferry trip back.

Cynwrig glanced up as I entered the kitchen and motioned toward a cozy-covered tea pot. I gratefully poured myself a cup, then wrapped my hands around it and leaned back against the Aga.

It sounded like he was talking to Lugh, which was surprising... until I remembered my phone hadn't been charged recently.

I returned to the bedroom to grab it. Yep, deader than a doornail. I connected the charger and plugged it into a point, then headed into the larder to find something edible. There was the usual range of condiments and jams, various cans of vegetables, soups, and baked beans, and several packets of biscuits. I settled on Jammy Dodgers simply because the shortbread and jam combination was probably the closest thing to a breakfast food in the pantry.

I tore the packet open, removed four biscuits, then pushed it across the counter as Cynwrig hung up. "What did Lugh want?"

Cynwrig plucked a Dodger free and took a bite. "He wants us to meet him in Swansea ASAP."

Excitement—and more than a little fear—surged. "He's found the cave and the church I saw?"

"Yes, and they just happen to be on a tidal island that runs by the name of Draig Y Môr."

"Meaning the Looisearch might already be there, given Vincentia gave them a heads-up."

Whether they'd be able to access the stone chest was another matter entirely.

"Oh, I think they'll definitely be there. As will Vincentia."

I frowned. "Why?"

"Because about two hours after she woke up in her car and walked back to the cottage, she and two men returned and drove to the airport. They took a plane to Swansea."

"And you didn't wake me? We should have gone after—"

"You were running on empty, Beth. That's always dangerous in this sort of situation."

"Yes, but if they get the sword—"

"You found the crown in that cavern, despite the Looisearch getting there first. Vincentia might know the island on which the sword rests, but she didn't see *where* it was, and it's very possible she won't be able to find it."

I knew he was right, but letting them get ahead of us again didn't sit well. "I take it you know all this because you arranged to have her followed?"

"That's a pretty safe assumption, given I'm not psychic."

I gave him a rather unamused glare, and he laughed. "My family has contacts in multiple locations, across multiple countries, and two hours is plenty of time to arrange a trace and clone."

"I take you don't mean cloning *her*."

He laughed again. "One of her in this world is more than enough. I meant her phone."

"She would have noticed someone stealing her phone."

"To clone a device these days is simply a matter of sitting close and using the right app. And even if her contact list proves unusable, having the clone means we can activate the tracker dot on the crown and find it, even if they move it again."

That would definitely be handy, especially if our presumptions were wrong and they *did* grab the sword. We needed to keep control of at least one of the Claws to thwart their overall plan—though I daresay each object in and of itself could cause plenty of damage if used by the wrong person.

Of course, I wasn't sure there *was* a right person when it came to the darker, more deadly godly relics.

"What's the range on the dots?"

"If it's in Deva, we'll find it." He glanced at his watch. "I did organize a private jet to take us back there this morning, but I'll contact them now and get the route changed while you grab your things."

I gulped down the rest of my tea, then rinsed the mug and headed back down the hall. Once I'd shoved on my still-damp boots, I grabbed our replacement coats, then opened the bottom drawer and pulled out a wooly hat. Not only was it highly likely the other cottage was still crawling with investigators, the Looisearch probably had people on watch here too. Vincentia might have left with two men, but that still left three unaccounted for.

Of course, they might well have been taken out—either permanently or temporarily—by the second explosion.

My borrowed coat was a little tight across my breasts, but the other jacket was an XXL, which would swim on me but definitely fit Cynwrig. I returned to the kitchen, tossed the new coat across to him, then pulled a hundred and twenty pounds—all the cash I had—from my purse and placed it on the counter to help cover the cost of us being here. It wouldn't cover the stolen coats, of course, but something was better than nothing.

I'd never make a good thief, I thought wryly, because the guilt factor would always get me.

Cynwrig headed into the laundry to turn off the boiler and electricity. I grabbed my phone and the charger, tossing them into the backpack before I slung it over my shoulder and followed him out. The howling wind showed no sign of abatement anytime soon, but it also said no one showed undue interest in this end of the street. Nor were there any watchers in the sky—though in truth, the near gale-like wind would have had all but the most determined bird shifter seeking shelter.

As Cynwrig relocked the door, I tugged on my hat and said, "I'm thinking it'll be safer if we don't suddenly appear on the street together."

"I agree." He motioned toward the end of the garden. "Which is why we'll use the graveled path beyond that wall. It skirts the forest's edge and leads into the road where the Uber will meet us."

"And if the forest is being watched?" I had no indication that it was, but I was very new to reading the nuances of the air and was too far away to hear the song of the trees.

"If it is, we'll deal with it." Though he touched my arm lightly, I felt it through every fiber of my being. "Let's go."

I followed him down the yard. The path lay several feet away from the half-height wall dividing the yard from the park. Alders lined the edge of the forest, and their song was sweet and strong. I lightly connected to their network, listening for the sounds of intrusion as we hurried along the old path. A slight vibration of movement echoed across the outer reaches of their song, but it wasn't moving in this direction.

Even so, I didn't fully relax until were well out of the park. Thankfully, the Uber was already waiting for us. I charged my phone on the way to the airport, and once it had rebooted, discovered missed calls from both Sgott and Lugh.

I glanced at Cynwrig. "Did you happen to call Sgott last night?"

"Didn't have time."

I raised an eyebrow. "No time, or no inclination because you wanted to give your people a head start?"

His expression was cool and unrepentant. "She is family—"

"And probably behind the attack on your twin *sister*."

"Which is why she'll face Myrkálfar justice rather than the courts. Trust me when I say she will fear the latter more."

His flat tone sent another chill through my body. I suspected Seryn's fate would be less about "justice" and more about retribution. About doing to her what she'd now done to many others.

It might even involve those pits he'd mentioned to Vincentia.

I fought the urge to edge away from him a little. He'd never physically hurt me—I was unreasonably certain of that—but that didn't mean I had to throw all caution away.

My hormones, of course, had other ideas when it came to distance.

My hormones needed to be bitch slapped.

"I'm not keeping information from Sgott," I said, a little more forcefully than was needed.

"I'm not asking you to."

I studied him for a second, then returned my gaze to my phone and sent a message to Sgott detailing everything we'd discovered. Cynwrig's people might have gotten an informational jump, but the IIT had the resource might of the law behind them. As races went, it should be fairly even.

We continued on in silence. At the airport, we were ushered into a private lounge and eventually escorted out to a small jet. Though there were ten—very comfortable—seats on board, we were the only passengers.

Thankfully, we had a tail wind, and it took less than an hour to get to Swansea. The minute I turned the phone's flight mode off, it dinged; Lugh, letting us know they'd arrived.

They'd? I glanced at Cynwrig. "Did Lugh say anything about bringing someone with him?"

Annoyance flickered through his expression. "Apparently Mathi has decided he needs to be useful."

A smile twitched my lips. "And he undoubtedly *will* be, especially if the Looisearch or Annwfyn attack."

He raised an eyebrow. "Why would the Annwfyn attack?"

"Because the sword will call to darkness the second anyone picks it up, and that unfortunately includes the shadowed folk."

He hesitated. "It's unlikely they'll attack unless our search takes us well into the night. For the most part, they avoid the sun."

"It's the 'for the most part' that worries me." I screwed up my nose. "Does that mean the myths of them not being able to move through daylight aren't true?"

He nodded. "It's a choice rather than a rule."

And he'd know. His people had done more than anyone else to keep the shadowed folk at bay; in fact, they were the only ones—aside from the Annwfyn themselves—capable of opening and closing the dark gates, though the latter didn't come with any sort of permanence.

"Well, the sword is only accessible through a cave in the dragon's head, and from what I saw, it's darker than hell in there, even in daylight."

"Then we'd better hope there's no gate on the island."

"You don't know? I thought the Myrkálfar kept track of them all, whether they're active or not."

"We do, but the problem is, humanity were once nomads and the gates shifted location with them. Records from those times are scant at the best."

As the flight attendant unlocked the door, Cynwrig offered me his hand, then tugged me into his arms. His kiss was very thorough indeed.

The attendant eventually cleared his throat. I stepped back, slung my pack over my shoulder, and said, "You did that for Mathi's benefit, didn't you?"

"Mathi has *never* figured into any of my actions." With his fingers still twined around mine, he turned and led the way out of the plane.

"So that kiss didn't come from a primeval need to assert territory?"

"It did not."

It was so flatly said I couldn't help but laugh. "Yeah. Believing that."

He didn't say anything. My grin grew, but I kept silent as we were guided across the tarmac to the small terminal building. Lugh and Mathi were waiting for us past the barriers, the latter's gaze scanning my length before rising to rest on my kiss-swollen lips.

Just as Cynwrig had no doubt intended.

Before Mathi could say anything, I held up a finger and said, "We haven't the time for any sort of macho posturing from either of you right now, so don't even start."

"And perhaps you should allow me to speak before you jump to unworthy conclusions."

"Unworthy they might be, but unfounded? I'm thinking not."

"And I'm thinking," Lugh said in exasperation, "that we need to get out of here and on the road ASAP if we want any chance of getting the sword before the tides and the competition make it impossible. We're already cutting it fine."

He turned and marched away. I followed, Cynwrig on one side, Mathi on the other. It wasn't often I had the opportunity to be bookended—in any way—by two divinely good-looking men, and I thoroughly enjoyed it.

"I spoke to my father before we left this morning," Mathi said. "The lawyer who interviewed the men who were killed in the cells is Carla Wilson, but he doesn't believe she had anything to do with the matter."

"He's spoken to her?" I asked, a little surprised. I'd half expected her to disappear as thoroughly as all our other suspects had.

"Yes, and the video evidence backs her statement."

"Videos can be altered relatively easily," Cynwrig commented.

And in this case certainly *had* been, given that in the Eye's vision, she'd admitted giving them Dahbree. "Have the autopsy results come through as yet?"

"Yes, but they're inconclusive."

I frowned. "Meaning what, exactly?"

"The initial blood work was contaminated. Secondary samples provided no evidence of drug or alcohol presence."

I didn't know anything about autopsies—other than what I'd seen on TV, and everyone knew they were written for drama rather than fact—but I would have thought more than one blood sample would be taken for that very reason.

"And did he in any way think *that* a little too convenient, especially when Dahbree is virtually only traceable via blood work in the first few hours of administration?"

His gaze shot to mine. "What makes you think Dahbree was used on them?"

"Heard the lawyer admit it in my vision." I raised an eyebrow. "You father didn't mention it?"

"No, but he likely wouldn't, given the contaminated blood sample."

We reached the car and climbed in—Cynwrig and I in the back and Mathi up front with Lugh. Once we were underway, I said, "Did your father or his people question the men before Carla arrived?"

"Yes. Quite extensively."

Knowing Ruadhán, that probably meant he'd squeezed all available information from them in a variety of legal and not so legal means well before Carla had even been called.

"And?" I prompted when he didn't continue.

"They said they were commissioned by an unknown broker to the steal the rubies, and that Gilda subsequently stole hers from them."

I frowned. "That makes no sense whatsoever. Gilda was a servant class fae with some ability to manipulate wood—why would she be involved in such a high-risk theft?"

"She wouldn't, but then, neither would those men. They gathered information using women as honeypots and then sold that information on to the highest bidder. My father believes their memories were manipulated."

"That still doesn't explain how Gilda got the ruby."

"Or why they'd even bother setting Gilda and her employers up," Lugh said. "That's a whole lot of effort for little gain."

"Not when you consider how much time the council has spent on first the singing bowl's appearance and now the ruby's," Cynwrig commented.

"It could also be a simple matter of greed," Lugh said. "Maybe there's a faction that simply wants to sell the lesser items for their own gain."

"I'd hardly call the Shield of Hephaestus a lesser item," Cynwrig said in a dry sort of tone. "It does give the wielder control over fire and volcanoes."

"Yes, but neither the shield nor the other two rubies have been found," Lugh said. "And while a ruby would no doubt have fetched a pretty price on the black market, would Gilda have had the knowledge or the contacts to sell it?"

"No," Mathi said. "The employment search she under-went would have picked up those types of links."

"Shame they didn't pick up the honeypot ones," Cynwrig said in a very bland tone.

An almost visible wave of anger rolled in from Mathi's direction, but before he could counter the barb, I quickly said, "If Gilda's acquisition of the ruby was a diversion, how did her partners know about it or the other two?"

"Perhaps by the same means that they knew about the council's decisions," Cynwrig said.

I gave him a warning look. He raised an eyebrow, but bedevilment danced in his eyes, and it obvious it had no intention of backing off.

But then, neither did Mathi.

"Even if other councilors had been placed in the same position," Mathi said, in a surprisingly even tone given that wave, "neither the shield nor the rubies were mentioned in any meeting after the theft of the hoard. I checked."

"Yes, but a list of hoard contents was tabled in the days following the theft," Cynwrig said. "All councilors have access to it."

"This is all useless conjecture and certainly a situation we can do nothing about right now," Lugh commented. "How about we concentrate on what we *can* do something about? Because we're about twenty minutes away from the coast and we need to have a plan of attack."

"We won't be able to park in the main parking area for that section of beach," Mathi said. "They're likely to be watching it."

"It won't matter where we park," Cynwrig said. "I checked Google Maps; the beach between the mainland and the island is wide and sandy. They'll spot us the minute we cross, no matter where our starting point is."

"Then we'll have to wait for darkness and another low tide," I said.

"That'll give them time to find the temple and get their hands on the sword," Mathi said.

"Except Vincentia didn't see where the temple was located, and the island is large and mountainous," Cynwrig said. "It'll take them time to explore."

"The other point in our favor is the fact she doesn't know how to open the chest that holds the sword," I said. "It can't be pried open, and it can't be stolen."

Not unless they had a dark elf capable of stone manipulation on hand, and even then, it was more than possible it wouldn't work. Whoever had hidden the sword would surely have catered for that situation.

"I don't like the idea of lying low until darkness," Lugh growled. "We can't afford to lose another Claw."

"We can't afford to get killed either," I said. "And remember, I'm the only one they need alive right now."

He grunted, an unhappy sound if ever there was one. Cynwrig pulled his phone out and began scrolling. "There's a pub with accommodation in Llyn Du—turn right at the roundabout about a kilometer ahead. The pub is about three klicks further along."

Lugh obeyed, and it didn't take us long to arrive at Llyn Du. It was a smallish village with a mix of stone and pebble-dash cottages. The pub was a two-story building in the center of the village, and had multiple Welsh flags hanging out the front. Lugh found a parking spot farther down the road, and we climbed out.

I drew in a deep breath, tasting the sea in the air despite the fact we were kilometers away from it. The storms that had plagued us in Ireland had swirled around this part of Swansea, and though the night was hours away yet, it promised to be still and cold. I wasn't sure that was a good thing, given the wind was the one weapon in my arsenal that neither Vincentia nor the people she worked for knew about.

We headed into the hotel and booked three rooms—one each for Lugh and Mathi, and one for Cynwrig and me. Mathi didn't look pleased about this situation but refrained from saying anything.

Color me totally surprised.

The manager happily escorted us to the rooms—it was off season, so room bookings were probably few and far between—then explained that though the bathroom was shared, there were two toilets, one for gents and one for ladies.

After telling us the kitchen was still open if we wanted to get something to eat, he handed us the keys and left.

"Food sounds like an excellent idea," I said. "Don't know about anyone else, but I'm absolutely starving."

"We did skip breakfast," Cynwrig said, in a way that implied we'd been too busy having sex to actually eat.

Mathi didn't bite, but I knew him well enough to see the subtle shift in his expression indicating displeasure.

"Given sunset hits around four in these parts," he said, "it's probably wise to grab something now rather than wait for dinner service."

"Meet you downstairs in ten, then," Lugh said.

"Make it twenty," Cynwrig said with a wicked look my way.

Lugh rolled his eyes. "Fine. If you must."

Mathi muttered something under his breath and disappeared into his room. Cynwrig opened ours, then waved me in. The room was basic but clean, with a small wardrobe and a handy washbasin in the corner. A kettle and a tea-tray containing two mugs, a selection of tea and coffee sachets, and half a dozen little tubs of milk sat on the table in the opposite corner.

I tossed my backpack onto the bed and then turned and stepped into his waiting arms. Twenty minutes wasn't a whole lot of time in the scheme of things, but by gods, it was utterly satisfying.

We basically had the pub's small dining room to ourselves and spent a good part of the afternoon eating while planning responses for various possible scenarios. In the end, it was decided that Lugh and I would tackle the cave while Cynwrig and Mathi kept watch from above using the energy hum of stone and foliage to track any approach. That did leave the sea open as a possible option, but the information Lugh had gleaned from the pub's owner about the cave suggested that even at low tide, such an approach would be treacherous. According to him, the climb up the wet and dangerous rocks that formed the dragon's jaw was one only an experienced climber should attempt.

As another round of coffee and tea arrived, I gathered my phone and asked the waitress where the ladies' toilets were. As she pointed me in the right direction, Lugh rose and said, "You shouldn't go anywhere alone."

"It's just down the hall, brother mine. And you know how loudly I can shout if needed."

His lips twisted. "Given my poor eardrums have been the recipient of said shouting more than a few times over the decades, I certainly do. But if you're too long, I'm coming in."

I rolled my eyes and walked to the end of the dining room and down the small passage the waitress had indicated. I had to go past the kitchen, several storerooms, and then through a door that led out into a small courtyard area before I found them.

Dusk had settled in across the sky, painting the clouds pretty shades of pink. The air was still but bitterly cold and made me wish I'd grabbed my coat. The courtyard was empty aside from a several dust-covered tables and a nearby stack of chairs. The toilet block lay to my left, and at the far end of it was a large waste bin. Something small and dark flicked around its base then dove into the deeper shadows, and revulsion crawled through me. Rats. Great.

After another quick look around, I headed into the ladies'. The lights came on as I entered, the sudden brightness making me blink. Both stalls were empty, so I headed into the cleanest. But as I closed the door, an odd scuff caught my attention. I froze, my heart pounding so rapidly it was practically all I could hear.

The sound wasn't repeated.

I hesitated, then bent and peered under the bottom of the stall, looking for shoes. Nothing. Maybe the scuff had come from one of the rats I'd seen; I knew from experience just how noisy the bastards could be.

But it was also possible that one of those rats was a shifter and I was about to be attacked.

I quickly used the toilet, looked for shoes under the stall wall again, then cautiously opened the door and peered out. There was no one here, but my instincts were twitching, and I couldn't escape the notion that what little luck we'd had was about to run out.

I washed my hands but didn't use the dryer; the last thing I needed was its noise masking any sound of an approach. I padded softly to the exit, pressed my back against the wall, and peered out. The courtyard remained empty and yet... instinct continued to prickle.

I glanced toward the pub's back door. The air in-between shimmered, and a wave of energy flowed around the building.

I swore, dug out my phone, and called Lugh.

"Get out," I said the minute he answered. "Someone is casting a spell and it's falling around the hotel—"

Another scuff, this time behind me. I spun, heart in my mouth. I had a brief glimpse of a thin, sharp face with beady little eyes, then something hit me hard, and the lights went out.

CHAPTER
THIRTEEN

I woke to the realization that luck had very definitely run out. My hands were tied behind my back, and I was nose down on some sort of channeled metal floor, each breath drawing in disgusting amounts of dirt and gods knew what else.

There was no conversation and no sound other than the nearby crashing of waves, which in itself suggested I was now a long way from the pub. I opened my eyes but couldn't see anything thanks to the fact I was facedown. I carefully shifted position, easing the weight off my nose but causing spot fires of pain across my body. My head was the worst; there were a dozen mean little men gleefully stabbing at my brain with hot pokers, and it hurt so damn much I could barely think.

But think I must if I wanted to get free.

From the little I could see through the shadows and the pain, it appeared I was in the back of some sort of van. It wasn't particularly large, and it definitely wasn't clean, and had a vague, fishy odor that made me suspect it had been "borrowed" from some poor fishmonger.

I rolled all the way over and discovered a big fat lump on the back of my head—one that didn't appreciate being touched in *any* way. My stomach rose, and I sucked in air in an effort to combat it.

And in that instant heard the soft squeak of leather. I wasn't alone after all.

"Well, well, well," Vincentia drawled from somewhere behind me. "Sleeping beauty awakes."

"What the fuck have you done?" I growled. "Where is Lugh?"

"Oh, he's perfectly fine," she said. "He, like everyone else in that hotel, is simply sleeping the night away. As I've already said, I'm not being paid enough to kill."

A comment that had worry stirring for two reasons: the first because she remembered what she'd said after the wall had exploded, and that suggested the compulsion hadn't taken full hold. The second because she wasn't running the show, and her bosses had a bad habit of murdering those who got in their way.

And we'd definitely gotten in their way.

Fear rose, but I pushed it down. Now was not the time.

But if they were dead, Vincentia *would* pay, blood curse be damned.

"How did you find me?" I asked.

"How do you think? I did warn you not to attempt deep control."

"I don't—"

"No, you don't, because your mother kept so much from you."

That was a truth I couldn't deny, and yet I knew it hadn't been done out of maliciousness but rather love. She simply hadn't wanted to burden me until she knew for sure I would come into the family power.

And by the time I had, it was all too late.

I tilted my head back but couldn't see Vincentia thanks to the dividing wall between us. The small sliding window in the middle of that wall wasn't big enough to climb through, and the rear door had no inside handles. That there was no easy means of escape wasn't surprising, but it was, nevertheless, annoying.

"Do you know *why* deep control of kin—or indeed, anyone—is forbidden?" she continued conversationally. "No? It's because a tenuous bond is formed between minds. I didn't have to follow you, dear Bethany, because I was aware of your presence at all times. I could even hear snatches of conversation."

Conversation, not thoughts, I thought with relief. The latter could have put us—me—into dire straits, given the Eye remained neatly tucked under my breast. Just because I believed the ceremony would prevent her using it didn't mean I was right. Especially given she'd been able to use the codex, even if only partially.

"If you can hear bits of conversation, why do you need me? You already have all you need to find the cave."

"Because I have no control over what I'm hearing and, unfortunately, I didn't catch all the relevant information. Better to have the source than fly blind."

Being kidnapped definitely sucked, but at least it gave me the chance to stop them. "Why did you leave Killiney and head to the airport rather than attack us? You knew we were still there."

"Because awareness did not mute the controls you placed on me. Coming here gave us more time to organize our trap."

"One of those controls was for you to pass on any infor-mation about the Looisearch's movements, so why didn't you?"

She smiled benignly. "You told me to report anything related to the Claws, but you never ordered me to report any action against you. Which was dumb, cousin."

It certainly was.

Her phone dinged. She was silent for a few seconds while she read the message, then added to me, "I hope Frances's refusal to catch you when you were felled hasn't impaired your ability to walk, because that would be rather inconvenient."

Frances being the rat shifter, no doubt. And while the idea of faking an injury to delay matters did have its appeal, they'd probably just resort to dragging me along by the hair. Caveman-style seemed right up these people's alley.

"If the restrictions are holding, then why are you even here?"

"Because you allowed me to continue working and you underestimated my cunning."

That was another truth I couldn't deny. "If you're talking about setting up a code word with Seryn to let her know whether you'd been magicked, I ordered you not to use it."

"Yes. Trouble was, I was expecting you to do that and had a countermand installed."

"Your mother," I said.

"Yes."

Meaning she'd been playing me from the moment I'd walked in that door—at least where Vincentia was concerned. It was a bitter realization that the only close family we had left had no qualms about betraying us.

I scanned the van again. There was nothing I could use as a weapon, nothing I could cut myself free with. I no longer had my phone, and I was mighty grateful that I'd left my backpack inside the hotel, even if it did leave me vulnerable to... The thought stalled. Fuck, had I been pixie magicked? Panic surged, but just as quickly died. I'd specifically ordered her *not* to do that, and she'd already said my restrictions were holding.

I'd find out the truth soon enough. "What's the plan from here?"

"You'll lead us to the sword, of course." Her sniff was somewhat disparaging. "And then you will use the codex to find us the ring."

And wasn't her nose put out of joint over that little fact? Though in all truth, she was damn lucky they still considered her useful, otherwise she might have met the same fate as many of Seryn's other contractors.

Another car approached ours, the crunch of tires on gravel abnormally loud on the still air. Wasn't it fucking typical that the one time I desperately needed the presence of the wind, it was noticeably absent.

Doors slammed, then footsteps crunched toward us. The van's rear door opened, and I raised my head. It was the rat shifter rather than Vincentia. Maybe the latter had realized getting close to me probably wasn't a wise move right now.

The shifter grabbed my feet, hauled me toward her, then stood me upright. The night briefly whirled, and warmth trickled down the back of my neck. The madmen renewed their vigorous stabbing, and for a moment, I thought I was going to puke all over the shifter's shiny gumboots.

Sadly, the urge went away.

Vincentia appeared around the corner of the van. Beside her was a thin woman I recognized even though I'd only seen her once before.

The infamous Maran Gordan herself.

"If you've hurt my brother or my friends," I said evenly, "I will cut out your goddamn heart and feed it piece by piece to the local rats."

Maran raised an eyebrow. "Such violence from someone in your position shows a great deal of bravery."

"It's bluster rather than bravery," Vincentia drawled. "The blood curse threat will impede any overly violent actions toward any of us."

I switched my gaze to hers. I wasn't sure what she saw in my expression, but her face paled.

Oh, yeah, I thought, *be afraid*. Be *very* afraid.

The shifter untied my hands, then grabbed my shoulder and pushed me forward. I stumbled briefly, then caught my balance and hobbled through the parking area and onto the sandy path that led through the dunes. The tide was still on the retreat, but the causeway between the beach and the island now sat high and dry.

My feet sank into the wet sand, slowing progress until I reached the granite "tail" of the island, which was basically a long serpentine series of rocky outcrops separated from the mainland by erosion. It loomed above me, majestic and yet somehow threatening in the darkness. The small "spines" of the dragon ran through the middle of the island in the same manner depicted in most drawings of the mythical monster. The cave was located at the creature's "head" at the far end of the island, and there were actually two—the mouth, which was entry point I'd seen in my dreams, and the creature's eye, which was where the church was located.

I stepped from the causeway onto the island and then paused, scanning the immediate surrounds, trying to decide what path to take. There were three, though the one straight up the middle was never going to be an option, given the madmen in my head were already complaining about the current level of exertion.

"Right path," Maran snapped. "And don't be thinking about slowing down, because we'll just start killing off the hotel's inhabitants. We have watchers there for that very reason."

I didn't say anything—though I certainly thought plenty—and moved to the right and the path that swept around the base of the dragon's "spine." There wasn't much vegetation to be seen other than scrubby clumps of grass, but the thick layers of bird shit that covered just about everything suggested there were plenty of seabirds using the island as their nesting grounds.

As we reached the middle of the dragon, the slightest whisper of air stirred. Only it wasn't just the wind that had arrived.

So had Beira.

Or rather, her metaphysical presence had.

I sucked in a breath and tried to contain the surge of excitement.

The storm comes, she said. *Use her power and use her wind, but do not, under any circumstances, call to the lightning. You will die if you do.*

I didn't reply. I didn't dare. Vincentia had admitted she'd been catching some snatches of conversation, and I couldn't risk her also being able to catch some of my thoughts now that she was closer.

I flexed my fingers to gather the gentle wisps of wind, then sent a stream toward the mainland. I needed to know what was happening at the hotel—needed to know whether Maran was speaking the truth about the spell and just how many guards they'd left behind.

By the time we reached the far end of the island, my vision was blurring, and the ache in my head was so bad I was beginning to suspect concussion.

There was nothing I could do if it was, of course. Mentioning it would only cause derision, and it wasn't like they needed me in tip-top condition anyway.

Several feet ahead of us, the narrow path split and moved down either side of the dragon's "cheeks." I paused. The wind's whispers were much stronger up here and the visual information it held far clearer.

My connection had definitely deepened since that whole lightning incident.

"Is there a problem?" Vincentia said, still keeping the distance between us. "Or is this nothing more than an attempt to waste time?"

Oh, I was *really* going to enjoy tossing her ass into the sea.

"I'm trying to decide which is the safer path." I cast her a glance. "Feel free to precede me and discover that for yourself."

"The left path has been used more," Maran said. "Get on with it or I'll fucking spell you into obedience."

I flicked my gaze to hers and said with a certainty that might well have been misplaced, "You can *try*."

She raised her eyebrows. "An Aodhán pixie without her knives is not immune to magic."

"*This* Aodhán pixie no longer needs the physical presence of the knives to be protected by them."

Maran's expression suggested she didn't for a second believe that statement, but she thankfully didn't test the truth of it.

I headed down the left path. Though the strength of the wind was increasing with every step down the dragon's face, I was wary of doing anything until the stream of air I'd cast earlier had returned with her information.

It surely wouldn't be too much longer. It was wind, after all.

Far below us the waves crashed against black rocks, a loud reminder of the fate that waited if any of us slipped. Sea foam flew high into the air, bright in the shadows, but between one blink and the next, it turned red, stained by the blood that now poured out of the cave sitting just above its reach.

It was a warning. Enter that cave and darkness *would* find us.

My steps faltered.

"Gods," Vincentia growled behind me. "What's the fucking problem now?"

"If we enter that cave, we'll be attacked."

Maran snorted. "Who by? The local birdlife?"

"There's a dark gate inside."

"Yeah," Vincentia drawled. "Believing that."

"The sword calls to darkness," I growled. "It's a logical location for a dark gate."

"If there is, I'll cast a spell to ward us," Maran said. "They won't get past that."

"They get past Myrkálfar locks," I growled back. "What makes you think your magic will fare any better?"

She didn't answer. The rat shifter pushed me on once again, and I had to clench my fists against the urge to push her into the sea. The path got progressively more dangerous, and I ended up edging down sideways over the last few meters, my back pressed against the rockface in an effort to keep away from the crumbling edge.

The relief of reaching the cavern's mouth in one piece was so damn strong, it left me shaking.

Maran and Vincentia stopped beside me and swept their lights across the darkness. Other than the odd flash of gold—the bats, not precious metal—there was little to be seen.

But it was what we couldn't see that was the problem.

The sense of evil riding the air was so damn strong, even Vincentia felt it. She sucked in a breath and said, "I'm not liking the feel of *that*."

"Oh, for goddess's sake," Maran muttered. "I'm surrounded by idiots."

She quickly cast a light spell. As the sphere rolled into the cave, the rivers of gold became hundreds of bats that rose in a cloud and flew straight at us. I raised my hands to protect my face and stop them getting tangled in my hair, then carefully edged deeper into the cave.

The sense of danger increased tenfold.

Despite Maran's sphere, shadows haunted the cave's walls, and it was hard to see anything deeper in. But I knew from my vision the steps lay to the left and wound up to the deeper darkness that still hugged the ceiling.

My stream of wind finally returned and quickly shared her findings. Images rose—men waking, fighting. A car destroyed, another stolen.

The cavalry was coming. I just had to hope they got here in time.

I flexed my fingers, marginally increasing the strength of the wind rolling around them. The storm was ten minutes away, Lugh and the others at least fifteen.

But it was pointless delaying things. The longer we dallied in this place, the more dangerous it became. The dark gate was definitely here. Its presence stained the air, making it difficult to breathe.

I moved left and found the steps. They were made of the

same Baltic stone as the island, and each one had definitely been designed for the stride of giants rather than humans.

We hurried up them, the sphere bobbing along beside us, though neither it nor the flashlights did all that much to penetrate the veil of darkness that hugged the walls and ceiling.

As we neared the cavern's roof and the stalactites became a forest of stone through which we had to move, I caught a glimpse of the old wooden door that divided this cave from the one in which the church stood. Dark tendrils of fog swirled slowly around the latch, and foreboding pulsed through me.

Touching those tendrils would *not* be a good idea.

I stopped several feet away and glanced at Maran. "Can you magically punch that door open?"

She immediately did so, using so much force that the poor old door simply disintegrated. I stepped over the splintered remnants, being careful to avoid those still-swirling shadows. The three women followed me, but Frances's arm brushed the shadow's edge, and their movement immediately stopped.

Then a bell sounded—a deep, unearthly resonance that made my skin crawl.

I had a *bad* feeling we'd just woken the dark gate.

"We need to move," Vincentia said with an edge in her voice.

Perhaps she was getting the same uneasy vibrations as me.

Maran cast her light ahead of us, and we hurried after it. The second cave was exactly as I'd seen in the dream but colder. Darker. More... wrong, somehow.

Shiny black stone had been used to construct the church and, in the sphere's light, it looked surreal. Though time and erosion had claimed three sides of the old building, the chancel end stood whole, the stained glass window beautiful and not dulled by time or grime.

That unearthly tone rang through the shadows again. I nervously glanced behind us. There was no sound or sensation of movement, but instinct was practically screaming that we needed to get out of here. *Now.* Before it was too late.

"You'll find the sword in the church." I stopped and called more the wind into the small cave, readying it for action even as I listened to her whispers and images.

Lugh, Cynwrig, and Mathi were on the island, but would they get here before the Annwfyn?

As much as I hoped so, instinct said otherwise.

Maran strode forward, Vincentia two steps behind her. When I didn't immediately follow, Frances gave me a shove. I half spun and half raised a fist, so very tempted to unleash the wind.

But I turned and stomped after the other two women instead.

We moved through the remains of the doorway into the nave and continued down to the chancel. The stained glass window loomed above us, seeming to glow under the sphere's bright light. The glass-black sword dominated the center window. Moisture ran down the fuller and dripped from its point, splashing wetly on the black stone chest that sat underneath it.

Just as I'd seen in the dream, but with condensation rather than blood.

But blood *would* flow in this place. Mine, and others.

I shivered and rubbed my arms. Vincentia walked around the altar and stopped in front of the chest. "The sword's in here."

Maran stopped beside her. "You sure?"

Vincentia nodded my way. "This is what she described when she was talking at the pub."

The tome sound again, closer and stronger than before. Darkness was coming, be it the Annwfyn or something else.

We had to get out of here. Had to run, while there was still time.

I took a step back, only to be stopped by a fist in my spine. I swore and elbowed her hard. As she "oofed" in pain, I swung around and growled, "Do not touch me again."

"Frances," Maran snapped, "go watch the door. Bethany, get your ass over here and open this chest."

"What makes you think I can open it?"

Vincentia looked at me. "I believe there was something about only a pixie gifted with prescience can unlock the final door? And I'm certainly not shedding any blood in this godforsaken place."

"If you heard that, then you'll also know that the minute a hand touches that sword, darkness will be called."

"Darkness has already been called, if I'm any judge," Maran growled. "So get on with it or I'll goddamn make you."

I stared at her for a minute, then stepped up the chest. "I need a knife."

Vincentia snorted. "As if either of us is stupid enough to hand you a weapon. Hold out your hand."

I did so. Vincentia caught it and pulled my fingers back to expose my palm more. Maran pulled a knife from a sheath strapped to her side and quickly stabbed it into my hand.

I cursed her and tried to jerk it back, but Vincentia's grip prevented me. As blood welled, she twisted my hand around and let the blood drip onto the chest.

One drop splashed.

A single beat in response.

Two drops.

The faintest fracture ran around the edge of the chest.

Three.

A rumble began, a distant thunder that grew stronger and stronger until it was all I could hear and all I could feel, both in my heart and in my body. It was almost as if the sword that lay within judged us, weighing us for worthiness. Then dark purple light ran around the fractured edge of the chest, and the lid clicked open a centimeter.

Shadows crept like skeletal fingers over the chest's rim and crawled down toward the floor.

Vincentia and I stepped away from them.

Maran did not.

My gaze snapped toward her. A smile touched her lips, and her eyes held a glow that was both triumphant and hungry.

The sword might have tested us all, but it had chosen *her*.

Fuck.

With a flick of her fingers, she spelled the lid away, then stepped forward. I lunged past Vincentia, trying to stop Maran, but those shadowy fingers wrapped around my ankles, making me stumble, pulling me down.

Maran reached into the chest and pulled free the sword. It flamed to life as it left the chest, the fire the same unearthly color that had run around the chest on the third drop of blood. It leapt up the fuller, wrapped around Maran's hand, and then disappeared into her skin.

My breath caught, but for several seconds, nothing happened.

Then Maran screamed, and everything went to hell

FOURTEEN

As her earsplitting sound of utter agony filled the darkness, the darkness moved, becoming creatures with thick yellow talons and claws that scraped across the stone as they flowed toward us.

I raised a hand and cast the wind in front of them, forming a howling barrier of air that would slow them down but not, in the end, stop them.

"Vincentia," I yelled, "give me the gun or fucking use it yourself. You have to stop her—now! Before the sword totally controls her."

Her gaze snapped toward mine. Her face was pale, her eyes wide. I was guessing she'd never seen the Annwfyn before.

"Gun!" I repeated. "Now!"

She blinked, then, like a sleeper coming out of a dream, slowly reached for the weapon strapped to her side. Too slow, and far too late.

Maran was suddenly between us, the black sword sweeping up and around, aimed at Vincentia's neck.

I swore and cast more wind, knocking the sword off its course and pushing Vincentia back. She stumbled and fell onto her rump. A claw appeared out of the gloom and arced toward her. She must have sensed it because she fell away, twisted around, and shot the bastard. As black blood sprayed, Maran turned and swung the sword at me. I scrambled back, only to be stopped by the black ribbon fingers wrapped around my ankles. I twisted and threw the wind at her, but it had no effect.

Magic protected her. Magic, and the sword itself.

I swore and lunged for the shadows, trying to pry them free as the black sword arced down.

A gunshot rang out. A shudder went through Maran's body, and the blow that should have cleaved me in two dug into the stone inches away from my left side instead.

Another shot. Another shudder.

Maran swung around, and magic rose, thick with darkness and intent. Vincentia's face was pale, her eyes wide and fearful, but she aimed the gun a third time and pulled the trigger.

The gun exploded in her hands.

As blood and gore and fingers sprayed across the shadows, Maran calmly stepped forward, raised the sword, and brought it down.

I did the only thing I could do.

I wrapped the wind around Vincentia and cast her out of the cave, out into the sea.

She could swim. I knew she could swim.

Whether she'd survive the blood loss from having her hands blown apart was another matter entirely.

The air screamed at me. I twisted around, saw the claws and the thin figure approaching at speed. Felt the storm roll in beyond the cave and pulled its power down, casting it at the Annwfyn, smashing him back against the cavern wall so hard that his spine came through his chest and his head exploded.

Another scream from the air.

I spun, saw Maran raise the sword, and redirected the storm's blast at her.

This time, it pushed her back several feet but otherwise didn't affect her. It hit the shadows moving behind her instead, and more Annwfyn crashed back against the walls.

I needed my knives. Desperately. But they were held secure in my backpack and well beyond reach.

Then I remembered my own words... *I don't need the presence of the knives to use them.*

I had no idea what I was doing, no idea if it would work, but I had to do something or I was going to get sliced in half or eaten by the damn Annwfyn.

I pushed a hand past the neck of my sweater, swept my fingers over my breast, and wrapped them around the Eye. Then I called to the knives.

As Maran pushed forward again and raised the gleaming black sword, the Eye pulsed, and suddenly there was weight in my free hand. I didn't stop to wonder how or why; I simply released the Eye, flipped one of the knives to my left hand, and then raised them high, crossing the blades as the sword descended. Metal clashed, and my arms gave way just a little under the force of her blow. I gritted my teeth, pushed the sword to one side, and then lunged forward, past her reach, into her body. The shadowy fingers pulled taut but not enough to stop me. Maran shifted her grip on the sword, obviously intent on thrusting it through my torso. I flung my arms either side of her and then called to the force of the storm and channeled it through the knives, then drew them in.

They cut through flesh, muscle, and bone as easily as water and cleaved Maran in two.

As her body crumpled and fell in different directions, I slashed at the fingers holding me captive. They shriveled away from the knives' touch and retreated to the safety of the open chest. I caught the wind, ripped the sword from Maran's grip, and threw it back into the chest. Then I slammed the lid back on top of it.

Which left me with the Annwfyn.

I sucked in a breath, drew on the last vestiges of my strength, and once again called on the power of the storm. I cast it at the Annwfyn, sweeping them up and throwing them far, far out to sea.

And hoped the bastards couldn't swim.

Every inch of me was trembling with exhaustion, but I couldn't give into it. I might have gotten rid of the Annwfyn from this cave, but the dark gate remained out there in the shadows, and I had no idea how much time it might take for another wave of the monsters to appear.

But at least for now, this cave was empty, and I was safe. And, even better, alive.

Claws scraped across stone. I tensed and clenched my fingers around the wind, but the sound was too soft to be Annwfyn. A furry figure bleeding from a dozen different wounds appeared out of the gloom and limped toward me.

A rat.

Frances.

I half snorted. "Trust a fucking rat to survive Annwfyn armageddon."

She shifted shape and sat down on the stone several

feet away from me. "This fucking rat was damned lucky they were more intent on reaching the sword than killing everything that moved." She sniffed. "What happens now?"

"We wait for the cavalry, and then you go to jail."

She cocked a bloody eyebrow at me. "You haven't got your phone, so how did you call anyone?"

I smiled and raised the knives. "I didn't have these before, either."

She looked at the knives, then back at me. "I think everyone has been underestimating you."

"Common problem with elves. Tell me, is Seryn the head of the Looisearch? Was Maran? Or is there someone else above them both?"

Frances shrugged. "I'm a grunt. It's not like they tell me anything important."

I smiled. "You're rat shifter. Secrets are like sweets to your people—you just can't resist them."

She laughed, though it fell away to an odd sort of groan. She gripped the wound in her side and said, "It's not like I owe them any allegiance. Not now. Maran and Seryn are the visible leaders. There's someone else behind them— someone no one has seen—pulling the strings."

"You never got a name? Never heard his or her voice?"

"No." She hesitated. "It's a male, I know that much. And his actions come from a place of deep revenge."

"That's hardly news, given the Looisearch was formed as a means of avenging the dead."

"Yes, but I'm talking a vengeance forty years in the making that has only found a voice in the last eight months."

Which was how long Lugh and Nialle had been researching the Claws. Coincidence? Probably not.

The wind stirred, sharing her secrets, and I smiled. The cavalry were in the larger cave. I sent the wind to keep a watch on them and shoved my knives into my belt. They weren't sheathed, and in any other situation, one wrong move might mean them ending up in my flesh but... I didn't think that would happen. Not with these knives. Not now.

Frances cocked her head, her expression intent. "I think your cavalry has arrived."

"Yeah." I glanced toward the doorway. Cynwrig slipped around the corner, at one with the shadows and almost invisible.

"There's no one here except us two and the dead," I said. "But I need you to call out the coast guard. I had to fling Vincentia out to the sea."

"She can stay there as far as I'm concerned," Lugh growled as he strode through the door. "She's no longer family in my books."

Mathi followed him through the door and, like Cynwrig, began a check of the multiple bodies scattered around the cave.

Lugh glanced at Frances and pointed a finger at her. "Move and there will be unpleasant consequences."

Frances snorted. "If I'd been able to move very far, I would have been out of here long ago."

Lugh grunted and squatted down in front of me. "How are you? I mean, you look like shit, but I can't see anything broken and there's not much in the way of blood, so I'm calling that a win."

I smiled tiredly. "A big win, considering everything."

His gaze went past me and settled on Maran. "What happened here?"

I told him and then added, "I'm not sure what we're

going to do now. We can't leave the sword here, and we dare not touch it."

He studied the stone chest for a few seconds, then glanced around. "Cynwrig, would you be able to bury it?"

"Yes, but Seryn will be aware of its location by now and can unearth anything I bury." Cynwrig bent to check a final body, then strode toward us. His gaze swept me, his expression a mix of relief and concern. "Lugh's right. You look like shit."

"Nothing like a bit of flattery to boost a woman's ego." Thunder rumbled, an ominous, angry sound that oddly seemed aimed at me. I couldn't sense Beira's immediate presence, but I nevertheless had the feeling she was keeping her eye on us. Or rather, me. Then I realized why. Use the wind, she'd said. *Use the power of the storm.* What if she hadn't meant as a weapon but rather a means of hiding a sword no one could safely touch? I drew in a breath and said, "What if we hide the sword in the storm?"

Lugh frowned. "Storms are transient and often dissipate as quickly as they form, so I hardly think that's an ideal situation."

"Yes, but we don't need to permanently store the sword in the storm. We just need to get it away from here long enough to find a more secure location."

Which, if my suspicion was right, might just be that mountain in Scotland.

"If it's possible, I think it's our safest bet," Mathi said. He stopped on the other side of Lugh and frowned down at me. "I've called in rescue and medics. They should be here in ten. The IIT will be here in five."

Frances groaned but otherwise remained silent. Perhaps she realized the IIT was a better bet, remaining-alive-wise, than the Looisearch—though given what had happened to Gilda's partners, I wasn't so sure.

"Then I'd better deal with the damn sword before they get here," I said. "You'd all better step back. The last time I opened the chest, creepy shadow fingers streamed out and grabbed me."

All three men raised their eyebrows, but otherwise, stepped well back as ordered. I drew in a deep, quivery breath, and then called to the wind and the storm again.

And found Beira within it.

With her guidance, I crafted a small storm that would self-perpetuate for a week at the very least—Beira had crossly informed me that if I'd bothered to keep some strength in reserve, I could have made it last a lot longer—then, with a finger of air, hauled off the chest's lid and wrapped a second finger around the sword and cast it into the center of my storm.

Then I sent it deep into the sea, where it would circle until I called it back in.

Then the local IIT people arrived, and the questions began.

Three days later, Lugh and I were back on a plane, heading across to Ireland. We had a council ruling to pass on and an aunt to sanction.

All because Vincentia still clung to the insane notion that the Looisearch would pay handsomely for her silence.

Of course, her silence was partially my fault. Maybe more than partially. Thanks to the sheer depth of control I'd attempted, I'd virtually made her immune to further pixie control—even mine. I couldn't even unpick the controls I'd placed.

Of course, there was another consequence—the pixie council. They were currently deliberating what level of punishment should be applied for my use of deep mind control. While they did understand the reasons, I suspected they also needed to send a message to the wider pixie community that this sort of behavior would not be tolerated. Cynwrig had said he'd speak to them on my behalf, but I wasn't sure that would help.

Sadly, Vincentia had learned nothing from either the murders she'd witnessed or from seeing just how dangerous a Claw could be. Not even losing her left hand and two fingers from her right had in any way changed her stance.

And now she and her mother would pay what for a pixie was the ultimate price.

Neither Lugh nor I said anything as we drove toward Galway. When we reached the driveway that led into our aunt's place, Lugh slowed the car and glanced at me. "You ready for this?"

I took a deep breath and released it slowly. "I wish we weren't the ones who had to deliver this ruling."

"We are her closest kin. By pixie law, it can't be done by anyone else."

I knew that. It didn't mean I had to like it. I motioned him on.

Lugh lifted his foot from the brake and continued down the beautiful forest that was about to become my aunt's prison.

The curtains twitched as we pulled up, but there was no other sign of movement. Not even from Peregrine's window. Lugh reached into the back seat of the car, picked up the sheathed knife that lay there, and then climbed out and followed me to the door.

He knocked three times and then said, "Riayn Aodhán, you have been judged by the great council and your actions found to be wanting."

Footsteps echoed, then the door was flung open and she stood there, her green eyes sparking with fury and heat creeping through her cheeks. "What the fuck do you mean by that?"

"The actions of your daughter have not only endangered the lives of kin, but also that of humanity itself." Lugh's voice was flat, showing none of the anger I knew bubbled underneath. "Under the rule of the council, and by the power of the great goddess Gaia, you are hereby excommunicated for a period of ten years. No longer will the earth or the trees respond to you, and you will be bound to this small parcel of land that you call home."

He unsheathed the knife and thrust the red blade hilt deep into the doorstep. The house shuddered and seemed to close in on itself. Its song remained, but it was one my aunt would no longer hear.

"You can't do this," she whispered, her eyes wide and frightened. "It's not fair. I didn't do—"

"*Anything*," I snapped, anger momentarily getting the better of me. "You didn't fucking do *anything*, even after I warned you. You could have stopped her, but you didn't. So her crimes become yours."

Lugh cast me a warning look. I clenched my fists and held back the torrent of words that burned at the back of my throat. Or maybe they were tears of frustration and hurt. She was my aunt. It shouldn't have ended like this.

"When Vincentia recovers from her injuries, she will be transferred here and share the sentence." Lugh paused and then added softly, "It is better than spending ten years inside the walls of a stone prison, and that was the only other option on the table."

"The council can't—" She stopped. The council could, and we all knew it. "What of our prisoner?"

"The council will remove her shortly. You are to continue looking after her until then."

"Fine," she muttered, eyes flashing. "But as you cut me off, so I cut you. My sister's offspring are no longer my kin. I revoke acknowledgement of them."

"Fine by me, Aunt." But it wasn't fine. It was a long way from fine. Especially when it was said by someone who not only looked so much like Mom but had meant so much to her.

I blinked fiercely, then turned and stomped back to the car.

Lugh followed but didn't say anything until we were beyond the boundaries of our aunt's new prison. "Are you all right?"

"Yes. No." I scrubbed my hands across my eyes. "What's our next move?"

"You mean aside from trying to find a safe place to stash the sword, relocate the crown, and try to reach the ring before the Looisearch do?"

A wry smile tugged at my lips. "Yeah, beside all that."

"We go home. There is sex to be had, remember?"

My eyebrows rose. "That's certainly true in my case, but I thought you were taking it slow?"

"I have decided slow is not so ideal. After all, we're up against some pretty fierce foes, and who knows when death will find us."

"And is Darby aware of this sudden change of heart?"

"Yes, although she did take some convincing that I wasn't ill or under some sort of mind control."

I laughed. "Then I won't expect to hear from you for a couple of days, at least."

"From your mouth to the gods' ears," he murmured.

I laughed and, for the very first time, felt like our luck had turned and everything was possible.

Only time would tell if that was a truth or yet another lie.

Also by Keri Arthur

Kingdoms of Earth & Air

Unlit (May 2018)

Cursed (Nov 2018)

Burn (June 2019)

The Outcast series

City of Light (Jan 2016)

Winter Halo (Nov 2016)

The Black Tide (Dec 2017)

Souls of Fire series

Fireborn (July 2014)

Wicked Embers (July 2015)

Flameout (July 2016)

Ashes Reborn (Sept 2017)

Dark Angels series

Darkness Unbound (Sept 27th 2011)

Darkness Rising (Oct 26th 2011)

Darkness Devours (July 5th 2012)

Darkness Hunts (Nov 6th 2012)

Darkness Unmasked (June 4 2013)

Darkness Splintered (Nov 2013)

Darkness Falls (Dec 2014)

Riley Jenson Guardian Series

Full Moon Rising (Dec 2006)

Kissing Sin (Jan 2007)

Tempting Evil (Feb 2007)

Dangerous Games (March 2007)

Embraced by Darkness (July 2007)

The Darkest Kiss (April 2008)

Deadly Desire (March 2009)

Bound to Shadows (Oct 2009)

Moon Sworn (May 2010)

Myth and Magic series

Destiny Kills (Oct 2008)

Mercy Burns (March 2011)

Nikki & Micheal series

Dancing with the Devil (March 2001 / Aug 2013)

Hearts in Darkness Dec (2001/ Sept 2013)

Chasing the Shadows Nov (2002/Oct 2013)

Kiss the Night Goodbye (March 2004/Nov 2013)

Damask Circle series

Circle of Fire (Aug 2010 / Feb 2014)

Circle of Death (July 2002/March 2014)

Circle of Desire (July 2003/April 2014)

Ripple Creek series

Beneath a Rising Moon (June 2003/July 2012)

Beneath a Darkening Moon (Dec 2004/Oct 2012)

Spook Squad series

Memory Zero (June 2004/26 Aug 2014)

Generation 18 (Sept 2004/30 Sept 2014)

Penumbra (Nov 2005/29 Oct 2014)

Stand Alone Novels

Who Needs Enemies (E-book only, Sept 1 2013)

Novella

Lifemate Connections (March 2007)

Anthology Short Stories

The Mammoth Book of Vampire Romance (2008)

Wolfbane and Mistletoe--2008

Hotter than Hell--2008

ABOUT THE AUTHOR

Keri Arthur, author of the New York Times bestselling Riley Jenson Guardian series, has now written more than fifty-five novels. She's won a Romance Writers of Australia RBY Award for Speculative Fiction, and six Australian Romance Readers Awards for Scifi, Fantasy or Futuristic Romance. The Lizzie Grace Series was also voted Favourite Continuing Series in the ARRA Awards. Keri's something of a wanna-be photographer, so when she's not at her computer writing the next book, she can be found somewhere in the Australian countryside taking random photos.

for more information:
www.keriarthur.com
keriarthurauthor@gmail.com

 facebook.com/AuthorKeriArthur
twitter.com/kezarthur
 instagram.com/kezarthur

9 780645 303148